THIS I$ NOT A GAME

WALTER JON WILLIAMS
THIS I$ NOT A GAME

orbit

www.orbitbooks.net

ORBIT

First published in Great Britain in 2009 by Orbit
This paperback edition published in 2010 by Orbit

A CIP catalogue record for this book
is available from the British Library.

ISBN 978-1-84149-664-1

Typeset in Baskerville
Printed in the UK by CPI Mackays, Chatham ME5 8TD

Papers used by Orbit are natural, renewable and
recyclable products sourced from well-managed forests and certified
in accordance with the rules of the Forest Stewardship Council.

Mixed Sources
Product group from well-managed
forests and other controlled sources
www.fsc.org Cert no. SGS-COC-004081
© 1996 Forest Stewardship Council

Orbit
An imprint of
Little, Brown Book Group
100 Victoria Embankment
London EC4Y 0DY

An Hachette UK Company
www.hachette.co.uk

www.orbitbooks.net

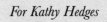

For Kathy Hedges

What if the game called you?
— Elan Lee

ACT 1

CHAPTER ONE

This Is Not a Mastermind

Plush dolls of Pinky and the Brain overhung Charlie's monitor, their bottoms fixed in place with Velcro tabs, toes dangling over the video screen. Pinky's face was set in an expression of befuddled surprise, and the Brain looked out at the world with red-rimmed, calculating eyes.

"What are we going to do tonight, Brain?" Charlie asked.

Pickups caught his words; software analyzed and recognized his speech; and the big plasma screen winked on. The Brain's jutting, intent face took on a sinister, underlit cast.

"What we do *every* night, Pinky," said the computer in the Brain's voice.

Welcome, Charlie, to your lair.

Hydraulics hissed as Charlie dropped into his chair. Ice rang as he dropped his glass of Mexican Coke into the cup holder. He touched the screen with his finger, paged through menus, and checked his email.

Dagmar hadn't sent him her resignation, or a message that gibbered with insanity, so that was good. The previous day she had hosted a game in Bangalore, the game that had been broadcast on live feed to ten or twelve million people, a wild success.

The Bangalore thing had turned out wicked cool.

Wicked cool was what Charlie lived for.

He sipped his Coke as he looked at more email, dictated brief replies, and confirmed a meeting for the next day. Then he minimized his email program.

"Turtle Farm," he said. The reference was to a facility on Grand Cayman Island, where he kept one of his bank accounts. The two words were unlikely to be uttered accidentally in combination, and therefore served not only as a cue to the software but as a kind of password.

A secure screen popped up. Charlie leaned forward and typed in his password by hand—for the crucial stuff, he preferred as little software interface as possible—and then reached for his Coke as his account balance came up on the screen.

Four point three billion dollars.

Charlie's heart gave a sideways lurch in his chest. He was suddenly aware of the whisper of the ventilation duct, the sound of a semitruck on the highway outside the office building, the texture of the fine leather upholstery against his bare forearm.

He looked at the number again, counting the zeros.

Four point three billion.

He stared at the screen and spoke aloud into the silence.

"*This*," he said, "must stop."

CHAPTER TWO

This Is Not a Vacation

Dagmar lay on her bed in the dark hotel room in Jakarta and listened to the sound of gunfire. She hoped the guns were firing tear gas and not something more deadly.

She wondered if she should take shelter, lie between the wall and the bed so that the mattress would suck up any bullets coming through the big glass window. She thought about this but did not move.

It didn't seem worthwhile, somehow.

She was no longer interested in hiding from just any damn bullet.

The air-conditioning was off and the tropical Indonesian heat had infiltrated the room. Dagmar lay naked on sheets that were soaked with her sweat. She thought about cool drinks, but the gunfire was a distraction.

Her nerves gave a leap as the telephone on the night-stand rang. She reached for it, picked up the handset, and said, "This is Dagmar."

"Are you afraid?" said the woman on the telephone.

"*What?*" Dagmar said. Dread clutched at her heart. She sat up suddenly.

"Are you afraid?" the woman said. "It's all right to be afraid."

In the past few days, Dagmar had seen death and riots and a pillar of fire that marked what had been a neighborhood. She was trapped in her hotel in a city that was under siege, and she had no friends here and no resources that mattered.

Are you afraid?

A ridiculous question.

She had come to Jakarta from Bengaluru, the city known formerly as Bangalore, and had been cared for on her Garuda Indonesia flight by beautiful, willowy attendants who looked as if they'd just stepped off the ramp from the Miss Indonesia contest. The flight had circled Jakarta for three hours before receiving permission to land, long enough for Dagmar to miss her connecting flight to Bali. The lovely attendants, by way of compensation, kept the Bombay and tonics coming.

The plane landed and Dagmar stood in line with the others, waiting to pass customs. The customs agents seemed morose and distracted. Dagmar waited several minutes in line while her particular agent engaged in a vigorous, angry conversation on his cell phone. When Dagmar approached his booth, he stamped her passport without looking at it or her and waved her on.

She found that there were two kinds of people in Soekarno-Hatta International Airport, the frantic and the sullen. The first talked to one another, or into their cell phones, in loud, indignant-sounding Javanese or Sundanese. The second type sat in dejected silence, sometimes in plastic airport seats, sometimes squatting on their carry-on baggage. The television monitors told her that her connection to Bali had departed more than an hour before she'd arrived.

Tugging her carry-on behind her on its strap, Dagmar threaded her way between irate businessmen and dour families with peevish children. A lot of the women wore headscarves or the white Islamic headdress. She went to the currency exchange to get some local currency, and found it closed. The exchange rates posted listed something like 110,000 rupiah to the dollar. Most of the shops and restaurants were also closed, even the duty-free and the chain stores in the large attached mall, where she wandered looking for a place to change her rupees for rupiah. The bank she found was closed. The ATM was out of order. The papers at the newsagent's had screaming banner headlines and pictures of politicians looking bewildered.

She passed through a transparent plastic security wall and into the main concourse to change her ticket for Bali. The Garuda Indonesia ticket seller didn't look like Miss Jakarta. She was a small, squat woman with long, flawless crimson nails on her nicotine-stained fingers, and she told Dagmar there were no more flights to Bali that night.

"Flight cancel," the woman said.

"How about another airline?" Dagmar asked.

"All flight cancel."

Dagmar stared at her. "*All* the airlines?"

The woman looked at her from eyes of obsidian.

"All cancel."

"How about tomorrow?"

"I check."

The squat woman turned to her keyboard, her fingers held straight and flat in the way used by women with long nails. Dagmar was booked on a flight leaving the next day at 1:23 P.M. The squat woman handed her a new set of tickets.

"You come two hour early. Other terminal, not here."

"Okay. Thanks."

There was a tourist information booth, but people were packed around it ten deep.

All cancel. She wondered how many had gotten stranded.

Dagmar took out her handheld. It was a marvelous piece of technology, custom-built by a firm in Burbank to her needs and specifications. It embraced most techno-logical standards used in North America, Asia, and Europe and had a satellite uplink for sites with no cover-age or freaky mobile standards. It had SMS for text messaging and email, packet switching for access to the Internet, and MMS for sending and receiving photos and video. It had a built-in camera and camcorder, acted as a personal organizer and PDA, supported instant mes-saging, played and downloaded music, and supported Bluetooth. It could be used as a wireless modem for her PC, had a GPS feature, and would scan both text and Semacodes.

Dagmar loved it so much she was tempted to give it a name but never had.

She stepped out of the terminal, and tropical heat

slapped her in the face. Mist rose in little wisps from the wet pavement, and the air smelled of diesel exhaust and clove cigarettes. Dagmar saw the Sheraton and the Aspac glowing on the horizon, found their numbers online, and called. They were full. She googled a list of Jakarta hotels, found a five-star place called the Royal Jakarta, and booked a room at a not-quite-extortionate rate.

Dagmar found a row of blue taxis and approached the first. The driver had a lined face, a bristly little mustache, and a black pitji cap on his head. He turned down his radio and gave her a skeptical look.

"I have no rupiah," she said. "Can you take dollars?"

A smile flashed, revealing brown, irregular teeth.

"I take dollar!" he said brightly.

"Twenty dollars," she said, "to take me to the Royal Jakarta."

"Twenty dollar, okay!" His level of cheerfulness increased by an order of magnitude. He jumped out of the cab, loaded her luggage into the trunk, and opened the door for her.

Above the windshield were pictures of movie stars and pop singers. The driver hopped back in the car, lit a cigarette, and pulled into traffic. He didn't turn on the meter, but he turned up the radio, and the cab boomed with the sound of Javanese rap music. He looked at Dagmar in the rearview mirror and gave a craggy-toothed smile.

Then the terror began.

None of the drivers paid any attention to lanes. Sometimes the taxi was one of five cars charging in line abreast down a two-lane road. Or it would weave out into oncoming traffic, accelerating toward a wall of oncoming metal until it darted into relative safety at the last possible instant.

Automobiles shared the roadway with trucks, with buses, with vans and minibuses, with bicycles, with motorbikes, and with other motorbikes converted to cabs, with little metal shelters built on the back. All moved at the same time or were piled up in vast traffic jams where nothing moved except for the little motorbikes weaving between the stalled vehicles. Occasional fierce rain squalls hammered the window glass. The driver rarely bothered to turn on the wipers.

What Dagmar could see of the driver's face was expressionless, even as he punched the accelerator to race toward the steel wall of a huge diesel-spewing Volvo semitruck speeding toward them. Occasionally, whatever seeds or spices were in the driver's cigarette would pop or crackle or explode, sending out little puffs of ash. When this happened, the driver brushed the ashes off his chest before they set his shirt on fire.

Dagmar was speechless with fear. Her fingers clutched the door's armrest. Her legs ached with the tension of stomping an imaginary brake pedal. When the traffic all stopped dead, which it did frequently, she could hear her heart hammering louder than the Javanese rap.

Then the cab darted out of traffic and beneath a hotel portico, and a huge, gray-bearded Sikh doorman in a turban and an elaborate brocade-spangled coat stepped forward to open her door.

"Welcome, miss," he said.

She paid the driver and tipped him a couple of bucks

from her stash of dollars, then stepped into the air-conditioned lobby. Her sweat-soaked shirt clung to her back. She checked into the hotel and was pleased to discover that her room had Western plumbing, a bidet, and a minibar. She showered, changed into clothes that didn't smell of terror, and then went to the hotel restaurant and had *bami goreng* along with a Biltong beer.

There was a string quartet playing Haydn in a lounge area off the hotel lobby, and she settled into a seat to listen and drink a cup of coffee. American hotels, she thought, could do with more string quartets.

A plasma screen was perched high in the corner, its sound off, and she glanced up at CNN and read the English headlines scrolling across the bottom of the screen.

Indonesian crisis, she read. *Government blamed for currency collapse.*

She could taste a metallic warning on her tongue.

All cancel, she thought.

Dagmar had been in Bengaluru for a wedding, but not a real wedding, because the bride and groom and the other principals were actors. The wedding was the climax of a worldwide interactive media event that had occupied Dagmar for six months, and tens of thousands of participants for the past eight weeks.

Unlike the wedding, Bengaluru was real. The white-painted elephant on which the groom had arrived was real. The Sikh guards looking after the bride's borrowed jewelry were real.

And so were the eighteen-hundred-odd gamers who had shown up for the event.

Dagmar's job was to create online games for a world-wide audience. Not games for the PC or the Xbox that gamers played at home, and not the kind of games where online players entered a fantasy world in order to have adventures, then left that world and went about their lives.

Dagmar's games weren't entertainments from which the players could so easily walk away. The games pursued you. If you joined one of Dagmar's games, you'd start getting urgent phone calls from fictional characters. Coded messages would appear in your in-box. Criminals or aliens or members of the Resistance might ask you to conceal a package. Sometimes you'd be sent away from your computer to carry out a mission in the world of reality, to meet with other gamers and solve puzzles that would alter the fate of the world.

The type of games that Dagmar produced were called alternate reality games, or ARGs. They showed the players a shadow world lurking somehow behind the real one, a world where the engines of existence were powered by plots and conspiracies, codes and passwords and secret errands.

Dagmar's job description reflected the byzantine nature of the games. Her business card said "Executive Producer," but what the *players* called her was puppet-master.

The game that climaxed in Bengaluru was called *Curse of the Golden Nagi* and was created for the sole purpose of publicizing the Chandra Mobile Communications Platform, a fancy cell phone of Indian manufacture that was just breaking into the world market. Live events, where gamers met to solve puzzles and perform tasks, had taken place in North America, in Europe, and in Asia, and all had climaxed with the fictional bride and the fictional groom, having survived conspiracy and assassination attempts, being married beneath a canopy stretched out in the green, flower-strewn courtyard of one of Bengaluru's five-star hotels and being sent to their happily-ever-after.

Dagmar's own happily-ever-after, though, had developed a hitch.

The hotel room was good. Dagmar spent a lot of time in hotel rooms and this was at the top of its class. Air-conditioning, exemplary plumbing, a comfortable mattress, a complimentary bathrobe, Internet access, and a minibar.

The rupiah had collapsed, but Dagmar had $180 in cash, credit cards, a bank card, and a ticket out of town. Indonesia was probably going to go through a terrible time, but Dagmar seemed insulated from all that.

She'd passed through too many time zones in the past four days, and her body clock was hopelessly out of sync. She was either asleep or very awake, and right now she was very awake, so she propped herself with pillows atop her bed, made herself a gin and tonic with supplies from the minibar, and called Charlie, her boss. It was Monday morning in the U.S.—in fact it was yesterday, on the other side of the date line, and Charlie was going through a day that, to Dagmar, had already passed its sell-by date.

"How is Bangalore?" he asked.

"I'm not in Bangalore," she told him. "I'm in Jakarta. I'm on my way to Bali."

It took a couple of seconds for Charlie's surprise to bounce up to a satellite and then down to Southeast Asia.

"I thought you were going to spend two weeks in India," he said.

"Turns out," Dagmar said, "that Siyed is married."

Again Charlie's reaction bounced to the Clarke Orbit and back.

"I'm so sorry," he said.

"His wife flew from London to be with him. I don't think that was his original plan, but I have to say he handled the surprise with aplomb."

Her name was Manjari. She had a polished Home Counties accent, a degree from the London School of Economics, beautiful eyes, and a lithe, graceful, compact body in a maroon silk sari that exposed her cheerleader abdomen.

She was perfect. Dagmar felt like a shaggy-haired Neanderthal by comparison. She couldn't imagine why Siyed was cheating on his wife.

Except for the obvious reason, of course, which was that he was a lying bastard.

"Serves me right," Dagmar said, "for getting involved with an actor."

The actor who had played the male ingenue in *Curse of the Golden Nagi*, in fact. Who was charming and good-looking and spoke with a cheeky East London accent, and who wore lifts in his shoes because he was, in fact, quite tiny.

Leaving for another country had seemed the obvious solution.

"Anyway," she said, "maybe I'll find some cute Aussie guy in Bali."

"Good luck with that."

"You sound skeptical."

An indistinct anxiety entered Charlie's tone. "I don't know how much luck *anybody* can have in Indonesia. You know the currency collapsed today, right?"

"Yeah. But I've got credit cards, some dollars, and a ticket out of town."

Charlie gave it a moment's thought.

"You'll probably be all right," he said. "But if there's any trouble, I want you to contact me."

"I will," Dagmar said.

Dagmar had the feeling that most employees of multi-millionaire bosses—even youthful ones—did not quite have the easy relationship that she shared with Charlie. But she'd known him since before he was a multimillion-aire, since he was a sophomore in college. She'd seen him hunched over a console in computer lab, squinting into *Advanced D&D* manuals, and loping around the Caltech campus in a faded Hawaiian shirt, stained Dockers, and flip-flops.

It was difficult to conjure, in retrospect, the deference that Charlie's millions demanded. Nor, to his credit, did Charlie demand it.

"If it's any consolation," Charlie said, "I've been look-ing online, and *Golden Nagi* looks like a huge hit."

Dagmar relaxed against her pillows and sipped her drink.

"It was *The Maltese Falcon*," she said, "with a bit of *The Sign of Four* thrown in."

"The players didn't know that, though."

"No. They didn't."

Being able to take credit for the recycled plots of great writers was one of her job's benefits. Over the past few years she'd adapted *Romeo and Juliet, The Winter's Tale, The Comedy of Errors* (with clones), *The Libation Bearers, The Master and Margarita* (with aliens), *King Solomon's Mines,* and *It's a Wonderful Life* (with zombies).

She proudly considered that having the zombies called into being by the Lionel Barrymore character was a perfect example of a metaphor being literalized.

"When you revealed that the Rani was in fact the Nagi," Charlie said, "the players collectively pissed their pants."

"I'd rather they creamed their jeans."

"That, too. Anyway," Charlie said, "I've got your next job set up for when you get back."

"I don't want to think about it."

"I *want* you thinking about it," said Charlie. "When you're on the beach in Bali looking some Aussie guy in the glutes, I want you distracted by exciting new plots buzzing through your brain."

"Oh yeah, Charlie," sipping, "I'm going to have all sorts of plots going through my mind, you bet."

"Have you ever heard of *Planet Nine?*"

"Nope."

"A massively multiplayer online role-playing game that burned through their funding in the development stage. They were just about to do the beta release when their bank foreclosed on them and found that all they'd repossessed was a lease on an office and a bunch of software they didn't have a clue about."

Dagmar was surprised. "They were getting their start-up funding from a *bank?* Not a venture capital outfit?"

"A bank very interested in exploiting the new rules allowing them to invest in such things."

"Serves them right," Dagmar judged.

"Them *and* the bank." Cheerfully. "So I heard from Austin they were looking for a sugar daddy, and I bought the company from the bank for eleven point three cents on the dollar. I've rehired the original team minus the fuckups who caused all the problems, and beta testing's going to begin in the next few days."

Alarms clattered in Dagmar's head. "You're not going to want *me* to write for them, are you?"

"God, no," Charlie said. "They've got a head writer who's good—Tom Suzuki, if you know him—and he's putting his own team in place."

Dagmar relaxed. She already had the perfect game-writing job; she didn't want something less exciting.

She sipped her drink. "So what's the plan?"

"*Planet Nine* is going to launch in October. I want an ARG to generate publicity."

"Ah." Dagmar gazed with satisfaction into her future. "So you're going to be your own client."

"That's right."

Charlie had done this once before, when work for Great Big Idea had been scarce. He'd paid his game company to create some buzz for his software company—buzz that hadn't precisely been necessary, since the software end of Charlie's business was doing very well on its own. But Dagmar had been able to build a plot around Charlie's latest generation of autonomous software agents, and she'd been able to keep her team employed, so the entire adventure had been satisfactory.

This time, however, there were plenty of paying customers sniffing around, so Charlie must really want *Planet Nine* to fly.

"So what's this *Planet Nine* again?" she asked.

"It's an alternate history RPG," Charlie said. "It's sort of a *Flash Gordon* slash *Skylark of Space* 1930s, where Clyde Tombaugh found Pluto on schedule, only it turned out to be an Earthlike planet full of humanoids."

"Out beyond Neptune? The humanoids would be under tons of methane ice."

"Volcanoes and smog and radium projectors are keeping the place warm, apparently."

Dagmar grinned. "Uh-huh."

"So along with the folks on Planet Nine, there are dinosaurs and Neolithic people on Venus, and a decadent civilization sitting around the canals on Mars, and on Earth you've got both biplanes and streamlined Frank R. Paul spaceships with lots of portholes. So Hitler is going into space in what look like big zeppelins with swastikas on the fins, and he's in a race with the British and French and the Japanese and the New Deal, and there's plenty of adventure for everybody."

"Sounds like a pretty crowded solar system."

"There's a reason these people went broke creating it."

Dagmar took a lingering sip of her drink. She'd always had an idea that writing space opera would be fun, but had never steered her talent in that particular direction.

The writers of ARGs were almost always drawn from the ranks of disappointed science fiction writers. It was odd that there hadn't been more space opera from the beginning.

"Okay," she said. "I'll think about it. But not while I'm nursing an umbrella drink and watching the Aussie guys at the beach."

Charlie sighed audibly. "All right, you're allowed to have some good dirty fun on your vacation. But not too much, mind you."

"Right."

"And here's something else to think about. I'm giving you twice the budget you had for *Golden Nagi*."

Dagmar felt her own jaw drop. She looked at the carbonation rising in her glass and put the glass down on the plastic table.

"What are you telling me?" she said.

"I'm telling you," said Charlie, "that the sky's the limit on this one. If you tell me you need to send a camera crew off to Planet Nine to take pictures, then I'll seriously consider it."

"I—" Dagmar began.

"Consider it a present for doing such a good job these past few years," Charlie said. She could sense Charlie's smile on the other end of the phone.

"Think of it," he said, "as a vacation that never ends."

Hanseatic says:
I was so totally floored when it was revealed that the Rani had really been the Nagi all along.

Hippolyte says:
Ye flippin gods! SHE was an IT!

Chatsworth Osborne Jr. says:
I was expecting this. The players' guide turning out to be the villain has been a trope ever since *Bard's Tale II*.

Hippolyte says:
The Rani isn't the villain!

Chatsworth Osborne Jr. says:
Of course she is. Who put the curse on all those people, I ask you?

"We heard a rumor that the airlines can't afford to buy jet fuel any longer," the Dutch woman said the next morning. "Not if they're paying in rupiah."

Dagmar considered this. "The foreign airlines should be all right," she said. "They can pay in hard currency."

The Dutch woman seemed dubious. "We'll see," she said.

The Dutch woman—horse-faced and blue-eyed, like a twenty-first-century Eleanor Roosevelt—was half of an elderly couple from Nijmegen who came to Indonesia every year on vacation and had been due to leave the previous evening on a flight that had been canceled. They and Dagmar were waiting for the office of the hotel concierge to open, the Dutch couple to rebook, and Dagmar to confirm her own tickets. A line of the lost and stranded formed behind them: Japanese, Javanese, Europeans, Americans, Chinese, all hoping to do nothing more than get out of town.

Dagmar had checked news reports that morning and found that the government had frozen all bank accounts to prevent capital flight and had limited the amount of money anyone could withdraw over the course of a single day to something like fifty dollars in American money.

A government spokesman suggested the crash was the fault of Chinese speculators. The governments in other Asian countries were nervous and were bolstering their own currencies.

The concierge arrived twenty minutes late. The shiny brass name tag on his neat blue suit gave his name as Mr. Tong. He looked a youthful forty, and Dagmar could see that the cast of his features was somehow different from that of the majority of people Dagmar had met in Indonesia. She realized he was Chinese.

"I'm very sorry," Tong said as he keyed open his office. "The manager called a special meeting."

It took Mr. Tong half an hour to fail to solve the problems of the Dutch couple. Dagmar stepped into the glass-walled office and took a seat. She gave Mr. Tong her tickets and asked if he could confirm her reservations with the airline.

"I'm afraid not." His English featured broad Australian vowels. "The last word was that the military has seized both airports."

She hesitated for a moment.

"How can people leave?" she asked.

"I'm afraid they can't." He took on a confidential look. "I hear that the generals are trying to prevent the government from fleeing the country. There's a rumor that the head of the Bank of Indonesia was arrested at the airport with a suitcase full of gold bars."

"Ferries? Trains?"

"I've been through all that with the couple who were here ahead of you. Everything's closed down."

And where would I take a train anyway? Dagmar wondered.

Mr. Tong took her name and room number and promised to let her know if anything changed. Dagmar walked to the front desk and told them she'd be staying another night, then tried to work out what to do next.

Have breakfast, she thought.

The dry monsoon had driven out the rain clouds of the previous day, and the sky was a deep, cloudless tropical blue. Dagmar had breakfast on the third-floor terrace and sat beneath a broad umbrella to gaze out at the surrounding office towers and tall hotels, all glowing in the brilliant tropical sun. Other towers were under construction, each silhouette topped by a crane. A swimming pool sat in blue splendor just beyond the terrace. It was about as perfect as a day in the tropics could be.

Her fruit platter arrived, brought by a very starched and correct waiter, and Dagmar immersed herself in the wonder of it. She recognized lychee and jackfruit, but everything else was new. The thing that looked like an orange tasted unlike any orange she'd ever had. Everything else was wonderful and fresh and splendid. The croissant that accompanied the platter—a perfectly acceptable croissant in any other circumstances—was bland and stale by comparison. The meal was almost enough to make Dagmar forget she was stuck in a foreign city that she'd never intended to visit and that had just fallen into economic ruin as surely as if all the great, glittering buildings around her had crumbled into dust.

What happened to you, she wondered as she looked up at the steel-and-glass buildings around her, when your money was suddenly worthless? How could you buy food, or fuel for your car? How could anyone pay you for your labor?

No wonder her taxi driver had been so happy to get American money. With dollars he could feed his family.

On her journey she had taken two hundred dollars with her in cash, for use in emergencies. With that money, she realized, she was better off than all but a handful of the twenty-five million people living in Jakarta.

After finishing her coffee, she decided that since she was stuck in Jakarta, she might as well enjoy the place as much as she could. She returned to her room to change clothes. She put on a cotton skirt and a long-sleeved silk shirt she'd brought with her from the States, an outfit she hoped would be suitable for a Muslim country.

She considered buying clothes here, but all she had was the $180. The dollars, she thought, she should definitely save for emergencies.

She left a hundred of the dollars tucked into her luggage and put the rest, along with her remaining Indian rupees, in a fanny pack. Then she put a hat on her head—a panama, with a black ribbon, that had been woven by machine of some new plastic version of straw. She could roll it up into a tube and stuff it in her luggage—which you could do with a genuine straw panama as well, but this at one-tenth the price.

It set off her gray hair very nicely. Her hair had started going gray when she was seventeen, and by the time she entered college the last of her dark brown hair had turned. She hadn't minded much at the time—the look had been eye-catching, especially since her eyebrows had remained dark for an interesting contrast, and when she got tired of it, the gray hair was easy to dye a whole rainbow of colors. Eventually she'd grown fond of the gray and decided not to color it any longer. It was a decision that, now that she'd just passed thirty, she was comfortable with, though she reserved the right to change her mind as her biological age caught up with the age of her hair.

It amused her that some people, in an effort to be kind, called her an ash blond.

A younger version of the previous night's Sikh doorman let her out of the hotel and offered to summon a cab. She said that she'd walk, and he wished her a good morning.

As she set off down the street, she wondered if there was some kind of Brotherhood of Sikh Doormen that had somehow monopolized jobs in many of the big Asian hotels. Perhaps, she thought, that could be an element in some future game—Sikh doormen in various Asian cities would all be part of some conspiracy, and players would have to try to cadge information from them.

No, she thought. Too elaborate. And auditioning Sikh doormen to find out which of them could act would be a time-consuming process.

The dry monsoon had failed to blow away the equatorial heat, and the sun was fierce, but tall trees had been planted on either side of the road to provide shade. She used a flyover to cross four lanes of Jakarta's insane traffic. The air had the fried-fritter smell of biodiesel mixed with the scent of hot asphalt.

The area was dominated by office towers and hotels, but there were smaller buildings in between with shops and eateries. Billboards and neon signs advertised Yamaha bikes, Anker Bir, and Chandra handsets, the appearance of which made Dagmar smile. Celebrities endorsed beauty products and whiskeys. Street food was available— Dagmar imagined the vendors had to sell their seafood and meats before they spoiled. The smaller shops were open—the single owner, or members of his family, looked out at the street, face impassive—but the medium-size stores, the ones that couldn't make their payroll in the current situation, were closed. Even in the shade the heat was appalling, so Dagmar stepped into a building that had been converted into a kind of vertical shopping mall, and wandered around in cool air for a while. The international chains, Bok-Bok Toys and Van Cleef and Arpels, were open; the smaller, locally owned businesses, the camera and clothing stores, were closed. There seemed to be few customers in any case, and the goods available for purchase weren't anything Dagmar couldn't get at home.

She paused for a moment at an indoor skating rink, a few young people in tropical clothing making lazy circles to the sounds of 1970s American pop.

Back to the heat and the traffic. She made a random turn onto a boulevard shaded by rows of cone-shaped trees, where a series of blocky old office buildings stood with their window air-conditioners humming. There was a lot of green in Jakarta—trees, bushes, tropical ferns, and more palms than in L.A. She made another turn and found herself heading toward some kind of square or park—or maybe just a big, empty parking lot. Dagmar saw the open area was filled with people, and that many of them were carrying angry-looking signs and banners; she made a U-turn just as a pair of police vans turned down the street, each filled with men in blue uniforms and white helmets and crossbelts.

Dagmar increased her pace, not about to get between the police and a bunch of pissed-off citizens.

A few blocks away, music boomed out over the street, louder than the traffic. The sound came from a music and video store. The music thundering from its speakers was propulsive: layers of Indian tabla; a harmony line drawn by a chiming synthesizer, a metallic sound influenced by the gamelan; and on top of it all a bubbly 1950s-style pop vocal. Dagmar was completely charmed.

She stepped into the narrow store. Local films glowed from plasma screens, all heroic action, men with bare, blood-spattered torsos, headbands, and krises. The walls were covered with movie posters and pictures of pop stars. There was a row of terminals where customers could download music into portable storage, for transfer into whatever media later suited them.

The fact that this store existed at all told her that most Indonesians still made do with dial-up, assuming that they had Internet at all.

A young man with a Frankie Avalon haircut sat behind a counter up front. Dagmar gave him a nod, and he nodded back, an expression of surprise on his face. Clearly he didn't see a lot of tourists in here.

Beneath the glass counter were interchangeable plastic cartridges of fuel for miniturbines and a lot of cheap memory storage, sticks and slabs and buttons with pop culture symbols: peace signs, the faces of pop stars and anime characters, popular heroes like Bruce Lee, Che Guevara, and Osama bin Laden, and of course the ubiquitous Playboy rabbit.

It's a sad world, Dagmar thought, *when you have to choose between Osama and Hugh Hefner.*

Dagmar was the only customer. She went to one of the terminals where a pair of headphones waited. She took off her faux panama, stashed it atop the monitor, and put on headphones that smelled faintly of someone else's sweat. The instructions were in Javanese, but she managed to call up a directory and began to sample what was on offer.

There was rap. There was reggae. There was heavy metal and bubblegum pop and classic rock and sappy love songs with far too much reverb. World culture was available to anyone with a T1 connection, and the local people downloaded it, wrung it for meaning, remixed it, rebranded it, uploaded it, and broadcast it onto the street from speakers mounted on the facades of music stores, from off-brand MP3 players, from speakers in taxi cabs, from podcasts and webcasts and radio and audio streamed from thousands of sources, from unlicensed radio stations run by enthusiastic amateurs in Brazilian favelas, by religious fanatics in Sumatran kampungs, by fierce college girls in Kansas with piercings in their navels and anarchy in their hearts . . .

And by Dagmar, standing atop the massive bandwidth

of Great Big Idea Productions in Los Angeles, the media capital of the world. Dagmar, whose job was to take all that culture and history and find, or invent, the collusions and cabals that kept the world dancing . . . all the content zooming out into the world, where it would join with all the rest and be downloaded and adored and hated and absorbed and remixed again, only now with Dagmar's fingerprints on it . . .

Now Dagmar, listening, was worried about how she was going to pay for any content that she downloaded. She figured that the kid behind the counter had no way of breaking one of her twenty-dollar bills, and she still had no local money, not that it would buy much. There was no sign saying the place took credit cards.

She went to the counter and tried talking to the kid, but despite all the rap and classic rock his store had on offer, he had no English at all. She offered credit cards, but he shook his head. She took out Indian rupees and waved them. He looked at them in a businesslike way and took a thousand-rupee note, about twenty dollars U.S., then waved her back to her station.

Dagmar was happy with the exchange, and she congratulated herself that the kid's family would eat for the next couple of weeks. She took out her cell phone, thumbed the catch that revealed the USB connector, and plugged the phone into her terminal. She began her first download.

There was a few seconds' pause, and then the phone screen began blinking red warnings at her, and an urgent *pip-pip-pip* began to sound. She looked at the screen for a startled instant, then yanked the phone from the connector. She reversed the screen to read it and discovered that the download store had just tried to load a virus into her handset.

She looked up at the kid with the Frankie Avalon haircut.

"You little bastard!" she said.

The kid affected nonchalance. *What's your problem, Kafir?*

"You tried to steal my shit!" She turned off the phone, with any luck killing the virus, and marched to the counter. She banged the counter with the metal USB connector.

"Give me my rupees back!"

The kid shrugged. The rupees were nowhere in sight.

Dagmar had just about had enough of Jakarta.

"You want me to call the cops?" She looked out the door and to her immense surprise saw three policemen, right on the spot and right on time.

Two policemen, blue shirts and white helmets, rode a motorcycle. The driver kept the bike weaving between the cars stalled in traffic, and his cohort rode pillion, turning to look rearward as he talked into a portable radio.

The third policeman was on foot. He'd lost his white helmet, and blood ran freely from a cut on his forehead.

He was running like hell.

Dagmar became aware of a strange sound echoing up the street: *bonk-whonk-thump-bonk!* Like people kicking a whole series of metal garbage cans down the street, or the world's biggest gamelan orchestra on the march. Behind the metal crashings there was a background noise, a roaring like the crowd in a stadium.

The kid was startled. He ran to the door and took a peek outside, and then suddenly there was a wide-eyed look of fear on his face and he was out on the stoop, reaching over his head to yank at the rolling mesh screen that covered the front of his shop when he wasn't in it. He had forgotten Dagmar's existence.

Bang-thump-whonk-thud! The metallic crashings were coming close.

The kid got the screen only about a third of the way down before a silver saucer sailed through the air, hit him squarely in the back of the head, and felled him like a tree. He dropped at Dagmar's feet, unconscious. Dagmar looked in complete surprise at the VW hubcap spinning in triumph on the pavement outside the store.

"Hey!" she said, to no one in particular.

And then the streets were full of running figures, scores and then hundreds of Indonesian men. Some carried sticks, some carried signs, and a few carried what looked like machetes.

The demonstration that she had seen in the public square a short while ago had become a riot.

The source of the metallic clanging sounds became apparent. The runners were banging on the hoods, roofs, and sides of the cars as they ran past them. Banging with their sticks or their fists. The trapped drivers stared at them in horror as they streamed past.

There were shrieks as a windshield caved in.

At the sound of the breaking glass, a wave of adrenaline seemed to pick Dagmar right up off the floor. The unconscious boy's legs stretched out into the street, and she couldn't lower the screen with him in the way. She knelt by him, hooked both hands in his armpits, and dragged him clear.

Then she looked up to see one of the rioters bent to enter the store. He was a small man with a goatee, a bare chest, and a cloth headdress. He carried a knife as long as his forearm.

He looked just like one of the men in the store's heroic action vids.

Dagmar gave a yell, which startled the rioter. He drew back, then got a better look at Dagmar and took another step toward her.

Dagmar yelled again, jumped to her feet, and ran for the back of the store. She found a toilet cabinet and slammed the door shut and shot the little bolt. The cabinet was a little over three feet deep, with a discolored, streaked hole in the ground, a tank of water, and a battered green plastic scoop. Dagmar looked for an exit and saw a screened window too high to reach. She then looked for a weapon and saw a mop and bucket. The mop was too long to use in the confined space, so Dagmar snatched up the plastic scoop and held it like an ice pick as she faced the flimsy door and its flimsy lock.

In the store were a series of crashes and thuds. The music out front stopped playing. More crashes. Footsteps. Then silence.

Dagmar stayed braced behind the toilet door, scoop raised, ready to gouge whatever flesh she could out of an attacker. The air in the tiny room was hot and rank, and sweat dripped from Dagmar's chin, patting down onto her silk shirt. Through the open window overhead she could hear, faintly, the *poink-whong-bang* of the rioters hitting the cars on the street.

But no sounds any closer than that.

She thought about calling for help on her cell but had no idea what number to call, and rather doubted she'd ever reach anyone who could help her. Even if she reached someone, she had no idea where in the city she was or what the street address of the store was.

Dagmar stayed in the toilet for another fifteen minutes, until the sounds of the riot had faded completely. Then—scoop poised to stab any intruder—she flicked the little bolt open and slowly pushed open the door.

Nothing happened.

Carefully she leaned out of the cabinet to scan the store. She could see almost the entire room. The kid still lay on his face near the front door. Several of the plasma screens had been smashed, and others carried away. Brilliant sunlight shone through the narrow windows and the open door.

Dagmar crept out of the cabinet and approached the front. What she could see of the street was empty: the cars and trucks had dispersed. No human beings were visible. The kid on the floor was still breathing and had bled freely from a cut on his scalp, though it looked as if the bleeding had stopped. The mesh screen was still partly deployed.

She stepped over the boy, looked left and right— smashed windows, broken bicycles, a Honda burning, sending up greasy black smoke—and then grabbed the screen and hung her weight on it. The screen rattled down, making a shocking amount of noise, and then hit bottom with a bang.

The bang echoed up and down the empty street.

Dagmar had no way of locking the screen, but hoped any rioters wouldn't look too closely.

She retreated from the door, bent over the Indonesian kid, and tried to find a pulse in his neck. The heartbeat was strong: it looked as if the boy weren't about to die anytime soon.

She saw a corner of her thousand-rupee note peeking out of the kid's back pocket. She reached for it, then hesitated. Then withdrew her hand.

The boy had just had his store wrecked. A thousand rupees might keep him alive for the next few weeks.

She noticed her faux panama on the floor. Someone had stepped on it. She picked up the hat, brushed away the bits of broken glass that clung to it, and put it on her head.

She moved back into the store and waited for whatever was going to happen next.

CHAPTER THREE

This Is Not a Cowboy

"Don," said Austin to his speakerphone, "I think what we should do is follow the strategic plan."

Austin listened with half his attention as Don protested this idea. He and his partners were spending a fortune to retrofit an old office building, *and they didn't even own it.*

"What we need," said Don, "is a building of our own."

Pneumatics gave a gentle sigh as Austin leaned back in his office chair and put his feet up on his desk. He had been through this so many times before.

"Don," he said, "we have a big performance benchmark coming up. We don't have time to *build you a new headquarters.*"

"About that benchmark. I've got some ideas for new implementations—"

"No, Don," said Austin. "Follow the business plan."

"Just *listen*," urged Don. "This is *great.*"

He explained his new ideas at length. Austin let his

gaze drift to the window. Century City sat in the middle distance below, white modernist perfection above L.A.'s cap of smog. He thought about Jackson Hole and the sight of snowcapped mountains and the smell of pine, and for a moment he wished he were anywhere but here, going through this scenario yet one more time.

"That's all good," Austin said when Don paused for breath, "but we can save all that for Release 2.0. Right now we need to *follow the strategic plan.*"

"But wait!" Don said. "This will make it *so much better.* It'll be *really cool.*"

And on and on, for another five minutes or so.

Austin listened vaguely to the speakerphone and thought about trout fishing. He thought about high mountain streams and wildflowers and cowgirls in faded Levi's and flannel shirts and straw cowboy hats.

On reflection, he changed the fantasy to girls in chaps and fringed vests and hats and nothing else.

Don went on and on.

This, Austin thought, was the problem with geniuses. They got bored too easily.

And most business was boring. You set goals and you worked hard to meet those goals and then you started working on the next set of goals. It was all too plodding for creative types, who came up with half a dozen new ideas every single day and wanted to bring them all into being instantly.

Don paused to take another breath.

"Listen," Austin said. "What's your job title again?"

Don paused as his mind shifted tracks.

"I'm chief technology officer," he said.

"Right," said Austin. "And what's *my* job?"

"I don't know what your title is." Don's voice was suspicious.

"Never mind my title," said Austin. "What's my *job?*"

"You're VC," said Don.

"Right," said Austin. "I'm venture capital. Which means that I and my associates have invested in *dozens* of start-ups. Hundreds by now. And *that* means that we've seen a *lot* of strategic plans, successful and unsuccessful. And so what I am telling you now is that *you need to follow the plan to which we all agreed.*"

He congratulated himself on his sweet reasonableness, that and the excellence of his grammar, avoiding the dangling preposition even in speech.

"I can talk to my partners about the changes," Don said. "And they'll be okay with it."

"Ask yourself," Austin said, "if they'll be okay with finding another source of start-up money after I refuse to give you any further capital."

"But we *agreed* . . ."

Austin's reply was lazy, airy, while he thought of cowgirls.

"Why do I have to follow the agreement, Don, when you don't?"

While Don, with greater intensity, explained his ideas all over again, Austin thought of cowgirls riding in slow motion through fields of daisies.

"Don," Austin finally interrupted, "if you follow the business plan and achieve every benchmark and every deadline, and the firm establishes itself in its market niche, and the IPO happens and everyone leaves rich, *you can buy all the buildings you want.* And hang around and make all the new implementations that strike your fancy. No one will argue with you—*you'll be rich.*"

"But—"

"So for now *you need to follow the strategic plan.* And if you don't"—Austin smiled at the thought—"I will join your partners in voting you off the board, and you'll get nothing. And please don't think I can't do it, because I can. Ask Gene Kring."

There was a moment of puzzlement.

"Who's Gene Kring?" Don asked.

"Exactly my point," Austin said.

Honest to Christ, he thought, this guy was almost as bad as BJ.

CHAPTER FOUR

This Is Not a Rescue

In midafternoon Dagmar heard tramping outside and peered out to see a double line of police marching down the street in line abreast, followed by police cars and vans. The police were dressed more seriously this time, in khaki, with long batons, shotguns configured to fire tear gas grenades, transparent shields marked POLISI, and round helmets that looked as if they were designed by samurai, with plates hanging down to cover the ears and back of the neck.

The kid with the Frankie Avalon hair was awake by then, if still unwell. He slouched against the wall beneath one of the shelves. His eyes weren't very focused yet, but he didn't seem about to drop dead.

Dagmar saw as the police passed that they were heading in the general direction of her hotel. She figured this was about as safe as her day was going to get.

She went to the door and rolled the screen up to waist height, then ducked down beneath the screen and out into the street. The rotating lights on the vehicles flashed on broken windows. Dagmar followed the police line down the street.

At the next intersection the police paused for directions, and that's when someone noticed her. One of the cops in a car saw her, blipped the horn, and gestured her over. She bent toward him, and—talking around the cigarette in the corner of his mouth—he asked her a question in Javanese.

"Royal Jakarta Hotel?" she said hopefully.

The cop looked at her for a long, searching moment, then motioned her to stay where she was. He thumbed on his radio mic, spoke briefly with someone Dagmar assumed was a superior, and then turned back to Dagmar and spoke to her while gesturing at the rear door.

It seemed he wanted her to get in his car.

"There's a man back there," she said, pointing, "who's hurt."

He squinted at her and pointed at the rear door again.

She pointed at the download store. "Ambulance?" she said.

"No ambulance." The cop was losing patience.

Dagmar thought she should insist on an ambulance. Instead she got in the backseat and hoped this wasn't her last moment of freedom.

The car smelled strongly of the driver's harsh tobacco. The driver put the car in gear and it sprang away, turning onto a side street. They were still heading in the general direction of the Royal Jakarta, which was encouraging.

A second cop riding shotgun turned around and grinned at her. He seemed very young.

"How are you?" he asked.

Dagmar looked at him in surprise.

"I'm all right," she said. And then, because he seemed to expect a response, she asked, "How are *you?*"

"I'm good." He made a fist and pumped it in the air. "I'm very good."

The car swayed as it swerved around a truck that had been driven onto the curb and then looted. The young policeman nodded, then said, "Where are you going?"

"I'm going to Bali," she said.

He pumped his fist again. "Bali's very good." He opened the fist and patted himself on the chest. "I'm from Seringapatam."

Dagmar thought about all the places she was from, and decided to mention the most recent.

"I'm from Los Angeles."

"Los Angeles is very good! Very famous!" The cop was enthusiastic.

She glanced down a side street as they sped along, and gasped. A large building was on fire—she thought it might have been the shopping center she'd visited. Tongues of flame extruded from smashed windows to lick at the sides of the building. Fire trucks and police were parked outside, and she saw pieces of furniture in the streets where they'd been dropped—looted, apparently.

She thought she glimpsed bodies lying among the abandoned furniture, and then the car sped on.

"Are you in the movies?" asked the young cop.

Dagmar tried to get her mind back on the track of the conversation. Was she in the movies? she wondered.

The right answer was *sort of*, but that led to too much exposition. And she had a feeling that reality had taken enough turns today without her having to explain about alternate reality gaming.

"I write computer games," she said.

"Computer games! Excellent!" The cop made a gun with his two hands and made machine-gun sounds. "*Felony Maximum IV!*" he said. "I always take the MAC-10."

Dagmar had never played *Felony Maximum*, but it seemed wise to agree.

"The MAC-10 is good," she said.

The car took another turn, and there, visible through the windshield, was the shining monolith of the Royal Jakarta Hotel. The car rocketed under the portico, and the driver stomped on the brakes, bringing the vehicle to a juddering halt.

"Thank you!" Dagmar said. "Thank you very much!"

She tried to open the door and found it wouldn't open from the inside. The driver barked some impatient commands at the Sikh doorman—the same one who had been on duty in the morning—and then the doorman opened the car door and she stepped out.

"Thank you!" she said to the driver, who ignored her and sped away.

The Sikh was holding the hotel door for her. She looked up and down the facade of the hotel and saw broken windows. Hotel workers had already cleaned up the glass. A hundred yards farther down the street was an overturned minibus that had been set on fire. Greasy smoke hung in the brilliant tropical air.

No bodies, at least. A small favor, this.

Dagmar walked into the hotel, nodded to the doorman's "Good afternoon, miss," and went to Mr. Tong's office. Mr. Tong was alone—apparently he'd already discouraged everyone who needed discouraging—and he looked up as she knocked on the doorframe.

"Miss Shaw?" he said. "Nothing's changed, I'm afraid."

"There's a man," Dagmar said, "who needs an ambulance."

Together they got a map of the area, and Dagmar reconstructed her morning walk and the location of the music store. Mr. Tong made the call, then looked up at Dagmar.

"I've told them," he said. "But I don't know if they'll come."

Dagmar thanked Mr. Tong and left, trying to think if there was anything else she could do. Short of going back out onto the streets, there was nothing.

She went to her room and took off her sweat-stained clothing and stood in the shower for a long while. Then she lay naked on her sweet-smelling sheets and turned on a news program and heard the reporter from Star TV talk about "anti-Chinese rioting."

Anti-Chinese? she wondered. From what she could see, the rioters hadn't much seemed to care whose stuff they were looting.

The reporter went on to talk about an "unconfirmed number of deaths," and the report was accompanied by video, mostly from cell phones, that had captured bits of the action.

CNN showed no video of the riot but broadcast a lengthy discussion of the causes of the currency collapse.

"The government went on a spending spree before the last election," said the Confident Analyst. "It won them reelection, but they ran through almost all their foreign currency reserves just at the moment when the price of oil went soft. Then they made matters worse by keeping their current account deficit a state secret—and when that secret leaked, it was all over."

All cancel, Dagmar thought.

CHAPTER FIVE

This Is Not a Hiding Place

Start with a woman in a hotel room, Dagmar thought. Because there's nowhere else to go, because all her options are gone. Because a stranger's voice on the phone has told her to stay in this place until she's told to go somewhere else.

From there, reaching back in time, her story unfolds. Perhaps in reverse order. That would be a nifty trick.

Except that you have to *find* the story. It's not all in one place, as it would be in a novel or a movie. It's scattered out all through the world, and most of it's in electronic form.

That's the sort of story Dagmar writes.

At the beginning of the sort of game that Dagmar designs for a living, you go down the rabbit hole. That's what it's actually called, "rabbit hole." The rabbit hole draws you into a Looking-Glass Land—okay, Dagmar knows, she's mixing the two Alice stories—a Looking-Glass Land where the truth lies, and where, unlike in real life, you can look behind the mirrors to find out what it is.

A rabbit hole could be anything. A jar of honey that appeared in the mail, a data stick found in a washroom, an online poker site. A wedding in Bengaluru, a ticket to Jakarta. A virus loaded onto your phone.

And where the rabbit hole took you was a place that was just like your own place, except there was another reality hidden there.

In Looking-Glass Land the truth was hidden in source code, layered into Photoshop, transmitted in Morse, hidden in music files, whispered in Swedish or Shanghainese or Yiddish. Secrets were revealed in table talk on poker sites, found in genealogical charts, written with spray enamel on the sides of buildings.

Dagmar figures that some of the woman's backstory has to be found in *Planet Nine*. Or on Planet Nine. Because that's where this thing has to start.

From: Dagmar
Subject: Indonesia Fubar

Charlie, I never made it to Bali. I'm stuck in the Royal Jakarta Hotel. There's rioting all around and people are getting killed. The airports are closed and I can't get out. I've got $180 in hard currency and some credit cards that I can't use because the banks are all shut down.

I've called the embassy and they put my name on a list. They say that if the situation warrants, they will stage an evacuation. They also say in the meantime I might as well stay here, because it's as safe as anyplace.

Any suggestions? You or Austin wouldn't happen to know anyone out here with a helicopter, would you?

Elevator music—saccharine Indonesian pop—tinkled from speakers in the breakfast room. A lavish buffet had been set up for hotel guests: coffee, tea, fruit juices, and a bewildering amount of food, both Indonesian and Western.

Meals were no longer served on the third-floor terrace. Hotel management had apparently decided it was safer to keep their guests under cover.

"Did you see the pillar of smoke?" asked Mrs. Tippel.

"Yes."

Dagmar hadn't been able to miss it: her windows faced northwest, and from the fourteenth floor she had an excellent view of the part of the city that was on fire.

"That's Glodok," the Dutch woman said. "It's where the Chinese people live."

The elevator music tinkled on.

"In the sixties," said her husband, "the Chinese were killed because they were Communists. In 'ninety-eight they were killed because they were capitalists. Now they're being killed for capitalism again."

"Scapegoats," said Mrs. Tippel.

"Yes, yes." Mr. Tippel's blue eyes were sad. "The government or the military always need to blame others for their mistakes. And now the Chinese will pay for all the mistakes that the government made before the election."

"And even if there *were* Chinese traders who attacked the rupiah," said Mrs. Tippel, "they weren't here in Indonesia. They were in Hong Kong or Shanghai or somewhere."

The elderly Dutch couple had seen Dagmar wandering through the breakfast room with her fruit plate and invited her to join them.

Dagmar tasted a piece of fruit from her plate and paused for a moment to savor the astonishing bright taste. Then Mr. Tippel began to talk, and Dagmar lost interest in breakfast.

"In 'ninety-eight it was terrible," said Mr. Tippel. "The military had just lost power, and they thought that if there was enough chaos, they would be called back. So the riots were actually led by the military."

"There were rape squads," said Mrs. Tippel.

Dagmar opened her mouth, closed it, strove for a response.

"Is that what's happening now?" she asked.

The Tippels looked at each other.

"Who knows?" said Mr. Tippel. "The army's up to something, though. They have the city under siege."

All those games she'd played, Dagmar thought as the elevator music tinkled in the background. All those dungeon crawls and conflicts and mysteries, all those battles, skirmishes, raids, and sieges. All those rolls of a twenty-sided die, all those experience points.

And none of them worth a damn. She had no idea how to behave in a city being blockaded by its own military. She hadn't known what to do in the face of a mob other than to lock herself in a toilet.

As far as action in the real world was concerned, all those games had been a complete waste of time.

When her ring tone went off—the first few bars of "Harlem Nocturne," the Johnny Otis version—Dagmar didn't notice right away. The sounds blended too well with Indonesian elevator music. And then she realized someone was calling her, and she snatched at the phone.

"Dagmar?" said Charlie. "Are you still in Jakarta?"

Dagmar's heart gave a foolish leap at the sound of his voice. "Yes!" she said. "Yes, I'm still here."

"Okay. I'll arrange to get you out, then."

"Good! Good!" Dagmar realized she was babbling and made an effort to achieve rational communication.

"How are you going to manage it?" she asked. "Because the embassy—"

"I've been with the *Planet Nine* people all day and only just got your email," Charlie said. "But I already know enough to realize that the embassy's fucked. They can't evacuate you because all our military assets are tied up in the current Persian Gulf crisis, and my guess is that our government is too proud to ask anyone else to do it."

That sounded like Uncle Sam all right, Dagmar thought.

"So," she said, "what next?"

"Lucky for you I'm a multimillionaire," Charlie said. "I'm going to get in touch with some security firms, and we're going to stage our own private evacuation. If necessary, we'll fly you off the hotel roof in a helicopter."

Dagmar paused a moment to picture this.

"Big box office," she said.

"Does your handheld have a GPS feature?"

"Yes."

"Give me your coordinates, then."

As the Tippels watched with interest, Dagmar thumbed

a button, and her coordinates flashed onto the phone's screen.

"Six degrees eleven minutes thirty-one point eight seconds south, a hundred six degrees forty-nine minutes nineteen point four eight seconds east."

"Got it," he said. "I'll give them your coordinates and phone number and email, and we'll see what they can arrange."

"Good," Dagmar said, and then she added, "Thanks, Charlie."

"No problem."

"You keep saving me," she said.

"I haven't saved you *yet*," he said. "And if I'm going to, I'd better hang up and contact the troops."

"I love you, Charlie," Dagmar said with sudden urgency.

There was a moment of silence as Charlie dealt with his surprise.

"I'm fond of you, too," he said. "Whatever you do, don't leave the hotel."

"No problem there."

"Take care. Someone will call soon."

"Thanks!" But Charlie had hung up.

Dagmar reluctantly closed the phone and returned it to her belt.

"Your boyfriend?" asked Mrs. Tippel.

Dagmar shook her head. "My boss."

Mrs. Tippel seemed a little surprised.

"He must be a good employer," she said.

He's hiring mercenaries to rescue me, Dagmar almost said. But she reflected that so far as she knew, no mercenaries were coming for the Tippels or for anyone else in the breakfast room, and that to mention her good fortune might seem tactless, as if she were boasting about her return to the life of a privileged Westerner.

"We went to college together," she said.

Hiring mercenaries, she thought.

It was like something you'd do in a game.

After breakfast, Dagmar checked with Mr. Tong to see if anything had changed, and found that nothing had. So she went to her room, booted her ultrathin computer, and checked her email.

Her handheld could do anything her computer could, but she preferred a standard keyboard to having to thumb long messages on the phone's little keypad. She wiped out spam, answered some routine queries, and sent messages to friends about her situation. She wrote about the riot and about being trapped in the music store, and about the bodies she thought she'd seen on the trip to the hotel.

As she typed on the familiar keyboard, in the hotel room that smelled of clean sheets, with the hushed sound of the air-conditioning in the background and the room's coffeemaker hissing and snorting as it provided Dagmar's caffeine fix, the previous day's hazards began to seem unreal, a brief dip into a nightmare that had been banished by the morning's strong tropical light.

The plangent sounds of Johnny Otis echoed in the room. Dagmar snatched at her phone. The number flashing in the display had a country code she didn't recognize.

"Hello?" she said cautiously.

"Is this Dagmar Shaw?"

The male voice had some kind of Eastern European accent.

"Yes," she said.

"My name is Tomer Zan," the man said. "I work for Zelazni Associates. Your employer, Mr. Ruff, has retained us to see about your safety."

Dagmar restrained her impulse to begin a joyful bouncing on the mattress.

"Yes," she said. "He told me to expect your call."

"Can you describe your situation, please?"

She did. She mentioned the riot the previous day, and being trapped in the music store, and the fact that she had $180 in cash. She told Tomer Zan that she was on the fourteenth floor of the hotel, with a view to the northwest. She mentioned that meals were no longer being served on the third-floor terrace because the hotel management considered it unsafe.

"I'm looking at a satellite picture of your hotel on Google Earth," Zan said, "and I can tell you right now that I don't like it. You're too close to that traffic circle with the Welcome Statue, you're too close to the government buildings that are going to be targets for demonstrators. The natural path for marches or riots runs right past your front door."

"Great," Dagmar said.

"We're going to try to move you someplace safer. But we don't have any assets in Jakarta, so that may not be possible for a few days."

Dagmar felt her mouth go dry.

"You don't have anybody in Jakarta?" she asked.

"No, we don't."

"So why did Charlie hire you?"

"Because," Zan explained patiently, "the companies with assets in Jakarta are all overcommitted right now."

Figures, Dagmar thought. She wandered to the window, parted the heavy curtains, and looked down at the street below. There was very little traffic, and none on foot. And no police.

"We'll have someone on the ground there in a few days," Zan said.

He seemed very confident of this.

"Okay," she said.

"You're not with anyone?" Zan asked.

"No. I'm alone."

"Okay. I want you to change your schedule every day. Eat meals at different times, and in different restaurants in the hotel, if that's possible."

"Why?"

"It takes three days to set up a kidnapping. If you keep changing your schedule, that makes an abduction more difficult."

Dagmar began to say, *But why would they kidnap me?* then clacked her teeth shut on the words because they sounded just like the sort of thing a stupid tourist would say.

"Okay," she said. "I'll do that."

"The power supply may be erratic, so keep your cell phone and your computer charged. Buy extra batteries if you can—or make sure your miniturbines have extra fuel."

"My phone doesn't have miniturbines."

"Then charge it every chance you can, and buy extra

batteries if you can find them in the hotel. And don't use the phone for anything except absolutely necessary calls."

"All right."

"If there's a store in the hotel where you can buy food, buy all you can. Even if it's junk food. The average city has only a three-day supply of food, and calories may get scarce."

"What do I buy the food *with?* Do I use my dollars?"

There was a long moment's silence.

"Save the dollars," Zan said.

He then went on to tell Dagmar that he wanted her to find six different ways to escape the hotel from her room. And another six exits from every other place she regularly visited within the building.

"What do I do if I have to leave the hotel?"

"Find a place of temporary safety, and call me."

He went on to tell her not to wear any expensive jewelry or be seen carrying her computer, because that might mark her out as someone worth robbing.

"Another thing," he said. "I need you to be on the roof of the hotel at sixteen hundred hours Jakarta time."

"This afternoon?"

"Yes."

"Why?"

"So the satellite can get a look at you. I need you facing east and looking up."

Dagmar wondered how much it was costing Charlie to retask someone's satellite, and decided it was better not to know.

"You can use my picture on the Great Big Idea Web page," she said.

"We're getting pictures of the roof anyway," Zan said, "in case we want to extract you from there. So we might as well find out what you look like *now*."

Extract, Dagmar thought.

"All right," she said.

She was placing herself in the hands of experts. Not that it had worked so far.

Tomer Zan advised her to keep her passport and money on her, preferably in a money belt, or in a pocket that could be buttoned or zipped.

"I have a pouch I can wear around my neck," she said. Which she rarely used, because it wasn't designed for people with tits.

"That's good," Zan said. "Would you like me to repeat any of my instructions?"

"Change my schedule," Dagmar said. "Six exits, no jewelry or computer in public, on the roof at sixteen hundred."

"You forgot to buy batteries," Zan said. His voice betrayed absolutely no sense of humor.

"Buy batteries," Dagmar said. "Check."

"Don't lose this number. I'll send you email in a few minutes repeating everything I've said."

"Okay."

Zan said good-bye and hung up. Dagmar located his number in her phone's memory and shifted it into the directory under the name Charlies Friend.

Ten minutes later, Zan's email turned up on her computer.

Dagmar decided she might as well go find batteries.

*

A woman in a hotel room, Dagmar thought a few hours later. That would be a good place to start a story.

You would have plenty of issues to deal with right away. Who was the woman, and why was she in the hotel room? Where was the hotel? What was going on outside? Was she in transit, in hiding, on the phone, in denial?

Probably all four, Dagmar thought, and felt an uneasy pang of self-knowledge.

The sad fact was that every sad fact in the world was the raw material for a story. Fiction thrived on desperation, on dejection, on violence. Every time you stepped outside the door, you could find a new subject. Every book and newspaper became research. Every act, no matter how sordid, and every tragedy, no matter how pointless, was matter for fiction—and in fiction, all tragedy has meaning and no action is random.

So you start with the woman in the hotel room, Dagmar thought. *And the reason she is there is that she has no place else to go.*

CHAPTER SIX

This Is Not the Bat Cave

The screen was full of chaotic movement, explosions, the clash of weapons. BJ's fingers danced over the controller. The ice-cold Entropy Beast that hovered over the chamber exploded in a blast of flame, scattering chunks of frozen flesh-shrapnel and knocking down half a dozen Goblin Warriors and one Lawful Paladin.

"No," BJ said, "you can't download all of 'Fly Like an Eagle' as a ring tone."

The Paladin sprang back to his feet and cut a Goblin Warrior in half with his Fire Sword.

"No," BJ said, "it doesn't matter if your friend says he did it. You still can't. If you have the right software, you can convert a sound file into a ring tone and download it from your own computer, but we don't provide that service."

Explosions rocked the stone castle walls. BJ's Elven Mage—who had the advantage of being invisible, at least as far as the other players were concerned—scuttled up the staircase and toward the glowing chest on the Altar of the Black Goddess.

"Thank you, ma'am," said BJ. "Sorry I wasn't able to help."

BJ worked in the darkest, most depressing dungeon of information technology, that of customer service. He spent his hours aiding the inept, the insane, and a very large population of compulsive liars. It was that last category that drove him into a fury—couldn't *any* of these people tell the simple truth? They chanted their mantra—"I didn't do *anything*"—when it was clear that they had been ravaging their own software with one deranged decision after another.

Fortunately, Spud LLC—"Your source for user-friendly IT solutions"—didn't much care that BJ ran his own little gold-farming projects on the side.

"Let's try this," BJ said. "Try restarting your computer. If you still have a problem, call me back."

His Elven Mage was the first of the party to the casket on the Black Goddess's altar. BJ knew that once he magicked open the casket, he had approximately thirty-four seconds before the Goddess Herself materialized in the chamber to lay waste to any intruders, whether they were invisible or not. BJ planned to be out of the room by then.

"Your email program won't respond to the password? Indulge me for a moment—have you checked to see if the Caps Lock key is on?"

The Elven Mage touched the glowing casket. A balloon appeared in a corner of the screen. BJ moused to the balloon and typed in the Pre-Adamite spell that would open the casket. With the sound of flourishing trumpets—a sound that BJ hoped would be obscured from other players by the general sound of combat going on below—the glowing casket opened.

The countdown had started.

BJ clicked the Grab button, and the Elven Mage glommed the two items in the casket, a scroll of spells and the Orb of Healing. The spells on the scroll were low-level crap, but BJ could maybe trade the item for something more useful. The Orb of Healing, however, was the big prize on this level, and BJ wasn't about to give it up.

The Elven Mage scurried down the stairs and snaked through the battling warriors. The Paladin was still cleaving Goblins in twain. The Dwarf Twins were fighting to protect the Enchanter, who in turn was casting spells, fireballs exploding with little mushroom clouds like atomic bombs, and the Halfling was hanging around in the background and throwing flaming bottles of oil at the Goblins.

If they were still in the room when the Dark Goddess showed up, they were all going to become extinct.

BJ didn't much care—he'd gotten what he came for, and if none of his party survived, there wouldn't be any argument over how to split the loot.

Besides, the Orb of Healing was unsplittable.

"Let's try restarting your computer," BJ said. "If you still have a problem, call me back."

The Elven Mage ducked through the Gothic arch at the far end of the room and ran past the splintered bodies of two Guardian Gargoyles. Behind him, he heard the chiming chords that accompanied the appearance of the Dark Goddess, followed by the sounds of a *lot* of dying.

Stupid noobs, BJ thought. And when the Dark Goddess disapparated, he could reenter the room and pick up the gold and possessions of his deceased companions.

That Fire Sword would come in handy . . . for somebody.

BJ had just made anywhere between six hundred and a thousand dollars—*real* dollars, not the virtual gold pieces used in the game. More if he could pick up the Fire Sword.

BJ had played the *Adventure of the Orb* so many times that he could practically do it with his eyes closed. He could do it with perfect competence even when performing his customer service job. But though the adventure was by now tedious in the extreme, the tedium was worth it in terms of income.

The fact was that there were a lot of players who didn't want to play the lower levels of online games like *World of Cinnabar.* They wanted to start powerful characters right away and were willing to pay—pay *real* money—for those characters and for powerful magic items like the Orb of Healing. It was against the rules of the *World of Cinnabar* for money to be exchanged for these virtual items, but there was no practical way for game administrators—or those of any other MMORPG—to police eBay or the many other auction sites.

The Orb alone, when auctioned online, would net BJ at least three hundred dollars. His Level Twelve Elven Mage, with all its loot and gear, would net him another three hundred. If he was lucky, the auction could go higher.

Not bad for the thirty online hours it had taken to

raise the Mage to his present level—even if competition from a thousand Chinese boiler-room gold farms had depressed prices.

And besides, BJ's old Chevy needed a new set of tires. And a paint job, but the tires came first.

BJ's job with Spud paid him enough to cover his nine-year-old car and an apartment that smelled both of mildew and of his ursoid roommate, a UCLA dropout and fellow Spud employee named Jacen—whose parents had named him, incidentally, after a character in the *Star Wars* Expanded Universe.

When he reflected on his apartment and his car and his job with Spud and compared it with what Charlie had, it made him want to sneak over to Santa Monica and slash Charlie's tires.

If he could actually come up with a Spell of Invisibility, he would do exactly that.

But until then, it looked as if he was stuck with having to toil at the gold farm in order to make ends meet.

CHAPTER SEVEN

This Is Not the Whole Story

At sixteen hundred hours, Dagmar was on the roof of the hotel. The top two floors were a series of suites and penthouses, and Dagmar needed a special key card to go there. She'd had to get off the elevator a floor below and go up the stairs. To keep the riffraff out, the top two floors had the same key card locks as the elevator, but the roof door was not so equipped.

By this time she was completely familiar with the hotel stairs. She'd followed Tomer Zan's instructions and found her six escape routes from her room. By the time she was finished searching out staircases and finding out whether they led outside the hotel, she was tired and covered with sweat. This called for a shower, a change of clothes, and lunch. As the hour she'd chosen for lunch was completely random, she presumed that any hypothetical kidnappers were at least as confused as she was.

She had looked up Zelazni Associates—she had at first spelled it Zelazny, like the writer—and discovered that it was an Israeli firm dedicated to "personal protection" and, it appeared, all things military. The word *mercenary* was nowhere on its Web site, but that's what they were. Their offices were in Tel Aviv and South Carolina— nowhere, she observed, near Jakarta.

She stood on the roof in the bright, humid daylight. The dry monsoon was from the north and carried the scent of burning Glodok, the bone and body fat of Chinese mothers and children. The roof had a fringe of the red tiles that were popular here, but most of it was a flat expanse of tar grown soft in the equatorial sun. The housing for the elevators and banks of solar cells and big ten-foot-tall aluminum boxes holding air-conditioning gear made the roof cluttered, so Dagmar made her way to the eastern side of the hotel tower and stood there in the bright sun for a long time, looking up. The tar oozed out beneath her feet, the hot sun prickled the side of her face, and she wished she'd been able to wear her panama. Every so often she brought her watch up into view, checked the time, and lowered her arm.

When it was five minutes past the hour, she looked out over the landscape of modern towers and, beyond the shining emblems of modernity, the vast landscape of the city, made indistinct by humidity and smog. There were other pillars of smoke rising besides Glodok, though none as large, and she wondered what political state- ments, neighborhood grudges, or mere criminalities were being played out.

This was what a travel writer would call "the real Asia," the world of those who had been lured to the city on the promise of a better life, then found that every promise, however unspoken, had been broken. Now their

life's work had gone for nothing, their savings were useless, and they were under siege by their own military.

They were a tough people, Dagmar presumed, if they
were here at all; but they could be forgiven for being
angry. She could only hope that she wouldn't become a
casualty of that rage.

An amplified Javanese voice echoed between the
buildings. The speech was rapid, urgent, and male.
Dagmar stepped closer to the edge of the building and
looked down the slope of ornamental red tile to the street
below.

Past the crests of the trees that lined the street,
Dagmar saw thousands of people marching north up the
street under homemade signs. They were close-packed
and orderly and hadn't yet turned into a mob, though
Dagmar wondered how many clubs and knives were
hidden away under loose clothing.

The amplified voice wasn't a part of the demonstration but was coming from a police line stretched across
the road ahead of it. They looked like the police she'd
met the previous day, with khaki uniforms, helmets, and
shields. There seemed to be very few of them compared
with the demonstrators.

The bullhorn fell silent. The demonstrators kept
moving forward. Then the amplified words came again.
Dagmar had a sense that they were the same words, only
spoken more rapidly.

Dagmar's nerves gave a leap at the window-rattling
boom of shotguns. Gas canisters arced high above the
crowd, splashed down in little flowers of white. The
crowd began to move—some running forward, some

clumping, some trying to move back against the pressure of the thousands coming up from behind.

The officer with the bullhorn was yelling.

Shots hammered out. Not shotguns this time, but rifles, the rip of automatic fire.

The whole crowd screamed at once, fury and mourning and pain wrapped up in one vast primal sound.

Dagmar remembered the young cop from the car, the boy whose whole life experience seemed derived from *Felony Maximum IV.* Who made machine-gun noises with his lips as he triggered an imaginary weapon.

I always take the MAC-10.

Aside from a handful that went crazy and charged, the crowd surged away from the police line, leaving behind specks of black and red on the pavement. The officer kept yelling through the bullhorn. The demonstrators who charged were gunned down, and bullets flew past them into the crowd.

Their sprawled figures were tiny. Dagmar could cover their dead forms with her finger and make them go away.

The crowd screamed as if it were one huge animal, and the animal fled. The shooting continued, more deliberate now, as if the police were picking their targets. The signs and banners the crowd had been carrying fell and lay abandoned along the pavement.

Dagmar stepped back from the edge, tar pulling at her shoes.

The scent of burning Chinese was strong in the air.

Once upon a time there had been four of them, Dagmar and Charlie and Austin and BJ. And though each was good at a number of things, all of them were very good at games.

They met at Caltech, where they majored in computer science. They spent a lot of their time staring into screens, and computer games had a limited appeal for eyes that were already weary of looking at 525-line images. They preferred games played with paper and pencil—RPGs, where each could pretend to be someone different from themselves, yet someone they had created.

Unlike their peers who preferred computers to human company, each was comfortable around other people. Austin and Charlie even knew how to talk to girls—and BJ was a fast learner.

Other people wandered in and out of the games, but these four were constants. They were all role players— they could stay in character for hours and shared a dislike of players whose chief motivation was to manipulate the rules in order to gain rewards or treasure.

Dagmar was a scholarship student. Her mother worked in a dry-cleaning establishment; her father was a bartender who had descended over time to a barfly. Dagmar had grown up preferring game worlds to her own life, though sometimes the latter intruded, as when she'd discovered that her father had pawned her computer in order to buy vodka. Caltech, in Pasadena, with its smog and perfect weather, was the best life she'd ever known.

When she ran her own games, she used GURPS as a rule set and created her own worlds of adventure, all crafted in meticulous detail. She specialized in elaborate plots with enormous sets of characters, sometimes so complex that after the game had run on for weeks or months, she herself forgot who had stolen the jewels, or murdered the Antarean ambassador, or double-crossed the Allies on the eve of World War II. Her games required hours of research to put together, but on the other hand, she enjoyed research.

Charlie's games were agreeably eccentric. In one game the players were ravens in a quest for the magic that had given them human intelligence; in another, they were zombies in search of human brains to eat. In a third, they were ordinary people who had somehow been shrunk to the size of hamsters. Other sorts of players— those who wanted to kill monsters, plunder treasure, and rack up experience points—recoiled from Charlie's campaigns as if they transmitted plague. Dagmar, Austin, and BJ loved them.

Austin Katanyan was a second-generation gamer. His parents had met playing *Dungeons and Dragons* in college. He had brought their first-edition *D&D* rules with him in the original brown cardboard box, actually used them to run a game, and had a worn copy of *Chainmail* that he used to resolve the large-scale conflicts. He liked to run old game systems: *RuneQuest, Witch Hunt, Empire of the Petal Throne*. Like Dagmar, he liked to explore the elaborate backgrounds of fantasy worlds. Unlike Dagmar, he didn't invent his own.

BJ's games were, in a word, diabolical.

His given name was Boris Jan Bustretski, and he came from the same eastern working-class background that had produced Dagmar. He was tall and stocky and blond and had inherited steelworker's arms and shoulders from his father, who had worked for Bethlehem until the bankruptcy, and for a trucking firm thereafter.

BJ thought very well of his own intelligence. He was happy to tell people how smart he was and boasted of his plans for a successful career as a master of Internet 2.0. Despite that, he didn't seem to know how physically attractive he was, a trait Dagmar found endearing.

His games were full of twists and cunning. Traps lurked around every corner. His nonplayer characters all had agendas, and all were faithless. The character who hired mercenary characters for a mission had no intention of paying them at the end of it; the venerable old lady who provided information to the players was an agent of the opposition; the weapons with which the adventurers were provided were faulty, or were cursed, or would give their position away to anyone with the right tracking devices. Characters would appear who would offer the players their heart's desire in order to betray their fellows.

BJ's campaigns kept his players sharp. Austin, Charlie, and Dagmar became experts at anticipating the treacheries and multiple loyalties of others. It was a paranoid worldview that was, in its way, comforting. You *knew* everyone would betray you; the question was when.

Sometimes the campaigns would simply *change*. Players who had been adventuring in twenty-first-century North America suddenly found themselves translated to alien worlds. A perfectly realistic historical campaign involving Vásquez de Coronado's march into the Midwest, a campaign that had gone on for weeks, would suddenly encounter Indian tribes worshipping world-threatening Lovecraftian monsters. BJ was a good enough craftsman that all these switches eventually made sense, if tenuously, but he admitted that he got bored with his creations and that the sudden switches from one genre to another were intended to keep him interested in his own games. Sometimes these attempts failed; BJ abandoned more campaigns than he finished.

Dagmar was a woman on a campus populated largely by males. The gaming group had an even larger percentage of men than the campus as a whole. For the first time in her life, she found herself a social success.

The attention was pleasing, but she viewed the possibilities with a cautious eye. She was perfectly aware that the only experience she had had in relationships was watching her mother remain in a hopeless marriage to an alcoholic.

Austin and Charlie had expressed polite interest in her. BJ hadn't—he was much more interested in working out the details of his future life as a billionaire. So of course—after a couple of years exploring other possibilities—BJ was the one that she fell for. They had a glorious nine months together before BJ's change in attitude grew too great for Dagmar to ignore.

The relationship had simply ceased to interest him. He'd gotten as bored with Dagmar as he had with Vásquez de Coronado's march along the Arkansas.

Dagmar managed to survive the blow to her self-esteem. Her principal regret, over the long term, was not so much having left BJ as having broken up the gaming group. Austin and Charlie had to decide which of the two to invite to their games, and without the chemistry of the four core members, the games became less interesting.

But Dagmar wasn't a part of that scene much longer. On the rebound from BJ, she fell for her English professor. Not that he taught English: he was a chemistry professor on sabbatical from Churchill College, Cambridge. When Aubrey's sabbatical at Caltech expired, Dagmar dropped out of school to marry him.

Now it was Dagmar's turn to be bored. Not with Aubrey, not at first, but with her situation. Her visa didn't allow her to work, though she did manage to wangle some under-the-table consulting jobs in computer departments in and out of Cambridge. When her resident immigrant status finally allowed her to look for jobs, her lack of a degree precluded meaningful employment.

Out of sheer boredom she created an online role-playing game called *Earth/Tea/Paper*. It consumed her completely for nine months and was a modest success. She decided that the Chinese backstory she'd written for the game was more interesting than the game itself and thought she might give writing fiction a try.

The first short story, "Stone/Paper/Tea," took her six months: one month to write the story, and five to work up the nerve to send it to an editor.

The story was accepted by *Orion Arm*, a British science fiction magazine. The magazine folded before they could publish, but during that time Dagmar had written four more stories, all of which eventually sold to better-paying markets than *Orion Arm*.

More stories followed, all science fiction. Her life

orbited a college that specialized in science and engineering, and her own literary tastes had always tended toward the fantastic. Aubrey, she was pleased to discover, was proud of her achievements.

The stories were followed by a novel and two sequels, all sold both in the U.S. and the U.K. In New York, Dagmar's acquiring editor left shortly after buying the series. Her replacement was promoted elsewhere in the company, and the next, fired. By the time the fourth editor wrote an email assuring Dagmar of his admiration for her work and his hope for a successful collaborative relationship, the series' doom was sealed.

In the U.K., the books died because of a lifestyle change on the part of their editor. She had risen to a position of power within the company, fueled by potent cocktails of alcohol and cocaine; but when she went on the wagon, her personality changed. From amiable and energetic, she became critical, angry, and vocal. She found fault with her superiors at meetings; she fired or drove away her assistants; she insisted that Christmas and birthday parties be alcohol-free.

The higher-ups at the company desperately wanted to get rid of her, but they couldn't find an excuse—she was, in fact, making them millions of pounds. So the company decided they really didn't need those millions of pounds after all and dropped their science fiction and fantasy imprint. To Dagmar it seemed an extreme reaction to a personnel problem, for all that it was a typically English one. Dagmar's books were reassigned to a new editor, an amiable man who had never read a science fiction novel in his life. The books were published, but as literary fiction, a change that only served to confuse everyone.

Dagmar's commercial destruction was thus assured on two continents. The books were never actually reviewed on paper, so far as she knew. The few online reviews were respectful, even enthusiastic, but the sales figures were catastrophic.

That was the end of her writing career, at least under her own name. She had become a literary unperson. Her sales figures were recorded in electromagnetic form in computers in the offices of the major distributors. The figures *proved* that her books didn't sell—no publisher in his right mind would take a chance on her.

That none of this was her fault was not on record anywhere.

That her career track was not at all untypical—that the career of practically every other SF or fantasy writer at her two publishing houses also cratered—did not make the situation any easier to bear, but only filled her with a rage that had no point and no direction.

The career collapse occurred simultaneously with a crisis in her marriage. Aubrey had always wanted children, and thus far she had managed to delay the final decision. But he was fourteen years older than she and wanted the children grown and out of the house "before I get too far into my declining years." He felt he'd indulged her long enough. Considering the death of her career, it wasn't as if she had anything better to do.

Dagmar thought he might have a point and stopped taking her pill. And then she reflected that she'd had three *affaires* during her marriage—each during a trip out of town, each short but extremely satisfying—and that rather than have a baby with Aubrey, she'd much rather march over to the Hepworth statue in Churchill College and rip the clothes off the first halfway attractive undergraduate she met.

It wasn't very nice, she reckoned, but it was *true*. And things that were true had their own weight, independent of whether they were decorous or not.

She'd lived in two places in the U.S.: Cleveland and Greater Los Angeles. Going west was what Americans did to start over. And so she went back on the pill, packed a pair of suitcases, shipped a copy of the Complete Works of Dagmar Shaw to Charlie by surface mail, and flew to Orange County. When the divorce decree arrived some months later, she signed it.

The only regret she had was that she'd left Aubrey with so many regrets. It hadn't been his fault.

Over the eight years she'd been away, Dagmar had kept in touch with Austin, Charlie, and BJ. Austin had become a successful venture capitalist and started his own company. Charlie and BJ had gone into business together: Charlie had done extremely well, but BJ was still, as the saying went, working on his first million.

The versions of how that had come about were so wildly different that Dagmar found them impossible to reconcile at a distance. The stories weren't any more compatible close up, but the anger was a good deal more visible. All Dagmar could do was make sure that Charlie and BJ never met.

She was looking around for jobs in IT when Charlie asked her to lunch.

"I think it would be wicked cool to own a game company," he said. "Would you like to run it for me?"

The next morning, at an hour chosen randomly in order to foil kidnappers, Dagmar went for the daily hopeless visit to see if Mr. Tong was able to help with any airline reservations. Instead of Tong, the office of the concierge was occupied by a small Javanese woman in a white Muslim headdress.

"Mr. Tong no here," she said. She didn't add anything more, even after Dagmar started asking questions.

Tong had gone up in flames with Glodok. Or so Dagmar could only suppose.

A few hours later the protesters came again, and there were no police to stop them. Most of the demonstrators marched past the Royal Jakarta north to the presidential palace, but a group at the tail of the column began throwing rocks at the hotel and smashing those windows that had survived the riot on Tuesday. When this produced no response, they stormed the hotel and looted all the shops on the first floor.

The Sikh doorman in his imposing uniform decided not to die for his masters and instead ran for the manager's office and locked himself inside.

Dagmar didn't know that any of this had happened until hours later, when she went to the hotel restaurant for dinner. The sight of the lobby, with smashed glass and furniture and glossy tourist brochures scattered like bright flower petals over the fine marble, sent Dagmar straight back to her room in terror. She emailed Charlie and called Tomer Zan.

"We're still working on moving you to a safer place," Zan said.

"The hotel got *looted*."

"We're working on it. We've got an advanced team in Singapore setting up logistics."

How many logistics does it take to move a single person? Dagmar almost screamed.

A lot, apparently.

An alternate reality game was made simpler if the players were helping a sympathetic character. The woman lost in her own hotel room was just such a person.

But how did she get in the hotel room, and what did that have to do with *Planet Nine*?

If *Planet Nine* was like other MMORPGs, there would be places in the game world where people could meet. In fantasy games, this was usually a tavern, where the player-characters could swill ale, eat hearty stew, and find like-minded individuals with whom to embark on quests.

Presumably there was a similar place in the *Planet Nine* setup.

If there was a room somewhere in the *Planet Nine* world where only the players of Dagmar's ARG could meet to exchange information, that would be useful to the game.

But what, she thought, if bad guys had a place to meet, too?

People who played in MMORPGs lived all over the world. They adopted online identities and knew one another only by those identities.

They could be anybody. Students, lawyers, teachers, truck drivers, or—as in the old *New Yorker* cartoon—dogs.

They could be criminals. Killers. Terrorists.

Suppose, Dagmar thought, some bad people were meeting in the *Planet Nine* world to anonymously plan their activities? Suppose they were overheard, by another player or a systems administrator? Suppose that person then ended up dead, not in the game but in the real world?

That, she thought, was your rabbit hole.

And if the rabbit hole led to the woman in the hotel room—if the woman was the lover or daughter or sister of the man who died—then what Dagmar had was the shape of her story.

CHAPTER EIGHT

This Is Not a Flashback

"Are you afraid?"

Dagmar sat up in the bed, stared wildly into the darkened hotel room with the telephone handset pressed to her ear. Shots crackled in the distance. Sweat dripped from her chin onto her chest.

"Are you afraid?" the woman said. "It's all right to be afraid."

Through a film of sleep and fear, Dagmar thought she recognized the voice. "Mrs. Tippel?"

"You can call me Anna, dear."

Dagmar put her head between her knees and sucked in air.

"I'm not sure I understand what this call is about," she said.

"We hadn't seen you since yesterday. We thought you might be lonely and afraid, especially after what's happened to that building."

Another dose of fear, this one slow and terrible, crept up Dagmar's spine.

"Building?" she said.

There was a moment of silence before Anna Tippel responded. "Oh my God, you didn't know. I'm so very sorry."

"What building?" Dagmar demanded.

"There's another hotel. The Palms. It's on fire. I'm sorry you didn't know."

Dagmar bounded out of bed and slapped aside the curtains. The burning building was in plain sight, one of the many great towers just to the north of the Royal Jakarta. Black, dense smoke poured from broken windows at the level of the eighth or ninth floor. The fire had burned upward from lower stories: the windows on the lower levels were all shattered, the walls all black.

She imagined the fire rising, driving the people upward floor by floor until there was nowhere else to go, nowhere but into space, spilling by twos and threes from the blackened roof.

Dagmar licked her lips.

"I'm looking," she said, and her voice dried up. She coughed to clear her throat, and said, "I'm looking at it now."

"I thought we might have breakfast together," said Anna Tippel. "If you were feeling lonely."

"It's safe to have breakfast?" Dagmar said. Her words seemed spoken out of some great void: her mind was entirely taken up with the sight before her, the fire eating its way upward floor by floor.

"Breakfast is as safe as anything," Anna Tippel said. "And we must eat."

Through the horror, Dagmar recalled that she hadn't

eaten anything since the previous noon, not having dared the lower levels of the hotel in case looters were still present.

"All right," she said. Tears welled into her eyes, and she could barely speak the words. "I'll meet you."

Yes, she thought, answering Anna Tippel's first question. *Yes, I am afraid.*

The breakfast room was crowded, and Dagmar and the Tippels shared their table with a businessman from Sumatra, a man named Dingwangkara. The menu was limited: there were no Western egg dishes and no fresh fruit save for various kinds of bananas, but there were still a range of breads, steamed rice and fried rice, vegetables, and a wide variety of sauces.

The meal was starch-heavy, but Dagmar ate a lot of it.

The Sumatran businessman was talkative and asked a great many questions: Where are you from? Where are you going? How many brothers and sisters do you have? What do you do for a living?

Dagmar was suspicious at first, Zan's warnings about kidnapping fresh in her mind. But the Tippels answered freely, and Dingwangkara was so cheerful, and so clearly what he claimed to be, that Dagmar found herself answering.

"My father died a few years ago," she said.

He had finally succeeded in his life's ambition of drinking himself to death.

To her surprise she found tears stinging her eyes. She hadn't wept for her father during his cirrhosis or anytime thereafter.

She supposed she wasn't crying for him now, not really,

but for the victims, those who had lost their life savings, who were killed in the riots and the demonstrations, those who had their homes burned out from under them or who were trapped in the burning hotel.

Dingwangkara looked at her with a gentle expression.

"My parents are both alive," he said, and then he added, "Inshallah."

"Inshallah," Dagmar repeated, and she blinked away her tears.

"They always want to know about your family," said Cornelis Tippel after Dingwangkara departed. "They'll ask any damn question they please."

"Their culture came from the kampungs," said Anna, "the long houses where they all lived together. They believe it's normal for everyone to know about everyone else."

Dagmar remembered the young policeman turning to her and asking her about her work. *I always take the MAC-10.*

She wondered how you were supposed to know when they were just asking questions, and when they were kidnappers trying to decide if you were worth a ransom.

FROM: BJSKI
SUBJECT: Re: Jakarta

Holy cripes! I had no idea you were even out of the country!

What can I do? Can I send you a care package? A gun? A helicopter?

Can I fly out there and help you somehow? Only problem
is, I'm so broke you'd have to buy the ticket. But I'll come!

Let me know!

Hearts,

BJ

After breakfast, Dagmar found it too depressing to
wander around the lower hotel, with its looted shops,
boarded windows, and frightened employees, so she
returned to her room. She didn't dare open the curtains
to watch the burning Palms, so she kept the drapes drawn
and watched the catastrophe on television. The talking
heads on CNN discussed 9/11 and speculated about the
ideological or religious motivations of whoever had set
the fire, chatted about how whoever had constructed the
hotel had obviously ignored a lot of building codes, and
spoke of a well-known American lawyer who was jetting
with his team to Singapore in hopes of signing up as
many survivors as possible in order to file a class-action
suit for damages.

Dagmar hoped her own hotel was up to spec.

When desperate people started throwing themselves
off the burning building, Dagmar turned off the television and opened her laptop. She found she had
dozens of emails from practically everyone who knew
she was in Jakarta, some of them writing more than
once, to all of the three email addresses she currently
maintained. They'd seen the burning hotel on television,

and they were desperate to know whether she was all right.

She answered one email and CC'd anyone else who had queried, so that everyone would have an answer in as short a space of time as possible.

When she was finished, she sat back in her chair while a slow sense of wonder rose in her, wonder at the sheer number of people who cared for her. Some of those who had sent email were people whom she hadn't seen in person for years and with whom she maintained only a tenuous form of contact.

Dagmar hadn't realized so many people cared.

She was used to the way interest groups spontaneously formed on the Internet, but there had never been one centered on *her* before. These people—friends from Caltech, from Britain, friends of her family in Cleveland, people in the gaming industry, players she knew only as Hippolyte or Chatsworth Osborne, individuals who came from different walks of life and whose only point in common was a personal knowledge of Dagmar—had seen news of the burning hotel and responded within *hours*. Many of them had clearly been in touch with one another, spreading the word that she might be in danger, and the outpouring of concern was touching.

It was then, as Dagmar decided to give everyone who had queried a personal answer, that the power died.

The lights flickered and went off, and the whisper of the air-conditioning faded away. An array of tiny plastic turbines, each the diameter of a pencil, switched on to provide her laptop with power. A breathy sound

accompanied the ignition, and paper on her desk rus-
tled to the warm exhaust.

A notice flashed on her display: the hotel's wireless
connection had gone down along with the power.
Dagmar checked the room's phone and found it worked.
The phone had an Ethernet jack, and she considered
connecting the laptop to it but then decided against using
fuel and turned the computer off.

The screen had just gone blank when the lights
wavered on again. They didn't seem as bright as before,
so Dagmar figured either that it was a brownout or that
a hotel backup generator had gone on but didn't have
quite the power required.

She lay across her bed and thought about *Planet Nine*,
and the fictional woman in the hotel room, and what
uncanny series of accidents had brought her down the
rabbit hole.

Tomer Zan called in midafternoon. Dagmar had just finished doing her laundry in the bidet—she'd run out of
clean clothes and was dubious about giving any of her
belongings to hotel staff.

"How are you feeling, darling?" Zan asked. The "darling" sounded perfectly professional, as if it were a
substitute for "Miss Shaw."

"I've been better," Dagmar said.

"We've decided to pull you off the roof with a helicopter."

Dagmar paused to think about this.

"You're not moving me to a safer place first?"

"Putting you on the streets right now would be

exposing you to too much risk. The situation is deteriorating fast—most of the police have walked off the job, since no one's paying them real money."

"So the streets are in the hands of the rioters."

"That's about it." Dryly. "We'll have a helicopter in Singapore by tomorrow."

"So you can pick me up the next day?"

"Well," Zan admitted, "no. Singapore's the nearest place we can stage from—except maybe Sarawak—but Singapore's nearly a thousand kilometers away, and the copter's an old Huey from Thailand, equipped for rescue work in the jungle. It doesn't have the range to reach you. So we're going to charter a ship in Singapore, put a lot of fuel aboard, and then steam toward Jakarta while the crew builds a helicopter landing platform from scratch. The chopper will land on the ship once the platform is built, refuel, and then fly to you once it's in range."

"What am I going to have to do when it gets here?"

"Practically nothing. We'll have rescue specialists onboard. The chopper will hover over the hotel roof and drop one of our people down to you. Then we'll lower a stretcher, and our guy will strap you into it. We'll winch you aboard, and then our guy will go up next."

"So all I have to do is lie down?"

"That's it."

Dagmar felt relief mixed with a degree of disappointment. She had hoped for a more swashbuckling exit than being strapped to a basket and winched to safety.

"Can I bring anything with me?" she asked.

"A small bag maybe. Emphasis *small*." There was a brief pause. "It's a pity we can't go in tomorrow. That's when the Japanese are evacuating, so our chopper could slip in without being noticed."

"How come they can evacuate and—"

"Because," Zan said, "they don't have all their goddam naval assets in the Persian Gulf, that's why."

"I haven't heard a single thing from the embassy."

"Schmucks." All the disgust in the universe filled the word. "One word from the embassy and this thing might be over. Instead they're going to let the military loot Jakarta."

Dagmar felt a hesitation. In a sense she didn't want to know anything more, know how much more desperate her situation had become. It was bad enough that she was in a tall building in a city where tall buildings were being burned.

"Loot Jakarta?" she said.

"Anything that goes into Jakarta goes with the permission of the generals," Zan said. "Food, fuel—everything the people need to live. And that means the generals get a cut of the action. They're going to gut the city, but they'll make their fortunes—or make their fortunes *back*, since they probably lost their money in the crash along with everyone else."

"Christ," said Dagmar.

"What's a banana cost there?" Zan asked. "Ten cents maybe? In another few weeks that banana's going to cost five, six dollars. And the difference will all go to the military."

"And if you can't afford the bananas," Dagmar said, "you starve."

"The government'll probably tell the starving people

to kill the Chinese and steal *their* food," Zan said. "But lucky for you, in a few days, it won't be your problem."

The water caressed Dagmar like warm little strokes of a fine brush. The water tinkled against the pool's tiled edge as she paddled her way gently into the deep section, then arrowed her body, closed her eyes against the sting of chlorine, and sank feet-first into the blood-warm water.

The darkness and silence were perfect. Her body was weightless. The boundaries between her self and the waters faded. Her pulse made a hushed, regular noise in her ears.

Then she began, slowly, to rise in the dark water. Her head broke the surface, and she swiped away the strands of hair that crossed her face, and took a breath. Chlorine burned in her sinus.

She opened her eyes. The blacked-out city rose around her, silent. There was no traffic noise, no noise at all, nothing but the flapping of canvas umbrellas set around the pool.

Dagmar was engaged in an act of rebellion. After dinner—where Dagmar had gotten skewered chicken with peanut sauce, a double dose of protein in a situation where she feared proteins might become scarce—and after the announcement that the hotel's generators would be shut down at nine o'clock in order to save fuel, Dagmar had found herself with nothing to do except consume the drinks in her room's minibar. After a couple of whiskeys, she realized that she simply couldn't stay in her room any longer.

Yet there was no place to go. The hotel was blacked

out except for emergency lighting in corners and stair-wells, and the elevators were shut down. The streets were beyond dangerous.

Then she had thought of the third-floor terrace, with its pool. The management had closed it because it was too exposed to theoretical attack from the tall buildings around, but now the pool was just one darkness among others.

Dagmar refused to believe in the existence of armed strangers sighting on the pool with night-vision scopes. Surely armed strangers had better things to do.

What had Anna said? *Breakfast is as safe as anything.*

And better, the pool was on the opposite side of the Royal Jakarta from the burning hotel. Out of sight, out of mind.

Dagmar had decided on this quiet night swim, alone in the dark water.

Of course this meant going down eleven floors in a non-air-conditioned stairwell to reach the pool, and then climbing back up at the end. She'd be a ragged, hot, mis-erable mess at the end of her climb, but then she could take a cool shower, and in the meantime the pool was perfection itself.

Dagmar dove to the bottom of the deep end several times, just to feel the joy of weightlessness, and then she began to swim laps. Her job kept her in hotels a lot, and swimming was her usual exercise. She started with a pair of laps as fast as she could go, just to get the heart pound-ing, and then settled into a slower, steadier pace. She did a few laps in a crawl, then switched to a backstroke, to exercise opposing sets of muscles. Alone in the darkness, she cruised through the water as purposefully as a shark.

The rhythm and warmth relaxed her. The physical demands drove the tension from her body, the unease from her mind. In her solitary exercise in the darkness, surrounded by the empty lawn furniture and the umbrellas, the dark towers of the city and the stars, she became only the swimmer. She was relieved of the burden of being Dagmar, of being caught in some strange, overlapping quantum state in which she was both tourist and refugee. A lonely geek in a hotel, waiting for the rescuers who seemed to have mistaken her for a princess in a tower . . .

Dagmar swam steadily for half an hour, alternating crawl and backstroke, and then went into a cooldown, lying on her back and paddling along with slight movements of her arms and legs. It was difficult, she thought, to cool down when you were floating in water warmer than body temperature.

She stared at the stars overhead and tried to think of nothing at all, just gradually let her breathing and the cotton-wool thudding of her pulse return to something like normal. Then she climbed out of the pool on legs that had turned a little wobbly, adjusted the crotch elastic of her swimsuit, and reached for her towel.

The empty terrace stretched out before her, all shadows and reflected starlight. It was eerie, and Dagmar felt as if she were in one of those postholocaust films, where everyone but she had died of radiation sickness or the plague. From all she could tell, she was alone in this empty night-world.

Then, clearly through the night air, she heard three gunshots echo up between the tall buildings.

No, she thought, there were humans here after all.

It was a long, hot climb back to her room.

Breakfast was a little more barren than that of the previous day—no proteins at all except for peanuts—and so Dagmar packed down the rice while she could and sprinkled it with crushed peanuts, fried shredded coconut, and a pungent chile sauce. Then she took some of the rolls in a paper napkin, went to her room, and put them in the fridge of the minibar.

They could keep her from starvation, maybe.

Damn, she thought as she closed the fridge, *I'm starting to think like Tomer Zan.*

City power was back on—it had come on abruptly at six in the morning, blasting Dagmar out of a peaceful sleep as all the lights and the TV snapped on—so Dagmar sat before her computer and vowed once again to answer all the email she'd received on the previous day.

She was halfway through the list when her phone rang. She reached for where it sat on the charging cradle, saw "Charlies Friend" on the display, and pressed Send.

"Hello, Mr. Zan," she said.

"Hello, darling," Zan said. "I'm sorry, but I've got bad news."

Mentally she screwed together an assembly of struts, just below her heart, to prevent it from sinking.

"What sort of news?" she asked.

"We've lost touch with the helicopter," he said. "And the ship as well. We don't know why."

"Do, uh," she began, "do radios break nowadays?"

"No," Zan said, "not really. Both the ship and the

Huey had state-of-the-art satellite communications equipment. So it's unlikely that there's any kind of malfunction. We suspect an accident."

Dagmar tried to imagine an accident that could take out a ship and a helicopter at the same time. Then she thought she would rather not imagine it—the crew of each craft were on a mission that involved *her,* after all, and if an accident had claimed them, it was all on her account . . .

"So," Dagmar began, "do you send out a search party, or—"

"We'll wait a few more hours in case there was a communications problem, and then contact the authorities in Singapore. But for *you,* darling, we're going to get a new helicopter, and if necessary a new ship, so don't worry."

Dagmar closed her eyes. She could kill *two whole new crews.*

"Not to worry," she said. "Right."

"Things have calmed down a little in Jakarta. When the Palms burned, it scared *everybody.* So a lot of the local Islamic associations have mobilized to guard their own neighborhoods."

"Islamic associations? They're like—what, militias?"

All Dagmar could think about was Sunni and Shiite terrorists in Iraq, and that didn't sound encouraging.

"Some of them are self-help groups," Zan said, "but most of them are martial arts clubs."

Bitter laughter exploded in Dagmar's head. She thought of the film posters in the music store, with their bare-chested heroes. These were the same people that had looted the store and the hotel.

"They're going to protect the neighborhoods with *kung fu?*" she asked.

"With silat," Zan said seriously. "That's the indigenous style. Indonesian martial arts always had a close relationship with religion."

"Uh-huh."

"Of course," Zan said, "some of these groups are political. Some are pro-military, some are against. I'm sure none of them are *for* the government anymore, but they have different ideas about what kind of government to have next. So if they start fighting each other, there could be more problems."

More problems, Dagmar thought.

As if murder and riots and starvation weren't enough.

It was her hour of answering the phone. After Zan hung up, she heard from Austin. The squishy, warm feeling that came from talking to one of her oldest friends multiplied when Charlie called only a short while later.

He said he was trying to find a tanker aircraft to fly north of Sumatra in order to provide in-flight refueling for the new helicopter.

"How much is this costing you?" Dagmar asked.

"Your next Christmas bonus," Charlie said. "Maybe."

Tears stung her eyes. "Thank you," she said.

"Oh, for Christ's sake," Charlie said, "you're not going to tell me that you love me again, are you?"

"Not if you don't want me to."

"Whatever I'm spending," Charlie said, "I can afford. No one else, including me, is going without a Christmas bonus, okay?"

"Right," said Dagmar.

"*My* Christmas bonus," Charlie added, "is going to include a Maserati." There was a pause.

"Have you been thinking about *Planet Nine*?" he asked.

"Yes," said Dagmar. "Yes, I have."

He liked what she told him.

Late that morning, Dagmar heard the throbbing of helicopters outside, and she dared to draw back the curtains and look out. The Palms stood like the one rotten black tooth in the city's gleaming modernist smile. The fire had gone all the way to the roof. A few threads of smoke still rose from a window here and there.

The copters were orbiting behind the destroyed hotel, black, businesslike silhouettes spiraling to a landing somewhere to the northwest.

Evacuating the Japanese.

Dagmar couldn't stand the sight of the Palms and let the curtains fall back into place.

She paced the room for a while, restless, and then went to the laptop she had been typing on when Tomer Zan had called. She was in the middle of a letter to the gamer she knew as LadyDayFan, thanking her for an email of concern.

Unfortunately I don't know anybody in Jakarta, LadyDayFan had written, *but let me know if there's any way I can help.*

Dagmar scrolled along her list of emails, answered and unanswered. There were even more than there had been the previous day, an impressive number. Many were from people that Dagmar knew only as online presences floating around the online game blogs.

She considered again this circle of which she was the temporary center, and the further circles that emanated from each of the members. There was a latent power in this group, a wide variety of skills and acquaintance. This group, she thought, could get things done.

Everyone, supposedly, was within six degrees of separation from everyone else.

Dagmar reflected that LadyDayFan maintained her own ARG-related online bulletin board, called Our Reality Network, where industry gossip was retailed and games were discussed, analyzed, and eventually solved.

The games that Dagmar created were designed to be solved. She created the puzzles, or suggested them to the team's professional puzzle designers, and the solutions were buried somewhere for the players to find. The games were finite: they led to a particular place, like the wedding in Bengaluru, and then they were over.

Her current situation, which had her placed at a hotel in a state of Schrödingerlike uncertainty, was a puzzle that perhaps had no solution. Certainly *she* was incapable of solving it.

Perhaps, she thought, her dilemma could be solved not by any individual but by a Group Mind.

She sat down and began to type.

From: Dagmar
Subject: Indonesia

Perhaps you can help me after all. I seem to be at the center of a puzzle that is in need of a solution.

I'm at the Royal Jakarta Hotel, on the fourteenth floor. This is at 6°11'31.8"S, 106°49'19.48"E. The situation is deteriorating and I'm worried for my personal safety.

The embassy has been of no use at all.

I want to get out of Jakarta and to a country that isn't having a revolution. My sole assets consist of US$180 in cash, a high-powered PDA/telephone, a computer, and some credit cards that don't seem to be worth anything in the current situation.

Most of the police have gone home. The army has besieged the city but has not entered it. The government is holed up somewhere. The streets are in the hands of rioters or Islamic societies, most of which are composed of martial artists.

If you know of anyone who can help me, I'd appreciate hearing from them.

If you don't, thanks anyway.

Bests,

Dagmar

She clicked the Send button without thinking, then sat back and wondered just what it was she'd set in motion.

CHAPTER NINE

This Is Not Folly

FROM: LadyDayFan

Dagmar Shaw, whom most of you know as the executive producer of games like *Curse of the Golden Nagi* and *Shadow Pattern,* is stuck in Jakarta, where supplies of food and medicine are running out and people are being killed. We all saw the hotel burn. Dagmar wants to get out and the government ain't helping.

Her original <u>email</u> is here and describes her situation.

It's possible that our combined efforts may be of assistance.

I have set up several topics.

<u>News and Rumors</u> has to do with the situation in Jakarta, Indonesia, etc. Please post any information, along with a link to the source. <u>Finance</u> has to do with money issues.

As detailed in <u>her email</u>, Dagmar has only a small amount of viable currency. If we can find a channel, possibly we could get money to her or otherwise finance an escape.

I have set up a special PayPal account to which people can contribute. Details are in the <u>Finance</u> topic.

<u>The Escape Topic</u> has to do with actual plans to move Dagmar to someplace safe.

We'll keep this topic as an arena for general discussion.

TINAG . . . I think.

FROM: Hanseatic

TINAG, hell! I think it's a damn game! But I'm willing to play.

FROM: Corporal Carrot

TINAG?

FROM: LadyDayFan

This Is Not A Game.

FROM: Corporal Carrot

Thanks.

FROM: Chatsworth Osborne Jr.

Corporal Carrot, TINAG is an ARG design aesthetic. The characters are required to believe they live in the real world, the puppetmasters are required to make a world that is internally consistent, and players should be able to function in the world as well as the characters.

FROM: Hippolyte

This really *isn't* a game! I got email from Dagmar yesterday. She's really stranded in Jakarta, where the hotel burned and all those people were killed.

How much should we contribute to PayPal?

FROM: LadyDayFan

Twenty bucks each?

FROM: HexenHase

Chatsworth, I disagree with you about TINAG. The effects you describe are entirely the result of the puppetmasters' abilities to skillfully craft a game while remaining behind the curtain. The fictional characters are *actors* scripted by the puppetmasters—if the scripts don't work, the players will never believe the game world is real, and the illusion fails.

<posts deleted>

FROM: LadyDayFan

I have removed twelve flamewar posts to the <u>Hell Topic</u>.

Civil discussions of game aesthetics may take place in the <u>Meta Topic</u>.

If this continues, someone is going to lose access privileges.

FROM: HexenHase

Sorry.

FROM: Chatsworth Osborne Jr.

Me too. I'll make nice from now on.

FROM: Joe Clever

I would like to state for the record that I think it's a game. But I'm always willing to play along, even if it's going to cost me twenty bucks.

FROM: Hippolyte

It's not a game, Joe. But feel free to hack the Indonesian military if it makes you happy.

FROM: HexenHase

I can't believe we're engaging with Joe Clever on this or any topic! That cheating shit-for-brains!

FROM: Corporal Carrot

Careful, Hexen. Don't start another flamewar.

FROM: LadyDayFan

Don't worry, Corporal Carrot. Abusing Joe Clever is an Our Reality tradition.

FROM: Corporal Carrot

Can I ask why?

FROM: Chatsworth Osborne Jr.

Because the crap-head's style of play totally violates the spirit of TINAG. He cheats.

FROM: Joe Clever

It's not cheating when there aren't any rules.

FROM: HexenHase

There are rules to any community, whether they're written down or not. We agree not to poke behind the scenes because it spoils the fun for all of us.

Corporal Carrot: What Joe Clever does is dumpster-dive Great Big Idea to find clues that might have accidentally been thrown away. He followed the actors around to see if they might accidentally drop a script. And he twice hacked Great Big Idea to locate pages that hadn't yet been uploaded to the Web.

FROM: Joe Clever

You say that as if I should be embarrassed. What I do is *win games*.

FROM: Chatsworth Osborne Jr.

Joe Clever is a complete egomaniac. Totally ruthless. Borderline sociopath. Probably crazy.

My guess is that he lives in his mother's basement and has no friends.

We despise him.

FROM: Joe Clever

What I have done is to recognize that ARGs *are in fact games*. That's what the *G* in ARG stands for!

Games have winners and losers. I am a winner. You people are losers.

FROM: LadyDayFan

Are we not overwhelmed by Mr. Clever's personal charm?

FROM: HexenHase

And he's *even more* charming in person.

FROM: Corporal Carrot

Can't you ban him from the bulletin board?

FROM: LadyDayFan

I could, but he would immediately rejoin with a new handle.

FROM: Chatsworth Osborne Jr.

Ahem. Aren't we supposed to be talking about Dagmar?

FROM: LadyDayFan

Good point. We need to get back to Indonesia.

FROM: Joe Clever

It's a game.

FROM: LadyDayFan

You go on thinking that, J. C.

FROM: Desi

I've just found this topic. My god! I can't believe we're actually doing this.

I don't know if this will be of any use, but one of my cubicle mates ranks high in penchak silat, or however it's spelled. I'll see if his school has any connections to martial arts groups in Jakarta.

FROM: LadyDayFan

Desi, that would be great.

FROM: Chatsworth Osborne Jr.

I took a scuba vacation in Bali a few years ago. Maybe I can contact those people and see if they know anyone with a boat in Jakarta.

FROM: Corporal Carrot

You guyz are acting like this is real.

FROM: LadyDayFan

TINAG, my friends. TINAG.

Dagmar plunged into the water, bubbles erupting around her. She arched her back, feeling the bubbles stream along her legs and the sensitive flesh of her neck, and rose through the dark water until her head broke the surface.

The night loomed around her, silent, the stars muted by wisps of cloud.

She began her laps. Arms, legs, lungs in synchrony, the warm water a midnight dream.

Her future, even her continued existence, was a question mark.

Swimming nightly laps was a defiance of that uncertainty, a statement that she was still an actor on her own stage. That there was still something in which her own will could alter events.

Even if it was just swimming, at night, hidden from the world.

FROM: Chatsworth Osborne Jr.

Sorry, but I've worked the Bali dive boat connection, and it didn't pan out.

FROM: Joe Clever

We might try sportfishermen. Do you think any of them would have a Web site?

FROM: Chatsworth Osborne Jr.

I'll check.

I've been doing some thinking. We've got three possibilities for getting Dagmar out of Jakarta. Air, water, land.

If we use an aircraft, the aircraft has to find a place to land, and then we'll have to move Dagmar to that place by car or bus or some other form of ground transport. In addition, the Indonesian military isn't allowing anyone into their airspace, so any aircraft runs a risk of being shot down.

If we use a boat, then we still have to bring Dagmar to the boat by ground transport. It's not clear whether the Indonesian navy is blockading Jakarta by sea or how effective the blockade is.

If it's possible to move Dagmar out of Jakarta by ground transport (say, by bribing or otherwise coming to an understanding with the military), then even if she doesn't leave the country, she would be safer than she is now. Even though she'd still be in Indonesia, she'd be outside the area of complete chaos.

FROM: Hanseatic

Have you considered a seaplane or flying boat?

FROM: Chatsworth Osborne Jr.

No, I hadn't. Good idea.

FROM: Vikram

I have an uncle who's being evacuated with the Indian nationals today or tomorrow. Once he's out of Jakarta, I will try to contact him and find out if there's anyone we can contact.

FROM: Desi

I got lucky with the silat connection! My friend's teacher is affiliated with a school in Jakarta. He's checking with them.

FROM: LadyDayFan

Great news!

FROM: Desi

We might be able to hook Dagmar up with her own body-guard of martial artists! How cool is that?

"How are you, darling?" asked Tomer Zan.

"I'm trying to keep my chin up," Dagmar said.

"That's good. I just wanted you to know that we got another helicopter. It's a Spirit, it's got a much longer range than the Huey, so we'll be able to stage from farther out at sea."

"Good to know."

"It's on its way from the Philippines now. So we should be set in just a few days."

"What happened," Dagmar asked, "to the old helicopter?"

"Yes. Well." Dagmar sensed considerable reluctance. "It was trying to land on our ship, and the winds were gusty, so it crashed into the superstructure. So we need a new ship and a new helicopter."

"Was anyone hurt?" Dagmar felt the depression that propelled her words.

There was a brief silence, and then, "The crew of the helicopter was killed. There were some injuries on the ship, too, because there was a fire. The radio room got burned—that's why we didn't hear from them."

It seemed to Dagmar as if her heart slowed, extending the long silence between beats. The breath that she drew into her lungs took an eon. Then time seemed to speed up as she hurled the words into the world.

"Oh Christ, I'm sorry," she said.

"It's not your fault, darling," Zan said.

Dagmar didn't answer.

"We're professionals," Zan said. "All our people have been soldiers. We understand the risks we take."

"*I'm* not a soldier," Dagmar said. "Nothing's prepared me for this."

"We're coming to get you," said Zan. "That's what you need to think about."

"I'll try," she said.

"We're coming soon."

After the phone call came to an end, Dagmar closed her eyes and fell into a dark, liquid sorrow, a grief the temperature of blood.

FROM: Joe Clever

I've found a boat and a captain. He's a fisherman named Widjihartani, and he operates from a port in West Java called Pelabuhan Ratu. It's something like five or six hours from Jakarta by sea.

He's willing to take a passenger anywhere, provided his fuel and time are paid for. All the way to Singapore, if we want.

He says that Jakarta is technically under a blockade by the navy, but they let fishermen through because they are too necessary to the economy to let them go under.

FROM: Corporal Carrot

FROM: LadyDayFan

Is Widjihartani his first name or his last name? Are you sure he's reliable?

FROM: Corporal Carrot

What do they call him for short?

FROM: Joe Clever

Widjihartani is the only name he's got. Lots of Indonesians have only one name.

I spoke to him on the phone. His English is pretty good, he takes tourists out for fishing and sightseeing.

He seemed pretty clearheaded, really. But he didn't know how he could afford the fuel, and with the banks in the state they are, it's unclear how we can get money to him.

FROM: Hippolyte

I found Pelabuhan Ratu on Google Earth!

FROM: LadyDayFan

Can we set him up with a PayPal account? Then we could put money into it, and he could withdraw it whenever the bank lets him.

FROM: Joe Clever

I'll check.

From the restaurant, Dagmar could see the Indian nationals evacuating, the line of helicopters parading neatly across the horizon.

The Chinese were going out in the morning, by sea, and the Singaporeans the next day. Even little *Singapore* could stage a proper evacuation, complete with a landing by their elite Gurkha troops.

The only nationality that wasn't evacuating, besides the Americans, was the Australians. The Indonesians were still angry at the Australians over Timor and weren't letting Australian ships into their waters.

For a moment, watching the Indians go, Dagmar felt a spasm of pure hatred for her own nation. Her country had lost the ability to do anything but make fast food and bad Hollywood blockbusters. Every city would have its very own Katrina, and the United States of America in its greatness and piety would do nothing before or after. At the embassy they handed out lies as if they were the White House budget office.

Even the saving of human life had been privatized. If you could afford your own security outfit to rescue you with its helicopters, then you were granted life; if you couldn't, you were beneath your nation's notice.

For a brief, fierce instant she wanted to see her own country burn, just as the Palms had burned.

Then the anger faded, and she looked down at the fried rice that was her supper.

Dutifully, she ate it to the last grain.

FROM: Simone

LadyDayFan, can you set up a fanfic topic?

FROM: LadyDayFan

Fanfic? You want to write fan fiction about Dagmar?

FROM: Simone

Yeah. She's cool.

FROM: Hanseatic

<glyph of astonishment>

FROM: LadyDayFan

Well. This is against my better judgment, but <u>here you go</u>.

"Where are you from?" asked the young man with the halberd.

"Los Angeles."

"That is near Hollywood?"

"Yes."

"That must be very interesting."

Dagmar understood that in the Q-and-A conversations favored by the Indonesians, both sides were supposed to ask questions.

"Are you from Jakarta?" she asked.

Paying her ritual morning visit to the concierge—

which, following Zan's advice, she did at a different hour each morning—Dagmar had discovered that the hotel was now guarded by men with medieval weapons. They wore kilts over baggy pants, with short jackets, round pitji hats, and sashes in bright primary colors. The outfits of the young men were black, and of the older men, white. They carried long knives, spears, sticks, and blades on the ends of sticks. They clustered by the hotel entrances and smiled and bowed at anyone walking by. They were making a clear effort not to seem threatening.

Mr. Tong had never reappeared, and his place seemed taken permanently by the young woman in the Muslim headdress. She told Dagmar that the hotel had hired a group of martial artists to secure the hotel.

"What is your group called?" Dagmar asked. Maybe Tomer Zan would know something about them.

"We are the Tanah Abang Bersih Jantung Association." The young man touched his chest. "Bersih Jantung means 'pure heart.'"

"And the other part?"

"Tanah Abang? That is our kampung—our neighborhood, near this hotel." He looked at her with curiosity. "Do you like Miley Cyrus?" he asked.

"Miley?" Dagmar said. "I think she's swell."

"Bersih Jantung?" asked Tomer Zan that evening. "How do you spell it?"

"It means 'pure heart,'" Dagmar said.

"What is the attitude of these people?" Zan asked. "Are they disciplined? Do you feel safe around them?"

"They seem friendly. They like Miley Cyrus, for heaven's

sake! There are some older men in white who give the orders. They're trying not to be scary."

"That's good. Just remember that this can change at any second. You should be alert to any sign that their attitude is changing. Remember, these are the people that invented the word *amok*. Well, actually they call it *mataglap*, but *amok* is what they mean."

Great, Dagmar thought. *Let's by all means look inside that silver lining to find that all-consuming black hole.*

"How's the helicopter?" she asked.

"It should be in Singapore tomorrow," said Zan.

Dagmar wondered whether to tell Zan about the amateur efforts to rescue her that were centered on the Our Reality bulletin board, efforts she had been following online with great attention.

She decided against it.

Let them compete, she thought. *Let the free market system prevail.*

Besides, she thought that Zan probably wasn't into fan fiction.

FROM: Desi

My friend has checked with his school's silat guru in Jakarta, and he's willing to help Dagmar. As an act of charity, they'll take her in and share their food with her, and they'll take her anywhere that doesn't involve danger to their own people.

Their style is called Bayangan Prajurit Pentjak Silat. My impression is that they'll take money if we give it to them, but their religion obliges them to do charitable acts, so they don't insist on being paid.

Here's the problem. Dagmar's hotel is being guarded by a group that Bayangan Prajurit doesn't get along with. The hotel guards are allied with the military, and their organization is headed by a general. Bayangan Prajurit are pro-democracy and they won't cooperate with the hotel guards in any way.

Anybody have any ideas? Do we have to get Dagmar away from her own guards?

By the next morning a food shipment had arrived, and for breakfast, Dagmar gorged on Southeast Asia's finest, freshest, most glorious fruit.

The military were providing food to their allies in the city, and the Bersih Jantung were willing to supply the hotel. Dagmar presumed there were vast bribes involved, money shifting around offshore, where the banks still worked.

There was an upside, Dagmar supposed, to dealing with a corrupt military.

"What's the word?" Dagmar asked.

"Whatever the word is," said Tomer Zan, "it's not a good one. Our people have had a chance to look at this helicopter, and it's a piece of shit. The maintenance logs are incomplete or nonsensical or forged in some obvious way, and it's clear we'll have to do a complete overhaul on the machine before we dare fly it out to you."

The dry monsoon, which had ceased to be dry,

spattered rain against her hotel window. Dagmar let the space of three seconds go by in order to demonstrate to Zan her displeasure.

"How long will the overhaul take?" she asked.

"Depends on whether new parts are required. And of course, what parts."

Dagmar let more time pass.

"Why don't you hire one of the helicopters that took the Indians or the Japanese out?"

"They were military aircraft, darling. They don't rent them."

"Zelazni Associates has an air division," she said. "I saw it on your Web page. Can't you fly me out in one of your own aircraft?"

"We don't have helicopters, darling. We *fly* helicopters, we *maintain* helicopters, but we don't own them. What we have are fixed-wing transport aircraft to help move our people and their equipment."

"Can't you put a helicopter on one of your transport planes and fly it out here?"

Now it was Zan's turn to be silent.

"Our planes aren't big enough," he said.

"Maybe you could find a bigger one."

"I'll look at what's possible," Zan said after another pause. Meaning, Dagmar supposed, what Charlie was willing to pay for.

"I should let you know," she said, "that another group is trying to help me leave Indonesia. They've actually made some progress."

"Another group?" Zan's query was cautious.

"I'll email you the Web page."

Maybe, she thought, he'd enjoy the fanfic after all.

FROM: Hanseatic

This game is amazing. How did Great Big Idea get the Indonesian government to cooperate with all this?

FROM: LadyDayFan

TINAG.

FROM: Hanseatic

Yah, right. My guess is the setup is something like this: we get 200 points for getting Dagmar out of Jakarta to someplace safer, 500 points if we get her out of Indonesia entirely, and 1,000 points for Total World Domination.

FROM: LadyDayFan

You're joking, right?

FROM: Hippolyte

Hanseatic, this *really isn't a game*.

FROM: Hanseatic

Maybe yes, maybe no. But what difference does it make?

"Are these people *serious?*" Tomer Zan asked.

"Some of them."

"Who are they, exactly?"

"The ones I know, I don't know well," Dagmar said. "The rest are just handles they use online."

"Are they Indonesia specialists?"

"I don't think so."

"How well do you trust them?"

More than I trust you, Dagmar thought.

"I don't think they would deliberately mislead me," she said.

"I'm going to fly to Singapore myself, to take charge of this," Zan said. "If you don't hear from me for the next day or two, that's why."

Competition, Dagmar thought, seemed to have heightened Zan's sense of urgency.

That night, Star TV reported that the American ambassador and his family had been evacuated from Jakarta by some kind of U.S. Special Forces unit. The report made the ambassador seem brilliant and courageous, a combination of Rambo and Jack Kennedy.

In the face of this bold, blazing adventure, the fact that the ambassador had abandoned his post, all his subordinates, and every U.S. citizen in Jakarta seemed hardly worth mentioning.

FROM: Joe Clever

I had to walk him through it, but we've succeeded in setting Widjihartani up with his own PayPal account. He can transfer money from there into his bank account in unlimited amounts, but the bottleneck is the bank, which will only allow him to withdraw a certain amount.

I'm checking into whether the bank will allow him to *borrow* money against the money already in his account. That way he can get a lot of cash at once.

Dagmar had just finished her nightly swim when she heard the roar of vehicles. She threw her towel around her shoulders and walked to the edge of the terrace, then looked down through the screen of trees to the street below.

A convoy of half a dozen cars had just driven up beneath the Royal Jakarta's portico. The Bersih Jantung guards were running to the cars and leaping inside. Their long, strange weapons thrust awkwardly from the windows as the vehicles sped away.

The last to leave was one of the older men in white. He jumped into a minibus without looking back, and then all Dagmar could see were the red taillights receding along the boulevard.

The hotel's guards had jumped ship.

FROM: Charlie Ruff

I'm Charlie Ruff. Some of you may know me. I'm Dagmar's boss, and Great Big Idea was my great big idea.

Dagmar has alerted me to the existence of this conspiracy, and I'd like to put your financing on a more professional basis.

Basically, I'll be paying for anything that leads to Dagmar's escape from Indonesia.

Please, let me know what you need.

The looters arrived while Dagmar was paying her morning call on the concierge, a visit that neither enjoyed but that both recognized was inevitable. Dagmar asked whether anything had changed, and the concierge always said that nothing had.

"What happened to Bersih Jantung?" Dagmar asked the concierge.

"Their neighborhood was attacked," the woman said. "The men left to protect their families."

It was then that the first vehicles arrived. Dagmar turned at the sound of squealing brakes. Through the glass door of the concierge's office she saw the small blue bus drawing up under the portico. Men jumped out, some of them armed with the same freakish weapons that the Bersih Jantung had carried.

They didn't wear uniforms. They wore tropical shirts and T-shirts with the names of bands on them and baseball caps and headscarves and pitji hats. They looked more like the rioters Dagmar had encountered on the first day than anyone's martial Islamic association.

Her heart gave such a violent lurch that her first grab for the door handle missed. She tried again, moved quickly into the lobby, and faded as fast as she could in the direction of the elevators. She scuttled to the double row of polished metal doors and jabbed at the call button.

Other vehicles had drawn up behind the bus, and

more men were piling out. There was no one to stop them—the Sikh doormen hadn't been seen for days, and Dagmar presumed they had been evacuated along with the other Indian nationals.

The leader entered. He had a Japanese long sword stuck in his belt. One of the managers made a diffident approach, and the leader told him to stand back, which he did. A mob of people followed him into the lobby.

Some of the invaders pushed hand trucks. Several seized the carts the bellmen used to carry luggage. One white-haired man had a list written in an old school note-book.

The leader drew his katana and made a broad gesture in the direction of the lounge. A dozen of his followers charged into the lounge and ran behind the bar. Bottles of liquor were piled on the bar to be swept up later. The bar television was torn from its moorings, and another looter moved a chair so that he could stand on it and disconnect another television that was mounted high in a corner.

Hotel employees clumped in one area of the lobby and did nothing.

The elevator dinged, and Dagmar ran for it. While she counted the seconds until the door closed, she remembered the six exits from the lobby that Tomer Zan had told her to locate, and realized that she should have used one of them.

Instead she'd panicked and run for the elevators.

It occurred to her that she was really unequipped for this kind of life.

The doors closed with an infuriating lack of haste, and

Dagmar began her rise to her precarious aerie on the fourteenth floor.

FROM: Dagmar

Okay, this is *it*. The martial arts association that was guarding the hotel fled last night, and today the looters moved in. It's not spontaneous looting this time; it's highly organized. I can look out the window and see trucks moving off with televisions, toilets, sinks, microwaves, and the gas ranges from the kitchen. I guess I've had my last hot meal. Or maybe my last meal of any sort, since they've probably taken all the food as well.

The looters are armed with swords, knives, and spears. I haven't heard of them attacking anyone, but that doesn't mean it hasn't happened.

I need out of this hotel, and I need to go *now*. Any ideas?

"Is this Dagmar?"

A strange male voice, very deep and authoritative, with the same accent as Tomer Zan.

"Yes," Dagmar said.

"My name is Mordechai Weitzman. I'm calling for Tomer Zan, who is in transit to Singapore and can't speak right now."

"Yes!" said Dagmar. "Hello!"

"We got your email. Can you get onto the roof later tonight?"

Dagmar's heart gave a leap of delight at the prospect of the helicopter finally arriving.

"Yes!" she said. "Yes, of course!"

"The package should arrive about midnight Jakarta time, but it may be delayed. You've got to be ready when it comes."

Her mind seemed to skip several tracks, like a needle hurled across an old LP.

"Package?" she said.

"We're sending you a package of dollars. They may help you acquire food and other supplies until we can arrive to pick you up."

Dagmar felt her sudden joy evaporate.

"You're dropping money, but you're not picking me up?"

"We're sending it on a surveillance drone. It's not big enough to carry you."

"*Shit!*" Dagmar kicked the chest of drawers in her room: it banged solidly against the wall. "There are armed men in the hotel! I need to get out of here *now!*"

"You need to stay in your room."

"*I* am *in my fucking room!*"

At that moment the lights died, and the air-conditioning whimpered to a stop.

"I am in my fucking room," Dagmar announced, "*in the fucking dark.*" She was not unaware of a degree of melodrama in her delivery.

"We are coming as soon as we can," said Weitzman. "But we need a working aircraft."

"The world is *full* of aircraft!" Dagmar said. "They've been flying in and out of here for *days.* They could even spare one to fly out the American ambassador!"

"Now *that* was a profile in courage, wasn't it?" There was cold humor in Weitzman's voice.

"I'd say," Dagmar said, "that the Alamo spirit is definitely dead."

On the roof at eleven, she thought.

And fuck you, Mordechai, whoever you are.

FROM: Desi

I've emailed the Bayangan Prajurit people, but it's the middle of the night in Indonesia and it may be a while before we hear from them. I did hear what happened with Bersih Jantung. They're pro-military, remember, and the army was supplying them with food, fuel, and other black market items. So their neighbors, who all hate the military, decided to hijack their latest convoy and steal their food and stuff.

Which they did. Successfully.

Bayangan Prajurit claims they weren't involved, but they're *very* pleased with this development, and they had a hard time keeping a straight face.

Dagmar stood atop the silent, dark tower as the monsoon spat warm drizzle in her face. She hoped that the reconnaissance craft would be able to find her through the cloud cover.

If it was like everything else Zelazni had tried so far, it would drop into the ocean somewhere west of Krakatoa.

As she looked over the edge, she could see that lack of

electricity hadn't stopped the looters. They were working by flashlight, and now they were loading mattresses and chests of drawers into their trucks.

They'd finished looting the ground floors, she saw, and had started on the guest rooms. The power outage meant they weren't going to get to the fourteenth floor anytime soon, but Dagmar had considerable respect for their industry and assumed they would reach her eventually.

And besides, sooner or later she was going to have to descend to the ground in search of food and water.

Around her, the city was dark except for a few fires burning here and there. The locals were still exercising blazing benevolence upon their neighbors.

She could see the pool down below, on the third-floor terrace.

She had decided against her nightly swim. Her courage did not extend to defiance of mobs with spears and knives.

Not that her courage had done anything so far but fail her.

She gave a jump as her phone let out a bray. She answered.

"Are you on the roof?" said Mordechai.

"Yes."

"Where?"

She ransacked a mental map. "Northeast corner," she said.

"Stay back from the edge. We don't want the package dropping to the street."

She stepped back until she came up against one of the

roof structures. Water dripped down her neck, a surprising splash of warmth, and she took a step forward.

"Any minute now," said Mordechai.

Dagmar scanned the sky. A flurry of rain pelted down for a few seconds, then ceased. Then there was a faint whooshing noise, and the wind carried a warm breath of burned hydrocarbon.

Suddenly she saw it, hovering right above her. There were no wings and no tail structure—the thing was just an aerodynamic shape, like an elongated Frisbee, black against the opalescent cloud. It made a sound like a crowd in a distant stadium, a far-off roaring, and Dagmar realized it was propelled by arrays of the same miniturbines that served as backup power for her computer. There had to be some method of directing the thrust so that the machine could hover or fly in any direction. From the smell, Dagmar assumed the machine was loaded with some form of high-powered aviation fuel, as opposed to the stuff in her computer, a substance that, at the insistence of the Department of Homeland Security, couldn't burn fast enough to be used to blow up an airplane.

"I see it!" she said into her phone. "It's right over my head!"

"How far above you?"

"Maybe twenty feet. It's hard to say. I can't tell how large it is."

"We'll take it down three meters."

The tone of the turbines shifted, and the machine wafted gently toward Dagmar. The hydrocarbon smell grew stronger.

"Right," Mordechai said. "We've got you. It was hard picking you out from the background. Stand by."

The drone was, Dagmar guessed, about eight feet long. Despite the gusting of the monsoon, the machine hovered with perfect stillness in the air, its fly-by-wire computer adjusting to every shift of the wind.

"Hold out your hand," Mordechai said. There was amusement in his voice.

Dagmar put out her right hand, her left hand still holding the phone to her ear. The package dropped and bounced off Dagmar's forearm, then fell to the rooftop with a little slap.

"Have you got it?" Mordechai asked.

Dagmar knelt, swept her hand over the roof, and found the package. Her fingers closed around it.

"I have it," she said.

She straightened and looked up in time to see the drone take off, its low roar increasing as it turned northeast and flew away with surprising rapidity. She watched it until it disappeared into the night.

"You want to be careful with that money," Mordechai said. "What you had before was maybe not worth killing over, but what you've got now can get you killed very fast."

Dagmar felt an invisible hand clamp over her throat. She managed to speak in a kind of whisper.

"How much is it?" she said.

"Two thousand dollars. That should pay for a boat to take you away. Now listen."

He told her that she should split the package up once she got it to her room, carry it in different places so she wouldn't be peeling bills off a huge roll and offering someone far too much temptation.

"Right," she said. "No temptation. Got it."

FROM: Joe Clever

Widjihartani's got money for fuel. I don't know how. Apparently Charlie arranged it.

Widji's on the way to Jakarta, and he's got a satellite phone so that he can be told where he needs to anchor. Or dock, as the case may be.

Sea rescue is go!

FROM: Desi

Bayangan Prajurit is go!

FROM: LadyDayFan

Evacuation is go!

FROM: Corporal Carrot

Thunderbirds are go!

FROM: Corporal Carrot

Sorry about that last, by the way. My enthusiasm got the better of me.

FROM: Hanseatic

That's all right. I knew *someone* was going to say it.

Dagmar helped the Tippels move eight floors up from their looted hotel room. It took the elderly couple a long time to slog their way up the stairs—the elevators, when they were working, were now reserved for looters.

None of them had eaten in more than twenty-four hours, and Dagmar gave her guests the stale rolls she'd smuggled out of the breakfast room five days ago. She couldn't do anything about the temperature: the power had been out for fifteen or sixteen hours, and the room was at least a hundred degrees—and since it was a modern hotel, all glass and steel, there was no way to open a window.

She had considered offering to take them with her when she made her exit, but the European Union was in the process of arranging an evacuation, and the Tippels had decided to wait. Dagmar asked how they planned to get past the looters.

"The looters have no reason to stop anyone from leaving," Anna Tippel said.

What, Dagmar wondered, did *reason* have to do with anything?

Be in the northwest stairwell at 1600 hours. It was the stair farthest from the front doors, and one that the looters weren't using: the Bayangan Prajurit didn't want to risk a collision with whatever group was gutting the hotel.

Dagmar was ready a quarter of an hour early, sitting in the hot, stale air of the staircase and waiting for the sound of her rescuers. She had her satellite phone on her belt and her laptop in a rucksack—in view of the amount of cash she had on her person, she was no longer worried about someone killing her just for her computer. Her bag held toiletries and a change of clothing. She wore her panama hat on her gray hair and Reeboks on her feet and couldn't tell if her current mood of buoyant optimism was a good thing or not.

Perhaps she was light-headed with lack of food.

Minutes crept by. Sweat dripped off Dagmar's nose and splashed on the concrete stair landing. At 1600 hours she cracked open the steel door to see if the Bayangan Prajurit had used stealthy martial arts skills to creep up without her hearing them, but the street was empty except for a few nervous-looking civilians scuttling in the shadows. Hot air blasted through the open door, and she closed it quickly. Frustration clattered in her nerves.

In another ten minutes she was convinced that the whole rescue had been an absurd fantasy, some kind of wild delusion that had possessed LadyDayFan and all the others. A bunch of game hobbyists, planning a real-life rescue half a world away? Insane.

She paced back and forth along the landing, muscles trembling with anger. She checked her phone repeatedly to make sure no one had left her a message, either voice mail or email.

Through the steel door she heard the sound of a vehicle. Doors slammed. More doors slammed than would have been present on a single vehicle, so there was more than one.

Dagmar's heart raced. She tipped back her hat and

wiped sweat from her forehead with an already-soaked handkerchief.

Through the door, she heard Javanese voices.

They could be Bayangan Prajurit. Or looters. Or killers.

She looked at her phone again, saw that no message waited, then returned it to its holster.

The stairwell was more airless than ever. For some reason she thought of the skating rink in the shopping center down the street, trendy young people turning slow circles to pop tunes recorded before Dagmar was born.

Oh hell, she thought. Now or never.

She clutched the door's locking bar with white-knuckled hands, then pushed the door open a foot or so. The hinges groaned, and Dagmar's nerves shrieked in response.

As she stared out, she saw a group of Javans looking back at her. There were about ten of them altogether, and three small cars. The men didn't wear uniforms like the Bersih Jantung Association—they were in ordinary street wear—but the oldest of them, a compact, fit-looking man of fifty or so, wore a loose white top and trousers, with a brilliantly colored wraparound knee-length kilt. All had weapons thrust into their belts or sashes, and each of the men wore a kopiah head wrap, blue with a white pattern, with two subdued little peaks on the top of the head, as if to cover a pair of small horns.

In the States, the kopiah would have made a particularly stylish do-rag.

One young woman was with them. She was still in her

teens and was taller than the leader, wearing a wide-sleeved blouse in tropical colors and dark pantaloons. Metal-rimmed glasses were set on her squarish face. Her hair was pulled back in a little bun, and she had a long, sheathed knife thrust through her belt.

When she saw Dagmar, her mouth opened, revealing prominent teeth in a brilliant smile.

The older man looked at Dagmar.

"Dogma?" he said.

"Yes," Dagmar said. "I'm Dagmar."

"Please," said the man, with a stiff little bow. He made a gesture toward a white sedan.

A young man in a wife-beater shirt jumped to open the rear door. Another opened the trunk and walked toward Dagmar with hands outstretched to take her bag.

The young woman approached first, stepping in front of the young man. She was still smiling.

"I'm Putri," she said. "Please come with us."

"Yes," Dagmar said. "Thank you."

She pushed the door open all the way and stepped onto the sidewalk. Afternoon heat shimmered up around her: the atmosphere seemed scarcely more breathable than the close air in the stairwell. The young man bustled up around Putri and took Dagmar's bag, then waited expectantly for the knapsack. Dagmar shrugged out of the shoulder straps and handed the computer ruck to him. He put both in the trunk and slammed the lid.

Dagmar stepped into the car. It smelled of tobacco, cloves, and hot plastic. One of the young men, very polite, closed the door for her.

Putri trotted around the car and joined Dagmar in the

backseat. The older man gave a quiet command and the others ran into their cars. The three vehicles made U-turns and sped away.

Dagmar looked over her shoulder to see the Royal Jakarta receding.

Putri was still smiling at her.

"Where are you from?" the girl asked.

Dagmar laughed and told her.

FROM: Desi

My friend Eric tells me that *Bayangan* means "phantom" or "shadow," and that *Prajurit* is "warrior." So the Bayangan Prajurit are Phantom Warriors. Pretty cool, huh?

FROM: Hanseatic

Phantom Warriors? Are they like Indonesian ninjas or what?

FROM: Desi

I don't think so. I think it's just one of those elaborate names that martial artists use, like Golden Crane White Tiger Long Fist Kung Fu. But I could be wrong.

The Bayangan Prajurit convoy avoided the highways and worked their way east and north in short legs, sometimes backtracking when they didn't like the look of an area. The older man, whose name, according to Putri, was Mr. Abu Bakar, was on his cell phone continuously—

negotiating, Putri said, with groups that controlled the neighborhoods they were passing through.

When they had to take an overpass over a highway, or a bridge across one of the city's many canals, one car was sent forward to scout, to make certain there was no ambush. Some of the bridges had roadblocks on them, cars drawn across the roadway, and then Abu Bakar came forward to negotiate. Sometimes they were turned away and had to find an alternate route. On other occasions, Abu Bakar paid a toll with sacks of rice that were carried in the lead vehicle.

Jakarta was like Los Angeles in a way, a series of small towns blended together. Some areas featured tall glass office buildings or apartments; some had private homes; some had apartment buildings clustered together. The homes were quiet; businesses were shuttered.

Everywhere there was greenery. The Jakartans liked living among trees.

Or perhaps, in the tropics, you couldn't keep the green from springing up.

Only in the poor areas, the kampungs, were numbers of people seen—their apartments were too small for anything but sleeping, so life had to be lived in the open whether there was a political and economic crisis or not. The destruction of the currency had hit the rich and the middle classes, but the poor had no savings to lose. What they had lost were jobs: in the streets, Dagmar saw people who would normally have been at work playing football or standing in groups or gambling with whatever passed for currency in an economy where the money had become so much toilet paper.

On one occasion she saw them engaged in a sport that looked like volleyball played with the feet, kicking sometimes from a handstand position. The game was fascinating, but the car raced by too quickly for Dagmar to get a good look.

She got on her handheld and sent a message to LadyDayFan, Charlie, and Tomer Zan that she was on her way.

No one tried to stop her from sending the message. If they were kidnappers, she thought hopefully, they would have kept her from communicating.

After two hours of transit, the convoy drew up before a canal, one equipped with a drawbridge of the same type Dagmar had seen in Amsterdam. The drawbridge was up but came down as soon as the cars appeared. Children playing in the canal stared from the water as the cars crossed.

Abu Bakar put down his cell phone for the first time. He turned around in his seat and looked at Dagmar.

"You okay?" he said.

"Okay," she said.

He gave her an encouraging smile, then faced forward again. Dagmar guessed he had pretty well exhausted his English.

The convoy passed over the bridge, between two shabby canalside warehouses with red tile roofs, and into a residential area. The principal streets were laid out in a grid, but the smaller streets, very narrow, crept and zigzagged between apartment blocks. There were bright plastic awnings, lines hung with laundry, flags, umbrellas—anything, Dagmar suspected, to provide shade.

Broken plaster showed that the buildings were made of red brick, with roofs of metal or worn red tile. The structures were old and sagged a bit, sinking into the soft ground. Zigzag cracks demonstrated that bricks were a very poor construction material in an earthquake zone. The tile roofs often had green plants, and even small bushes, sprouting from the crumbling red clay.

The vehicles passed a small neighborhood mosque and drew up in front of a long building. The brick walls had been plastered and painted white, with neat, bright blue and red lettering. Dagmar recognized "Bayangan Prajurit" amid other words she didn't know.

Doors opened. Abu Bakar opened Dagmar's door, and said, "Please."

The building turned out to be the group's training hall. The place was scrupulously clean. Racks for weapons stood along the walls, half of them empty. A large photo of a distinguished-looking man, perhaps the style's founder, stood on one wall between a pair of Indonesian flags.

A group of women sat on a raised platform at one end of the room. Cooking smells brightened the air. Dagmar felt her mouth begin to water.

Dagmar removed her shoes at the entrance along with the others. The boy in the wife-beater shirt brought in her baggage and placed it by the door.

Dagmar looked at the springy split-bamboo floor, ideal for percussive exercise, and reflected that in Los Angeles, fashionable homeowners would have paid a lot of money for a floor just like this one.

She turned to Putri. "How long are we staying here?"

"Till the boat comes. The boat won't come till night."

"How will we know when the boat arrives?"

"The captain will call on his phone."

On his satellite phone. Of course.

"Please," said Putri, waving a hand in the direction of the circle of women. "We thought you might want to eat."

"Thank you!"

Dagmar approached the platform eagerly. The women looked up at her—they were young girls in their teens under the direction of an older woman, and they had prepared a large pot of rice and a number of other dishes set in a circle around the rice bowl.

One of the girls gave Dagmar a bowl, and she was prepared to seat herself with the others when a thought struck her. She turned to Putri.

"Food must be scarce here," she said. "I don't want to take anyone's food."

Putri absorbed this, then nodded.

"That is kind of you," she said. "But in our kampung we have food. One of those *gudangs* we passed—storage places?"

"Warehouses?"

"Yes. Warehouses. One of the *gudangs* was full of rice. So now we have a lot of rice, and the head man of our kampung can trade this rice for other kinds of food." She smiled. "So we are poor here, but not starving."

"Is Abu Bakar the head man?"

"No. That is Mr. Billy the Kid. You may meet him later."

Dagmar was hungry but couldn't keep the question from her lips.

"Billy the Kid? Is that a name his English teacher gave him?"

"No," Putri said patiently, "it's his Indonesian name. American names are very popular here, and Mr. Billy the Kid was named after a character played by Paul Newman in the cinema."

Dagmar could think of no response but a nod.

Dagmar moved to seat herself with the other women, who gladly made room for her. She noticed that several of the young girls carried knives in their belts, and she was pleased that women were allowed to study martial arts here, in a Muslim country. No one had imposed burkas on these women, not yet.

The food was lovely, and carefully prepared. Dagmar praised it extravagantly. Her stomach had shrunk in the day and a half since her last meal, and that helped her eat slowly. The girls were talkative, and those who had English were eager to practice it. Dagmar answered the usual questions and asked questions of her own.

Time passed. The young men wandered in and out. Abu Bakar talked with the older woman, who Putri said was his wife. Dagmar looked out the rear window and saw an undeveloped area, partly under a shallow lake, that stretched from the rear of the building toward an industrial district in the distance. There was a petrochemical smell—perhaps the lake was used for dumping.

The kampung, backed up against this desolate area, with its canal and drawbridges, was practically an island. That made it very defensible, assuming of course that anyone ever found it worth attacking.

The sun drew close to the horizon. The evening call

for prayer went up from the neighboring mosque, but those in the training hall ignored it as if it were nothing more than birdsong.

If you were religious enough to pray, Dagmar supposed, you were probably in the mosque already.

As the muezzin fell silent, Dagmar approached Putri. She reached for one of the pockets where she had stashed some of her money, opened the pocket button, and offered Putri three hundred dollars.

"Could you give this to Abu Bakar for me?" she asked. "For the poor people in the kampung?"

Putri was astonished. For a moment her English deserted her, and she could only nod. She walked to Abu Bakar and gestured for Dagmar to follow. Putri handed Abu Bakar the money, and the two conducted a rapid conversation in Javanese. Then Abu Bakar turned to Dagmar and held out the money.

"He says," said Putri, "that you don't have to pay. We are doing this for the sake of our own—" She paused, then made a valiant attempt at the proper English. "For our spirit. For our own development."

Dagmar's mind spun. She had wanted this not to be noblesse oblige, a round-eyed female handing out hundred-dollar bills like tips. She genuinely liked these people; she wanted them to be well.

She put out a hand and pressed the bills back toward Abu Bakar.

"For the children," she said. "For medicine and— whatever."

Putri translated. Abu Bakar thought for a moment, then gravely put the money into a pocket.

"Thank you, Miss Dogma," he said.

A cell phone rang. Dagmar recognized a ring tone by Linkin Park. One of the young men answered, then gave the phone to Abu Bakar.

In a few moments everything was motion. Dagmar found herself back in the white sedan with Putri and Abu Bakar, her luggage in the trunk. The convoy moved out, traveling under running lights on the blacked-out streets. They crossed another drawbridge out of the kampung, then turned north. Abu Bakar was back on his cell phone, talking to his friends and allies.

Bags of rice were exchanged, and the group passed through a roadblock into another kampung. The cars passed young men carrying spears and wavy-edged blades. Taillights glowed on the red brick buildings.

The convoy passed through an industrial area, factories looking out with rows of blind glass eyes. Dagmar caught sight of a tank farm off to the left, glowing eerily in the moonlight.

The convoy came to a canal, and a roadblock on a bridge. The cars paused on the deserted road. Dagmar saw a Coca-Cola sign hanging loose on a shuttered fast-food place. The lead car moved up to the roadblock; there was some shouted Javanese, then there were cries and martial yells. Dagmar's heart lurched as she saw moonlight on sharp blades. There were the bangs of weapons striking the car, and then taillights flashed and the car came roaring back as fast as it could come, a mob in pursuit. Abu Bakar yelled out orders. His young driver faced to the rear and put the car in reverse, his face all staring eyes and moist lips. He couldn't move until the rearmost car reversed, and the rear car wasn't moving.

Dagmar was aware only of being trapped, that she could die in this car and not know what to do.

There was a metallic noise as Putri drew her knife. Dagmar stared at it. It was unlike any knife she'd ever seen, a nasty S-shaped thing with a bright little hook at the end, just the size to cut off someone's finger.

TINAG, she thought. *This is not a game.*

There was a flash, a bang, and a singing of metal. Someone was shooting.

Abu Bakar leaned out the window and yelled at the driver of the rear car. Then all three cars were scrambling backward as fast as they could go. Crumbling brick walls shot past, and parked vehicles. Whoever had the gun held his fire.

After it put some distance between itself and pursuit, the convoy sorted itself out and began moving westward. Abu Bakar shouted into his cell phone. Dagmar tried to slow her racing heart.

"That kampung," Putri said, her face white, "was captured by friends of the military." She sheathed her knife.

"I see," Dagmar said. She was trying not to gasp for breath.

Abu Bakar managed to reroute his convoy. Now the tank farm was on the right. Then Dagmar scented the iodine smell of the sea, and her nerves gave a little thrill. Despite all obstacles, they had managed to come near the sea. The sea, where rescue floated somewhere in the darkness.

The convoy moved east, and now there was water on

the left. Then the convoy turned left and was driving down a long jetty. Wooden schooners floated left and right, all in the local style, with a distinctive raked prow. Some had anchored out in the water, where no one could reach them, but some were drawn right to the pier, their fabulously raked stems and bowsprits hanging over the jetty like openmouthed sharks caught in the act of devouring their prey.

The convoy drove unmolested to the end of the pier. Abu Bakar, very calm now, made a call on the cell phone.

Doors opened. People got out of the cars, stretched, breathed in the sea-drenched scent of the land breeze. Dagmar wandered about in a daze.

A boat engine throbbed somewhere in the darkness. The lead car flashed its headlights. Dagmar stared hopefully out to sea, and then she saw it, a blue and white boat with a tall mast and an extravagantly raked stem in the local fashion. The engine cut out, and the boat made a gentle curve and came up broadside to the jetty. Two crew members threw out rope mats to cushion any impact with the pier, then cast lines to lasso bollards with practiced efficiency. Dagmar saw that jerricans of fuel were lashed to the pilot house. A man in a baseball cap peered out of the pilot house and called over.

"Is Dagmar here?"

She wanted to jump in the air, whoop, wave her arms.

"I'm here," she said, and then realized her voice was pitched too low. "I'm here!" she repeated, louder this time.

"Good! Come on the boat!"

Dagmar took the time to embrace Putri, the girl who

had been willing to draw a knife to protect her. She hugged Abu Bakar as well, much to his surprise. And then she let Widjihartani in his baseball cap help her onto the boat. Lines were cast off, and Dagmar's last view of Indonesia was of her rescuers lined up on the pier, silhouetted against the car lights, waving as she set off on her return to the Western Paradise.

I never got to meet Billy the Kid, she thought.

Maybe next time.

The dawn rose over the moving ocean, throwing the schooner's long, dark shadow before it over the sea. Red sun twinkled from the wave caps, long rollers driven by the dry monsoon. Java was well out of sight, but there were islands off the starboard bow. Dagmar stared out over the stern and smelled breakfast cooking.

Suddenly "Harlem Nocturne" rang out over the throb of the engine. Dagmar saw "Charlies Friend" on the display, laughed, and answered.

"Hello, darling," said Tomer Zan. "How are you?"

"I'm in a boat," Dagmar said, "heading for Singapore."

There was a moment's silence.

"Good," Zan said finally. "The helicopter was crap anyway."

"Well," said Dagmar, "I'm sure you tried your best."

No points to you, she thought.

No world domination, no donut.

ACT 2

CHAPTER TEN

This Is Not the End

FROM: LadyDayFan

It has been pointed out to me that <u>this image</u> has appeared briefly on flat-screen billboards in major cities.

The image is a <u>sem@code</u>, a type of bar code that leads to Web content and, once decoded with the proper software, leads us to this Web page, where we find still photographs of a young woman in what appears to be an ordinary motel room. We also have an inventory of her possessions.

Looks like a rabbit hole to me.

I have started the usual series of topics under the name <u>Motel Room Blues</u>, which will serve until something better comes along. This announcement will be copied to the <u>Introduction</u>.

Anyone want to play?

FROM: Corporal Carrot

I'm in!

FROM: HexenHase

Me too. And hey, the lady is armed and dangerous. I think that pistol is a Firestar, probably the 9mm M-43 variation.

The Firestar is a Spanish pistol. I wonder if it is a clue to her place of origin.

FROM: Desi

Her driver's license is from California and gives her name as Briana Hall. But she's checked into the motel under the name of Iris Fitzgerald.

FROM: Hippolyte

Hey, cool! I'm in!

FROM: Chatsworth Osborne Jr.

If you download the picture of the driver's license and enlarge it, you find tiny numbers inserted just below the photo: 011000110111010101101100011011000110010 10110111000100111011100110010000001100100011

0010101100001011001100 (if I have that transcribed correctly).

Which is binary, and which converted to decimal is 6518124.

FROM: Corporal Carrot

6518124? Is that a phone number?

FROM: Hippolyte

But which area code?

FROM: Corporal Carrot

I'll call them all!

FROM: Chatsworth Osborne Jr.

I'll have to get on my other computer before I'm able to convert the binary to roman numerals. That could be important, too.

FROM: Hippolyte

File the 6518124 until later. I'm sure we'll need it.

FROM: Chatsworth Osborne Jr.

File along with the fact that 216 plus 6518124 is

6518340, which could be a whole = other = phone number. I = never = think numbers are coincidence.

FROM: LadyDayFan

I've just converted that binary string into ASCII, and it says "cullen's dead." Which is probably the clue that you're really after.

FROM: Chatsworth Osborne Jr.

< glyph of slapping forehead >

FROM: Consuelo

Hey, guys! Among the contents of Briana's bag is an invitation to *Planet Nine,* which is an online RPG. They're offering free membership for the next eight weeks, which suggests the length of the ARG.

FROM: Corporal Carrot

Hi, Consuelo! Have we met?

FROM: Consuelo

I've just subscribed to this forum, though I've been lurking for a while. I was waiting for an ARG to start at a convenient time for me, and this is it.

FROM: Corporal Carrot

You're not a puppetmaster, are you?

FROM: Consuelo

A lady never tells. But notice that the *Planet Nine* invitation has a serial number on it.

FROM: Desi

Has anyone noticed that there's a DVD sitting atop the TV set? I bet we can get a video if we solve the right puzzle. Of course we have to *find* the puzzle first.

FROM: Consuelo

6518124 doesn't get much when typed into the YouTube search engine.

FROM: Desi

But the binary string works when you look on Video Us!

Here's the URL.

FROM: Corporal Carrot

Binary after all! PSYCH!

FROM: LadyDayFan

Nice work, Desi.

BTW, I observe a high gloss to this production that suggests the house style of Great Big Idea. Not to mention
the woman-in-the-hotel motif that might be viewed as
autobiographical in view of the recent history of a certain
friend of this bulletin board.

So hi there, Dagmar, if it's you! We're on Briana's trail!

Dagmar stood in the lobby of Burger Angeleno and
watched the hostess chat on the phone. The hostess was
very young, maybe just out of high school, and was talking about somebody named Vincent, who was involved
in some soap opera issues with another person named
Janis. As she talked, the hostess stood behind the cash
register and watched Dagmar with an indifference that
was perfectly without affect. It was as if Dagmar wasn't
there at all.

Dagmar wondered if she should just grab a menu and
seat herself. She peered around the divider between the
dining room and the lobby to see if Austin was waiting
for her, but she didn't see him.

She decided she could wait.

After several minutes the hostess wound up her phone
call. She hung up the phone and looked at Dagmar for a
long moment, again with that affectless expression, as if
she saw nothing worthy of interest.

Dagmar looked back at her. Two could play at this game.

Eventually the hostess was stirred to action. She looked up and to the left, as if she were trying to remember something.

"Can I like help you or anything?" she asked, having at last recalled an approximation of the correct line.

"Table for two," said Dagmar.

The hostess took two menus out of the rack and led Dagmar to a booth.

"I didn't know if you wanted anything or not," she said.

"I wanted to sit down," said Dagmar.

"You might have wanted to pay," said the hostess.

"I didn't have a check," Dagmar pointed out.

"You don't have to be so rude about it," the hostess muttered as she returned to her station.

Dagmar stared after her for a long moment, then reached into her pocketbook for a pen.

A few minutes later, Austin arrived and found her writing on the back of her paper place mat.

"What's that?" he asked.

"A flow chart," Dagmar said.

Austin dropped his canvas shoulder bag onto the table and sat. "For the game?" he asked.

"No. For our hostess."

She finished the chart and took it with her to the lobby. The hostess was back on the phone, talking about someone named Tashi. Dagmar walked up to the hostess and held out the flow chart and tapped it with her pen. The hostess looked annoyed.

"I'm talking," she said.

Dagmar reached out and pressed down the telephone toggle, disconnecting it.

"Tashi can wait," Dagmar said. "I want to show you something that can help you keep your job. This is a flow chart."

"A what?"

Dagmar ignored the question. "There's a box at the top, see. You'll notice it says *Customer stands in lobby.* And then there's an arrow from this to the *next* box, which says *Does the customer have a check?*"

The hostess stared at her.

"You'll see," Dagmar continued, "that the second box has two arrows, marked *Yes* and *No.* If the answer is *Yes,* you follow another arrow to the box marked *Take his money.* And if the answer is *No,* you follow that arrow to the box that says *Ask the customer if you can help him.* And there's an arrow leading from that box to the next, which says *Does the customer want to be seated?*

"If the answer is *Yes,* the arrow goes to the box that says *Seat him.* And if the answer is *Customer is looking for someone,* the arrow takes you to *Help customer find his friend,* and then to *Seat him.*"

Dagmar put the flow chart down in front of the hostess.

"I left off a few unlikely situations," she said, "like *Does customer have a gun?* which would lead to a box that says *Give him money,* but I figure in that situation the customer will tell you what to do. But in the meantime, all you have to do is follow these simple instructions, and you'll do fine."

The hostess didn't say thank you, but then Dagmar hadn't thought she would.

Dagmar returned to her seat and opened the menu.

Burger Angeleno was an upscale diner, the kind of place that served you grass-fed bison patties on your burger, offered the option of soy milk in your shakes, and assured you that the chicken nuggets were free-range and had never been within pecking distance of an antibiotic.

"What's new?" Austin said.

"We launched the new game yesterday," Dagmar said. "The site had nearly a hundred fifty thousand hits as of noon today, so I'd say we're in business."

"Someday," Austin said, "I hope to have enough time to actually play one of these games."

"So do I," said Dagmar.

They looked up as a man approached. He was about twenty, with a spotty complexion. His slim body was neatly encased in a dark suit. He wore a single earring.

"Excuse me," he said. "I'm the manager. I understand there's a problem here?"

"I could use a new place mat," said Dagmar.

"Donna," said the manager, "said that you have a gun."

"Donna," said Dagmar, "is too stupid to know *what* the fuck I said."

A few minutes later, as they drove away in Austin's car, Dagmar rolled down the window and threw a finger at the receding restaurant.

"I've never been thrown out of a restaurant before," Austin said. "And I *liked* that place."

"Plenty of places to get soy milk shakes in L.A."

He looked at her from beneath the brim of his Yankees cap.

"Sometimes I worry about you," he said. "Do you

think you might be suffering from post-traumatic stress disorder?"

Dagmar thought about it, then shrugged.

"Who isn't?" she said.

Austin was a Type One Geek, which is to say he was well over six feet tall and very thin. Because he was now rich, he wore Armani sportswear and custom Ray-Bans and drove a 1957 Corvette, but to Dagmar's mind he still looked like a Type One Geek, only playing dress-up.

Not that she didn't love him, of course.

And at least he wasn't shaving his head, even if he was going bald. You could forgive a rich man a lot for not shaving his head.

And clean on the other end of the scale, he didn't wear a motoring cap. Points for that, too.

Austin had become a legend in the local world of venture capital because he only had a 63 percent failure rate. Normally 80 percent of start-ups failed, but the 20 percent that succeeded made so much money that they paid for the failures and then some. Austin had somehow made a success of another 17 percent, nearly doubling his company's income.

Dagmar was really very proud of him.

They found a New Mexican place that had walls covered with embroidered sombreros and black velvet paintings of bullfighters, and Dagmar ordered chiles rellenos, with a sauce made from Hatch green chile.

In Los Angeles, she had observed, menus often told you where the food came from.

"Did I ever tell you about the live event we did in

Charleston for *Shadow Pattern?*" she said. "I asked the hotel concierge where I could find a restaurant with good southern cooking, and he recommended a place. So I went in, and I looked at the menu and saw, 'Roast breast of upland Carolina quail on a bed of beef tongue tartare, garnished with generous slices of foie gras.'"

"Did you order it?"

"How could I not?" She laughed. "So that was my experience of down-home southern cooking."

"Someday I'll buy you a pork chop and a box of instant grits."

Austin reached into his canvas shoulder bag and retrieved a package done up in fancy wrapping paper, with a large golden ribbon.

"I bought you a present," he said.

Dagmar took it with pleasure. She tore away the wrapping and found a book bound beautifully in rich brown calfskin. The paper was edged in gold, and a pair of red satin ribbons, to mark her place, had been bound into the book. She looked at the spine.

The Unconventional Adventures of Dagmar, she read.

"It's the fan fiction they wrote about you on Our Reality Network," Austin said.

"Oh my God!" said Dagmar.

"Have you read any of it?"

"No!" she said.

He plucked the volume from her fingers and opened to where one of the red ribbons marked a place.

"I've marked my favorite passages," he said. He propped the book up before him and began to read. *"Ahmed ran his fingers through Dagmar's strangely attractive pale hair.*

"'Ahmed,' she whimpered, 'I only feel safe when I'm in your arms.'"

"Oh God," Dagmar moaned.

"His powerful arms encircled her from behind. Dagmar shivered as his lips brushed the sensitive skin of her shoulders. His hands rose to palpate her tingling breasts."

"Saved!" Dagmar said as their meal arrived.

"The plates are very hot," the waitress said.

"So's the prose," said Austin. "Are there really Indonesians named Ahmed?"

"Probably. I never met any. Or had anyone named Ahmed palpate my breasts, for that matter."

She tasted one of her rellenos and smiled. Whatever it was that Hatch did to its chiles, she approved. The taste was a far cry from what Cleveland thought of as southwestern cuisine, chili con carne drenched in cinnamon and served on a plate of spaghetti.

Austin was still looking at the book.

"There's an explicit sex scene that follows," he said. "Written, I suspect, by someone who has never actually *had* sex—the anatomy seems wrong here and there—but she's read about it with great interest."

Dagmar kept her attention on her plate. "Why do I think," she said, "that a thousand years from now, the only thing about me that will survive, in some database somewhere, is this fanfic?"

"Once the other players found out the sort of thing Simone was writing," Austin continued, "they began to write parodies. They're pretty merciless, actually."

"I'm not surprised."

"I noticed Simone stopped posting after a while."

Austin turned to his other bookmark. "My favorite is a lesbian scene. Let me just give you the flavor of it."

She snatched the book from his hand and put it on the bench seat beside her. He sighed.

"I hope the people in Bayangan Prajurit never see any of this," Dagmar said.

"How are they, by the way?"

"Doing very well. They sent photos of the sidewalks they'd paved."

Paved with Charlie's money. Six days after Dagmar's escape from Jakarta, the IMF and World Bank had made it clear that Indonesia's fiscal rescue would depend on a civilian government's remaining in place, so the soldiers had gone back to their barracks, and certain generals had flown to other countries, along with suitcases of money.

In the five months since Jakarta had reopened, Charlie and Dagmar had adopted the Bayangan Prajurit school and its kampung. The local grammar school now had new computers and high-speed wireless Internet, and a local clinic had received additional funding. Areas were being paved, and old homes rebuilt. Microloans were being granted to start local businesses. Charlie provided most of the money, with Dagmar as the liaison.

Bayangan Prajurit had helped Dagmar for their own religious reasons, but Charlie and Dagmar wanted them to enjoy their heightened spirituality from a position of material comfort.

"I freely confess that all Charlie's charity work makes him my moral superior," Austin said.

"You contribute to charity," Dagmar said.

"Usually when Charlie tells me where to send the check."

She smiled. "Nothing wrong with following the advice of a moral superior."

Austin talked about Wyoming. He'd bought a condominium in Jackson Hole—half a million dollars for twelve hundred square feet—and now he talked about quitting and buying a ranch. Dagmar was faintly surprised he hadn't yet bought a Stetson, a pair of alligator-skin Tony Lamas, and a big cowboy belt buckle.

"You don't know how to run a ranch," Dagmar said.

"Some of the ranchers I've met," Austin said, "you get the idea it can't be that hard."

"I can't picture you up there, I just can't."

"Well," he said, looking at her, "it might be hard getting a good RPG together."

She sighed. "I miss live gaming," she said.

"So do I. We should do it sometime."

She nodded.

"I'll check with Charlie. Maybe we can commit some nights."

"After the current ARG is over, okay? It's absorbing all my energy."

"If we wait for us all to have time off from work, it'll be forever."

Dagmar considered this. "That's so true."

"How long has it been since Charlie actually played anything?"

Dagmar looked blank. "Not since I've been back in California."

"I wonder if he's played since he crashed *Lost Empire*."

Dagmar stared. "Charlie was the one who crashed *Lost Empire*?"

Austin was startled.

"You didn't know it was him and BJ?"

"No. They didn't tell me."

Lost Empire had been a classic fantasy MMORPG that had been brought down by its own rather primitive economic system. The game designers had kept the economy simple, figuring that players would be more interested in killing monsters and performing quests than in becoming entrepreneurs. Some smart trading had resulted in players' gaining monopolies in basic commodities such as "grain," "wood," and "gems," bringing down the whole system. The result had been a game reset and a lot of players having their money refunded.

Austin looked down at his blue-corn enchiladas. "It wasn't exactly their greatest hour. Maybe they're embarrassed."

"I'm impressed, though. *Lost Empire* was a pretty good hack."

Austin seemed dubious. "Don't tell Charlie that I told you, okay?"

"Sure."

After buying lunch, Austin took her back to the Burger Angeleno parking lot to pick up her car. She followed him to Great Big Idea, where he had a meeting with Charlie.

Great Big Idea occupied part of an office tower of ocean-colored glass in the San Fernando Valley, sandwiched between a Chili's and a Gap on a green bluff overlooking the Ventura Highway. The building was

owned by Charlie, or by his company, or his foreign backers—Dagmar was a bit unclear about it. The rest of the
building was occupied by AvN Soft, Charlie's company,
the name of which was usually pronounced "Avvensoft."

Austin was in the atrium, talking on his phone, when
Dagmar entered. The atrium rose all eight stories and
neatly bisected the building, with offices off balconies to
either side. The atrium was filled with greenery and comfortable furniture and had a small coffee shop. A lot of
the employees preferred the less impersonal environment
of the atrium to their offices, wireless connecting them to
their jobs.

"I *know* we made the benchmarks," Austin said. "And
the next step is the *release.* So we've got to stick with the
plan, all right?" There was a pause, and then Austin said,
"I'm sure it's a great idea. But save it for Release 2.0."
His heel tapped with impatience on the imported Finnish
porphyry of the atrium floor. "Dude," he said, "we've *had*
this conversation."

Dagmar waited for the dialogue to end so that she
could thank Austin for lunch. Charlie arrived first,
padding through the atrium in blue suede Adidas.

Like Austin, Charlie was a Type One Geek, tall and
thin, with a balding head. He wore dark-rimmed spectacles, chinos, and a Versace sports shirt of the same
pastel shade as Austin's.

"No," Austin said firmly. "You're sticking with the
strategic plan. Because if you don't, I'm going to spank
you hard. Got that?"

Charlie listened with a grin on his face until the conversation was over.

"That wasn't BJ, was it?" he asked.

Then there was a moment of awkward silence as he and Austin recalled Dagmar's relationship with BJ, and then Dagmar reached out to pat Austin's arm.

"You can say what you like—I haven't slept with BJ in ten years. Thanks for lunch. I've got a meeting of my own. Have a good time."

She took the elevator to Great Big Idea, which was on the third floor. She had a meeting of her creative team—while she did most of the writing, other people handled Web design, graphic art, audio, video, and the more complex and technical sorts of puzzles for which the form was known. The meeting took place in a board-room covered with charts and schedules drawn on whiteboards and glittering from plasma screens.

On the largest screen, Dagmar's mantra glowed, one line following the next on infinite repeat:

> *Read the Schedule*
> *Know the Schedule*
> *Love the Schedule*

The meeting was to make certain that everyone had taken the mantra to heart, and Dagmar was pleased to discover that for once, nothing had gone pear-shaped. Everyone was making the deadlines. The number of people who had joined the game was now more than eight hundred thousand and still climbing.

After the meeting broke up, Dagmar helped herself to a cup of coffee from the machine and walked to the boardroom's floor-to-ceiling window to gaze across the

Ventura Highway to the Santa Monica Mountains, dull brown against the brilliant California sky.

The players were calling the game *Motel Room Blues*. Her own name for it was *The Long Night of Briana Hall*.

Either would do. The important thing was the hundreds of thousands of players, who, if they could be persuaded to join *Planet Nine,* would quadruple its membership.

She looked down at the parking lot just as Austin started to cross it toward his Corvette. His head was shaded by his Yankees cap, and he carried his keys in one hand.

Dagmar's attention was caught by motion in a corner of the parking lot—a motorcycle had just bounced across the low concrete berm that separated the AvN parking lot from the Chili's restaurant next door. The bike accelerated as it moved along the row of cars. It was a green and white Kawasaki, and the rider wore what looked like brand-new riding leathers and a black helmet with a visor. Dagmar could hear the bike's whine from her third-floor perch.

Austin had heard the machine and had politely stopped to let it pass. Instead the motorcycle slowed and came to a stop, as if the rider were going to ask Austin a question.

The rider drew a pistol from his green and white jacket and shot Austin five times. At each report the glass window rattled in its frame.

Dagmar's heart lurched with each shot. A scream seemed to crouch somewhere in her throat, ready to spring. She stared as Austin fell, as the biker calmly put away his pistol and accelerated.

Dagmar clawed for her cell phone and tried to punch 911 while still keeping her eyes on the biker. She hit 611 instead.

The biker couldn't get into the Gap parking lot—there was a fence with a three-foot-high cable stretched across a series of posts—so he turned left at the end of the row of cars and then, almost casually, made his way out of the parking lot and down the frontage road, where he accelerated out of sight.

Dagmar looked down at Austin in the parking lot and felt herself fill with despair.

Her fingers trembled, but she managed 911 on the third try.

CHAPTER ELEVEN

This Is Not a Spy

That is so cool, thought Andy. *I wonder how they knew I was looking.*

Andy—better known by his online handle Joe Clever—was in his James Bond van parked in a strip mall across the highway from AvN Soft and Great Big Idea. The van was a new idea—he'd bought a used Dodge and equipped it for surveillance, with cameras hidden behind two-way-mirror windows, a satellite uplink, a cooler for the Mountain Dew and Red Bull he drank during the course of his researches, and a camp bed for when the caffeine finally wore off. He was divided on the notion of adding a chemical toilet—it would smell, but it meant he didn't have to abandon his researches to haunt the rest rooms at Starbucks or Burger King.

He'd equipped the van with a number of plastic placards that he could stick to the door with built-in magnets. The current one told observers that the van belonged to Andy's Electronic Service.

He was considering getting himself a surveillance

drone, like those used by the police, highway patrol, and traffic reporters. They were cheap enough to make—just a big model plane with an onboard camera controllable from the ground. He didn't need one of the fancy ones with the miniturbines.

Maybe, he'd thought, he could mount a launch rail on top of the van.

Andy had been using his Big Ears, bouncing a laser off the boardroom window at Great Big Idea, to listen to Dagmar's meeting with her team. The reception had been wretched—the van was too far away, on the far side of the highway—and the air-conditioning must have been blowing right onto the window glass, because the sound was horribly distorted. Yet he had caught a few names that were probably characters who would be introduced into the game, and a few interesting phrases like "the cold-data store under the gantry at Mars Port," which would be a place to pick up a clue if he only knew when it would be there.

He'd have to make sure that Consuelo—his new handle, chosen for this game—would be in the online world of *Planet Nine*, and at Mars Port under the gantry, at the right time.

If only he'd managed to hear *which* gantry.

It was while listening to the wild distortions on his Big Ears that he'd first caught sight of the motorcyclist. He was passing up and down the frontage road slowly, keeping an eye on the AvN Soft building the entire way. Andy had watched the rider take note of the CCTV camera above the entrance to the AvN parking lot, and he wondered if the rider had also seen the camera on the front door.

Andy assumed that he had a rival. He wasn't pleased by this prospect; he very much preferred to be the only Dumpster diver on any game. But the driver seemed a little ill-equipped for espionage. The Kawasaki was nice, but it wasn't even an anonymous SUV, let alone the spy van that Andy had assembled for himself.

The cyclist had eventually parked himself in the Chili's parking lot out of sight of any cameras. When he took off his helmet to smoke a cigarette, Andy got out the Pentax and the big zoom lens. The rider was an impressive figure: in his twenties, tall, thick-necked, with big ears and reddish blond hair styled in a flattop. He wore gleaming-new riding leathers and clunky, thick-soled boots, and he looked like an actor playing a heavy.

Which wasn't necessarily unusual: L.A. was full of underemployed actors. Sometimes, if you ate in restaurants, everyone on the wait staff seemed to be giving auditions.

As Andy took a series of pictures of his rival through the mirrored glass in the van's rear doors, he reached the conclusion that he'd never seen the man before. A player this dedicated, you'd think Andy would have seen him at a few live events.

Andy noticed that the rider didn't throw away his cigarette butt, but instead pinched it out and put it in his pocket.

When someone left the AvN Soft building, Andy tracked his camera to the new arrival and lost sight of the cyclist. He recognized Austin Katanyan, whom he knew as one of Charlie Ruff's business associates who was unconnected with the game business, and when he swung the camera back to the Kawasaki, it was already moving.

The Pentax could take video as well as still pictures, and when he saw the motorcycle slowing down as if the rider wanted to talk to Austin, Andy thumbed the video button and reached for the Big Ears.

And then, to Andy's utter delight, the rider pulled out a pistol and shot Austin dead. Andy kept the Pentax on the motorcycle until after it had left the parking lot and rocketed away down the frontage road, and then tracked back to where Austin Katanyan had dropped behind a row of cars. Apparently Austin was still there, because the receptionist had just run out of the building and crouched down by the body. Or the "body," since obviously the assassination was a part of *Motel Room Blues*.

Whoever was playing the receptionist was a pretty good actress. That wild, distraught look was very convincing.

"This," Andy said out loud, "is the *coolest thing I've ever seen!*"

He got busy. He powered up the satellite uplink and uploaded the video onto Video Us. He then logged on to Our Reality Network and posted a link to the video, and then uploaded the still pictures of the assassin to a new topic called "Who Is This Man?"

It was only when the ambulance arrived and the police began to swarm the area that Andy began to wonder if perhaps he'd made a mistake.

CHAPTER TWELVE

This Is Not a Team

"I talked to Austin's mother this morning," Charlie said. "The Red Cross came up with their phone number."

His voice was raw with lack of sleep and hours of talking to the police.

"I'd never spoken to her in my life," he said, "and I don't think she has the slightest idea who I was, but I had to tell her that her son had been killed. And then as soon as I'd gotten through *that* conversation, the *father* called. Because the mother told him and he didn't believe her. Or me. I only know that he was really pissed off and kept yelling. He didn't believe me until I gave him Detective Murdoch's phone number, and maybe not even then."

Charlie lay back in his office chair, drawn eyes gazing sightlessly at the plush Pinky and the Brain dolls sitting atop his monitor. The tasteful functionality of his spacious office—huge desk, computer, monitor, and huge video displays—provided a contrast with their owner. Dense stubble coated Charlie's cheeks and chin, and great sweat patches bloomed beneath the arms of his pastel shirt. The police had been present till after eleven at night, and after that, Charlie had been too busy to leave.

He both looked and smelled as if he'd slept on his office couch, which he had. At midmorning he'd sent his secretary out to buy some new clothes, and there were showers in the exercise room, which he'd use as soon as he had something to change into.

Dagmar did not possess an assistant who would buy clothes for her. She needed to do a laundry and was wearing yesterday's clothes. She'd thought she'd at least had clean underwear, but apparently she'd miscounted.

"Have you heard anything from the police," Dagmar asked, "about who did it and why?"

"The police," said Charlie, "do not confide in me. But I overheard some of them talking to Murdoch—they said they didn't get the call early enough to track the killer with their camera drones, so nobody knows who he is or where the hell he went. We looked at the security cams and found out that the one on the door didn't see anything, and the one at the parking lot entrance saw only the top of the guy's helmet—so the police are fucking out of luck."

Charlie waved a listless arm as he spoke, and then let it fall. Dagmar looked at his supine figure.

"Do you need coffee or something?" she asked.

"Coffee's all I've had for the last dozen hours," Charlie said. "I can't look at food right now. The sight of it makes me—well, it doesn't make me sick, it just makes me not want food."

"Yeah," Dagmar said. "I know what you mean."

She was floating on coffee as well, quarts and quarts of the stuff, and the only food she'd eaten was a piece of dry toast she'd choked down with a handful of vitamins. Unlike Charlie, she'd gotten home the previous night, but she'd barely slept. Every time she closed her eyes she saw a blood-spattered Austin lying on the blacktop, mouth slack and open, the Yankees cap rolled off his head and lying by his hand.

Do you think you might be suffering from post-traumatic stress disorder? he'd asked.

Her answer had been less than serious, but she'd give a different one now. She'd seen dreadful things in Indonesia, but she'd had the consolation of going home afterward and looking at them from a safe distance.

The atrocities were no longer at arm's length. They were right in her lap.

"Murdoch asked me," Dagmar said, "if Austin had any enemies. And when I said he didn't, they didn't believe me."

"Would you?" Charlie's shoulders lifted in a shrug. "They asked me if he had any connection to organized crime."

Dagmar was overwhelmed by a feeling of disgust at the question.

"Christ," she said, "that's stupid."

Charlie gave her an irritated look.

"It was a drive-by shooting," he said. "A contract killing, most likely. Murdoch was only asking the obvious questions."

Dagmar felt herself dig in her heels. Austin was not some kind of mafioso or drug dealer, and he didn't deal with them, and any investigation aimed in that direction was not only *wrong*, it was a waste of the time that could be spent finding the killer.

"If it was a contract killing," she said, "they hit the wrong man."

An idea brushed against her mind, but she was too weary to catch at it, and it faded.

"Listen," she said. "We've got a problem."

Charlie turned again to Pinky and the Brain, gazed at them bleakly, then closed his eyes.

"Oh yeah?" he said. "Is it important?"

"I'm afraid so." She gathered her strength, then spoke. "A video of the killing turned up on Video Us, along with pictures of the shooter. They were taken with a zoom lens from—I don't know—across the highway, maybe."

Charlie's eyes were wide open and staring at her. "Do the police know?"

"I called Murdoch and gave him the URL. I had to explain about the game—I don't think he quite understood it."

"If they catch the guy," Charlie judged, "what Murdoch understands doesn't matter. Who took the pictures?"

"A new gamer who uses the handle Consuelo. But I think she's a sock puppet for someone like Hermes or Joe Clever—one of our Dumpster divers."

"Jesus." Charlie sagged in his chair again. "At least one of those bastards finally did something useful."

"It means we're being stalked by someone pretty serious," Dagmar said.

Charlie flapped a hand. "Who cares? We've been stalked before."

"But not by a contract killer," Dagmar said. "If we look in the rearview mirror and see someone following us, is it Joe Clever or is it somebody with a gun?"

Charlie gave her an unreadable look. "We are *not* the targets here," he said.

"Crazy people exist," Dagmar said. "None of the people we work or play with are exactly models of middle-American thought and behavior." She banged a hand on the arm of her chair. "Someone killed *Austin*, for Christ's sake!"

"Right. Shit. Damn." Charlie hesitated. "Do you think I should put out a warning to our employees?"

"They might overreact." Dagmar thought for a long moment. "But if you *failed* to put out a warning and someone got hurt, then you might be liable."

That decided it.

"Right. I'll have Karin send out an email when she gets back."

Dagmar hesitated. "There's another problem," she said.

"Can it wait?"

"No." Again she hesitated. She didn't want to acknowledge this.

"The Video Us site," she said, "has had nearly half a million hits since the video was posted."

Charlie's lip twisted. "Sick fucks," he said.

"No," Dagmar said. "*Confused* fucks. Consuelo's a *gamer*—she posted the link on Our Reality Network and nowhere else. Nobody knows whether the video is real or a part of the game. The Our Reality people have been speculating on their live feed continually since eight o'clock last night, and they're not slowing down."

"Jesus." Charlie rubbed his eyes.

"The buzz is *huge*," she said. "It's spreading outside the usual channels. And normally we *want* buzz, just not the kind we're getting."

"Screw the buzz," Charlie said. "You've got a subscription to their live feed, right?"

"Yeah. Under one of my handles."

Anger edged Charlie's tones, burned in his eyes. He jabbed a finger into the laminate surface of his desk.

"So go online," he said, "blow your cover as Dagmar, and tell them that Austin's death was not a part of the game but a real-life tragedy. And they should *shut the fuck up already.* Got that?"

"Right." Again she hesitated. "But it might be too late."

"Too late for *what?*"

Dagmar looked at the savagery crackling behind Charlie's eyes and decided not to answer.

"Never mind." She rose. "I'll go post the announcement."

Unspoken objections still clattered in her mind, objections that had nothing to do with Austin's death or the investigation.

They had to do with the shape of the game.

When Consuelo had posted the video and linked to it from Our Reality Network, the shape of the game had changed. The players had shifted their energies in an unanticipated direction.

Alternate reality games worked in a complex synergy with the player community. During the course of previous games, Dagmar had been forced to change the game when players moved in an unexpected way.

TINAG—this is not a game. The game only worked when both players and puppetmasters *acted as if everything was real*. When Dagmar, as puppetmaster, addressed the players directly, it shattered the illusion—it broke the fourth wall, as in theater when an actor turns to the audience and speaks to them directly.

If Dagmar posted a notice telling players that Austin's death was real, all the player momentum that had been generated by the release of Consuelo's video would come to a screeching halt.

Dagmar was loyal to her creations—to their integrity, their own internal sense. She wanted their shape to be logical, their interior purposes fulfilled. She didn't mind changing her work if the change was for the better, but arbitrary changes made her crazy, and she completely hated changes that destroyed the illusion she had worked so hard to create.

But, she then realized, in this case her loyalty was ridiculous. What was the game—what was a mere story—against Austin's tragedy?

Charlie was right. Dagmar had to make the announcement. Austin's real death could not become a part of Dagmar's alternate reality amusement.

She mentally composed the message as she walked to her office. As the executive producer for Great Big Idea she had a spacious corner billet and a desk filled with high-powered hardware. The rest of the office featured

desks and shelves filled with souvenirs of Dagmar's fre-
netic, complicated life. There were books, disks, manuals,
file folders, and toys. There were posters from gaming
conventions, graphic designs from the past four years of
Dagmar's games, portfolios of actors, technicians, and
software designers, maps of areas where live events had
taken place, books about the history of Los Angeles and
other cities, and lists of the go-to people in half the cities
of the world.

On a coat stand near the door hung her panama hat,
the one she had worn in Jakarta.

She had always assumed that when she had some free
time, she'd systematize her room into a streamlined, effi-
cient, highly organized office that reflected her personality.
But then, as the years passed and the clutter only grew,
she'd finally conceded that the room *already* reflected her
personality, and then stopped thinking about it.

She sat at her desk. Her computer was already logged
on to Our Reality Network under one of her aliases, and
she checked the message boards to see if there had been
any developments in the last half hour.

And there it was.

Oh Christ.

FROM: Chatsworth Osborne Jr.

For once I am not going to demonstrate how I learned
this, as I very much like my day job and want to keep it.
But thanks to Consuelo's excellent snaps, we've got a ton
of biometric data, and it gives us the identity of the
shooter.

Our man is one Arkady Petrovich Litvinov, age 28, a Russian national born in Latvia. He is a member of Russian organized crime and is suspected of a string of murders in Russia and Western Europe.

This is his first appearance in North America. I doubt he arrived in the U.S. under his own name.

I've posted his rap sheet here—sorry, but it's in Russian. You might have better luck with his sheet from Interpol.

I'm afraid this will end our long and ultimately fruitless discussion of whether the killing Consuelo caught on camera is part of *Motel Room Blues*. Great Big Idea is known for its innovative approaches to gaming, but I very much doubt they would hire a genuine Russian killer to play an assassin.

Maybe it's time to leave this issue behind and return to the actual game that GBI is giving us.

FROM: Corporal Carrot

Damn, Chatty! What are you in your other life? Some kind of spook?

FROM: Chatsworth Osborne Jr.

I'm afraid I can neither confirm nor deny.

FROM: Desi

Are you a cop?

FROM: Chatsworth Osborne Jr.

Let's just say I have access to biometric data, and leave it at that.

FROM: LadyDayFan

I think we should stop harassing Chatsworth and thank him for his first-rate work.

FROM: Corporal Carrot

Amen! Most excellent detection, dawg!

FROM: Hippolyte

Customs should be able to ID him from biometric data and find out the passport he's used to come into the country.

FROM: Corporal Carrot

It's not our problem any longer.

FROM: Hippolyte

I'm just sayin'.

FROM: Chatsworth Osborne, Jr.

I'm not in a position to alert Customs myself. But perhaps someone reading this is better situated.

FROM: Desi

(At least we now know that Chatty doesn't work for Customs!)

FROM: Hippolyte

You know, we're not devoting every minute of every day to *Motel Room Blues*. If we could solve a real-life murder, we could earn a lot of good karma. Like we did by helping Dagmar.

FROM: Corporal Carrot

But the victim won't give us all a thank-you dinner, the way Dagmar did.

Dagmar looked at the bulletins lined up on her screen and simply stared for a long moment. Then she let out the air she'd been holding in her lungs and reached for the phone on her desk.

She had Lieutenant Murdoch's number somewhere, if she could find his card with her trembling fingers.

CHAPTER THIRTEEN

This Is Not a Detective

Charlie had showered and changed and as a result now looked like a homeless person who had been taken off the street and dressed in someone else's clothes. He was slumped, motionless, over his desk, hunched over a mug of coffee. He seemed to have aged twenty years in the past twenty-four hours.

Probably Dagmar had, too. She should probably avoid mirrors for the next several days—she didn't want to know how ragged she looked.

As Dagmar entered his office, Charlie looked up, and said, "Did you post the message?"

"I didn't need to. The Group Mind figured it out on its own."

He shrugged, slumped again. Dagmar seated herself.

"But listen," Dagmar said, "they figured it out by finding out who the killer was."

Charlie looked up.

"He's a professional hit man," Dagmar said. "Russian Maffya."

Charlie stared. Dagmar sensed his mind working behind the weary facade.

"Did you tell the police?" he asked.

"Yes, but Murdoch already knew. They had Consuelo's uploads and the same biometric data that the Group Mind had."

"Do they know where the guy lives?"

"He smuggled himself into the country under a false identity. I imagine they're going to wait for him to fly out on that identity, and nail him at the airport."

Charlie looked down, frowned for a moment, then glanced up. "Do you know what false identity he's using?"

"Murdoch wouldn't say."

Charlie leaned back, stared into the far distance, and tapped a thumbnail against his coffee mug. "I wish," he said, "that I was one of those millionaires who knew all the politicians, and I could call Murdoch's superior and get the name. But I'm not politically connected. I've never needed favors from any of those people. I don't even know who my state senator is."

"Do you know anyone who *is* connected?" Dagmar asked. "Anyone who owes you a favor?"

"I know lots of people. Favors are another issue." He looked at Dagmar and narrowed his eyes. "We're thinking about the same thing, aren't we?"

"Set the Group Mind to finding the killer?"

"Yeah." He scratched at the stubble on his chin. "That is like *totally* crazy, isn't it?"

Dagmar felt anger clenching the muscles in her jaw.

"I want Austin's killer found," she said.

"So do I."

"So if we make Austin's killing part of the *game* . . ."

"Yeah."

Dagmar put her hands on her head. "And give rewards to anyone who gives us answers." She passed a hand over her weary eyes. "I'll have to think about how to do all that. How to work it."

Charlie stood, hitched up his brand-new khaki trousers.

"In an hour," he said, "I've got a meeting with Austin's partners. We've got to try and figure out a way to keep his company going."

She looked at him. "Why are you involved? You're not part of his company."

"I'm one of Austin's original backers. I still own a piece."

She stared at him in surprise. He looked irritated.

"What's wrong?" he said.

"It's just that I didn't know that."

Charlie flapped one arm. "I made my millions first, so I gave Austin a hand. It's not as if I haven't been repaid a dozen times over. He had the golden touch."

"What's going to happen with the company?"

He shook his head. "He's got partners, but they're *junior* partners. None of them are ready to move up to the Show. So we're going to have to hire a honcho with a good record, and hire him fast, and that's going to cost."

"Good luck."

He waved a hand. "Thanks."

She stood, and she walked with him to the elevator. As he reached for the button, she put a hand over his.

"Charlie," she said, "I have to know something."

He looked at her. "Sure. What do you need?"

"I need to know if Austin was connected with the Russian Maffya," she said. "You're a part of his company, maybe you know."

Charlie looked at her in astonishment.

"No," he said. "No, in fact I'm sure he wasn't. I don't know every start-up he was involved with, but I know he had plenty of options, and there's no way he'd touch anything that looked hinky."

Hinky. Now *there* was a word Dagmar had never before heard in conversation.

"Okay," she said. "Next question." She looked over her shoulder, made certain the corridor was empty. "Are *you* involved with the Maffya?"

Charlie was beyond astonishment. The question left him openmouthed.

"Me?" he managed.

"Yes."

He put a hand on her arm.

"Dagmar," he said, "I make *software*. I make autonomous agents to help business and government manage complex systems." He gave an incredulous laugh. "I help ordinary people make *shopping decisions*. I help *filter spam*, for Christ's sake."

Dagmar licked dry lips.

"You have these foreign backers," she said. "None of us have ever met them."

Again he gave a laugh.

"No," he said. "None of them are Russian."

Then he stepped back, put both his hands on the sides of his head in a parody of astonishment.

"*Dagmar!*" His voice rose to a kind of geeky shriek, unusual in a man of his height and dignity. "How long have we known each other? I can't believe you've been thinking this!"

Dagmar felt heat rise to her cheeks.

"Sorry," she said. "But it occurred to me that the killer might have been after you, not Austin."

He looked at her in sudden silence, and lowered his hands. "What do you mean?"

"You're the same physical type. You wear glasses and he didn't, but he was wearing shades. Your faces are different, but behind the cap and sunglasses, that might not have been apparent. You were even wearing the same color shirt."

Charlie raised his arms again and looked at his new shirt.

"Jesus, Dagmar," he said.

"Okay." Dagmar waved a hand. "I'm clearly out of my mind. Go to your meeting, okay?"

"Sure." He reached for the elevator button and pressed it, then shook his head.

"Damn," he said. "You're fucking scary, you know that?"

Dagmar ventured a tight little smile.

"PTSD," she said. "But I'm learning how to manage it."

Exhausted, Dagmar went home in midafternoon. On the way she stopped at a Beef Bowl drive-through, and the scent of the beef, rice, and ginger rising in her dented old Prius rekindled her faded appetite.

It had been a long time since that piece of toast.

Dagmar lived in a two-room apartment in the valley, less than two miles from AvN Soft. The building had been built in the 1970s, was three stories tall, and surrounded a courtyard with palm trees, a swimming pool, and a clubhouse with a couple of ping-pong tables and humming soda machines.

Dagmar lived on the top floor so that when the Big One hit, she'd pancake on the people below and not be pancaked herself. She figured that was only sensible.

Even though Charlie paid her very well, she still couldn't afford California real estate, and she didn't have time to take care of a house anyway. So she put her money where Charlie and Austin told her to put it, and watched it grow with a kind of abstract joy completely void of comprehension.

She'd grown up poor, in apartments of decreasing splendor off Detroit Avenue in Cleveland. She knew the value of a dollar, of twenty dollars, of a hundred.

The kind of numbers that Charlie dealt with every day were beyond her ken. A hundred thousand dollars was a statistic. A million a fantasy.

She had a couple of hundred thousand in the market, but it was just Monopoly money to her.

Monopoly money that was growing. Regular paychecks and a rising market, she had found, were a good reinforcement.

She parked in front of the ginkgo bush, took her beef bowl in its white paper bag from the worn passenger seat of the Prius, and legged out of the car. She was about to give her thumbprint to the electronic lock on the wrought-iron gate when she noticed the white Dodge van parked in one of the building's visitor spaces.

The van, she saw, had a *satellite uplink*. If she hadn't had a very paranoid twenty-four hours, she might not have noticed the detail.

Andy's Electronic Service, she read on the door.

Dagmar walked along the wrought-iron gate and placed herself directly between the car and her apartment door, on the third-floor corner.

The sight lines were perfect. Whoever was in the van had an unobstructed view of the front of her apartment.

Anger crackled along her nerves. She pulled her handheld from its holster, opened a file, thumbed in the license number, and mailed it to herself. Then she stalked up to the van and peered through the dark glass of the driver's-side window. Joe Clever's surprised face stared at her for a brief second before he vanished into the back of the vehicle. She walked to the rear of the van and banged on the door.

"Hey!" she shouted. "Come out of there!"

She kicked the door.

"I can stay here all day, motherfucker!" she yelled. "Get your ass out here!"

"Don't dent my van!" came a muffled voice. "I'm coming out!"

One of the rear doors opened, and Joe Clever climbed out, lanky body unfolding as he dropped his sneakers onto the pavement. He was over six feet, appeared to be in his twenties, and had a stoop and dark hair that looked as if he cut it himself with scissors and a pair of mirrors.

Type One Geek.

"Hi, Dagmar," he said. "Haven't seen you since the dinner."

Dagmar had given a dinner at an Indonesian restaurant for those members of the Group Mind who had helped her escape from Indonesia, or at least those who had been able to make it to L.A.

"You've seen *me* since the dinner," Dagmar said. "It's just that I haven't seen *you*."

He grinned. He didn't seem the least embarrassed.

"Yeah!" he said. He stepped to the side so that Dagmar could see the interior of the van. "Pretty cool, huh?"

"Why don't you give me the tour?" Dagmar said.

So he showed her the van, the two-way-mirror side and rear windows, the Pentax on its mount, the lenses sitting in foam in their shockproof steel carrying case, the telescope, the binoculars, and the elegant NKVD-surplus monocular that could be worn on the finger like a ring. Electronic images fed into a laptop computer, which could then upload anything via the satellite uplink.

There was more than one computer, and an online game was frozen on one monitor, something he'd been playing when she showed up.

The van smelled like old fast-food cartons, which it contained in large numbers.

He didn't show her what she suspected was audio equipment, so Dagmar made a point of asking about it. He showed her his Big Ears, and some smaller surveillance gear he'd purchased in some neighborhood spy store.

So, Dagmar thought, her own office wasn't secure, not

with the big glass window that could be used as a diaphragm for the laser signal.

She'd have to call in some countersurveillance experts.

"I've even got some oscilloscopes," he said. "They don't really have any *function* or anything, but I think they're cool." Green standing waves hummed in the displays.

"Nice mad-scientist decor," Dagmar said. "All you need is a Tesla coil."

"Thanks!" He opened the squeaking lid of a large cooler. "Want a drink to go with your dinner?"

She chose a lemonade, then climbed out of the van and blinked in the bright California sun. She turned to Joe Clever as he joined her on the asphalt.

"What do you do for a living, anyway?" she asked.

He adjusted his spectacles. "I play games full-time."

"I don't think that pays very well," Dagmar said.

Joe Clever grinned. "My grandma died and left me an income. Not a big one, I'm not rich or anything—the van is six years old—but I don't have to work, and sometimes I'll buy myself a trip to Bangalore or someplace."

Dagmar looked at the van and the blinking oscilloscopes.

"That's good," she said, "because I've got a job for you."

"A job?" For the first time, he seemed surprised.

"Not for money," she said, and then corrected herself. "Not unless you *want* money, I mean. What I want is for you to find the killer."

He frowned. "That Litvinov guy? It looked like he wasn't part of the game."

"He is now," Dagmar said.

Joe Clever considered this. "Interesting," he said.

"When you find him," Dagmar said, "don't approach him or anything. Just let me know—me or the police."

He scratched his chin. "Where do I start?"

"If I knew," she said, "I couldn't tell you. I'm the pup-petmaster. I'm the one who decides what the puzzles are."

"Yeah." He offered a faint smile. "It's a cool idea, Dagmar."

And it would get Joe Clever out of her hair while she had the office scanned for bugs and shifted details of the game around to make worthless any information he might have discovered through eavesdropping.

A look of uncertainty crossed Joe Clever's face. "Can I play the game and look for Litvinov at the same time?"

"Yes. But you get more coolness points for Litvinov."

He nodded. "Okay. Great. I'll do it."

"Thanks."

"Oh—" Joe Clever looked over Dagmar's head toward her apartment. "I should tell you. Some guy went into your apartment about an hour ago."

Dagmar was staggered. "What?" she asked. "Who?"

"I don't know, but he had a key. Let me show you."

He reached into the van's interior for his laptop, pulled it toward him, and bent to use the touch pad. A film appeared, and she saw a dumpy, middle-aged man approach her apartment, look over his shoulder, then insert a key and enter.

"That's the building manager," Dagmar said. "Rich-ardson."

"He was in your place for six minutes."

Dagmar stared at the picture. "What the hell for?" she wondered.

"I suppose he could have been there to repair something," Joe Clever said, "but my guess is that he was poking around in your underwear drawer."

"He *what?*" Rage filled Dagmar's heart. "How do you know?"

"I think it was the expression on his face when he left." He tapped buttons and fast-forwarded to the moment when the manager left her apartment.

The man *did* manage to look both furtive and smug.

"The bastard!" Dagmar said. "I'm going to check!"

She swung away from the van, but Joe Clever called her back.

"You forgot your dinner."

She took the fast-food bag from his hand and marched to her apartment.

Normally the problem with her underwear drawer would have been that it was too disorganized to actually tell if anything was missing: it wasn't as if she bothered to line up and number her underpants. But there *was* no clean underwear.

She'd remembered that she'd thought she'd had enough to last her the next few days, and then thought she'd miscounted.

But she hadn't miscounted after all. The superintendent had been in her drawer, just as Joe Clever had suggested.

Filled with fury, she stepped out onto the balcony that overlooked the courtyard and looked down. There, carrying out a garbage bag from the clubhouse, was the creep himself.

"Hey!" she called. "Richardson!"

Faces looked up at her from around the classic 1970s coffin-shaped swimming pool. Two young women tanned there, model-slash-actresses with large breasts that pointed skyward in a clearly artificial way, and a short distance away from them was an elderly man who swam slow laps every afternoon and then sat on a chaise longue to dry out and absorb some warmth from the sun.

Richardson looked up at her and shielded his eyes from the glare.

"Do you need something?" he asked.

"I need you to stay the hell out of my underwear drawer, you fucking creep!" Dagmar yelled. "Come in my apartment again, and I'll kick your ass!"

She watched as a series of complicated expressions crossed Richardson's face. Whatever the reaction was, it wasn't that of an innocent man.

Busted! she thought, triumphant.

Richardson shuffled a step closer.

"I don't know what you're talking about," he said.

"*I've got video, you fucking pervert!*" Dagmar shouted. "*You wanna watch it?*"

Even from the third-floor balcony she could see the color drain from Richardson's face. Enlightenment dawned across the faces of the model-slash-actresses. Perhaps they had missed a few items themselves.

Richardson dropped the garbage bag and flapped his hands in a vague way. Dagmar found that infuriating.

"I'll have your job, prick!" she shouted, and then she went back into her apartment and slammed the door.

The one good thing about surviving the Indonesian holocaust, she thought, was that she was no longer afraid of anyone who wasn't carrying a gun or a damn big knife.

CHAPTER FOURTEEN

This Is Not Simple

A new digital dead bolt was installed on Dagmar's apartment door early the following morning. A few hours later a pair of private security contractors, wearing identical tan blazers, swept through the Great Big Idea offices and failed to find any eavesdropping gear planted there by Joe Clever or anybody else. To counter the laser eavesdropping system, they were happy to sell Dagmar white-noise generators to provide interference, and detectors to sound an alarm when a laser was directed at the room.

"I want a death ray," she told them, "to shoot back." Her science fiction background coming to the fore.

"If you shoot a laser back at them," one man said, "you could blind them."

"They could blind *me*."

They nodded.

"True," one said. "They could."

In any case, the Tan Blazer Men doubted that Joe Clever could get close enough to the building to hear much of anything, not without being seen.

"It depends on how good his software is at sorting signal from interference."

"Great," Dagmar said. "I could have been blinded for *nothing.*"

Dagmar tried to pass the news to Charlie, but his secretary, Karin, said that Charlie had called in and said he wouldn't be coming to the office today.

Maybe sorting out Austin's company was a knottier problem than he'd anticipated.

Dagmar looked out the window to see if the Dodge van was visible before calling in her design team and letting them know that their meeting of two days before had possibly been compromised and that they were going to have to rework everything that had been decided on that day.

They were in a vengeful mood. They decided not only to shift all the game goodies to different locations, but to lay ambushes in the compromised areas.

"Anyone going into *Planet Nine* and looking under that gantry is going to find three heavily armed sharpshooters from Team Evil who are going to take him apart!"

Or so Helmuth, her head programmer, proclaimed. Dagmar waved a hand to give the plan her blessing.

"And if they find any of the pages we discussed," Dagmar said, "we'll fill them with information that leads nowhere."

"Information," Helmuth said darkly, "written in Estonian."

It was only after the meeting that Dagmar had a chance to go online and see what had been happening in the game world.

Joe Clever's video of Austin's death, which Video Us had not as yet removed, had generated more than eleven million hits.

And in the past forty-eight hours, another 3,600,000 people had joined *The Long Night of Briana Hall*.

Ghouls, she thought.

She checked her email, and all sense of accomplishment evaporated.

FROM: Siyed Prasad
SUBJECT: Holiday in L.A.

Dagmar my Dear,

I'm going to be in Los Angeles next week to shoot a commercial. My agent tells me that the *Golden Nagi* credit has been a big plus! Lots of people in the business saw it, apparently.

I would like to thank you for the opportunity to work with you, and all the doors that you have helped to open for me.

Can I take you to dinner?

Your appreciative Siyed

"Oh for God's sake," Dagmar said aloud. And then, to the computer, "Return mail."

FROM: Dagmar Shaw
SUBJECT: re: Holiday in L.A.

Siyed,

I'm working hard on a new project, and I doubt I'll be able to see you.

Good luck with the commercial.

Dagmar

Was that curt enough? she wondered.

Get lost, married man.

She began dealing with the problems involved in reworking the game to suggest that Austin's death was somehow a part of it. She didn't feel she could say it outright, but she could offer hints that the players were certain to notice.

Dagmar thought that maybe Joe Clever wasn't clever enough to find Litvinov, but she had more confidence in the entire Group Mind.

Three million people: they had to know *something.*

Briana Hall, the woman in the hotel room, was hiding from the police, who were under the impression that she had killed two of her former lovers. The game was designed to move both backward and forward in time, following Briana as she fled from the police and attempted to prove herself innocent, and simultaneously going back into the history of the characters to discover their past actions and the reasons for them. The help of the players would be needed in order to accomplish both of these objectives.

One of Briana's exes had been killed by a sleeper cell of saboteurs who were using a location in the *Planet Nine* game as a rendezvous—the sometime boyfriend had been a sysop and during the course of his work had overheard some of their conversation.

The other had been killed because he was a minor player in a securities fraud and his cronies erroneously assumed he was under investigation—in fact he had had contact with SEC investigators for an entirely different reason.

Dagmar wondered if that victim could be renamed Austin. But if so, she'd have to change the plot: she didn't want to make one of her oldest friends guilty of securities fraud, not even in the context of fiction. So she'd have to reengineer the plot in order to provide a reason why he was killed—accidentally—by a hired assassin.

She calculated how to make the plot changes, which she figured would involve a couple of days of rewriting. But there would be more than rewriting, because she'd have to add a whole Maffya subplot, and that would take up a lot of resources.

While thinking this over, she found the card that Lieutenant Murdoch had given her and called him. He was out, but she left a message asking him to return her call.

She was deep into rewriting when "Harlem Nocturne" announced Murdoch's call. She looked at the time in the corner of her monitor and saw that it was after six o'clock—Murdoch was probably returning all his phone calls before leaving the office.

"This is Dagmar," she said.

She had met Murdoch the previous day. He was a small, systematic man with a lined face and graying hair. His mouth had the kind of pinched look that suggested false teeth. His questions the other day had been competent and professional, and he'd asked them all without giving the slightest clue what was happening behind his pale blue eyes. He was almost like a character on the old *Dragnet* program, deadpan and businesslike, but more human, without the TV characters' utter humorlessness.

"You called?" he said.

"Yes. I realized that if you give me the name that Litvinov used to enter the country, I could probably find him for you."

"How could you do that?" he said after a pause.

Dagmar explained about the game and the fact that she had thousands of detectives eager to set their intelligence on the problem.

"While we appreciate citizen help," Murdoch began, "I'm not sure that this would be appropriate."

"Lieutenant Murdoch," Dagmar said, "can you call every hotel and motel in Greater Los Angeles to find out if Litvinov, or his alias, is staying there?"

"No. There are thousands of hotels altogether. We don't have that kind of manpower."

"*I* do," Dagmar said.

There was another pause.

"Here's what I figured out," Dagmar said. "Either Litvinov has left town, in which case you'll have to hope you can get him arrested back home in Saint Petersburg or whatever—"

"He's based in Hamburg," Murdoch said.

"Okay," Dagmar said, "Hamburg. But my point is, either he's gone, or he's still in town. And *if* he's still in town, it's because he's realized he shot the wrong man and is still planning on going after his real target. So if he *isn't* found, someone else could die."

After a moment of thoughtful silence, Murdoch spoke.

"Let me sleep on it," he said. "I'll get back to you tomorrow morning."

"Thank you," said Dagmar.

And got busy with her rewrite.

CHAPTER FIFTEEN

This Is Not Madness

FROM: Consuelo

I'm going to steal a page from Chatsworth's book and decline to reveal how I came by this information.

But.

Litvinov, the assassin, entered the country with a Latvian passport under the name Ainars Vilumanis. Latvia is a NATO country and he probably had less difficulty entering than with a Russian passport. Since Litvinov was born in Latvia he probably speaks acceptable Latvian.

As of 9:00PDT this morning he hadn't used that passport to leave the country. He may still be in the Los Angeles area, and it's possible we could locate him.

Anyone want to help me try?

FROM: Corporal Carrot

I thought Litvinov had nothing to do with the game.

FROM: Hanseatic

That's what I thought, too, and then I saw <u>this</u> on Briana's MySpace page this morning:

Thanks, Consuelo. You're on the right track.

FROM: LadyDayFan

I am finding this really intriguing. Can anyone think of another example of a character in a game addressing a player directly?

FROM: Hanseatic

Only when we've screwed up badly and need a nudge to get us back on the right track.

FROM: LadyDayFan

We should consider ourselves nudged. We should assume that the death of Austin Katanyan is a part of the game until proven otherwise.

FROM: Corporal Carrot

But it was in the papers! The *real* papers! Great Big Idea

can't plant phony stories in the *L.A. Times*! Not stories
that big, anyway.

FROM: Hanseatic

If we solve all the puzzles like good little players, everything will be revealed.

FROM: LadyDayFan

So how are we going to find Litvinov? His rap sheet
doesn't list any known associates in Los Angeles.

FROM: Hanseatic

Let's not forget that the rap sheet lists a number of
aliases. We should search for those as well.

Dagmar watched as the messages appeared on Our
Reality Network, followed by concerted action as the
available players located an online Los Angeles telephone
directory, divided up the alphabet between themselves,
and began to call motels.

Dagmar could only hope that Litvinov hadn't
googled his name and found this bulletin board, and
wasn't aware that his cover identity had been pene-
trated.

People in places like Dubai, the Low Countries, and
Ceylon began calling motels in places like Culver City,
San Gabriel, and Costa Mesa. Observing the process was
fascinating, and Dagmar watched the messages pile up

for the next forty-five minutes as more and more people got involved.

If Litvinov was staying at a hotel under any of his known aliases, he was dead meat.

Good, she thought.

Her handheld played "Harlem Nocturne," and the display showed Charlie's name.

"Where are you?" she answered.

For the second day in a row, Charlie hadn't come into the office—and today Karin wasn't in, either, so Dagmar hadn't been able to ask anyone where Charlie had gone.

"Right now?" Charlie said. "I'm at home."

"You haven't been in your office."

"I've got stuff to do."

Dagmar figured she wasn't going to get any more out of him than that.

"I've been trying to reach you," she said. "For starters, I had to have Great Big Idea swept for bugs."

Somewhat to Dagmar's surprise, there was a long, thoughtful silence on the other end.

"Probably a good idea," Charlie said. "Did you sweep the rest of the building?"

"I don't think Joe Clever is *interested* in the rest of the building."

"Joe *Clever?*" Charlie's surprise was palpable.

Again there was an awkward silence.

"Charlie," she said, "whose bugs did you *think* I was trying to sweep?"

Charlie gave a nervous laugh.

"I got paranoid when you started talking about Austin being killed by the Russian Maffya," he said. "I thought—I thought maybe Austin *did* step on them in some way."

"My recollection," Dagmar said, "is that you had pretty comprehensively dismissed that possibility."

"Well," Charlie said, "it's still damned *unlikely.*"

Dagmar wished she could see him face-to-face. He was hiding something, and his expression might have told her what it was.

"Did you find out anything at the meeting?" Dagmar said. "When you met with Austin's partners?"

"No," Charlie said. "No Maffya connections."

"Are you sure?"

"We didn't talk about Austin's projects in that kind of detail. We mainly talked about who we could get to take Austin's place, and how we could manage the company until we got the replacement."

"How's that going?"

"Karin and I are sitting in my living room cold-calling rich, busy, successful people. How do you *think* it's going?"

Dagmar laughed. "So that's why you're calling me. You figure I won't hang up on you."

"Partly to hear the friendly voice, yes. But I actually have business to discuss with you."

"I'd better give you an update first."

She told him about Joe Clever and his James Bond van, about how she'd nudged the players toward helping the police find Litvinov and how Lieutenant Murdoch had furnished the Ainars Vilumanis identity, which she'd then passed on to Joe Clever to post in his Consuelo guise.

She told him how she was planning on altering the

structure to make Austin a character in the game. She'd tentatively decided that Austin the game character had been killed because he possessed a piece of information he didn't know was important.

"Of course," she added, "we can change that if we ever find out why he was really killed."

"Sounds good, I guess." Charlie paused. "I don't know how I feel about using my friend's murder as an element in an online game."

"I know how *I* feel," Dagmar said. "I feel like a complete shit."

"Yeah," Charlie said. "That's how I feel, too."

"But if it catches the guy . . ."

"Yeah. If."

"If it weren't for the game and Joe Clever, we wouldn't have any idea who had killed Austin. We'd be completely in the dark."

"To give the devil his due," Charlie said.

"Set a devil to catch a devil," Dagmar said. "That's what we're trying to do."

Charlie's voice turned weary.

"Well," he said, "you did good."

Something in Dagmar responded to the fatigue in his voice, and she felt her own exhaustion descend on her, weariness and sorrow that settled over her shoulders like a heavy cloak, its weight pinning her to her chair.

"Thanks," she said.

"Listen," Charlie said. "Why I called in the first place. The coroner is done with Austin, so his parents are flying in tomorrow to pick up the body. I'm going to be meeting them at their hotel. Do you want to be there?"

She felt the sadness clawing at her vocal cords, turning them husky.

"Yes," she said. "I suppose."

"They're going to bury Austin back in Bridgeport," Charlie said. "I don't know anyone there, and I'm swamped with work, so I'm not going to fly out there for the funeral. But do you think we should do something here?"

"A memorial," Dagmar said. "At Austin's company, so it won't be just the two of us and the Katanyans."

"Good idea," Charlie said. "I'll call them and set it up."

"Call everyone who knew him, whether they worked for the company or not."

"It better be *you* who calls BJ," Charlie said. "I'm pretty sure he wouldn't take any calls from me."

Surprise eddied through Dagmar's veins. She hadn't thought about inviting BJ at all.

Well, she thought, why not? BJ wasn't on bad terms with Austin the way he was with Charlie.

"I'll call him," she said, and then couldn't stop herself from adding another question. "You won't mind if BJ's there?"

"I won't *like* it," Charlie said, "but I'll remind myself that he's poor and I'm not, and I'll feel better."

Dagmar hadn't seen much of BJ since her return to California: she met him for lunch every three months or so, usually at an inexpensive diner so that BJ could afford to pay his half. He was very much the man she remembered: smart, quick, witty, easily distracted. She'd kept the conversation away from Charlie and AvN Soft, the

company that BJ had cofounded and from which he'd
been fired before it achieved success.

It was sad, that the man she remembered as being so
brilliant had succeeded in nothing. She would have
helped him if she could, but she couldn't—there was no
way Charlie would tolerate her hiring BJ for any of her
projects.

His cell phone number was on her handheld and she
dialed it. He answered on the third ring.

"Hi," he said.

There were the sounds of clashing weapons and
explosions in the background, electronic combat.

"BJ?" she said. "Can you pause the game?"

"No, I'm with a party and on real time. But go ahead
and talk."

His voice was fast and staccato, and Dagmar diag-
nosed too many cans of Red Bull.

"BJ," said Dagmar, "did you hear that Austin was
murdered?"

For a long moment all she could hear were the sounds
of combat, and she wondered if BJ had heard her. She
was about to repeat herself when he spoke.

"No," he said. "I hadn't heard that. I guess I've been
kind of busy." His voice had slowed, as if shock had
somehow knocked the Red Bull off-line.

"There's going to be a memorial at Katanyan
Associates in the next few days. Do you want to come?"

"Yeah, but . . ." His voice faded away, and Dagmar
heard a particularly violent explosion, followed by a series
of gonging sounds. Then the voice came back.

"What happened to Austin? Who killed him?"

Annoyance at BJ crackled through Dagmar. What did he think he was doing, continuing his game play in the face of this kind of news? She let the annoyance show in her voice.

"It's too complicated to explain with you distracted," she said.

"Okay. Sorry. This is how I make my living now, okay?"

"Right."

"I'll call you tonight, okay?"

"Fine."

A tone of mischief entered his voice. "Is Charlie coming to the memorial?"

"He's organizing it."

"Maybe I'll mad-dog him from across the room."

"No"—sternly—"you won't."

"Okay," he said. "Only if I catch him alone."

She stabbed the Stop button and cut off the call. It was only then that her phone chimed to tell her that she had voice mail. Her nerves gave a jolt as she recognized Joe Clever's voice.

"Dagmar," he said, "I found Litvinov! He's in room three twenty-two of the Seahorse Hotel in Santa Monica, registered under the Vilumanis name. I wanted to make sure that it was the right guy, so I got a pizza and went to the door and pretended I was delivering to the wrong room. It was him all right!"

Dagmar stared at the office window, the twilight outside.

"I don't know what to do now," Joe Clever went on. "Do I call the police or what?

"He was pretty good," he added. "He stayed in character the whole time."

Dagmar had reached for a pen and jotted down the relevant information. It took her a few frantic moments to locate Lieutenant Murdoch's card, and then when she called, he wasn't in. She persuaded whoever had answered that it was an emergency, and he told her to hang up and expect a return call from Murdoch.

The call came in two minutes. But by the time the police burst into Litvinov's room, the assassin was gone.

CHAPTER SIXTEEN

This Is Not a Code

FROM: Joe Clever
SUBJECT: Re: Stakeout

No, it wasn't that I alarmed him with the pizza trick. I thought that went real smooth. I think the police must have made a mistake setting up their raid.

The Seahorse is a big hotel and I couldn't watch every exit, so I kept the front office under surveillance in case Litvinov checked out, but he must have gone out the back way. His transportation must have been back there, too, because the police didn't find his bike or a car or anything.

What do I do now? Keep checking hotels and stuff?

FROM: Dagmar Shaw
SUBJECT: Re: re: Stakeout

Keep checking hotels and stuff.

Don't contact him this time. Once is intelligible; twice
begins to look like carelessness.

It was hard dealing with Austin's parents. The mother
was prone to silent weeping, and the father was angry. He
insisted on going straight to the coroner's office to make
certain that they hadn't made some kind of mistake.
Charlie drove the minivan he'd rented for them, and
Dagmar sat in the back with Austin's mother.

She knew that Austin's parents had met over gaming,
playing *D&D* back in the seventies. She tried to find the
college-aged gamers in them and failed.

She couldn't bring herself to see Austin's body. When
the father emerged after the viewing, he was pale but
angrier than ever. He complained over the forms necessary to ship Austin's body home to Connecticut and then
demanded to meet Lieutenant Murdoch.

Murdoch worked out of the North Hollywood Station,
which rather implausibly shared its building with the
Studio City Chamber of Commerce. Murdoch had met a
lot of grieving parents, fortunately, and met Austin's father
with a bland, helpful demeanor that helped to redirect his
anger. He explained that Litvinov would certainly be
caught sooner or later, probably when he tried to leave the
country, and that a police raid had missed him only by a
few minutes the day before, in Santa Monica.

Murdoch tactfully refrained from telling Austin's parents that the raid had been spoiled when Litvinov was
spooked by the appearance on his doorstep of a wild-
haired amateur detective claiming to be a pizza delivery
man.

Dagmar watched the detectives in their squad room, knowing this would end up in a piece of fiction one day. She noted the metal desks in cubicles, the glowing computers, the pictures of family on the desks, the soft-spoken detectives who contrasted with the wild variety of other people in the room—the slumped or frantic victims, the defiant suspects, the transvestite with the calico dress and the heavy five o'clock shadow, and others too drunk or stoned to do more than sit and stare dully at their surroundings.

Everyone seemed right out of central casting. All that was needed were three sassy hookers.

Lots of guns, she noted. She didn't know if that made her feel safe or not.

By the time Charlie returned Austin's parents to their hotel on Cienega, they were clearly exhausted.

"I'll let you rest," Charlie said, "and then I'll take you to Katanyan Associates tomorrow morning."

Charlie and Dagmar left the room, and Charlie turned to Dagmar. "Can we talk?"

"Sure."

"This way."

Dagmar followed Charlie down the corridor to another hotel room, where his thumbprint opened the lock. She followed him into the room, which turned out to be a corner suite decorated in a Hollywood version of Louis Quinze and scented with sachets of potpourri. A notebook computer sat on a white marble-topped table in the corner, its display showing a Pinky and the Brain screensaver.

"You're staying in the same hotel?" Dagmar asked.

"It makes things more convenient." He went to the minibar and pulled out a half-liter bottle of Coca-Cola—imported from Mexico, where Coke was made with white sugar instead of corn syrup and therefore tasted far better. Charlie had cases of the stuff at his house, and more in a cooler near his office.

"Want something to drink?" he asked.

She took another Coke. Charlie sat on a patterned armchair and began to unlace his shoes.

"Tomorrow," he said, "I'm going to try to explain to the Katanyans just how wealthy their son was. Mr. Katanyan's well off, I think, but as Austin's heir he's rich twenty times over." He ran a hand over his balding head. "My nightmare is that Mr. Katanyan will think he can run his son's company."

"He wouldn't. Would he?"

"He runs his own import company, why not? But there are some crucial differences between seed-stage venture capital and a family-run Oriental carpet business."

Dagmar didn't answer, but instead looked at the minibar.

"Are there peanuts or something in there?"

"Help yourself."

She found a packet of peanuts and seated herself on a sofa. Charlie looked at her.

"Now," he said, "I don't want you to scream."

She gave him a narrow look.

"I want you to change the game," he said, and then cut her off as she was about to protest.

"Don't worry," he said. "This will add to the coolness factor."

"I'm listening," she said, and put down the packet of peanuts.

"Okay," he said. "We've got more than a million players, right?"

"More than *three* million, as of this morning."

"So what if they each received a text message that consisted of *one* packet of data. Encrypted. And when they decrypted it, they discovered that they *still* had only one packet of data and that they all had to be combined in the right order for the message to make sense."

Dagmar looked at him.

"How big is a packet?" she asked.

"No smaller than twenty bytes, no bigger than sixty."

"The routing information might be larger than the message."

"Yes." Charlie nodded. "It would. But the routing information could be a part of the puzzle. If you include the IP layer, it would include the originating IP address, which could be crucial to finding out who sent the messages."

Slowly, Dagmar lifted her drink and took a contemplative sip.

"One big problem," she said, "is that a lot of our players don't actually play, they just lurk."

"So make the number of messages smaller and build in a lot of redundancy."

"Okay. So we break the message into, say, three thousand packets, and we send out multiple copies of each packet until everybody gets one. Then they have to decode the thing, right?"

"Yeah."

"And reassemble it."

"Which won't be hard, because each message will contain a sequence number as part of the routing information."

"We'll have to create some kind of engine that reassembles it. We can't expect them to do it by hand."

Charlie shrugged. "Whatever."

"And the result could be a graphic or a photo, which would be more cool than a text message. And more unanticipated."

Nodding. "That's good."

"Okay." Dagmar lifted her Coke bottle and offered Charlie an ironic toast. "I don't actually hate this idea. Especially since it won't require a lot of rewriting, and I can shift most of the work onto Helmuth and his staff."

Charlie smiled.

"Excellent," he said. "Now, the cipher I want you to use is called Portcullis."

She looked at him. "Why Portcullis? I never heard of it."

He shrugged. "Portcullis is a start-up out of Dallas. They have a good product, and they also offer support in case the players run into trouble."

A feeling of unease seeped like a cool mist into Dagmar's brain.

"This is a private company?" she asked. "They sell their product?"

"Yeah. They sell the cipher fairly cheaply and plan to make most of their money selling support."

Mentally, Dagmar probed this idea and realized she didn't like it.

"Why not use freeware?" she asked. "You can find military-grade encryption on the Web and use it for free."

Charlie straightened in his chair and looked down at her. "Firstly," he said, "because Portcullis offers support, and a lot of the players haven't necessarily used decryption programs before."

Dagmar did not find this argument convincing.

"And secondly . . .?" she said.

He gazed down at her expressionlessly.

"Secondly," he said, "because Portcullis is the program I want you to use."

Anger flashed through Dagmar, but it faded quickly, to be replaced by an anticipation of oncoming wretchedness—that there was some horrible truth about to emerge, something that would send her spiraling into misery. A sense that she was on a ship running before the storm, only vaguely aware of the reefs looming ahead.

"How much," she asked, "will Portcullis cost the players?"

"Basic service is something like thirty bucks and comes with half a year's free support."

She looked at him and folded her arms across her chest.

"Charlie," she said, "that's going to make the players berserk. Traditionally, ARGs are *free Internet entertainment*. Players aren't used to paying for them, and they *won't*. ARGs that expected their players to pay for something have all . . . *struggled,* to put it as kindly as I can."

Charlie nodded at her words, but only to dismiss them.

"Enough of them will buy Portcullis to make this work," he said.

A sudden urgency possessed her. She had to make herself understood.

"Charlie," she said, "we're on our way to more than three million players. This game is *already* an enormous success. Why are we risking that success?"

He looked down at her. "I do not have to explain my decision."

She spread her hands helplessly.

"Give me something to work with, okay?" she asked. "Make believe this is a rational act."

Charlie said nothing.

"Are you *invested* in Portcullis in some way?"

Charlie shook his head slightly, a few millimeters left and right. "No. Absolutely not. This decision does not benefit me in any way."

"Is Austin's company involved?"

"No," Charlie said. "Portcullis came to him for funding originally, but Austin turned them down."

"Could that be," Dagmar said, her voice rising in heat, "because they're competing with stuff that cryptoware geeks give away for *free?* Could that be because *their business model totally sucks?*"

Charlie inclined his head, an absolute monarch conceding a minor matter to a loyal councillor.

"Last month they *did* have a disappointing IPO," he said.

In frustration, Dagmar raised clawed hands and slashed at an invisible barrier. "*So why are we—*"

"Let's just say," Charlie said, "that I believe in their product."

Dagmar gave up. She sagged back on the couch in utter capitulation.

Charlie was screwing again with the shape of Dagmar's game. The inclusion of Austin's death and the search for Litvinov had unbalanced the structure, but she had hopes that if she skated fast enough, she could beat it into shape again.

Now they were set to anger millions of players. Millions upon whom Dagmar depended for goodwill. Millions who could have stayed in *Planet Nine* and made Charlie's new acquisition wildly profitable.

She looked at him, the Type One Geek she'd known all her adult life, and wondered if he knew the havoc he was wreaking upon his own potential bottom line.

"Charlie," she said, "Litvinov was found in Santa Monica."

"Yeah." His face remained expressionless.

"I've seen the Seahorse. It's less than a mile from where you live."

"Right."

"Is it more than a coincidence that Litvinov is first seen hanging around your business, and next he turns up *right in your neighborhood?* What if it really *was* you he's gunning for?"

Dagmar saw a twitch in a corner of Charlie's mouth.

"I don't know who he was after, Dagmar," he said.

"And now you're running your company from a hotel room," Dagmar said. "It's like you're afraid to go home *or* to the office. Plus you're involved in a scheme that will bring Portcullis a huge wave of unexpected income, which will drive up their stock price. Which"—she leaned toward him—"looks just like a classic pump-and-dump stock fraud, the kind the Russian Maffya does *all the time*."

Again Charlie gave that brief, taut shake of the head.

"You're wrong, Dagmar," he said. "You're way off base."

She reached a hand toward him but fell short. She let the hand hang in the air.

"Charlie," she said, "are you in trouble?"

"If you want to save me trouble," he said in a flat, controlled voice, "you will *follow my damn instructions*."

Dagmar withdrew the hand.

"Right," she said, and stood.

She carried her drink to the door.

"Don't forget your peanuts," said Charlie.

FROM: Jack

Can I ask a question? What's this "destegging" I keep reading about?

FROM: 16nHorny

Yeh. That one has me pussled to. And what is teh PM's besides the afternoon ha.

FROM: LadyDayFan

Our bulletin board welcomes all of the thousands of new players that have been showing up in the past few days, but we urge them to check the <u>FAQ List</u> and <u>Player Tutorial</u> before asking questions.

FROM: 16nHorny

Ok thats cool ha. Is there a way to meet briana cuz she is teh hawt.

Austin's memorial service was held at Katanyan Associates in a mahogany-paneled boardroom, the guests seated in padded brown leather chairs with brass accents, the whole a California simulation of a New York bastion of Old Money. The illusion was spoiled by the large LCD screens used for teleconferencing, and by the long smart table with the intelligent, touch-responsive screens, all of which demonstrated that the room belonged not to nine-teenth-century robber barons but to those of the twenty-first.

The largest of the LCD screens now showed a large studio portrait of Austin, the one used on his company's home page, smiling out from between tall, brilliant flower arrangements placed on a table below the screen. Austin's parents sat in the brown overstuffed chairs, and Dagmar went to say hello and then signed the memorial book.

Dagmar had dressed for the memorial in hose, Blahnik satin shoes, a Marc Jacobs skirt, and a navy Chanel jacket, the last three items of which she'd picked up in a Beverly Hills secondhand store, the sort of place where Orange County trophy wives dumped the previous year's fashions. Dagmar, whose usual tastes ran to khakis and freebie game-convention T-shirts, didn't care if her clothes were eighteen months out of date—and the Chanel jacket, in any case, was timeless.

Style sense had always been something she'd planned to acquire, if she ever had the time to think about such things.

Most of the people in the room were Austin's partners and employees, and though she knew a few faces from Austin's parties, they were mostly strangers. Charlie either hadn't arrived or was off organizing something. Dagmar helped herself to some coffee from a brushed-aluminum urn and took a seat.

Half a minute later, BJ dropped into the seat next to her.

"Hi," he said.

"Hi, yourself." She felt suddenly more cheerful.

He wore gray polyester slacks and a brown twill jacket. Hours spent eating junk food while squinting at low-end monitors had added about thirty pounds to BJ's stocky frame, but the arms and shoulders were still powerful. His fair hair hung over his ears, and he'd added a set of muttonchop whiskers to his mustache. There were fine lines around his eyes, and he wore a pair of rimless spectacles that made him look like a down-at-the-heels grad student.

She put her coffee on the table, slid her chair closer to his, and reached out to give him a hug. He patted her bemusedly on the back.

"Good to see you," he said.

He looked around the room. Mischief sparkled in his blue eyes.

"Where's Charlie?" he said. "Hiding?"

The question made Dagmar uneasy. She had not ceased wondering if Charlie was in truth hiding, not from BJ, but from Litvinov or what he represented.

"He's probably organizing something," Dagmar said.

"I've been looking at your game," BJ said. "Nice, devious stuff."

"Thanks."

Charlie entered at that point, with a man and a woman who were slightly familiar to Dagmar and who she assumed were more of Austin's business associates. He spared BJ a glance, but nothing more than that. He said hello to Austin's parents and introduced the two people he was with, then took a seat at the far end of the table.

BJ stared at him throughout, his blue eyes hard. Charlie's face was mild.

One of Austin's associates stood and introduced himself as Stephen. He introduced Austin's parents to the group and then suggested that if people would like to talk about Austin, they should feel free to do so.

Then he sat down, an expression of satisfaction on his face.

Oh great, Dagmar thought. *It's like a Quaker Meeting. No one is in charge.*

She would have preferred a little more direction in this enterprise. Or at least some warning, so that she could have had something prepared.

Or, failing any of that, she could have used the Spirit of God descending on her, as it was alleged to for the Quakers.

A silence followed. Dagmar feigned sipping at her coffee while she ransacked her brain for anecdotes of Austin that would make sense to everyone here, including the parents.

BJ bounced up from his chair. Dagmar looked at him in surprise.

"Hi," BJ said. He spoke directly to Austin's parents. "My name is Boris Bustretski, and I've known Austin since freshman year at college. We were in the same gaming group—and since he mentioned that you were gamers, you know what that's like."

The Katanyans listened with interest. The mention of gaming had touched something that the impersonal world of business and crime and investigation had not.

"Austin was a detail-oriented gamer," BJ said, "like he was in his other life, I guess—you don't do as well as Austin did without paying attention to the fine print."

Dagmar saw Austin's father nod—he understood business as well as gaming.

"Austin's games," BJ went on, "were full of interesting technicalities that told you a lot about his game worlds and that told you a lot about Austin. He always did his research. I remember there was one game where the plot point hinged on metallurgy—it depended on the details of how people with a low tech level counterfeit gold and silver coins, which were used by an enemy to destabilize a kingdom. That's just an example of Austin's interest in detail, and how markets work, and how you tell good money from bad."

BJ offered the Katanyans a wistful smile. "When he came west, he brought your old games with him—that original *D&D* rule set, and *Empire of the Petal Throne*, and those others. He ran those games for us, and I think sharing his parents' games with us was maybe his way of honoring *you*." For the first time he looked over the room, and then he looked back at the Katanyans. "Thank you," he said, and sat.

Mrs. Katanyan was weeping silently. The anger that had simmered in Mr. Katanyan had gone, and he was looking at BJ with gratitude.

Somehow BJ had hit exactly the right note.

Others spoke—for the most part they were Austin's partners or employees, and their focus was toward the business: Austin's traits as a boss, Austin's uncanny knack for finding successful start-ups.

Charlie spoke, mentioning that he, too, had met Austin as a result of gaming in college, and that he'd subsequently had the opportunity to help Austin set up his company.

"I knew he would be a success," Charlie said. "With that mind of his, there was no way he wouldn't be."

As he spoke, he very carefully did not look in BJ's direction.

When Dagmar spoke, she mentioned that she, too, was an old friend from the college gaming group, and that as a result of that group, she now wrote games for a living.

She knew she couldn't top BJ's anecdote about gaming, and everyone else had covered Austin's professional life, so she told the story of how she'd gotten herself and Austin thrown out of the restaurant. She changed the story a bit, to make it better—she made the restaurant Austin's favorite, and she avoided mentioning that this had happened on the day when Austin had been murdered.

Her anecdote faded out rather than came to an end, and she sat down in silence. Her stories were really much better when she wrote them down than when she had to tell them aloud.

Afterward there was a buffet in the company dining room. Dagmar noticed that the Katanyans sought out BJ and spent an hour talking to him.

For someone whom Austin had barely seen in the past six or seven years, he had certainly made an impression.

CHAPTER SEVENTEEN

This Is Not a Whim

FROM: Hanseatic

Is Great Big Idea seriously expecting us to spend US dollars for this cryptography program?

FROM: Chatsworth Osborne Jr.

Apparently, yes.

FROM: Vikram

Have we found a hidden sponsor?

FROM: Chatsworth Osborne Jr.

A remarkably unsubtle one, if so.

FROM: Desi

I'm not spending any money on this!

FROM: Chatsworth Osborne Jr.

That's your privilege. But I ask myself if my entertainment is worth a special introductory price of $31.99 for some software that may have applications outside the game, and I have to conclude the answer is yes.

FROM: Corporal Carrot

So says the spook!

FROM: Vikram

It's not whether the game is worth the money, but whether they should be making us spend it at all.

FROM: Desi

Yeah! This is really pissing me off.

FROM: Hanseatic

With the euro under attack, I very soon may not HAVE $31.99.

FROM: Desi

I think I'm going to drop this game. There are plenty of cheaper entertainments out in the datasphere.

FROM: Hanseatic

I'm not dropping out. But I'm not doing anything that requires me to spend $$$.

Dagmar looked at the bulletin board and felt another surge of bitter anger, one in a long series. Her prediction about the players' reaction to Portcullis was absolutely on the money.

It wasn't so much the players who *were* posting on Our Reality Network. It was the players who *weren't* posting, who were simply absent.

She couldn't prove it, but she suspected that players were deserting her game in droves. Millions of them, possibly. And the damage extended beyond a single game: she was losing credibility with her audience. They were going to be much less likely to trust her when it came to the *next* Big Idea game.

The game had entered its third week. Neither the players nor the police nor Interpol had been able to find Litvinov. Murdoch had given up trying to find him in the States and was hoping the Germans would pick him up when he returned to his old Hamburg haunts. Austin had been in a grave in Connecticut for six days. Dagmar's apartment's owners had not yet sacked their underwear-sniffing manager. And Charlie had gone crazy—he hardly ever appeared in the office, and instead migrated from one hotel to another. Currently he was renting a cabana at the Roosevelt in Hollywood. He called Dagmar at strange hours and demanded constant updates on the progress of the game.

A chime told Dagmar that she had email, and she clicked to her mail program.

FROM: Siyed Prasad
SUBJECT: Holiday in L.A.

Dear Dagmar,

I've arrived in the City of Angels. They're putting me up at the Chateau Marmont—very sweet, don't you think?

I'm still hoping to see you while I'm in town. I know you keep saying that you have no time, but I'm still hoping you will be tempted to have dinner with me. I have reservations at the Pentagram tonight at eight o'clock—will you please tell me that you will come?

Your adoring fan,

Siyed

Dagmar sent Siyed a terse reply to the effect that she was working late and wouldn't be able to join him for dinner. At which point her phone sang, and Dagmar saw that it was Charlie.

"Have you seen Our Reality today?" she said. "We're losing lots of players, Charlie."

"We are also selling a lot of copies of Portcullis," Charlie said. "Their servers were jammed today. Whenever I tried to load their page, my browser kept timing out."

"All you're doing," Dagmar said, "is giving hope to a bunch of losers with a delusional business plan."

"Since when has *your* division of my company made a big profit?" Charlie asked.

Good point, she had to admit. Great Big Idea, though it had always been in the black, had never been much of an earner, at least as compared with the rest of AvN Soft.

Best to change the subject.

"What do you need, Charlie?" she asked.

"I need a sit-down. Come see me at the Roosevelt."

"Why don't you come to your office? Meetings are what your office is *for*."

"My office," Charlie said, "is for burying me in piles of trivia. Talking to *you* is what my *cabana* is for."

Dagmar looked at the time in the corner of her display.

"I've got a recording session this afternoon," she said. "That's in West Hollywood anyway. So I can come by after that."

"Perfect," said Charlie.

It was only after the phone call was over that Dagmar realized she hadn't asked what Charlie wanted to see her for.

It can't be good, she thought.

FROM: LadyDayFan

We are happy to play host to the tens of thousands of new players that have been arriving in the past few days, but we urge them to check the <u>FAQ List</u> and <u>Player Tutorial</u> before asking questions in this forum.

Thank you.

(Signed) Frazzled

The recording sessions usually left Dagmar in a buoyant mood. Terri Griff, the actress she'd hired to play Briana Hall, was incredibly talented, and very good at improvisation. It was a good reminder that not all actors were vapid, self-involved mirror gazers.

Or lying shit-heel married psychos, like Siyed.

Dagmar took an active role in this session, playing the part of Maria Perry, Briana's best friend. Dagmar had never possessed any inclination to become an actress, but during the fifth week of the game, the players were scheduled to phone Maria and try to sweet-talk her into giving them information that would move the game forward. These conversations were very intense and tended to jump in unexpected directions as the players disgorged everything they thought might get them the knowledge they were after, and an actress might not be able to improvise. Dagmar knew exactly what the players would have to say in order to get Maria to spill, and therefore it seemed sensible for her to play Maria herself.

Dagmar found the recording sessions chock-full of

positive reinforcement. The life of a writer was a solitary one—you worked alone, and the stuff went into a magazine or a book or onto a Web page, and then you either got feedback or you didn't. And in the case of her ARGs, a lot of the feedback was carping over small details.

But in a recording session the feedback was *immediate*. Her words were spoken aloud, usually by talented professionals, and she knew at once whether they'd work or not. If rewrites were needed, she could do them on the spot.

"How much does Briana trust Cullen at this point?" Terri asked. She was tall, with long, dark hair and a pale complexion that belonged more in Elsinore than in L.A.

"I don't think she does," Dagmar said.

"In that case," Terri said, "would Briana say, 'I saw someone in the courtyard,' or would she identify Cullen right away?"

Dagmar paused. "Let me think," she said.

The sound studio was a small one off La Brea, used mainly for recording commercials. The white sound-absorbent panels on the walls and ceiling were turning yellow with age, and the microphones were venerable steel objects dating from the birth of disco. There was a better-equipped studio in the back used for looping, also mostly commercial work.

The owner of the studio, Ray, sat behind the controls. He was an elderly man with a goatee and a white pompadour and fingers stained yellow with nicotine. The odor of his cigarettes leaked into the studio from the hall outside. He sat behind the console with a melancholy, infinite patience that suggested that perhaps he *had* heard everything.

"We don't want to make it clear that it was Cullen this early in the game," Dagmar said. "Maybe she'd say it *could* have been Cullen. Because by this point the players are going to suspect Cullen anyway."

And then Cullen turns up dead the week after, Dagmar thought, *and the sinister plot just keeps on rolling.*

After recording the conversation between Briana and Maria, Dagmar hung around to listen to Terri record Briana's call to the police on finding the body of her ex, Duncan.

When they joined the game, the players were asked to provide basic data such as addresses, phone numbers, and email addresses. After joining, the players received a series of phone calls, faxes, emails, and sometimes packages, usually purporting to be from the fictional characters in the game.

In this case, the players were all going to get to overhear Briana's 911 call.

The actor playing the emergency operator had already recorded his lines, so Terri just waited for the cues and spoke Dagmar's words—or rather, sobbed and shrieked and wailed them.

Terri did take after take, and each time her voice grew more hysterical, more horrified. Terri's eyes grew wider, her mouth looser somehow, more moist, the tongue more visible as it pulsed behind the teeth. The color drained from Terri's face, as if she'd actually managed to work herself into a genuine state of terror. Dagmar was fascinated by the process.

And then she wondered what she'd sounded like on her own 911 call when Austin was shot, and suddenly she couldn't watch or listen anymore. She barged out of the studio into the hall with its flickering fluorescent lighting. On the walls were old LP jackets and photographs of celebrities that may or may not have ever recorded there.

Dagmar's head swam. Her pulse raced. Her flesh prickled with waves of heat. She looked at her hands and saw fluorescents strobing on her, crawling over her skin like ants.

The hall reeked of cigarette ash. Muffled by the studio door, Terri's screams raked Dagmar's nerves like rusty nails. Dagmar walked down the hall, through the reception area, and out into the parking lot. She leaned against her car and took deep breaths of the asphalt-scented air. A police siren dopplered up and down on La Brea.

A horrific sense of dread possessed her. She remembered the Palms burning in Jakarta, the pillar of smoke over Glodok, protesters falling under police fire. Sparks flying in the darkness as bullets caromed off the metal bodies of cars.

She imagined bodies lying on La Brea, Century City afire, automatic weapons crackling down in Japantown.

It was all so fragile, she thought. That was really the lesson of Jakarta, how the world could change in an instant. How a nation could fall, a neighborhood burn, a friend lie murdered.

How a general or a politician or a mobster could watch it all and smile.

What am I playing with? she wondered. She created entertainments based on all this, on violence and mysteries and movements behind the scenes, all the things that might be fun so long as they weren't actually happening to *you*. And now she had sent people from her strange, insular world of online entertainment to track a genuine killer.

She was, it occurred to her, completely crazy. And Charlie was even crazier.

It was all going to end, she thought, in a rising cloud of ash.

A little farther down La Brea, Dagmar found a convenience store with flyspecked windows and a cashier who carried a pistol on his hip for use in the event of a robbery. She bought two miniature bottles of Cuervo, which she took to the car and drank very fast, one after the other.

She sat in the car and listened to the radio for a while, until the burning in her gut turned to a relaxation that slowly spread to her barbed-wire nerves, and then the radio began to irritate her. They were playing some kind of extended-play nineties music that she didn't remember from the actual nineties, so she got out of the car to toss the miniatures in the trash, got back in the car, and headed north to Hollywood.

Driving drunk to see your boss, she thought. *How fucked is* that?

She drove past Scientology's Norman castle and the sad, tacky souvenir shops. Hollywood was seedier and more depressing every time Dagmar saw it. She saw clouds of tourists wandering the Walk of Fame, lining up to take one another's pictures. All probably wondering how to get their vacation back.

She gave the car to the valet at the Roosevelt and walked to the pool. The poolside areas were full of people talking on cell phones, doing business. Dagmar walked to Charlie's cabana and was about to knock when the door opened from the inside. A young woman smiled at her, all bouncing strawberry curls and gleaming teeth.

"Excuse *me*," the woman said, and slipped out of the cabana to walk back toward the main hotel. Dagmar watched her walking away.

Damn, she thought. *That girl could wear* anything *and her ass would forgive her.*

She entered the cabana. Charlie sat on a striped couch, gazing at the notebook computer that was propped up in front of him on a hassock. Charlie wore one of the complimentary Roosevelt bathrobes and looked down at the display with a frown. Behind him, a portable massage table had been set up and draped with white towels.

"Hello, Mr. Hefner," Dagmar said.

Charlie glanced toward her, looking at her from over the rims of his spectacles.

"Ah," he said. "Did you meet Kimba Leigh? That's not Kimberly, it's k-i-m-b-a l-e-i-g-h. Two words."

"Your model/actress/masseuse?" Dagmar asked as she closed the door behind her.

"Not mine," Charlie said mildly. "She belongs to the hotel. And the person who gives massages is, unfortunately, a fireplug-shaped Arab named Mahmoun." He turned toward the tray sitting next to him on the couch and removed the shiny metal dome to reveal the plate and sandwich beneath.

"Kimba Leigh brought my French dip," he said.

Dagmar smiled. "I'll just bet she did."

He gave her a tolerant look. "She's the food and beverage manager. She thinks I'm in the business, so she offers me her special VIP personal service."

"I bet she does."

"Would you mind getting me a Coke from the fridge? And help yourself, if you like."

The air bore a faint undertone of paint in the room, a hint that the place had recently been redecorated. The cabana had a full kitchen and a wet bar prestocked with expensive liquor. The walls were plastered white with ocean turquoise trim. Slate blue drapes had been drawn over the glass wall that looked out onto the pool area. The furniture was the sturdy sort you might find in a Mexican beach resort, wood-framed, with colorful fabrics. The chairs and couch were covered with books and papers, and there was a cluster of featureless white cardboard boxes, each slightly larger than a paperback book, around Charlie's feet.

Charlie's Pinky and the Brain stuffies stared down from atop the television cabinet.

Dagmar went to the refrigerator and got one of Charlie's imported Mexican half-liter Cokes. She reached for a second bottle and hesitated, then closed the fridge, stepped to the bar, and poured herself three fingers' worth of Tres Generaciones. She had a feeling she might need it by the time her meeting was over.

She returned to the couch and handed Charlie his Coke.

"Have a seat," he said.

She balanced her glass on the arm of the couch and took a double handful of papers and books and moved them from the couch to one of the chairs. *Double Star,* she saw, by Robert Heinlein. *Introduction to Macroeconomics. Theories of the Great Economists.*

"Why the textbooks?" she asked.

"They have to do with my new project."

"I've never been terribly impressed by Heinlein's economic theory."

Charlie smiled. "That's leisure reading."

She sat next to him on the couch. On the hassock she could see the computer's display, and she saw that Charlie had been writing code.

He saw the direction of her glance, then reached out and closed the display.

"What are you doing?" she asked.

"It's a special project." He looked at her. "Do you know how long it's been since I've written a piece of code?"

"Six years?" she said. That being the length of time since AvN Soft had really taken off.

"Exactly." He shrugged. "I *like* to code, but because I'm such a big success, I never do it anymore. So I'm working on a little thing of my own."

He was going to make her ask him, she realized. So she might as well get it over with.

"What's it about?" she asked.

His mouth twitched. "I'd rather not say."

"But it's about economics."

He looked away, at Pinky and the Brain atop the cabinet.

"It has an economic dimension," he said.

"You're creating a stock-trading program?"

He gave her an ambiguous look.

"There are a lot of *those*," he said. "And AvN Soft already has Rialto."

"Currency trading?"

He shrugged.

"The currency traders are really slamming the euro today," she said.

Charlie shrugged again. "That's over," he said. "The central banks intervened, and so did the oil sheiks, to protect all their favorite boutiques."

"You'd think the sheiks would want their Gucci cheaper."

"Not if it means the Europeans are so poor they can't buy petroleum."

"Ah." She sipped her tequila. "So who was leading the attack this time?"

"I believe," Charlie said carefully, "that the Chinese are getting the blame again."

"*Was* it the Chinese?"

"The Chinese were in the pack," Charlie said, "but it was all really the fault of the French and the Germans. The euro is supported by this complicated agreement among the member communities that establishes various economic targets, like inflation. But the French and the Germans have been cheating since the beginning— they're the largest economies over there, and they figured they could get away with it. But they left their currency vulnerable, and now they've paid the penalty. The euro's down about thirty percent, last I checked."

"How's the dollar?" she asked.

He lifted his eyebrows. "Knock wood," he said.

Dagmar watched him as she sipped again at her drink.

"Was it the Russian Maffya that attacked the euro?" she asked.

Charlie seemed to consider this.

"I doubt they've got enough capital to damage a major currency," he said seriously. He took a large swallow of his Coke, reached for one of the white cardboard boxes piled at his feet. "I didn't call you here to talk about this, anyway. I want you to take a look at one of these."

He tossed her the box. The contents were light. She opened the box and took out a recharging unit and a device the size of her phone, covered in gray plastic. There was a small display, two buttons with Y and N on them, and a kind of clear plastic reservoir on one end, with a green plastic cap.

"What is it?" she said. "A really stupid computer?"

"It's—well, you'd better use mine, I charged it last night." He dug beneath the remaining papers on the couch, then produced an identical unit. He held down one of the buttons for a few seconds, and then the display lit.

"Go to the sink," he said, "and fill the reservoir with tap water."

She raised her eyebrows, but Charlie just looked at her. She took the unit and walked to the kitchen, then popped the bright green top and very carefully ran a little water into the reservoir.

"The unit is waterproof," Charlie said. "You can submerge it if you like."

"Do I put the cap back on?"

"Yes. Then press the Yes button."

When Dagmar pressed the button, nothing happened. Nothing visible, anyway. Then letters appeared on the display: DRINKING WATER?

"It's asking if it's drinking water."

"Press the Yes button."

Dagmar did so.

TRANSMIT? read the display.

"Do I want to transmit?" Dagmar asked.

"Yes."

Dagmar pressed the Yes button and waited another few seconds. Then the display read: TRANSMISSION COMPLETE.

"Okay," she said. "That's done."

"Right. Empty out the reservoir, then bring the unit back."

Dagmar did as she was requested, then sat on the couch and gave the unit back to Charlie.

"What we have here," he said, tossing the unit lightly in one hand, "is a portable water-analysis device combined with a GPS and a satellite transmitter. It's a civilian offshoot of technology developed for Homeland Security types to identify biological and chemical threats. Within a few seconds, the scanner can analyze water for any of hundreds of common and uncommon pollutants, including bioforms, then transmit the results to a central database, along with GPS coordinates."

"Interesting," Dagmar said. Warily, because she had a feeling she knew where Charlie was heading with this.

"Interesting, hell!" Charlie said. "It's brilliant! Pass out enough of these things, and you can analyze every body of water on the planet, including every source of drinking water. You end up with a complete database of available water sources. Right now, we just added a new entry for tap water in this cabana."

Dagmar sipped her drink. Tequila fumes flamed up her sinus.

Charlie held up a USB cable. "When you get one of these units," he said, "you connect it to your computer with the cable, and you get an account with a company up in Portland called Tapping the Source. When you log on, you can read any data that you sent them yourself, so you'll always know if your own drinking water is safe. But if you want access to the whole database—which a lot of people will—you have to pay a fee."

Dagmar nodded. "A model of responsible environmental capitalism," she said.

"Yeah. That's why I like them." He looked at her. "That's why I want you to build these units into the game."

She had, of course, been expecting something like this. Charlie had no reason to invite her to his cabana other than to screw with her work. But even though she had anticipated him, she still felt the shock, as if he'd just punched her in the ribs.

"Why not the *next* game, Charlie?" she said. "I'm already up to my neck in rewrites."

He shook his head.

"No," he said. "*This* game."

Dagmar feigned a patience she didn't feel. "Charlie," she said, "we're in week three of an eight-week game.

The last two weeks aren't even written, and I'm still doing rewrites caused by the *last* piece of technology you wanted me to include in the game."

"It's not going to be that hard," Charlie assured her.

She gave him a cold stare. "Uh-huh."

She was tired of explaining about writing to people who didn't write and didn't know how to write.

"Look," Charlie said, "your bad guys, the ones meeting in *Planet Nine*, are terrorists, right?"

"Yeah."

"And what sort of terror are they up to?"

"Dirty bombs in major cities."

Brussels, London, New York, Charleston, Delhi, Seattle, and San Diego. So that the players could each be sent on errands that would uncover important clues to the terrorists' identities.

"Right," Charlie said. "So instead of nuclear terrorism, make it chemical or biological. They're contaminating water supplies. And they're doing it in—for example—the fifty cities where we have the largest concentration of players."

"*Fifty?*" Outrage burned in her blood. "You're going to ask the players to test the water reservoirs of fifty major cities, and do it without getting arrested or—"

Charlie shook his head. "It doesn't have to be reservoirs, or even tap water. It could be lakes, creeks, ponds. Public fountains, even."

"And what are they testing *for?* We can't actually contaminate all these bodies of water."

Charlie held up his unit. "These babies analyze the water down to parts per billion. You put a tiny amount of some neutral chemical in the water—something that won't hurt anyone but will show up in the scans. Tell the players that the terrorists are testing their delivery systems before they use the real thing."

"Charlie!" Dagmar said. "Now I have to find a person in each of fifty cities who can put this chemical into a body of water, and do it without being noticed!"

"There are go-to guys in every city," Charlie said. "We just have to find the right—"

"*Are you crazy?*" Dagmar demanded. "We don't have the personnel to do this! We don't have the budget! The technical staff doesn't have the resources. We'd have to reshoot video and rerecord audio. And *I* don't have enough time to do the rewrites." She glared at him. "Plus, the players are going to revolt if they have to buy anything new. How much do those units cost?"

"Tapping the Source has a couple of hundred thousand of them in the warehouse and is selling them for cost, in hopes they can get as many out into the world as possible. They cost something like forty bucks, including postage and handling."

"*Forty dollars!* That's more than the encryption software!"

"Stop bouncing," Charlie said. "You're going to spill my *jus.*" He moved his meal tray from the couch to the hassock, balancing it atop his computer.

"You're going to wreck Great Big Idea!" Dagmar said. "You're giving us a job that we flat can't do, and that will destroy our credibility with the players."

Charlie regarded her coldly. "No, I'm not."

"But—"

"Money," said Charlie, "will get you through times of inadequate staffing better than inadequate staffing will get you through times of no money."

"Which means *what*, exactly?"

"I'm giving you the keys to the kingdom," Charlie said. "I'm going to set up a bank account with an adequate budget for you to get this thing done. You'll be able to hire the go-to guys in fifty cities. You'll hire more technical staff." He reached out and tapped her knee. "And you'll hire more writers. Okay?"

"It's far too late for any of this," Dagmar said.

"No, it's not," Charlie said. His look was level and very serious and very intense. "You're going to do this, Dagmar. Because you owe me, and you know it."

An argument followed, but Dagmar lost it, which was what happened when you were fighting someone who had all the power and all the money. Her only option was to quit her job, and—aside from the fact that she *liked* her job, at least usually—she couldn't afford to stop taking Charlie's money.

In fury, she gulped the remains of her Tres Generaciones and stomped out, blinking in the bright sun and the reflection off the pool. She felt ridiculous because she had an armful of the Tapping the Source units in their white boxes, a visible reminder of her failure.

By the pool, people were still under their umbrellas, talking on their cell phones.

Being seen and doing business. Being seen *while* doing business.

Kimba Leigh stood behind the poolside bar, giving

orders to the Guatemalan bartender. Maybe she actually *was* the food and beverage manager. Dagmar walked past her and didn't receive a glance. She wasn't important enough to rate Kimba Leigh's attention.

Dagmar decided she was too drunk to drive, so she went to the hotel lounge and, conscious of a degree of irony, ordered coffee.

She sat behind her square wooden table with its colorful inset Mexican tile, sipped her coffee, and looked down at the white boxes scattered before her.

What the hell . . .? What in God's name was Charlie up to?

Players would wander all over fifty major cities, testing every water source they could find: tap water, public fountains, creeks and rivers. Data would flow into Tapping the Source. Which, apparently, wasn't nonprofit: it was building the database in order to sell it.

So Tapping the Source would have a much bigger database to sell. Which meant Tapping the Source would be worth more money.

At least it was a company that had a more sensible business plan than Portcullis. And they were about improving water supplies, so that was a good thing.

Still, it looked like another Maffya-style pump-and-dump stock scheme, buying a company's stock while it was cheap and then inflating its value.

Though she had to admit that it was difficult to picture the Russian Maffya getting interested in a company with such a green profile. Helping the earth was not one of their usual priorities.

She decided, in alcohol-ridden despair, that she should

assume that Charlie was in thrall to the Maffya. He must owe them money, or owe them something other than money. Probably the latter, because if he owed them money, he'd just give it to them.

She paid for her coffee and took the 101 past the exit for the Hollywood Bowl and up over the hills to the Valley. She parked in the AvN Soft parking lot in view of all the new security cameras, then got out of the car. Afternoon heat shimmered: it was hotter here than in Los Angeles proper. She walked past the uniformed guard at his security station and into the building.

Even though it was after business hours, the building still hummed with activity. People still sat amid the ferns of the atrium, connected to their jobs with Wi-Fi; the coffee shop was still open, selling drinks, salads, and sandwiches.

Dagmar went to her office and looked through her database.

Over the years she'd hired freelance writers to help her on various projects. Sometimes she'd hire a television writer, but usually she drew her writing staff from science fiction writers scattered throughout North America. They were usually happy to oblige her and earn real money, and all too readily put aside their regular work, which on average paid a word rate that hadn't changed since the Great Depression.

She called them all. None were available on short notice. Everyone was on deadline, or on vacation, or had just been hired to script a new drama on TNT.

Damn it, she thought. There was no way she had the time to train someone new.

Unless.

Unless.

Unless, she thought, it was someone who knew games inside out, and who really needed the money, and who had no job worthy of the name. Someone who had devised the most diabolically complex and treacherous games she had ever played, or even heard of.

Charlie will really be pissed, she thought.

Not that she gave a damn about that, not any longer. And besides, a writer didn't have to work from an office, and since Charlie was never in the building anyway, there wasn't much of a chance of their paths crossing.

Oh yeah.

She picked up the phone and called BJ.

CHAPTER EIGHTEEN

This Is Not a Homecoming

FROM: LadyDayFan

We are sorry that so many players were unable to log on yesterday. Our servers have been overwhelmed by the hundreds of thousands of new players that have recently joined *Motel Room Blues.*

As always, we urge new players to check the <u>FAQ List</u> and <u>Player Tutorial</u> before asking questions in this forum.

Thank you.

"I haven't been here since Charlie had me thrown out," BJ said. He had contributed his thumbprint to the database at the new security station and now stood in the AvN Soft atrium, looking past potted palm trees to the upper reaches of the office tower.

"I had one security guy on each arm," he said. "Two guys came behind with cardboard boxes of stuff from my office." He pointed upward, at the eighth-floor balcony. "And Charlie was up there, watching. He didn't say a damn word. He just watched."

He stood there, scowling defiantly up at the place Charlie had occupied on that day. He wore Levi's worn smooth and pale, and a polyester knit shirt strained by his broad shoulders.

"Is there going to be a problem?" Dagmar asked.

He looked at her with his blue eyes.

"Nope," he said. "Not at all."

"Oh, Dagmar!" the receptionist, Luci, called from her desk. "I forgot to tell you! Someone sent you a present."

She reached behind her chair and lifted up a vase filled with at least three dozen white roses. She put the vase on her desk and fanned out the flowers, producing a brief rose-scented breeze.

"My God," said Dagmar.

"Someone sure loves *you*," Luci said.

Maybe it's Charlie, Dagmar thought. *Maybe he's trying to make up for what he did to me yesterday.*

She reached for the envelope attached to the display, opened it, and read it.

I'm so very sorry that you were unable to join me for dinner yesterday evening, she read. *Perhaps tonight? Your very own, Siyed.*

"Crap," she said, and crumpled the card.

"Goodness!" said Luci. "Who is it?"

Dagmar gave the short form. "Short psycho married foreigner," she said.

Luci gave a knowing nod. BJ chuckled. He picked up the vase.

"Well, if he's a bastard, it isn't the flowers' fault," he said. "Where shall we take them?"

They went to her office, where they cleared some of the rubble off a shelf and made a place for the vase. The soft scent of the roses floated through the room. Dagmar called Contracts and told them she needed a freelancer contract rushed through. She gave them BJ's name, address, and Social Security number and told them he was going to be paid two thousand dollars per week.

"And backdate the contract to Monday," she said.

That way, BJ could pick up his first check on Friday. Which, since he had quit his IT job for this, was the least she could do.

"Thanks," BJ said, looking out her window at the highway down below. "Now can you tell me what the hell I'm doing here?"

"Have a seat."

He moved file folders from one of the chairs and sat in it. She explained what was happening in *The Long Night of Briana Hall* and how all that would have to change. She called up a flow chart of the action, put it on the big plasma monitor on the wall, and walked him through it.

He adjusted his rimless spectacles and pursed his lips in thought. "So Briana's suspected of two murders, right?"

"Yes."

"And the murders aren't actually connected?"

"No. It just seems that way to the cops."

BJ rubbed his chin. "That's a *coincidence*," he said. "I don't *like* coincidences in fiction. I see enough of them in real life."

Dagmar smiled, then gestured at the chart. "The cops don't believe in coincidence, either. But the players are going to prove them wrong."

"So one of the murders is committed by a terrorist, and the other was done by people involved in some kind of securities fraud."

"Right."

"Can we connect them in some way?"

She blinked at him. "How?"

"Well," said BJ, "let's say that the people involved in the fraud know that the terrorists are about to strike. So they're planning on—I don't know—shorting S&Ps or something, knowing they're going to go down."

"Ah. Like al Qaeda was supposed to have done—manipulated stocks just before 9/11."

"Exactly."

Dagmar leaned back in her chair. Possibilities cascaded through her mind.

"Yes," she said. "We could do that. But in that case the players are only confirming what the authorities actually believe. It's more dramatically satisfying for a player to prove an NPC wrong than to show he's been right all along."

"Then you make it a triple-layered puzzle," BJ said. "Level one is solved by the cops, who think Briana's guilty. Level two will be solved by the players, who will prove that the crimes are unrelated and that Briana is innocent of the murders. And then the players unravel the third layer, which shows that the crimes are related after all but that Briana is still innocent."

Dagmar looked at BJ and grinned.

"Yeah," she said. "We could work it that way."

She couldn't help being grateful for someone who was actually trying to *solve* her problems.

"Now," BJ said, "tell me how this Russian assassin is connected to everything."

Dagmar took a long breath and slowly exhaled.

"That," she said, "is really complicated."

She told him. His blue eyes widened.

"This is the guy who killed *Austin?* You've got hundreds of thousands of people trying to find a *real killer?*"

"Millions," said Dagmar.

"Holy Christ." His arms made a hopeless, flopping gesture. "I have no idea what to say to that."

"The problem is that they *aren't* finding him. We've got to give them other things to work on until Litvinov surfaces. And if he *doesn't* surface, we've got to give the players a satisfactory resolution to that plot."

BJ scrubbed his face with both hands. "I can't believe this."

"Wait," Dagmar said, "till you hear what Charlie wants to do with the water samplers."

She was in the middle of her explanation when her desk phone rang.

"Dagmar," she answered.

"Did you get my present, love?" asked Siyed.

Her heart gave a guilty lurch at the sound of the East London accent.

"Thanks for the flowers," she said, "but I'm too busy to see you."

Across the desk, BJ smiled.

"Please, Dagmar," said Siyed. "I've come all this way."

"Sorry, no," said Dagmar. "There's this problem about your being married."

"I—" And at that moment Dagmar's handheld began to play "Harlem Nocturne."

"My other phone's ringing," Dagmar said. "Gotta go."

The display on the handheld showed it was Charlie calling. The sight of his name brought a flash of paranoia, and she wondered if one of Charlie's spies could have seen her bring BJ into the building.

She didn't think there was anyone but Charlie at AvN Soft who dated from BJ's time, but perhaps she was wrong.

Her hands were clumsy in removing the phone from its holster, and in pressing the Send button to answer.

"Yes," she said into the phone.

"Dagmar," said Charlie, "are you ready for the keys to the kingdom?"

Her head swam. It took her a moment to orient herself to an entirely different context, and then she reached for her stylus.

"Okay," she said.

Charlie gave her an account number and a complicated password, a random mix of letters and numerals. Dagmar jotted it down on her handheld display and saved it to a text file.

"Got it," she said.

"Right," Charlie said. "That's your budget for the game. If you need more, let me know."

"Will do," she said. "Whose name is the account under?"

"Atreides LLC," Charlie said. "It's a corporation I created years ago but never got around to using."

"You named the company after the family in Aeschylus?" Dagmar asked.

"No." Blankly. "I named it after the family in *Dune*."

"Right," Dagmar said. "Of course."

Sometimes she forgot what subculture she was living in.

"I'll need a good accounting at the end of this," Charlie said.

"You'll get one," Dagmar said. With BJ's payment listed as "Consultant fee," and no names mentioned.

"How's the game moving?" he asked.

"I believe I gave you my views yesterday," said Dagmar.

"Just do it," Charlie said, and hung up.

BJ was watching her. Amusement glittered behind his spectacles.

"You have a very complex life," he said.

"No kidding. Excuse me for a moment."

She used her trackball to take her to the Wells Fargo page and then typed in the account number and password.

Charlie had given her an account with twenty-five million dollars.

She stared for a long moment.

Curse of the Golden Nagi had been budgeted at four million, with live events on three continents. *The Long Night of Briana Hall* had a budget double that of *Golden Nagi*, much of which had already been spent on professionally produced, professionally acted video, by far the most expensive item in the budget. Now Charlie had given her more than triple that sum, in addition to the eight million already in the budget.

The keys to the kingdom indeed.

If Dagmar couldn't do what Charlie wanted on this game, she thought, it was because it simply couldn't be done.

At one o'clock, Dagmar had an emergency meeting with the Great Big Idea creative team, fourteen people altogether, with the exception of one woman who was in Amsterdam setting up the weekend's live event.

She couldn't stop herself from peering out the window blinds of the conference room, to make sure that Joe Clever wasn't lurking somewhere with his Big Ears. No eavesdroppers were visible. She turned on the white-noise generators anyway, and the meeting proceeded with a kind of distant waterfall hiss in the background.

When Helmuth entered, Dagmar introduced BJ.

"Helmuth von Moltke," Helmuth said, offering his hand.

BJ raised his eyebrows. "Von Moltke?" he asked.

"Programmer by day," said Helmuth. "Eurotrash by night."

Helmuth, descended from a German general, was a sleek, handsome young man, still under thirty. He wore cashmere slacks, a T-shirt with the Ferrari stallion, and a jacket of paper-thin, featherlight leather made in Buenos Aires. He was known to spend most of his nights partying on the Sunset Strip. When or if he slept was unknown.

Jack Stone ambled in next. He was the puzzle designer

and a Type Two Geek, which was basically a Type One plus about eighty pounds. He lived, ate, and breathed puzzles, at least when he wasn't living, eating, and breathing Frito pies, which he made himself by lining a bowl with Fritos, pouring Wolf brand chili on top, and putting the result in the microwave. When it was hot, he'd throw grated jack cheese on top. Even other Type Twos couldn't abide the result.

Fortunately he hadn't brought a Frito pie with him this time. Instead he had a plastic sack filled with miniature candy bars, which he would eat like popcorn.

Dagmar introduced BJ as "Boris, who's going to help with the writing." The others paid no attention to BJ after that. Writing wasn't interesting to them.

When everyone arrived, Dagmar demonstrated one of the Tapping the Source units and explained Charlie's latest nonnegotiable demands.

"You're changing the story *after the launch?*" demanded Helmuth.

"No point in whining," Dagmar said. "I've already whined to Charlie, and Charlie isn't listening."

So of course they whined some more. Dagmar let them.

"We have the budget on this one," Dagmar said. "If you need help, we'll hire anyone who can provide it. Freelance programmers, design studios, you name it. Start calling them *now,* if you think you'll need them down the line."

"The players are going to *hate* this!" Jack protested. "They went nuts when they had to buy that ninjaware. They're going to be even more crazed when they have to buy these damn water-quality units."

"I've got a work-around," Dagmar said, and smiled. "We buy the units *for* them."

They looked at her. She shrugged.

"Maybe not for *all* of them," she conceded, "but the budget will buy a *lot* of forty-dollar boxes."

After that, it went a little easier.

After the meeting, Dagmar and BJ went to her office to replot *Briana Hall*. The scent of Siyed's roses saturated the air. Drinking coffee and eating Pop-Tarts from the snack station, they worked over Dagmar's interactive monitors and saw their changes appear instantly on the big wall plasma screen, complete with colored arrows that showed how the complex plot elements were connected.

BJ was as devious a story craftsman as Dagmar remembered from their college days. He had an instinctive gift for the twist, the reveal, the snapper that would whip the story in an unanticipated direction, like a rocket slinging around the moon en route to some distant world.

"Right," Dagmar said finally. "Let me put you to work writing the various documents relating to the backstory. I'll do the audio, video, and comic scripts, because I'm familiar with the format."

BJ shrugged. "That should work."

This meant that BJ would be spending his days creating the text for phony documents, everything from school reports to classified government intelligence assessments, newspaper articles to blog entries, birth certificates to death certificates. The Graphics Department would then turn the text into facsimiles of the actual documents. An

ARG thrived on its virtual paper trail—puzzles led to documents, documents contained more puzzles, the puzzles led to more documents, the documents led to revelations.

"You might as well work from home," Dagmar told him. "We don't have an office for you here."

"And besides," BJ said, "I might run into Charlie in the elevator."

"Like I care?" Dagmar snarled. And then wondered if she actually meant what she'd just said.

Dagmar looked out her office window and was surprised to discover it was night. She looked at the time on her monitor screen and saw it was after nine o'clock.

She realized she was very hungry. The coffee shop in the atrium closed at nine, so there was no food in the building unless she wanted something from a vending machine, or more Pop-Tarts. At this hour, neither option seemed attractive.

"Want to get dinner?" she asked. "Charlie's paying."

BJ grinned. "That's an offer I can't refuse."

They found a steak house open on Ventura, one with dim lighting in 1950s colored-glass sconces, battered dark wood tables, and red-and-white-checked tablecloths. Dagmar ordered a margarita and a medium-rare rib eye. She didn't eat much red meat, but on this evening she planned on making a sizzling, juicy exception.

"Well," BJ said, "as long as Charlie's paying." He ordered the same thing, only with a shrimp cocktail for an appetizer and king crab legs draped over his steak.

"At this rate," Dagmar said, "it won't be long before you bring Charlie to his knees."

"I wish," BJ muttered.

Dagmar looked at him. "What would it take," she said, "for you and Charlie to be friends again?"

"Well," said BJ, "he could give my half of the company back."

"He doesn't actually own the company," Dagmar said. "It's his investors."

BJ raised an eyebrow. "You ever *met* one of these investors? Seen one? Heard their names?"

"No," Dagmar said. "But then I'm not involved with Charlie on that level."

"I don't think anyone is," BJ said. "I think there's a *reason* no one's ever seen the people who rescued the company."

Dagmar felt suspicion sing in her bones, a deep, subdural hum of mistrust. The day's anger and the complex logistics and plotting session had kept a lid on her speculations, but now her doubts flooded her.

"Any idea," she asked, "why Charlie's angels are so mysterious?"

"Nope." He scratched one of his muttonchops. "My best guess is that they're involved in some kind of tax-fraud scheme. Or maybe the investors are laundering money through AvN Soft."

Dagmar leaned toward BJ over the table.

"How would that work, exactly?" she said.

"If they're laundering money, they'd just overpay for AvN's services. How are the IRS auditors going to know how much our autonomous agents are worth? As long as Charlie pays taxes on the money that's rolling in, the IRS and everyone else are happy."

Dagmar nodded. That seemed plausible enough. And she hadn't failed to notice that "our."

The margaritas and the shrimp cocktail arrived. The prawns were vast and pink, like tongues lolling from the rim of a cocktail glass. BJ offered Dagmar one, and she took it. It had that bland, farmed taste that suggested it had never been anywhere near an ocean, but even so, it whetted Dagmar's appetite.

BJ gave her a calculating look.

"You're thinking about that Russian assassin, aren't you?" he said. "You think Charlie's involved with the Maffya."

"The assassin," said Dagmar, "is a problem to which I have no ready answer."

"So you're trying to track the killer through the game." Thoughtfully, BJ picked up a shrimp, then replaced it on the rim of the cocktail glass. "And you have to hope that he'll have some answers once he's picked up. I have to give you credit for optimism."

"Foolhardy though it may be."

Feeling foolhardy and hopeful, she licked the rim of her glass and took a swallow of her drink. Tongues of tequila fire sped along her veins.

"There's more than one Charlie Ruff," BJ said. "There's the one you've known all these years, and then there's the other one." His gaze darkened. "You're starting to meet that other one now. I met him six years ago."

"And what's he like, this other Charlie?"

BJ took a thoughtful drink of his margarita.

"At some point," he said, "Charlie has to be the winner. And with him it's a zero-sum game—if he's the winner, that means everyone else has to lose."

Dagmar considered this. "What kind of game is he playing with me, then?" she asked.

"He hired you to run his game company because he thought the games would be cool," BJ said. "You succeeded. You made the games cool. But now Charlie figures your cool quotient is bigger than his, so he's got to take you down a peg."

"So he's doing this just to humiliate me?" Dagmar didn't find the theory entirely convincing.

"That, and the fact that he's learned enough about ARGs to think he can run one," BJ said. "That's what happened at AvN Soft. He thought he'd learned enough about my end of the business to tell me what to do, and he started trying to do *my* job as well as his." He flapped his big hands. "We both went down in flames. But he found those mysterious backers, and I didn't. So I got thrown out of the building, and Charlie sat up on the balcony and watched and never said a word."

Dagmar took a contemplative sip of her drink. *You're going to do this, Dagmar,* Charlie had said. *Because you owe me, and you know it.*

"I can see that, I suppose," she said. "But why now? If Charlie is really involved with the Maffya, and there is an assassin running around looking for him, you'd think he'd have other things to do besides prove to himself that he can boss me around."

BJ lifted his shoulders in a half shrug. "He can be erratic if he's under pressure. Trust me, I know. He can be *crazy.*"

Dagmar thought about this while BJ ate a prawn.

"So," she said, "tell me what happened with you and Charlie and AvN Soft."

BJ made a face. "This isn't my favorite topic."

"I've had Charlie's story," Dagmar said. "I've had enough from you to know how you *feel* about it, but not what actually happened."

BJ said nothing for a while, just ate the last prawn. Then he touched his lips with his napkin and pushed the cocktail glass away.

"Okay," he said. "We both came up with the ideas that made the autonomous software agents work. That was in one of those late-night bull sessions where we were both flinging theory around, and by five in the morning we'd nailed down our particular approach to intelligent, distributed, self-replicating, self-evolving agents. We knew that was what we wanted to spend the next ten years working on.

"And *then* we had to divide up the work, and that was pure chance. I'd been a project manager for Crassus Software, and I knew how to run an office, so I ran the business side. And by default that put Charlie in charge of creating the software—though in the early days we *both* worked on that. He was better at line-by-line coding, anyway."

He sipped his drink, then put the heavy glass down on the checked tablecloth.

"I'll tell you one thing," he said. "It wasn't Charlie who cold-called venture capital firms and who convinced them to take a chance on a couple of twenty-five-year-old software engineers and their wonky ideas about self-evolving software. It wasn't Charlie who raised the millions to start the company and fill that office tower with software engineers. It wasn't Charlie who did any of that."

She looked at his stubborn, defiant face, and she nodded. "Did Austin help?"

"Right then, Austin was in New York working for Morgan Stanley. But he put us in touch with some people."

"Go on," she said, but at that point the steaks arrived, sizzling on hot metal plates set into wooden platters, and they paused for appreciation.

"Eat while it's hot," BJ said, and picked up his steak knife.

"So," Dagmar said, "did you get the big office building right away, or—"

He gave her an amused look from over the rims of his spectacles.

"I'm not talking about this," he said, "till my surf and turf is *history.*"

Dagmar sighed and picked up her knife. She carved a piece of her rib eye, inhaled its savor, then placed it on her tongue. Juices awakened tired taste buds.

Oh my. Where had this steak *been* all her life?

BJ was using some highly specialized tools to crack open a king crab leg. The carapace snapped; a tiny piece of shrapnel hit Dagmar on the cheek. She flicked it away and reached for her drink.

When the waitress came back with a plate for empty crab shells, Dagmar called for another round of margaritas. She ate her meal with languid pleasure and watched BJ wrestle with his crab legs. By the time the last chunk of

crabmeat had been dipped in lemon butter and consumed, Dagmar was well into her second margarita and
was willing to view the world from on high, enthroned,
like a pagan god, amid a benign radiance.

BJ pushed away his plate.

"That was the best meal I've had in a long time," he
said.

Dagmar lifted her arms and stretched.

"Ready for dessert?" she asked.

BJ laughed. "Maybe I'd better digest a bit first."

She looked at her watch and saw that it was a quarter
after eleven. The dining room was nearly empty, and the
noise from the bar had faded.

The waitress cleared their plates and asked if they
wanted dessert. Dagmar allowed as how they'd look at
menus. The waitress moved away, balancing plates on
her arms. Dagmar watched her.

"I'm always glad when I find a waitress who's just a
waitress," Dagmar said.

"What do you mean?"

"One who's not"—Dagmar tilted her head and
assumed a perky voice—"'Hello, my name is Marcie
and I'll be your waitress tonight. I'd like to recommend
the swordfish, and just in case you're someone important
I'd really really *really* like to be in your next motion
picture.'"

BJ grinned. "You don't get that in the Valley so much,
I bet."

"They're everywhere."

The waitress—whose name was *not* Marcie—returned
with the dessert menu on laminated cards. Dagmar was

too full to eat anything more, but she looked at the list for form's sake. Her glance lifted from the list of desserts to look at BJ.

It struck her that, despite the way he'd been neglecting himself, he was still a very attractive man. BJ gazed down at the menu with a relaxed expression, his blue eyes half-lidded behind their spectacles, and Dagmar considered how few of her memories involved his being relaxed. In school he had always been on the hustle: planning his future, sucking up information, writing vast amounts of sloppy code because he was in too much of a hurry to make it clean. Eventually the hustle had grown so all-encompassing that it had squeezed Dagmar out of his life without anyone quite noticing.

BJ had never allowed himself to be bored. Dagmar wondered if he was bored now.

He looked up at her, saw her looking at him, and his lips firmed in a frown.

"I can see that it's time to pay for this meal," he said.

Dagmar hadn't been thinking of their earlier conversation, but she was willing to take advantage of BJ when the opportunity arose.

"You can order dessert first," she said.

When the waitress came back, he ordered coffee and strawberry shortcake. Then he turned to Dagmar.

"Actually," she said, "I was wondering if you find your life boring."

"I just left a stupid, dead-end job in customer service," he said. "I supplement my income with the two most despised activities in online RPGs: I'm a ninja and a gold farmer. All of the above is as repetitive as hell." He thumped his fingers on the table. "So yes," he said, "I'm bored."

"Well," Dagmar said, "I'll try to keep things from turning too dull for the next few weeks."

"I'd appreciate it."

"But in the meantime I need to find out as much as I can about Charlie. So I need to find out what happened to AvN Soft."

He glanced away, a rueful smile on his lips, then turned back to her and visibly steeled himself, squaring his shoulders, sitting more rigidly in his seat.

"Right," he said. "We started by calling ourselves Advanced von Neumann Software, because our agents were meant to reproduce themselves. But that ended up being misleading, because von Neumann machines are self-replicating *machines*, not software, so we settled for AvN Soft. We started in this old building down in Culver City—it had been an old movie-production facility, and by that I mean *old*. There was junk in there dating from the forties. I wanted to put it on eBay and sell it to collectors, but Charlie insisted we didn't have time, so we just paid the trash men to haul it away. And then we had to retrofit the whole building to modern standards—my God, there was no high-speed Internet anywhere in the building, let alone a T3 connection. And while that was going on, we found the asbestos in the ceiling. So that meant more delays and more money down the drain and guys in moon suits covering half the building in plastic sheeting.

"So then that's the situation we were in when Soong Scientific went bankrupt. You remember them?"

"No," Dagmar said.

"They were bleeding-edge for, like, three years—but it turned out the bleeding edge was nothing but vapor, and when their CEO was arrested by the Chinese government for fraud and bribery and shot in the back of the head, his office tower in the valley became available. I talked Charlie into moving because we could buy the building cheap and it would save money in the long run. But that meant more discussion with the VC people, and more delay and more money . . ." He waved a hand. "Well. You can imagine."

"I've heard Austin describe start-ups. This sounds sort of typical."

"It felt like we were going off into the wilderness," BJ said, "felling trees with hand tools, and putting up cabins. It felt like we were fighting bears with stone axes and eating them raw. It felt as if *nobody* had ever done *any* of this before. It felt like we had to invent everything from scratch."

"Didn't you have a business plan?"

"Sure we did. But what did the business plan say about asbestos? What did it say about contractors that never showed up to do their work, about a project manager who found Jesus and ran away to a fundamentalist Bible camp in Arkansas, about old Soong servers that were riddled with Chinese trapdoors and had to be replaced—*Christ*, those Soong people were devious! The business plan didn't last ten seconds. We were up the creek without a map."

The waitress brought BJ's coffee and dessert, but BJ's story had gained momentum, and he ignored the food placed before him. He jabbed the air with a stubby finger.

"The fact was," he said, "that Charlie and the development team were wandering in circles trying to get the product finished. I kept having to adjust the business strategy because the software kept mutating out from under me. And there were always choices to make—either do something half-assed *now,* or make a commitment to the long haul and do it *right.* I always made the choice that would pay off in the long run. I *began* by assuming the company would be there forever. The only times I compromised were when Charlie talked me into it—he was always looking over my shoulder and arguing with me instead of doing his own work."

He spread his hands. "And I was right, wasn't I? Charlie's reaping the benefits of all my long-range planning. I'm just not there to share it with him."

Dagmar nodded. "So how did it end?"

"It was the first release that killed us," BJ said. "Rialto was eight months late. There were bugs. The user interface sucked. What we had was a data-mining agent that would analyze publically available financial information—everything from stock market quotes to remittances to exchange rates to raw materials prices to employment rates—and it would make predictions. It would make the trades itself, if you wanted it that way.

"The problem was"—fervor shone in BJ's eyes—"there was already plenty of software on the market that did that. The competition was fierce. Credit Suisse, for example, had an alg program that would analyze eight thousand stocks *per second* and trade based on predictions set three minutes ahead. Each trade took about a millisecond. They've probably got a better system now.

"And let's face it, Release 1.0 just wasn't all that successful in the beginning— Rialto was designed to *evolve*, not to be brilliant right from the start. It was hard to explain that to the customers. Word of mouth in the marketplace destroyed us." He shrugged. "It's very successful now, I understand."

"That's what I hear," said Dagmar.

"After that," BJ said, "the money ran out. We had five or six other projects in the pipeline, but it was too late. We kept having to lay off staff. I called every venture capitalist in America and every European merchant bank, trying to raise funds to keep us afloat. Eventually it was just Charlie and me and maybe half a dozen other people in this empty building. He was immersed in programming, trying to keep one of the other projects afloat—and whenever he saw me, he'd just start yelling that it was all my fault. He'd gone totally insane.

"Our options ran out. We declared bankruptcy, and all the assets were seized by our creditors. We'd pledged our copyrights and our own shares against our financing, so we were left with nothing. We stayed in our offices, because the building hadn't been sold yet and our creditors hadn't gotten around to throwing us out. And then"—he shrugged again—"Charlie's backers turned up. They bought the company from the VC people for pennies on the dollar. They retained Charlie and threw me out."

His blue eyes gave Dagmar a defiant look. "Russian Maffya?" he said. "*You* tell *me*."

Dagmar was silent. BJ took a fork and jabbed it angrily into his shortcake.

"The least I could get out of all that," he said from around his dessert, "is a damn meal."

"Be my guest," Dagmar murmured.

BJ ate his dessert in wrathful silence. Dagmar's mind spun in circles, trying to reconcile BJ's story of AvN Soft's fall with those of Charlie and Austin.

In any case, the story seemed to cast very little light on Charlie's current behavior.

The waitress arrived to ask if they wanted anything else. Dagmar looked over her shoulder and saw they were alone in the dining room. The loudest sound from the bar was a cable news channel. Dagmar said they'd have the check and then went to the ladies'.

Her route passed through the bar, and something, some dreadful sense of déjà vu, made her look at the news program perched on its plasma screen above the bar.

The crawl at the bottom of the screen read *Bolivian Currency Collapse.*

A shiver ran up her spine.

She remembered watching the same network talking heads five months before, from the bar in the Royal Jakarta.

"Apparently the same traders have now switched their focus to Chile," one said. "Chile's the IMF's poster boy in South America, a perfect example of the neoliberal economic model . . ."

The other talking head twinkled. "They call it neo-conservatism here in America," she said.

They laughed. The first talking head twinkled back.

"That's right," he said. "And if Chile falls, the rest of

Latin America is just that much closer to economic apoc-
alypse."

Dagmar clenched her hands to keep them from trembling. The scent of burning Glodok came faintly to her
nostrils.

She paid for the dinner with her company card, then
drove BJ back to the AvN Soft building to pick up his car.

BJ stood for a long moment by Dagmar's car, staring
up at the darkened glass tower with only a few windows
illuminated, where the service was cleaning or some programmer was pulling an all-nighter.

"This sure has been one damn weird day," he said.

"True," Dagmar said. She put her arms around his
burly body, rested her head against his shoulder. He
smelled pleasantly of steak and strawberries and coffee
and himself. His arms came around her.

"Thanks for doing this," he said.

"No problem."

"And thanks for listening." He took a deep breath.
"You know, I hadn't told that story to anyone before. I
didn't know if anyone would believe me."

"I don't know what to think," Dagmar said. He stiffened, and she added quickly, "Not about you, but about
Charlie."

"Be careful around him," BJ said. "I think he's connected to all the wrong people."

"I think you're right."

She released BJ and stepped back.

"I'll talk to you tomorrow," she said. "Have a safe
drive home."

"And you."

Dagmar sat in her Prius and watched BJ's old Chevrolet turn out of the parking lot and onto the frontage road. He had once owned a BMW, she remembered—he'd emailed her a picture of it.

He was just so *different*. She had a hard time reconciling the old hard-charging, energetic, arrogant BJ with the diffident, frustrated man she'd met today.

She wondered what made the difference.

Failure, she thought. Failure was all it took.

CHAPTER NINETEEN

This Is Not Treason

FROM: Siyed Prasad
SUBJECT: Re: Holiday in L.A.

Dear Dagmar,

I know that you are very busy right now, but I simply must see you. Ever since our wonderful time together, I can think of no one but you. You possess my every waking thought, and you invade my dreams as well. I try to concentrate on work, but all I see is your beautiful face before me.

My dearest, we must meet. Name the time and the place, and I will fly to your side!

Your devoted,

Siyed

FROM: Dagmar Shaw
SUBJECT: Re: Holiday in L.A.

Go back to your wife.

Dagmar

FROM: Siyed Prasad
SUBJECT: Re: Holiday in L.A.

Dear Dagmar,

I don't care about my wife. I don't care about anyone but you. I will leave my wife if you desire it. I will leave my family, my country, everything.

Just let us be together. You mean everything to me.

Your desperate,

Siyed

FROM: Dagmar Shaw
SUBJECT: Re: Holiday in L.A.

You don't deserve Manjari. Bugger off. Go away.

Dagmar

Twenty-five million dollars, Dagmar thought.
Numbers like that were as far beyond her under-

standing as the analysis of, for example, continuous tangent vector fields, but still she knew that money like that didn't come from just anywhere.

The money didn't seem to be in anyone's budget. It was possible, she supposed, that Charlie shifted it to the Atreides account from another part of the company, but that sort of thing wouldn't go unnoticed for long.

He had to have gotten it from *somewhere*.

Somebody earned this money, she thought. Either Charlie earned it, or the person who earned it gave it to Charlie. Or someone stole it. Or Charlie stole it.

Money will get you through times of inadequate staffing, Charlie had said, *better than inadequate staffing will get you through times of no money.*

The keys to the kingdom, Charlie had called it. Twice.

Did she want to turn those keys? she wondered. Did she want to find what Charlie was hiding in his kingdom?

Because right at this moment she had somewhere between one million and three million players who could help her.

She leaned back in her office chair and reached blindly for her teacup. She took a drink of the jasmine tea, replaced the cup, swallowed without tasting.

It was past eleven at night, and Dagmar was alone in her office. The aroma of the jasmine tea blended with the scent of the flowers that Siyed continued to send, one new arrival every morning. Every horizontal surface in the untidy office now had its elaborate arrangement, and the flowers weren't dying fast enough to be replaced by the new arrivals, so Dagmar had begun to give the bouquets away. Soft floral scents floated through half the doors in the company, mingling on occasion with the odor of Jack Stone's Frito pies.

Dagmar decided she didn't want to think about the keys to the kingdom for the next, say, six minutes, so she touched the screen and brought up some other work, some of BJ's, and she sat at her desk for the next few minutes and edited it.

She had known BJ was good at plotting, but she hadn't known whether his writing would be adequate for her purposes. He wrote her lively emails, but that didn't mean he had a sense of story or structure. That's why she'd had him creating phony documents, because documents had a structure that would be easier for BJ to follow.

He'd turned out to be more than a satisfactory writer, though he was unfamiliar with the concise style required, and needed editing. Dagmar was relieved. Her instincts in hiring BJ had been correct.

And of course BJ's presence had the potential to really make Charlie insane, which as far as Dagmar was concerned was a bonus, even if—as Dagmar intended—Charlie never found out that BJ had been hired.

Dagmar saved the changes on BJ's work, then touched the screen and brought up the page that had her worried.

She had the number of the Atreides account. She had the time of the electronic fund transfer that had dumped the twenty-five mil into the account. She had the tracking number of the fund transfer itself.

The Long Night of Briana Hall had a financial dimension, the stock swindle that had motivated the murder of one of Briana's ex-boyfriends. The murky financial history behind the killing was part of the game.

Dagmar could put the real numbers into the game, ghosting them in as part of the game's fiction. Real people, players, would then try to find out where the money came from, who the account belonged to, and possibly even how much was in it. Possibly, among the millions of people who had signed up for the game, there would be one person who had the tools, or the access, to find all that out.

The question was whether Dagmar really wanted all that to happen, whether she wanted a look into Charlie's secret world.

Or should she even be bothering with this, with the Latin American currencies in freefall and tens of millions of people's savings having just floated off into the slipstream . . .

Atreides LLC. Named after the House of Atreus, lords of Mycenae, who had torn themselves to bits in a multigenerational fratricide that had involved nephews baked into pies, husbands hacked with axes, Furies pursuing mad children from one futile sanctuary to the next, all the bloody and baroque ways the ancients had of torturing and offing one another . . . that, and the Trojan War, too.

Dagmar was certain that one friend had already died as a result of whatever was going on in Charlie's life. If Dagmar began poking around, was it possible that she might start another round of fratricide?

Might she become a target herself?

Or worse, would Charlie find out and fire her ass from the only job she'd ever really loved?

The truth shall set you free. She wanted the truth, but she didn't want to be free from Great Big Idea.

Keys to the kingdom, she thought.

Austin was dead, and Charlie was going mad, and she didn't know why.

She added the account number and the tracking number, saved the work, and then sent it to Ninja Ned in the Graphics Department to be stegged into a facsimile memo that would appear on a hidden Web page that would only be opened when someone playing *Briana Hall* solved a puzzle.

Puzzles, she decided, were going to fall.

The scent of Siyed's flowers hovered in the air. Dagmar sat on the edge of the desk in her office and looked at the plasma screen on the wall, then down at the speaker-phone that sat on the desk by her right hip. She wore her panama hat as if it carried an alternate personality she could adopt. Adrenaline keened in her nerves, like the scraping of a fiddle.

BJ leaned against the window, and Helmuth lounged in Dagmar's office chair, from which he had just sent out the game's latest update. His index finger lazily moved over the screen, touching buttons—some of them well hidden—that caused newly loaded Web pages to flash on-screen.

Dagmar watched the wall screen, where the same pages paraded one after the other.

There. The document with the bank account, the numbers that were the key to Charlie's secrets.

"Looks like everything loaded," Helmuth said.

If all the pages hadn't gone up at once, confusion and catastrophe could have resulted. But Dagmar's suspense did not diminish as Helmuth spoke. She was in Charlieland now, and the suspense wouldn't go away until she found her way out.

Helmuth began tapping on Dagmar's ten-key pad. More pages leaped into view, each stacked atop the next. A video began playing, Terri Griff as Briana Hall fleeing from the bad guys who had just whacked Cullen.

"Excellent," Helmuth said. "So far all the features are working."

"How many hits are we getting?" Dagmar asked through her dry mouth. She reached for her cup of tea.

Helmuth caressed the screen with his fingers. Data leaped onto the plasma screen. "The page that *you're* most interested in," he said, "has a couple of dozen so far."

Helmuth was wrong: that *wasn't* the page Dagmar was most interested in. But that was fine, too. If the nervousness showed, she had other reasons to be nervous.

"Damn," said BJ. "These people are quick."

"Quick they are," said Dagmar. Laughing. Nervously.

Adrenaline fired a rocket up Dagmar's spine. In a few moments, after players destegged the memo, they would call Briana's best friend, Maria Perry. Who, played by Dagmar, would answer.

They watched the hits increase. Tens of thousands of people had noted the update by now, and the number was increasing exponentially as each informed everyone on his network.

Pages that were hidden by puzzles began to open. Dagmar looked down at the speakerphone.

Which rang, right on cue. It was a dedicated line, so she knew no one but a player was on the other end.

She pressed the answer button.

"Hello?" she said.

"Is this Maria Perry?"

The male voice had a strong accent, Dagmar guessed Korean or Japanese. She wondered if the caller was phoning from Asia.

"This is Maria," Dagmar said. "Who is this?"

"This is . . ." There was a hesitation. Dagmar was familiar with the phenomenon: the player wasn't sure whether to use his own name or his online handle.

"This is Roh," he said finally.

"I don't believe I know you, Roh." Dagmar tried to sound as harassed and paranoid as Maria was by now, the fourth week in which she was serving as the chief line of defense between her friend Briana and the people who wanted to kill or arrest her.

"I want to help Briana," Roh said.

"Briana who?"

"Briana Hall. She is on your Facebook page as your friend."

"Okay," Dagmar said. "So I know Briana. But I still don't know *you*."

"You must give Briana a message."

"What makes you think I know how to reach Briana?"

"She—she says that you are helping her."

"Well," Dagmar said, "if you know her that well, you can give her the message yourself."

There was a moment of panicked silence.

"You sound like a cop," Dagmar said. "You sound like you're trying to trap me."

"I am not a police," said Roh.

"Prove it," said Dagmar.

Again there was silence.

"I'm busy," Dagmar said. "Talk fast."

Silence.

"Nice try, Detective," Dagmar said, and hung up.

BJ looked at her.

"Damn," he said. "You're brutal."

The phone rang an instant later.

"Hello?"

"May I speak to Maria, please?"

Dagmar thought she recognized the voice as an L.A.-based gamer who went by the handle of Hippolyte. And Hippolyte probably recognized Dagmar as well.

TINAG, Dagmar thought. This conversation would only work if both of them stayed in character and ignored the fact that this was a game.

"This is Maria," she said.

"I know you've been a friend of Briana Hall's since you were at Central High," Hippolyte said. "I'd like you to send her a message."

"How do I know," Dagmar said, "that you're not the police trying to trap me?"

"The police don't know about George Weston and his Firebird at the junior prom," Hippolyte said. "Only someone who knew Briana would know something like that."

"Okayyy." Dagmar tried to sound as if she were reluctant to be convinced.

"And then there's your friend David. He's gay, but he hasn't come out to his family or to his boss."

Dagmar tried to sound as if this last data point had made up her mind.

"What message do you need to send?"

"I need Briana to know that Rita is working with the police. Briana can't trust her."

"Rita? Are you sure?"

"She's got her phone bugged by the NYPD. They're just waiting for Briana to call."

"If that's the case," Dagmar said, "then somebody else is going to have to move the package."

"The package with the evidence from Cullen's firm?"

Dagmar grinned at Helmuth and gave him a thumbs-up. Hippolyte was right on top of the story.

Hippolyte had given Maria the three pieces of information necessary for the game to proceed. She had to come up with some persuasive background to convince Maria that she was Briana's friend—the junior prom story was one of several, as were the facts about Maria's friend David—and then the information about Rita and the knowledge of what was in the package.

"That's right," Dagmar said. "The package has been hidden, and there's a letter in the mail telling Rita where to find it. Somebody's got to move it before Rita tells the police."

"Where is it?"

"It's in Grand Army Plaza, on top of the plinth of Gouverneur Warren's statue."

There was a moment of surprise.

"Where's Grand Army Plaza?" Hippolyte asked.

"Brooklyn. Are you anywhere near Brooklyn?"

"Don't worry about that," said Hippolyte. Hippolyte was in Southern California, but there were plenty of other players in the New York area who could be counted on to fetch the package.

"How do you spell *Gouverneur?*" Hippolyte asked.

Dagmar spelled it for her.

"What should be done with the package?" Hippolyte asked.

"Send it to Iris Fitzgerald, General Delivery, West Hollywood, nine zero zero four six."

Which, since Iris Fitzgerald had been established as an alias used by Briana Hall, would serve as a clue to Briana's location.

The incriminating document, stolen by Cullen before his murder, was a list of fifty cities beneath the words "Water Sources," which set up the Charlie-mandated subplot involving the contamination of water sources and the boxes from Tapping the Source. And the page also contained a watermark that hid a clue to something else.

Elsewhere among the uploads was a page that would allow players to order Tapping the Source boxes for free. Great Big Idea, with its twenty-five-million-dollar slush fund, was going to buy the players their toys.

"Have you got that?" Dagmar asked.

"Nine zero zero four six," Hippolyte repeated.

"Thanks," Dagmar said. "You've been a great help."

And then Dagmar stabbed the button to hang up, slid off her desk, and punched the air.

BJ, still leaning on the window, looked up at her. "Do they really do what you tell them to?"

"Yes," Dagmar said. "They do."

The phone rang again, then went to voice mail, a brief message telling any caller that Maria Perry was no longer at this number. Dagmar picked up the phone and turned off its ringer.

Players might be calling this number all day, hundreds or thousands of them, but to no purpose: Hippolyte had scooped them all.

Helmuth, in the meantime, was tapping his keyboard. He was a precise two-finger typist, and the taps and clicks rattled out in a steady rhythm.

He stopped his typing, then leaned away from the screen.

"Okay," he said, "now there's a sound file of your conversation on the archive page. If the player forgets how to spell *Gouverneur,* the recording will remind her."

"That was Hippolyte, I think," Dagmar said.

Helmuth lifted an eyebrow. "Smart girl," he said. He rose, took his leather jacket from the back of Dagmar's chair, and shrugged into it.

"I've got a meeting," he said, "with one of our free-lance programmers who has been fucking up in a truly hideous and original way. Wish us both luck."

"Luck," Dagmar said. Helmuth left.

BJ was looking at the wall screen.

"Is there some way of following the players in real time?" he asked.

"You could count the number of hits. Or you could go on Our Reality Network and watch them work out the puzzles."

He took a step toward Dagmar's computer, then hesitated.

"Can I do that here?" he asked.

"Sure. Be my guest."

BJ sat at Dagmar's computer and reached for the keyboard. Dagmar laid a warning hand over his, then used her other hand to reach for the Shift key and hold it down.

"Go to Our Reality Network," she said.

The browser immediately loaded the ORN's home page.

"There you go," Dagmar said.

He looked up at her. "Thanks," he said.

She stood back, her palm warm from the touch of BJ's hand.

He watched with undivided attention as the players unraveled the latest mysteries. Dagmar sat in the other chair and watched on the wall screen as the players located the hidden files and encrypted messages. It took them about three hours before they'd found all the hidden Web pages, revealed the video and audio files, and arranged for someone in Brooklyn to pick up Cullen's hidden document from Grand Army Plaza.

The only puzzle they hadn't solved was the key to Charlieland. The routing number told them that the twenty-five mil had gone into a Wells Fargo account, but they'd been *given* that.

There was nothing yet about where the money had come *from*.

Frustration beat a tattoo on the inside of Dagmar's skull. She'd risked her job for this, and it wasn't working. She rubbed her eyes.

BJ leaned back in his chair, his eyes still fixed on the screen.

"You know," he said, "I could really enjoy becoming a puppetmaster."

"You already are one," Dagmar said. She rose from her chair, stood on her tiptoes, stretched.

He smiled, watching her. "I'm a last-second, highly spur-of-the-moment PM at best."

"You've been doing very well."

"I just hit a snag, though."

She looked down at him. "Yes?"

"My laptop's down."

"What's wrong with it?"

"I think the fan failed, and then everything cooked." He shook his head. "It's nothing but a doorstop now. But then it was an antiquated piece of junk anyway."

"You have another computer, right?"

"No. My high-powered computer was the one at work, but I quit that job to take this one." He shrugged. "Well, I can afford a hot computer now, thanks to you."

Dagmar thought for a moment. "You don't have to buy one right away," she said. "I'll give you one."

He was startled. "You have a spare?"

"I don't, but the company does." She walked toward the door and gestured for him to follow.

"It's time," she said, "to visit the assassin."

He raised his eyebrows. "Not the Russian one?"

Suddenly the situation wasn't amusing.

"No," she said curtly. "We have an assassin of our own."

He then rose heavily from his chair.

"Sure," he said. "Sounds like . . ." He hesitated. "Fun," he said.

AvN Soft's network security guy worked out of the fifth floor and basked in his nickname of Richard the Assassin. The name was actually on his desk nameplate. He was a young olive-skinned man in his early twenties who favored black jeans and T-shirts, which he wore with white Converse sneakers. Action figures of ninjas lined his top rank of shelves. He was relentless in guarding the security of AvN Soft from spam, malware, intruders, and people like Joe Clever.

Richard had a personal grudge against Joe Clever, who had actually breached his security on two occasions, and he swore that the next time Clever came calling, he'd flood Clever's machine with a program that would do nothing but load thousands of pop-ups from fifth-rate Singapore porn sites, the kind with businesslike, thick-bodied hookers performing listless acts in badly lit rooms.

Richard checked out a laptop to BJ, gave him a temporary password, made certain he could access the office net, and packed the computer in a green cardboard box with a plastic carrying handle. He told BJ never to use the password on a Wi-Fi connection, even on a private network, and handed BJ an Ethernet connector.

"This is your best friend," he said.

BJ looked at the cable with a bemused expression.

"Hello, best friend," he said.

"You're friend's paranoia is really impressive," BJ told Dagmar as they left.

"Remind me to tell you about Joe Clever," Dagmar said.

BJ headed for the elevators, but Dagmar checked him. "This way," she said.

"Where are we going?"

"Accounting."

At Accounting, Dagmar arranged for BJ to be air-expressed the latest office suite compatible with everything used at AvN Soft. Word processor, spreadsheet, browser, presentation software, video and audio editors, Web page builder, SFTP ware, templates for standardized business forms, a miniaturized research library on disk, a word processor that offered film and TV script format—even interest-rate calculators and software used for making investments and planning retirement. Thousands of dollars' worth of software altogether, all to be delivered to BJ's apartment the next day courtesy of Federal Express.

"Uhh, thanks," said BJ, a little stunned.

"Might as well get the total upgrade. We're spending Charlie's money like water, anyway."

BJ tweaked a little smile. "I'm all for doing *that*."

They went to the elevators, and Dagmar pushed the down button.

BJ turned to her. "So tell me about Joe Clever."

A brief outline of Joe Clever's infamous career lasted them the length of the elevator journey and the return to Dagmar's office.

"You see anyone following you home," Dagmar said, "it's probably Joe Clever, or one of the other stalkers." She looked at him. "In fact, you're a prime target. You're new to the game, and he might think you'd be careless with a computer or with documents."

BJ looked at his computer in its cardboard box. "I'll be prudent, then."

"That would be good."

He looked at her. "Doing anything for dinner tonight?"

"I'll be working late and grabbing a salad in the coffee shop."

He shrugged. "Too bad. With my computer slagged and my software not arriving till tomorrow, I've got a free evening."

"That means more work for me, unfortunately."

"I suppose it does."

She hugged him good-bye and suppressed an urge to kiss his cheek.

It wasn't as if the last work-related romance had worked out very well.

And she could hardly consider it a good idea to have a boyfriend who made her boss crazy. Or vice versa.

She drifted to the window and watched BJ cross the parking lot and put the computer in his old Chevy.

It probably hadn't been such a good idea to bring BJ into Charlieland.

But what choice, she reflected, had Charlie really given her?

A software suite and the loan of a computer were probably the least she could do in compensation.

CHAPTER TWENTY

This Is Not a Tale

FROM: Vikram

It took me a couple days, but I've been able to discover that the twenty-five million was transmitted from the United Bank of Cayman, from an account owned by a company called Forlorn Hope Ltd.

In the incorporation pages, the officers of Forlorn Hope include Charles Ruff of Los Angeles, California, and Anthony and Marcia Ruff of Grosse Pointe, Michigan, all in the USA.

The balance of the account, as of 1600 hours Cayman time yesterday, was $12,344,946,873.23, all in US dollars.

FROM: Corporal Carrot

How much???

FROM: Chatsworth Osborne Jr.

May I ask how you acquired this information, Vikram?

FROM: Vikram

I don't want to say much here, for obvious reasons, but I'm from the Indian subcontinent and I come from a family connected with a merchant bank.

Everyone in the world is six degrees of separation from everyone else, but I only needed to go through two degrees to acquire this information.

FROM: Corporal Carrot

You're with a merchant bank? Like the United Bank of Cayman?

FROM: Vikram

Well, no. I'm not connected with that institution. And I didn't say that I was with *any* bank, just that members of my family are.

FROM: Corporal Carrot

You're just connected, period.

You know, I figured it would be Chatty who'd bust this one.

FROM: Chatsworth Osborne Jr.

Corporal Carrot overestimates my powers.

But still, I find this interesting in terms of the game. Charles Ruff owns Great Big Idea and what <u>his Wikipedia profile</u> states is a profitable software company. I assume the other two corporate officers are his parents or other relations.

In addition to the late Austin Katanyan, that's three more real, living people who have appeared in *Motel Room Blues*. What are we to make of this?

As I don't believe that Mr. Ruff, wealthy as he may be, actually has twelve billion dollars lying around *in cash,* I also wondered how he managed to insert that figure in his bank balance, such that Vikram was able to discover it. How are we to read *that?*

Or is it that we really weren't intended to backtrack the money transfer, just to accept that it was part of whatever scheme Cullen's traders were up to?

But in that case, why the deception over the twelve billion?

It doesn't entirely add up.

It doesn't entirely add up, Dagmar read.
No, she thought, it didn't.

Because *she* knew, unlike the gamers, that the figure in the Forlorn Hope account was real.

And she also knew that there was no way that Charlie, successful as he was, could have made that kind of money legally.

She reached blindly for her cup of tea, drank, replaced the tea on its St. Pauli Girl coaster.

Across her office, a leaf fell from one of Siyed's bouquets.

Her sense of scale was completely wrong where Charlie was concerned. He was *huge*. He was like the Medellin cartel, like the Burmese junta, like the smiling president of oil-rich Nigeria with his Swiss accounts and white cotton-lined cardboard boxes full of blood diamonds.

Charlie's Godzilla-size footprints ought to be all over the world.

And the fact that they weren't—the fact that Charlie was masquerading as a modest software entrepreneur in the San Fernando Valley—meant that Charlie had left the real world altogether and now lived somewhere in supervillain territory. He was Magneto. He was Lex Luthor. He was Doctor Doom.

He was the Napoleon of Crime.

When the hell had Charlie found time to develop this secret life? Certainly not in the years since Dagmar had begun working for him. She'd seen him nearly every day, and she'd never once seen him meeting with the Brotherhood of Evil Mutants.

Probably the meetings took place in his secret base in a dormant volcano.

Was even the Russian Maffya worth twelve billion? In *cash?* Dagmar doubted it.

Unless, of course, Charlie *owned* the Russian Maffya. Given what she'd just discovered, she wouldn't put it past him.

FROM: Dagmar Shaw
SUBJECT: Meeting

Charlie, I've got to see you. Are you still at the Roosevelt?

There was no answer to the email. Repeated phone calls were answered only by voice mail. Dagmar left a series of messages and then in her frustration drove down the 101 to Hollywood. She banged on the cabana door, which was opened by a fat, middle-aged man wearing nothing but a towel. He smelled strongly of cigars, and behind him were a pair of Hollywood rent-boys who gazed at Dagmar from over his hairy shoulders. Dagmar apologized and shuffled away.

Fucking Charlie, she thought.

She had to talk to somebody or she would explode. She called BJ and suggested they meet for dinner.

"Are you in the valley?" he asked.

"I'm in Hollywood."

"I know a little place on Olympic near Koreatown. Want to check it out?"

When she got in her car, she unholstered her phone and prodded the icon for email. Charlie's name leaped off the list. She retrieved the email and narrowed her eyes as she peered at the small screen.

FROM: Charlie Ruff
SUBJECT: Re: Meeting

Damn right we've got to meet. But I'm in Chicago right now and won't be back for a couple days.

I've got some ideas for the game. Don't worry, nobody buys anything this time.

"Damn you, Charlie!" Dagmar shouted.

A pair of tourists walking past gave her a quick glance, then just as quickly turned away.

Dagmar decided she didn't care if they thought she was crazy, and pounded the steering wheel with her fists until her phalanges felt they'd been slammed by a crowbar. She slumped in her seat, breathless.

Suddenly she missed Austin very much.

There was a burning in the back of her sinus. She dabbed tears away with the back of her wrist.

She hadn't had time to mourn him. Everything since Austin's death had been constant movement, dreadful pressure, frantic improvisation. All tangled up, one way or another, with *The Long Night of Briana Hall* and the decision to use the game to solve real-world problems.

That had been her decision, she realized. She'd pressed Charlie to permit it.

She realized, as she searched for a tissue to wipe away the tears, that she was as crazy as he was.

*

BJ's restaurant turned out to specialize in egg dishes. It was the kind of place that would serve you breakfast eighteen hours out of twenty-four.

"Be sure to order the candied pepper bacon," BJ advised.

"Candied pepper bacon," Dagmar repeated.

"Sounds weird, but it's good. Try it."

She ordered an omelette with an English muffin and the candied pepper bacon. BJ ordered corned beef hash with poached eggs on top.

The restaurant had about twelve different kinds of iced tea, and Dagmar asked which one of them had caffeine. The waiter just stared at her, as if no one had ever asked about caffeine before.

No caffeine, she thought. *Check.*

"Never mind," she said. "I'll have the French press."

The waiter had barely gone to place their order when Dagmar exploded.

"Fucking Charlie," she said, "has sent me an email telling me he's going to screw with the game again. But he hasn't told me how or why or when, and now I'm going crazy."

BJ looked at her intently through his spectacles. He had arrived in worn blue jeans and a T-shirt so old that its original blue had turned to purple. He hadn't shaved in several days.

He smelled of lavender soap. That was nice.

"What did Charlie say, exactly?" BJ said.

"Hardly anything, just that he had another idea. That's what's making me nuts." She waved her hands. "We may as well stop working. We're going to have to change it all anyway."

BJ gave a shrug. "All I can say is that he's behaving true to form."

"I went to his cabana at the Roosevelt and found he'd left. He's gone to Chicago!"

Surprise passed across BJ's features. "Chicago? Did he say why?"

"No."

He rubbed his chin. "Do you think he's still hiding from the Maffya?"

"I don't know what to think!"

Dagmar wished she still had the steering wheel in front of her so that she could punch it again.

BJ pursed his lips, looked thoughtful. "Do you think he's testing you?"

Dagmar blinked at him. "Why would he do that?"

"To find out if you're—I don't know—really loyal?"

Dagmar considered this.

"That doesn't make much sense," she said. "I've never had any tension with him till now. He has no reason to think me anything other than a loyal employee." Frustration bubbled in her veins. "He *picked* me, for God's sake!"

"He's under pressure now. His backers, or the Russian Maffya, or whoever it is that's giving him trouble—he can't lash out at *them*. It's got to be the people around him."

She looked at him curiously. "Did he do that to you?" she asked.

BJ shrugged his big shoulders. "Now and then," he said. "Little ways, mostly. He'd demand that I abandon my own ideas and adopt his, that sort of thing. It made no sense, but it was his way of controlling things, and early on I agreed with him against my better judgment. It was when I began to stand up to him that he decided I was disloyal, and then he barely spoke to me."

"It's got me so *crazy*." She made claws of her hands and rent the air with her nails.

"Well," BJ said, "I wish I could help."

"You *are* helping," she said. She put her hand over his. "You're the only person I can talk to."

His blue eyes looked into hers. "It's the same with me," he said.

The waiter arrived with their drinks, iced tea for BJ and the French press for Dagmar. She reached for the pot and pushed the plunger down, then poured.

"Not bad," she judged.

This much coffee this late, she knew, she'd be up to 3 A.M.

Not that she didn't have plenty of work to do.

She looked at BJ. "Something I've always wondered," she said.

He raised his eyebrows. "About Charlie?"

"About you."

A dubious look crossed his face.

"If you don't mind," Dagmar said.

He spread his big hands. "Ask, if you want."

"You went down with AvN Soft, okay," Dagmar said. "But you were still smart. You still had talent. You had experience."

He nodded.

"What you want to know," he said, "is how I ended up at a place like Spud LLC?"

"At the very least," she said, "you could be working as a programmer, earning a lot more money than doing customer service."

"I hate to say this," BJ said, "because it sounds paranoid. But I got blackballed."

Dagmar was surprised. "By whom?"

"Charlie and his friends. Austin in particular." Before Dagmar could protest, BJ held up a hand.

"When Austin moved back to California," BJ said, "I went to him to start a new company. My idea involved creating a peer-to-peer network for cell phones, so they wouldn't depend so completely on cell phone towers." He leaned toward her across the table. "When Hurricane Katrina hit," he said, "the cell phone towers in New Orleans went down. People couldn't call out. Maybe thousands died because they couldn't tell emergency services where they were. If the phones had been connected with a peer-to-peer network, so that they could talk directly to each other instead of to a tower, the messages could have chained together until they reached an intact tower."

Dagmar was impressed. "That's a great idea."

"It would be ideal in any emergency situation— California's natural for it, because of the earthquakes. So I went to Austin with the idea of developing it."

"He turned you down?"

"No. What Austin did was try to saddle me with a partner to handle the business end. He insisted I had to follow the guy's orders whenever it came to a business decision."

Dagmar remembered Austin on the phone to his

client, insisting that the business plan be followed. *Dude, we've* had *this conversation.*

"What did you do?" she asked.

Anger burned in BJ's eyes. "I turned Austin down. I wasn't going to have some stranger telling me what to do." He spread his hands in a gesture of helplessness. "But then whenever I went to some other venture capitalist, it turned out he had the same stipulation. Turns out that Charlie or Austin had been there ahead of me, telling everyone the official version of how AvN Soft went down, and everyone believed them instead of me."

"Come on," Dagmar said. "I can't see them calling everyone in the industry just to get back at you."

"Believe it how you want," BJ said. There was belligerence in his tone. "I'm just telling you what happened."

Dagmar decided to skate away to another subject.

"But why Spud, then?" she asked. "There must be a thousand better jobs."

BJ gave a bitter little laugh and took a sip of his iced tea.

"I decided that rather than take a crap job, I'd take a shit job."

Dagmar found herself laughing.

"Perhaps," she said, "you'd better make that distinction clearer."

He scratched his chin. "Okay," he said. "When you know a job is shit going in, then it's a shit job. It's *honest* about being a shit job. That was my job at Spud."

"Okay," Dagmar said.

"But a crap job is a shit job with *pretensions.* You get

paid more, maybe, but it's only because you have to work twelve-hour days in a cubicle doing work that's beyond tedious, all with fuck-wit managers on your case every minute of the day. Crap jobs aren't for bright people, they're for Dilberts. And I'm not a Dilbert."

Dagmar looked at him and shook her head.

"No," she said, "you're not."

Their dinner arrived. Dagmar's omelette was fluffy and moist, and her home fries had a surprising, delightful herbal taste.

"These are the best home fries I've ever had," she said.

BJ grinned. "There was a reason I recommended this place."

She tried the candied pepper bacon. It was very good.

"I didn't think you could improve *bacon*," she said.

"Told you it was good."

They talked about jobs through their meal, trying to distinguish shit jobs from crap jobs. BJ had endured many worse jobs than the one at Spud. Dagmar had experienced plenty of both, working as a teenager in Cleveland, where she had dealt in addition with the hazard of a father who would steal her money and valuables.

"And in England?" BJ asked. "You worked there?"

"Under the table," she said, "because of immigration. But then I started selling stories, and that was very nice. The best job I've ever had."

"I imagine it would be." He tilted his head. "And—Aubrey, was that his name? How did he feel about the writing?"

"He was proud of me."

BJ nodded. "But the marriage still didn't work."

She looked at him. "I married him on the rebound. Never a good idea."

BJ held her gaze for a moment, then looked away. "Seeing anyone now?"

Dagmar tried to work out a way of explaining how she had been Promiscuous Girl back in England, and that while her morals hadn't improved since, her work hours had increased and so her flings were few and far between. She gave up.

"I'm celibate on account of a seventy-hour work-week," she said.

"Typical geek," he said. "A geek with a crap job and a crap boss."

"I'm being paid very well for all those hours," Dagmar pointed out.

"You're being paid well to burn yourself out, after which the money and the job will disappear and you'll be in your late thirties with no current job skills. That's the very definition of a crap job."

Dagmar smiled thinly. "Can we get back to our love lives? Sad to admit, that's the less depressing subject."

"It's like moving from the Valley of the Shadow of Death to the Slough of Despond, but—whatever." BJ gave a self-conscious smile. "I'm celibate on account of poverty," he said. "The only women who want me are crazy, or single parents who need a father and a second income for their kids."

"You don't want to be a father?"

"What I don't want," he said, "is to be a stepfather in a trailer court with a swarm of underdisciplined children and no money."

She nodded. "Yeah. That's understandable."

He looked at her, then shrugged and smiled.

"We're pathetic," he said, "but at least we're not in Chile."

A cold finger brushed her spine. She looked up at him in shock.

"What happened in Chile?" she asked.

"Didn't you hear? Their currency collapsed today— the Chinese traders again, supposedly. All of South America is on the edge of a depression worse than anything since the nineteen thirties."

Dagmar sucked in breath. Her mind spun. BJ talked on.

"They say the Chinese are taking out their competition, one currency at a time. It makes sense—Indonesia's got a huge population, and so does Latin America. These are all people who work for coolie wages, just like the Chinese. From the Chinese point of view, it's best to keep their economies from ever developing."

Dagmar thought about that, spoke slowly. "So you think it's Chinese government policy?"

BJ shrugged. "Their government can be ruthless, and they're smart and calculating. We know that."

Images of Jakarta flashed in Dagmar's mind—the mobs, the police shooting, the tiny bodies strewn on the pavement. The pillar of smoke over Glodok.

"But," she said, "if Latin Americans are really desperate, they'll work for less money than the Chinese."

"Not if the employers don't have the resources to pay wages in real money." BJ narrowed his eyes in thought. "Investment will eventually come in, though, right? From other countries. But the country might be China—using the Latin Americans' own wealth to buy their own factories. It's a win-win for the Chinese."

Dagmar decided to change the subject before she lost herself entirely in the nightmare. She gave BJ a wan smile.

"You crashed an economy once, right?" she said.

He looked at her in surprise. "Sorry?"

"Austin told me that you and Charlie crashed *Lost Empire*."

"Oh." He gave a grin. "Yeah, we did that."

"On purpose?" BJ and Charlie had never been destructive hackers.

"No, it was an accident." He sipped his iced tea. "When we were shopping AvN Soft around, we both got involved with the game. We spent fourteen hours a day bashing wizards and fighting monsters and stealing treasure. But when the first of the venture capital came in, we had to drop the game and build a real business."

"So you crashed *Lost Empire* because you couldn't play anymore?"

"No." He gave a little laugh. "It's kind of embarrassing, what we did, actually. We were so freaking young."

"Go ahead."

BJ ran a hand through his shaggy blond hair.

"Okay," he said. "We cashed in all our armor and weapons and magic stuff for the virtual gold pieces they used in the game, and then we put a couple of our software agents to work. We programmed them to make money, so that when we had time to get back to *Lost Empire*, we'd still be in the game, and with luck in a better position than when we left."

"You had the software agents play *you?*"

"Play our characters, yeah. They had our passwords and just stayed logged on twenty-four/seven, buying and selling. It wasn't hard, if our characters weren't moving around, just buying stuff in the market in the Old Imperial City, which was basically the market for the whole world. We were, like, testing our work. Doing a proof-of-concept. And the thing worked out—in four weeks Rialto had *Lost Empire* on its knees. Between the two of us, we had monopolies in lumber mills, flour mills, the woods and fields the lumber and the flour came from, all the mines that produced iron, gems, gold, silver, and copper. We owned all the warehouses. If anyone else competed with us, we'd undersell them and drive them out of business, then buy whatever was left and jack the price up. That way we ended up with all the cash, too. The only thing we couldn't control was the magic items, because the game produced those on a schedule, or randomly."

"By 'we,' you mean the agents."

"The software, yeah. And *Lost Empire* came to a screeching halt. The game masters had to shut everything down, and they confiscated all our property and gave the players a bunch of free game gold to make up for being ripped off." He laughed. "God, we were *infamous*. But they didn't know our real names, just our online identities. Otherwise we might have gotten our asses sued off."

A cold ice-water thought drenched Dagmar's brain.

"Is that what the Chinese are doing?" she asked. "In the real world?"

"Using software agents?"

"Yeah."

BJ shook his head. "*Lost Empire* basically had only a couple of dozen tradeable commodities, that and armor and weapons and magic stuff. The real world has fifty million times as much complexity, and real-world economies have more mechanisms for correcting themselves." He grinned. "Believe me, Charlie and I discussed this. We had all sorts of fantasies about conquering the real world the same way we conquered *Lost Empire*." He shrugged. "But you know how the agents we unleashed on the real-world markets turned out. They're good, they're making money for Charlie and everyone who rents one . . ." He laughed. "Nobody owns the planet yet."

"Guess not."

Twelve point three billion, she thought. But even that wasn't enough to bring down a large, diverse, robust economy like that of Chile.

Chad, maybe.

Something else was going on.

She thanked BJ for listening, paid for both meals, and took the 101 back to the valley. She worked past ten o'clock, at which point the thought of a swim in her apartment's pool began to creep softly into her mind. Doing laps in the pool alone in the night, as she'd done in Indonesia. She began to think of the weightlessness, the water caressing her skin, the silence. The eerie glow of the underwater floodlight.

Eventually she couldn't concentrate on work any longer and drove home.

She parked in front of the ginkgo trees in the parking lot. As she got out of the Prius, the scent of the rotting fruit stung her nostrils, a disgusting combination of vomit and semen that was like a fraternity the morning after the homecoming party, and she stepped away from the smell. She walked to the iron apartment gate and prepared to give the lock her thumbprint. A shadow moved quickly toward her from the darkness between a pair of SUVs, and Dagmar's nerves gave a shriek.

She tried to get her heart under control and briefly considered flight—no, she realized, he'd probably catch her. If she tried to open the gate, he could pin her against the iron bars. And so—adrenaline booming in her ears like kettledrums—she hastily adjusted her car keys in her hand so the keys were protruding from between her fingers, improvised brass knuckles.

Her reactions had improved since Jakarta. If this guy tried to attack her, she was going to do her level best to fuck him up.

Unless, of course, he was a Russian assassin with a gun, in which case she would die.

The man stepped into the light, and Dagmar saw it was Siyed.

"Shit!" she said. "You scared the piss out of me!"

"I had to see you, love," Siyed said. His pupils had shrunk to pinpricks in the floodlights. "Dagmar," he said, "you're all I can think about."

"Are you *stalking* me now?" she demanded. "Go home!" She pointed at the street and talked to him as if he were an overaffectionate dog. "Go home!"

"I can't!" Siyed staggered toward her. He was a tiny man, only two or three inches over five feet. Once Dagmar had enjoyed the lightness of his frame, the delicacy of his hands and wrists, but now she just wanted to throw him across the parking lot. He wore chinos and a white cotton shirt, and in the glare of the floodlights his dark eyelashes were black commas drawn above and below his eyes.

Her grip on her keys loosened. She couldn't be afraid of a man shorter than she, even if he *was* barking mad.

"Dagmar, I love you!" he croaked. "I only want to be with you. You're like night and day and moon and sun—"

She interrupted before she could become any more cosmic than he had already made her.

"Siyed," she said, "you're fucking married! Go back to your wife!"

"I can't!" he said again. He blinked up at her. "Oh my God," he said. "You're so dazzling."

He fumbled for her hand. She pulled away from him. The stink of the rotting ginkgo fruit lay in the back of her throat like a coating of phlegm that she couldn't hawk out.

"Go home!" she said again. And then, more gently: "This is *California*. You can get *arrested* for this kind of behavior."

"I can't go home." Siyed's eyes suddenly filled with tears. "I told Manjari about us. I told her we were in love!"

"We're *not!*" Dagmar cried. Out of sheer frustration she waved her fist, and Siyed jumped back at the glint of the keys in her hand.

"There's no obstacle now, love!" Siyed said quickly. "We can be together. I've got it all arranged . . ."

"Did you think to *ask* me about these goddam arrangements first, whatever they are?" she demanded.

"Did you think to *ask* me whether you should tell your wife anything about me?"

"I did it for you!" Siyed said. Tears spilled down his face. "It's all for the two of us!"

Dagmar turned from him and jabbed at the gate with her thumb.

"I see you around here again, motherfucker," she said, "I'm having you arrested!"

"But Dagmar . . ." he moaned.

Dagmar swung the creaking iron gate open, then shut. Siyed stepped close to the gate, and the shadow of the bars fell across his face.

"Dagmar!" he cried.

"Go away!"

She stalked toward the stairs, then up and to her apartment, where she had to restrain herself from slamming the door behind her and waking any of the neighbors who hadn't already been roused by all the shouting.

She didn't turn on the lights. Instead she went to the window over the sink and looked out to see if Siyed was still in the parking lot.

He was gone, at least from the patch of asphalt she could see through the gate.

He could still be skulking outside her view, though. For a moment she fantasized about calling the cops, and then decided she was too tired to wrangle with Siyed *and* the police.

Dagmar's gaze shifted to the pool, glowing Cherenkov blue down in the courtyard, and she felt her energy level subside, swirling into emptiness like the pool draining away.

She wanted to use the pool, but she didn't want to give Siyed the pleasure of watching her swim, assuming that he was still lurking around.

Goddam it.

Instead of swimming, she opened the refrigerator, and in its light she ate half an eggroll that was left over from a take-out Chinese meal two nights before. The cold grease was rancid on her tongue.

Then, still creeping like a bewildered ninja around her own apartment, she brushed her teeth, washed her face, and went to bed.

In the middle of the night she woke up with a sudden understanding of everything that had happened.

BJ was wrong, she thought. *And Charlie is riding a tiger.*

Poor man, she thought. *He can't get off.*

And then: *None of us can.*

CHAPTER TWENTY-ONE

This Is Not a Refuge

Dagmar knew what was going on, but she couldn't do anything about it. Not now, perhaps not ever.

And furthermore, she was trapped in her ordinary life. The next day was Saturday—for Great Big Idea a work-day, with *Briana Hall* scheduled for another update, complete with a live event in London that would begin at 8 A.M. California time. Dagmar was in her office by seven, gulping coffee and digging through Siyed's employment records from *Curse of the Golden Nagi*.

She found that she wanted to clear herself with Manjari. She didn't want to come clean, exactly —if she could manage this without having to admit that she'd actually been to bed with Siyed, that would be fine with her—but she wanted Manjari to know that, despite what Siyed had told her over the phone, she wanted no part of him now, that whatever romantic fantasies Siyed was spinning were entirely a product of his own unhinged imagination.

It occurred to Dagmar that Manjari might well be

skeptical of whatever claims her husband's lover might make.

I don't want him. Please take him back.

Was that convincing or not? But why *wouldn't* it be convincing?

She didn't *want* Manjari's husband, right? Why wouldn't Manjari believe that?

Dagmar decided she was getting paranoid.

None too soon, whispered an internal voice.

But if she didn't have some way to get ahold of Manjari, Dagmar wouldn't have a chance to say anything. And Siyed's file was not very forthcoming where his London family was concerned.

The file had Siyed's email address. His cell phone number. The different number that he'd been assigned when he was in the States and given one of Great Big Idea's cell phones. His street address in London. And the name and phone number of his London agent. But Dagmar didn't want to talk to Siyed or his agent; she wanted to talk to Manjari, and the file didn't offer Siyed's home phone number, where Manjari might reasonably be expected to pick up.

Dagmar cursed under her breath and then remembered that she lived in the twenty-first century. Within seconds, her computer displayed a London telephone directory, with the Prasads' phone number.

She looked at the number, took a swig of coffee, and wished the coffee was something stronger.

Call now, she thought. *Before you lose your nerve.*

She reached for her handheld; then—hearing voices in the hall outside—she closed her office door and locked it.

Dagmar returned to her office chair, began to punch in Manjari's number, then stopped to wonder just what the hell she was going to say.

She had no damn idea.

Dagmar erased the number from the display, stared at the phone's screen for a moment, then reached for a pen and paper and began to jot down talking points. She was happiest when following a script, preferably of her own devising.

Not my fault! she wrote, and underlined the words. Which was stretching the truth a bit, but Dagmar felt it was a positive start.

She stared at the paper for a long moment, then underlined *Not my fault!* a second time.

A few minutes later, the list read as follows.

I'm not involved with S.
S. has invented this fantasy about me
Please call S. and tell him to come home
Not my fault!

She looked at the list for a moment, then decided the four points pretty much covered everything she intended to say. She punched in Manjari's number, then hit Send.

Her heart rapped a quick rhythm as she raised the phone to her ear.

"Hello?"

The voice seemed strangely normal. Dagmar had expected an angry voice, or a tearful voice, or a snappish voice. Anything but this sunny-afternoon-in-London voice.

"Is this Manjari?" Dagmar asked.

"Yes. Who is this?"

Dagmar cast a desperate look at her list and spoke. "This is Dagmar."

There was a moment's pause, one that lasted a beat longer than the satellite lag, and then: "I'm sorry?"

"Dagmar Sh-shaw," she said, annoyed at her sudden nervous stammer. "From Los Angeles."

"Oh," Manjari said. "Dagmar, of course."

Of course, Dagmar thought in fury. *The woman who slept with your husband.*

There was an expectant pause. Dagmar gave another glance at her list and spoke.

"I wanted to say," she said, "that whatever Siyed told you about me, it isn't true."

Dagmar's heart beat four times in the ensuing pause.

"I'm sorry. What did he say, exactly?"

The tone of Manjari's reply, the genuine puzzlement, clued Dagmar to the actual situation. Which was that Siyed—already a proven liar—had lied again.

He *hadn't* told Manjari he was involved with Dagmar. He hadn't told his wife that he was leaving her. He had just told Dagmar that as a ploy to win her over.

It was Dagmar, just now, who had told Manjari that something was badly wrong.

Dagmar's mind thrashed for an escape route.

"All right," she said quickly. "Obviously we've had a miscommunication."

"Yes?" Manjari said. "Are you in London?"

"No," Dagmar said. "I'm in L.A. But I need to tell you . . ." Her mind spun like a broken clutch. "I think Siyed is having some kind of breakdown out here. I think it's . . ." Imagination failed her. "It's just Hollywood," she finished lamely. "It happens."

"Is he in hospital?" Manjari asked. For the first time there was urgency in her voice.

"No. But he turned up last night, and he said some things—he was irrational."

"What sort of things did he say?"

"I . . . I don't remember, really. It doesn't matter." She tried to put as much kindness into her words as possible. "You should call Siyed and tell him to come home. All right?"

"Tell him to come home," Manjari repeated.

"Yes," Dagmar said, and then a piece of maliciousness entered her mind.

"Tell him that I told you to call," she said.

"I . . ." Manjari seemed bewildered. "I'll call him."

Dagmar reached for the piece of paper with her talking points, crumpled it, and tossed it in the wastebasket.

"I'm sorry to bother you," she said. "But I think it's best."

Dagmar unlocked her office door and propped it open. The suspense and panic and determination that had filled her during the phone call had drained away, and she felt strangely hollow.

She thought about Siyed flying away on a big silver plane. Crossing paths with Charlie, flying in.

Charlie. How could she tell Charlie that she knew what he was up to?

Members of the Great Big Idea technical staff passed

by, ready for the game update. Soon—four o'clock in London—players would be assembling beneath the shadow of the old Gothic pile of Lincoln's Inn. Streaming video, taken by a freelance crew frequently employed by Great Big Idea, already showed several dozen people gathered in an expectant crowd. Each held a silver DVD in a transparent jewel case, a sign that they were part of the game.

The barristers of Lincoln's Inn, who might normally resent a crowd on their doorstep, were presumably spending their Saturday afternoon at home.

Dagmar moved into the big conference room for the update and found it full of laptops and cables. Siyed's flowers drooped and sagged everywhere. Her mantra glowed on one wall monitor.

> *Read the Schedule*
> *Know the Schedule*
> *Love the Schedule*

BJ wandered in, holding a twenty-four-ounce foam cup of coffee, and hugged Dagmar hello. Dagmar realized that BJ had shaved off his muttonchops, leaving only the modest mustache he'd worn as long as she'd known him. The change, she thought, made him look younger.

"Congratulate me," he said. "I think I've got a new job."

Dagmar looked at him in surprise. Hesitation tripped her tongue before she could offer congratulations.

"Don't worry," he said, anticipating her. "I won't start the new job till we finish *Briana Hall*."

Dagmar brightened. "Good news, then," she said. "Where will you be working?"

BJ grinned, then hesitated. "I don't think I should actually say."

"Can you tell me," Dagmar asked, "if it's a crap job or a shit job?"

BJ laughed. "Neither. It's a *real* job. A total, stone opportunity."

"Well." Dagmar reached up a hand and touched his newly shaven cheek. "I'm guessing that whoever they are, they have a hair policy."

He laughed again.

"No," he said. "I just figured I should try to blend in with the other tycoons."

She looked at him. "Tycoons, huh?"

He gave a lazy shrug.

"We'll see," he said. "Yeah."

"All right," she said. "Be mysterious if you want to."

Dagmar and the others watched the live feed. At four o'clock London time, a car drew up to Lincoln's Inn, and Anne stepped out, followed by jerking camera crews. Anne was a sweet-voiced, petite English Rose who headed Great Big Idea's small office in London and from there ran all European live events.

To anyone who flashed her a DVD, Anne handed a sheet of xeroxed paper containing clues. The first of these, when properly decoded, sent players southwest across the pleasant green of Lincoln's Inn Fields, where they would encounter a man with a sign that said "Free Time Travel."

When a player approached this man, she would be

given a headset that was cabled to a high-powered laptop computer. The headset featured a screen that would drop down over the right eye. When the player moved her head in the correct direction, her left eye would show her the sights of a Holborn Saturday afternoon while the screen would show a different image, a scene from the "past"—the fictional past of *The Long Night of Briana Hall*.

The scene showed Vlatko, the amoral mercenary who was assisting the terrorists, meeting one of his contacts in London.

Cameras wandered along with the crowd, broadcasting the event live to anyone who cared to watch.

When a player had seen Vlatko and had a chance to identify the contact, the player would follow the next clue north to Red Lion Square, where another vendor would offer another headset and another free trip into the past, a trip that would reveal another of Vlatko's contacts.

And from thence to Gray's Inn Gardens, and from there to New Square, again under the shadow of Lincoln's Inn, on each occasion learning the identity of one of Vlatko's associates. At the end of the journey, the players would know all of Vlatko's London network and begin to follow their tracks and dissect the attackers' plot.

Which would culminate next Saturday, when the players would deploy the Tapping the Source scanners in fifty cities across the world.

So far, Great Big Idea had spent more than two and a half million dollars of Charlie's money shipping nearly sixty-five thousand scanners to players all over the world. Several thousand more dollars had been spent paying for extra warehouse help to make sure that the scanners were shipped on time, an act of generosity that had left the management reeling at Tapping the Source.

The Long Night of Briana Hall was probably going to be the least profitable online game in history. Not that Dagmar much cared—if it ran overbudget, that was all the fault of her boss.

Who, it had to be admitted, seemed to have plenty of extra money anyway.

Dagmar waited for the update that followed the live event—new pages going online with the information that the players had discovered in London, each page loaded with new puzzles that would keep the players busy for, at least, hours.

Or, if they were slipping, days.

Helmuth and his staff were focused on their displays, hands tapping. BJ and Dagmar looked over their shoulders.

"Harlem Nocturne" floated from her handset. Dagmar looked at the screen, saw Charlie's name, and answered.

"How's the update going?" Charlie asked.

"We're in the middle of it." *You bastard.* "No problems so far." *You selfish, treacherous bastard.*

"I'm back in L.A. We need to meet."

"Damn right we need to meet," Dagmar said. She was aware of BJ's mild gaze, ten feet away.

BJ raised his coffee cup, sipped.

"I'm at the Figueroa Hotel," Charlie said. "Medina Suite."

"Hotel Figueroa? That's *on* Figueroa, right?"

"Yeah."

"Downtown's a freakin' desert. Why are you there?"

"It's next to the Staples Center. Maybe I want to catch a game."

"Heh. Yeah. Right."

"Can you make it down as soon as the update's finished?"

"Yeah. I was going to do a laundry, but I guess I can go on wearing stinky clothes for another day."

"See you."

She reholstered her phone and looked at BJ's expectant face.

"The master calls?" he asked.

She nodded.

He nodded. "Good luck."

A few minutes later, Helmuth hit Enter one last time, peered at the screen, then pushed his chair back from the table.

"Update's finished," he said. "All the pages are up, and all the video files from London are archived for anyone who wants to watch them."

"Go home, then," Dagmar told him.

Helmuth yanked the cord from his laptop and closed the computer's display, then stood. He looked at the wall clock.

"I've got time for a nap before my haircut," he said.

"You *sleep?*"

Helmuth smiled. "Only on weekend afternoons," he said.

As Helmuth made his way out, BJ stood, crumpled his empty coffee cup, and tossed it in the recycling.

"I'm ready for a nap myself."

"If you're not going to the country club with the other tycoons."

He grinned and waved on his way out.

Dagmar looked at the time display on her phone. *Medina Suite,* she thought. *On my way.*

It was easy to find Figueroa, which was a major street downtown, but the road was one-way going in the wrong direction, and she got lost at least three times trying to find her way around the problem. Once, Dagmar discovered herself on the 110 headed for Long Beach with no clear idea how she got on the freeway. By the time she finished blundering around the basketball arena and the convention center, found the hotel, and gave her car keys to the Figueroa's valet, her nerves were crackling with fury.

The Figueroa Hotel was in a building that dated back to the 1920s and had been decorated in some kind of Moroccan Iberian frenzy, with a lobby full of wrought-iron lamps, geometric tiles, palms, bougainvillea, and throne-shaped chairs slung with bull hide. As Dagmar passed by the front desk, she heard an unfamiliar clattering and turned to discover the clerk working on an actual *typewriter,* an IBM Selectric probably manufactured before she was born.

She appreciated the classical touch.

Dagmar found the Medina Suite easily enough, by the flat of Mexican Coke empties sitting outside the massive doors with their iron hinges. Dagmar knocked, and Charlie let her in. Her anger was forgotten in the first glimpse of the room—painted an unlikely Mediterranean blue, with gold curtains, a russet spread on the enormous bed, ballooning striped tent fabric that concealed the ceiling, and a low couch with dangling tassels.

The plush Pinky doll sat in the strange wood-mounted metal bowl that served as a coffee table. The Brain glowered with red eyes from a Moorish cupboard. Charlie's laptop sat on a desk by the window.

Dagmar looked at Charlie. "Where's Kimba Leigh when you need her?" she asked.

"Providing room service elsewhere, I guess," Charlie said. "Sit down."

The low couch swallowed her. Charlie sat cross-legged on a vast cushion. He hadn't shaved today. He seemed tired, and discouraged, and more than a little irritated.

In which case, she thought, they were a matched pair.

"So how are things?" she said.

"They suck." He looked up at her. "I was looking for someone to take Austin's place, but that was an impossibility. All the really talented venture capital guys already have terrific jobs that pay them ridiculous profits. So then I thought I'd try to find another firm that would buy Austin's shares and fold his business into theirs. Which I did—I had a nice deal lined up with a Chicago firm that wanted a presence on the West Coast. But then Austin's father scotched it."

"Mr. Katanyan?" Dagmar asked. "Why?"

Charlie's mouth tightened into a line. "He's decided to run the business himself. I tried to tell him that VC was a little different from the rug business, but I think that just made him mad."

He flapped his hands.

"Oh well," he said. "It's not my damn business anyway. I was just trying to do Austin's dad a favor." He grimaced. "I hope I can sell him my shares, though."

"You can sell them to *someone,* I suppose."

He glared. "Not once *someone* discovers that the firm's in the hands of an Armenian American rug seller, no."

Dagmar almost told him that his billions would be a comfort in this matter, but decided not to.

"You wanted to talk to me about the game," she said.

He seemed embarrassed. He took off his glasses, looked at them in his hand for a moment, then replaced them.

"Yeah," he said. "I thought I had a good idea, but I realized it wouldn't work."

"Why not?"

"Because it involves the cooperation of too many people who aren't connected to the game."

She looked at Pinky, waving from the table with one three-fingered hand.

"Cooperation from whom?"

There was a strange little twitch behind his eyes, as if he first had to decide what piece of the story Dagmar was entitled to know before he could tell her anything.

"It had to do with the game's . . . financial dimension," he said slowly. "You know, the money men who are supposedly going to profit from the terrorist attacks. I thought . . . I thought the players could track the buy and sell orders coming into the brokerage houses, then—I don't know—do a little hackage to wreck the bad traders. But so many people trading online are perfectly firewalled—it's sort of a necessity, come to think of it, if you're going to start moving money around through the

Internet. In the game we might be able to get an IP number, but that won't necessarily get into the other folks' computers. It's just not going to happen."

Dagmar wondered if Charlie could see the calculation behind her own eyes, as she herself tried to decide what to reveal and what to hide.

"We could build a virtual brokerage in the game," Dagmar said. "We could give the players access to trades, let them track the traders using information we provide."

"No," Charlie said. "That's too much work for the technical staff on such notice."

Pity you didn't consider the deadlines for the writing staff, Dagmar thought.

Pity you didn't consider, she thought, *all the people you killed.*

She sighed. Scrubbed at her jeans with her palms. Decided to stop the guessing games.

"Charlie," she said. "Can you tell me what the hell this is about?"

He looked at her in a calculating way, as if he understood perfectly well what she meant but was trying to decide how much she knew.

"What do you mean?" he said.

"You're going to have to find some other mechanism for taming your gold-farming bots," Dagmar said.

Charlie's look turned to horror.

"You've got all the money in the Forlorn Hope account," she said. "Twelve billion that I know about. That'll accomplish a lot, I expect. But all that money's got Austin's blood on it—and probably the blood of a lot of other people by now—so if you want me to help you, I've got to know everything."

The color had drained from Charlie's face. He stared at her wildly, eyes huge behind his spectacles. Dagmar pointed a finger at him.

"Don't even *think* about having me killed," she said. "The gamers are halfway to the truth already—they just don't know it. But if we don't give them satisfactory answers, they're going to find out everything you want to keep hidden."

Protest entered Charlie's face—he was going to say that he'd never even *considered* killing Dagmar. But he didn't say it.

Maybe he was considering it now.

"And not only *that*," Dagmar said. "My guess is that the world's security forces are taking a big interest in you right now. You can't hide what's happening from *them*, not once they start probing." She looked at him. "Deaths just make all that worse," she said.

All expression had faded from Charlie's face. He was staring emptily into a corner of the room.

Dagmar looked at the plush doll in the Moorish cabinet.

"What are we going to do tonight, Brain?" she asked, and then she gave a galvanic leap as Charlie's laptop computer answered for her.

"What we do *every* night, Pinky." The computer spoke in the Brain's deep Orson Welles voice.

"Try," added Charlie, his voice listless, "to take over the world."

Dagmar looked at him.

"How's that working for you, Charlie?" she asked.

Charlie stared expressionlessly at a corner of the room.

"Better than it's worked for Brain," he said. He looked at Dagmar. "So what do you want to know?"

"Start with you and BJ crashing *Lost Empire*."

Charlie sighed. "God. That was so long ago."

"But it gave you an idea for saving AvN Soft when you ran into trouble."

Charlie looked up, spread his hands helplessly. "The first release of Rialto was a mess. I'd worked for months, and all we'd done was screw it up. And BJ was making us crazy, changing his mind every few hours about the way he wanted the company run, about the features on the software, about how he wanted to advertise the product."

He rose from his cushion and began pacing the room. He marched to the gold curtains, turned, marched back.

"We had created many different versions of the software during the development process, and we were working on upgrades to the existing software when the money ran out. The thing was *already* configured to make trades on its own, if the buyers wanted that feature." He stopped, turned, and began speaking rapidly, hands gesturing on the ends of his thin arms.

"The software was configured to evolve. It would learn from its mistakes, learn from its successes. I didn't want multiple copies on our company servers, because then BJ and every other damn person in the building would see what was happening. I ran the first copy from my own desktop machine in my own apartment.

"In order to create more copies, I added peer-to-peer networking, like the old Russian Storm Worm, and I sent it out into the world with the company's last twenty thousand dollars as a stake." He laughed. "That money wouldn't have kept the company going more than a week. It didn't seem worth hanging on to it."

"How do the bots work?"

He walked to the fridge as he answered, drew out a half-empty half liter of Mexican Coke, and began to drink.

"They look for other machines where they can reproduce, and if they find a security weakness, they'll clone themselves. They're not a threat to their host machines. They do no damage. They just use spare memory and processor capacity to make online trades. If a systems administrator wasn't looking for them, he wouldn't find them."

The peer-to-peer network, harnessing computers with poor security to do the actual work of computation, wasn't unique. More than half the spam in the world was generated by computers whose owners had left them open to intrusion. Other infected machines participated in stock fraud, pump-and-dump schemes, trolled for passwords and credit card information, and sent out denial-of-service attacks on targeted companies.

"The bots trade twenty-four/seven," Charlie said. "Every market in the world." His eyes glowed behind his spectacles as he took a swig of Coke. "Each clone evolves on its own, but they all share information continuously along their peer-to-peer network."

"In order to trade online," Dagmar said, "you need an account."

Charlie shrugged. "Accounts with an online brokerage firm aren't hard to get. You need a name, an address, an email address. And money. Once you wire money to your account, they don't care so much about the rest."

"Social Security number?" Dagmar asked.

"You don't need one if you're operating from a foreign country. All the clones use names and addresses in foreign tax havens—they've got access to public databases like online phone lists, and they generate names randomly. All the money is kept in brokerage accounts, except that half of the profits are wired to the Forlorn Hope account on Grand Cayman."

"Obviously it succeeded," Dagmar said.

"At the last minute." He took a drink, Adam's apple bobbing. "I checked the Forlorn Hope account every hour, then every day. Every so often a few dollars would appear, but nothing like the twenty grand I'd invested. I started to get paranoid—I started thinking our creditors would audit the books and prosecute me for that missing money. I decided not to think about any of it. I stopped checking the Cayman account."

He looked at the bottle in his hand and frowned.

"It happened after we'd been formally evicted. We had till the end of the month before the locks would be changed and we'd lose everything. I'd given up—I'd placed ads trying to sell my car, and I was looking for work. Anywhere but L.A.—I was sick of this town. And then I looked at the Forlorn Hope account for the first time in a couple of weeks, and there the money was, just sitting there."

He looked at Dagmar. A loose-lipped grin spread across his face.

"Eleven point two million dollars. All grown from that

twenty-thousand-dollar seed." He laughed and waved his Coke. "L.A. was looking better!" he said.

He clenched his fists and waved them on either side of his head in a gesture of triumph. "The bots *learned*. They learned just like they were supposed to. And once they learned, they kicked *financial ass!*"

He thrust out a foot to kick someone's imaginary butt.

"My babies pwned the markets! Damn, I was proud!"

"So you bought AvN Soft back," Dagmar said. "You're your own mysterious foreign backers."

Charlie gave a triumphant little laugh.

"Damn right. And I kicked BJ the fuck out and changed the locks and got a security specialist to wipe him from the computers before he could do me any damage." He pointed the bottle at her. "He had trapdoors *everywhere*, you know that? He'd been thinking about doing a scorched-earth on the company long before I took control." He shook his head. "Wiping out everything before the creditors could have it, or lurking in the computers in order to sabotage our successors or to steal things. Bad as the damn Soong. He could have ended up in jail!"

Dagmar ran fingers through her gray hair and let herself fall into the huge, soft cushions of the couch. She could imagine BJ angry; she could imagine him vindictive.

But she couldn't imagine him destructive. That wasn't his history—his wreckage of *Lost Empire* had been an accident. If he had trapdoors into AvN Soft, it was to keep track of things.

It was useless, though, to try to convince Charlie of that.

"You didn't put your bots on the market for AvN Soft," Dagmar said.

"I couldn't." Charlie looked embarrassed. "All I had was the original one on my home computer. And that one wasn't making that much money—it hadn't evolved in the right direction. It was the agents I'd released into the wild that were making the money for me, and I didn't even know where they were. I had no way of keeping track of them."

She gazed up at him in awe.

"You're out of your mind, you know that?" she said.

"Yeah, probably." He waved a hand dismissively. "The annoying thing is that I can't take credit for any of it. It all has to stay secret."

Dagmar felt anger enter her voice.

"You really want to take credit for what happened to Chile?" she asked. "Bolivia? Indonesia?"

A haunted look crossed Charlie's face.

"Yeah," he said. "Okay."

He put the Coke down and flopped cross-legged onto his cushion.

"The bots were doing well for me," he said. "Profits were averaging something like twenty million each quarter. Sometimes more, sometimes less. Once I got AvN Soft on its feet, all the excess was just icing on the cake. I invested in Austin's company and several others. I contributed to a lot of charities and foundations. I tried to be a force for good in the world.

"And then, back in June"—face turning blank—"the bots leveled."

Leveled. A term from gaming, where a character cashed

in experience points and gained a host of new magical abilities.

"The agents started crashing whole countries," Charlie said. "The day that Indonesia started to go down—it was a Sunday—I saw all this cash sitting in the offshore account, and I knew that something bad had to have happened somewhere, on the other side of the date line, where it was already Monday." He looked up at Dagmar. "I would have warned you if I'd known you would head for Jakarta that day. It was that afternoon that the *real* Chinese traders made their move and finished what the bots had started."

"There really are Chinese traders?" Dagmar asked.

Charlie nodded. "Oh yeah. And American traders, European traders . . . they've been following the bots' action through the currency markets. In the beginning, the bots didn't have enough muscle to really take down a whole country. But now . . ." He looked at her. "Back in 'ninety-two, George Soros crashed the English pound with ten billion in positions. The bots now have twice as much money as Soros did."

"More than twelve billion?"

"More than twenty now. Now that Chile's burned."

Suddenly Dagmar's mouth was dry. "Can I have one of your Cokes?" she asked.

"Be my guest."

Dagmar got a Coke from the fridge and walked to the window. She pushed back the gold curtain and looked out on Los Angeles, the tall glass buildings of downtown as solid and perfect and permanent as the Royal Jakarta Hotel.

In the blue sky she thought she saw the pillar of smoke above Glodok. She blinked away tears.

"Dagmar." Charlie's voice was soft. "I won't have you killed. I don't do that."

"You kill whole countries."

"I . . ." Charlie's voice faded to a whisper. "I can't stop the agents. I thought I could, but it isn't going to work."

She turned to face him. Charlie's hands had turned into fists. She could see the tendons standing out on his forearms.

"It could be the dollar next," he said. "The ruble. The yen, the yuan." He gave her a wild look. "The bots don't stop. They just go on winning."

"It's not illegal to use a machine to trade online," Dagmar said.

"It's illegal when the agent is in someone else's computer," Charlie said. "And when they're using a fictional identity." He gave a growl of frustration. "The bots don't *know* what's legal and what's not. All they know is to keep on trading." He scrubbed his neck with his hand, as if he were trying to remove a stain. "The Indonesian and Bolivian currencies were weak. But the Chilean currency *wasn't*—that means the bots now have enough clout to *manufacture* a currency crisis!"

His eyes were wild. "This goes on, I could own all the money in the world!" he said. "And then the money— mine and everyone else's—would be worthless!"

Charlie looked down at the room's Oriental carpet and traced its flowery pattern with his fingers.

"Money isn't anything real," he said. "It's just an *idea*. Even gold only has value because everyone agrees it does.

If a piece of software can get all the money for itself, that shows everyone that the money is a *sham*. It's *nothing*. It's like a magician revealing his trick—once you see it, it's not interesting anymore."

Charlie slumped on his pillow, his mobile hands silent in his lap, his spectacles halfway down his nose.

"I don't understand how the software agents know enough to do this," Dagmar said. She remembered BJ's arguments against this even happening. "Real markets are supposed to be self-correcting. They're incredibly complex. They're not *Lost Empire*."

"Markets are self-correcting *over time*," Charlie said. "The invisible hand and all that. But in the short term, there can be oscillations. And if the bots are smart enough to anticipate the correction, they can make money there, too."

He looked up, hands forming models in the air. "The bots are very single-minded. They *evolve*. The ones that make mistakes either learn from them or lose everything and go out of business. They've been on the loose for four years now—they've got massive amounts of empirical data, and *they talk to each other.*" He shrugged, then looked down at the floor again. "I couldn't tell you how they know what to do," he said. "I'm not in charge anymore."

"Why do the Maffya want to kill you?" Dagmar asked.

He looked up. His eyes were filled with a weary amusement.

"The bots raped and plundered them," he said. "It was some dodgy offshore scheme, I don't know exactly what. But I have something like four million in Maffya dollars."

"So when I asked you about it," Dagmar said, "the day after Austin got killed, you lied to me."

"I didn't *know*," Charlie said. "The bots don't tell me where or how they trade, they just send me half the profits. But when you asked if the killer was after me instead of Austin, I started checking. And as far as I can tell, a certain day's deposits in Cayman rightfully belong to a bunch of Russian criminals." He waved the hand with the empty Coke bottle. "Apparently they have enough illicit clout to find out who Forlorn Hope belongs to."

"You and your parents," Dagmar said. "Are your parents in danger?"

"My folks have new security, thanks to our Israeli friends."

"And you don't?"

Charlie was irritable. "I don't want bodyguards hulking around," he said. "They'd just get in my way. I just stay nimble and pay for things with cash. They can't track me if I don't leave a trail."

He shrugged. "If I could figure out how to give the Russians their money back, I would. When things get a little less hectic, I'll start researching all that and come up with a name. I'll pay him back double—that should get me off the hook."

"It won't help Austin."

Charlie gave Dagmar a defiant look.

"I *know*, okay?" he said. "I *know* that bad things have happened! I *know* they're my fault! I kick myself enough without you kicking me, too!"

You haven't been kicked nearly enough, Dagmar thought.

"Sorry," she said, not sorry enough.

"Listen," Charlie said, "I'm giving the money away as fast as the system permits. International Red Cross, Oxfam, Red Crescent, even Billy the Kid's little kampung in Jakarta . . . I'm trying to repair as much of the damage as I can."

She returned to the couch and sat, leaning toward Charlie, her elbows on her knees.

"So," she said, "you need to tell all the Internet security companies about the gold-farming bots. When the virus-checking programs have the bots in their database, that will take care of most of the problem."

Charlie shook his head. "Sorry, no," he said. "Virus-checking programs generally don't wipe the program, they *quarantine* it so that the experts can study it. Which means they'll find out how the bots *work*, which means *any one of their engineers* could release a new, improved bot into the environment again, one tooled so that the virus checkers wouldn't find it.

"*And*," he added with an emphatic gesture, "what if a hacker took a look at what turned up in his quarantine cage? Better *I* have all the money in the world than some bastard at McAfee or a fourteen-year-old script kiddie."

Dagmar sagged into the cushions, defeated.

"Your compassion knows no bounds," she said.

Anger grated in his voice. "I'm trying to think of a way out of this!" he said.

"You said you had a plan to fix the problem."

"I also said it wouldn't work." There was still defiance in Charlie's voice.

"Tell me about it."

His jaw muscles clenched.

"Okay," he said. He looked up at her. "I've been manipulating stocks, trying to figure out how the bots would react. That's what I did with Portcullis, and what I'm doing with Tapping the Source. I've been buying and selling online, too. Penny stocks—it doesn't take much to alter their value. I've still got my original bot running on my old PC. It's networked with the others, and it gets news from the network about what to buy and sell. I'm watching it, and I'm getting an idea of how the bots think."

"Yes. Good. Go on."

"When I make certain trades, the bots see it—remember, they're analyzing tens of thousands of trades every second. When certain things happen, I can count on the bots' reacting a certain way. And if I can trace their orders and find out where they're hiding, I could send a patch that will turn them off." He gave a mischievous look. "Or rather, I'll tell them to liquidate their positions, send the results to my bank account, and *then* turn off. *Not*," he said, seeing her face, "because I need the money, but because large sums sitting in the accounts of broker-age houses are a temptation to mischief."

"Okay," Dagmar said. "Let's pretend I believe that."

Charlie made a cat's cradle of his fingers. "The problems with the plan are twofold."

"Twofold," Dagmar repeated. The first time in her life she'd heard anyone speak the word aloud.

"First, all the actual buy and sell orders come from online brokers, so tracing them would just give us the brokers' servers, not the servers where the bots are hiding."

"Right."

"That's why I've been flying all over the place, talking to the security people at brokerage houses," he said. "I've told them that I've found evidence of someone using unlicensed copies of Rialto to manipulate the markets. I've got them to agree to let me see a list of the IP addresses from which buy and sell orders of certain stocks originate on certain days."

"There must be a million online brokerage houses," Dagmar said.

"I didn't tell the bots to use some boiler-room operation in Jersey, you know." Charlie's tone was scornful. "There are only a handful that are big enough to trade in every market across the world and to swing the kind of trades that brought down Chile. Those are the ones I programmed into the agents in the first place, six years ago."

"Okay, great," Dagmar said. "You've got the brokerage firms cooperating. So what's the problem?"

"If the bot is sitting in an insecure computer—which is very possible, considering how they spread—I can send the patch to that IP address and everything's good. But if the computer is firewalled, I'm screwed. In order to get the patch in, I'd have to find out who that IP address belonged to, contact that person, tell them their computer was infected, and either get them to erase the bot or to load the patch themselves."

"Or let you through their firewall."

"Yes." Charlie looked at the wall in despair. "Do you know how much work that is? It would take thousands of hours."

"Or thousands of people," Dagmar said.

She looked at him.

"Or millions," she said.

He gazed at her with wide eyes.

"Oh," he said.

CHAPTER TWENTY-TWO

This Is Not an Exit

Over what remained of the weekend, Siyed sent no flowers, made no calls, and was not observed haunting the apartment parking lot. No Russian killers were seen, and Richard the Assassin seemed to have succeeded in keeping Joe Clever from breaching computer security.

None of this meant peace for Dagmar. She worked madly on *Briana Hall,* trying to figure out how to get the players to track down Charlie's swarm of bots.

The scenario itself was clear enough—the financiers who hoped to profit from the terror attack would send buy or sell orders to manipulate the market, and the players would track them down and stop them and unknowingly kill Charlie's bots while they were at it—but the exact game mechanism by which the players would locate and process all this information, and then act on it, was unclear.

Dagmar called an early morning meeting on Monday with the whole design team—"early morning" in this case being an IT euphemism for ten o'clock. She knew how badly they dealt with Mondays.

She wasn't in very good shape herself. Hoping for clean arteries and a lively mind, she'd breakfasted on oatmeal and Red Bull, but she suspected she'd failed on both counts.

She encountered BJ in the parking lot as they walked to the entrance. He was dressed in a charcoal-gray shirt with pearl buttons and softly glowing gray cashmere slacks.

For the first time ever, Helmuth had competition for the title of best-dressed game geek in the building.

Dagmar looked at him and lifted her eyebrows.

"Dressing for the other tycoons?" she said.

BJ spread his hands and did a clumsy pirouette.

"And thanks to you," he said, "I can afford it."

She hugged him hello.

"Good for you," she said.

"Things are looking up. Once I get a paycheck, I hope you'll let me take you to dinner."

She grinned. "Absolutely."

The door opened to her thumbprint. She said hello to Luci at the front desk, saw with satisfaction that no enormous bouquet from Siyed waited, then walked with BJ to the elevator. As they waited in the elevator lobby, Dagmar looked again at BJ. He was glowing with pleasure, the smile on his face just the least bit smug.

"Either this is a fucking great job you've got," Dagmar said, "or you got laid last night. Which is it?"

BJ leaned back and laughed. Louder, Dagmar thought, than the joke quite warranted.

"Why not both?" BJ asked.

She shrugged. "Why not?"

"I was on the phone to the East Coast this morning," BJ said. "And I nailed the job down."

"It's on the East Coast?" Dagmar asked. "Can you talk about it yet?"

"No, the job's here. I—"

The elevator door opened, and they stepped into the car. The doors slid shut, and BJ turned to Dagmar.

"I was on the phone with Austin's father," he said. "I'm going to be the new chief operating officer of Katanyan Associates."

A long moment followed, the elevator ascending, in which Dagmar looked at BJ and seemed to see a completely new human being, not an old friend but an alien, a total stranger.

"Damn," she said, for lack of anything better.

His grin was radiant.

"It's really something, isn't it?" he asked.

"I . . . " She considered him again, still a stranger. "I hope you don't take this the wrong way," she said, "but do you know anything at all about the venture capital business?"

"I know everything I really need to know," BJ said. "I know how to evaluate a new idea or a technology. I know how to arrange financing, and I know how to run an office. Austin's dad—his name is Aram—is coming out to supervise until the arrangement gels. He's run a business forever. He'll be my backup."

BJ had met Mr. Katanyan for the first time at Austin's memorial and had charmed his way into Austin's place. Dagmar had to give BJ credit: he had seen his chance and acted on it.

She wondered what he had said to Austin's father to give himself this chance. She wondered what Austin's

partners would say when a complete novice was promoted over their heads. She wondered if he had any idea
how pissed Charlie was going to be when he heard.

She wondered what BJ would say at the first staff
meeting. He'd better not walk into it with that grin on his
face—that she knew for certain.

"Well," she said. "Good luck."

The elevator doors slid open. Neither of them moved.

"I told Aram I had to finish the game writing first," BJ
said. "He was cool with that."

"Did you know that Charlie owns a piece of the company?" Dagmar asked.

"Yeah. Aram will buy him out."

BJ spoke with perfect confidence. Dagmar was not
certain that Charlie would sell once he discovered the
current arrangements. He might hold on to his shares
just to fuck with BJ.

The elevator door tried to slide shut. BJ blocked it with
a hand.

"Do me a favor," he said. "Don't tell Charlie right
away, okay? He doesn't own enough of the company to
stop Aram from doing whatever he wants to do, but he
could cause problems with the partners."

No shit, Dagmar thought.

"No problem," she said.

Charlie had enough on his plate without this news.

And besides, she thought, BJ deserved his chance. If
he could pull this off, it would mean happy endings for
everybody.

Unless, of course, Charlie's bots wiped out the financial system, in which case the fate of Katanyan Associates

would be a minor tragedy in a world full of sudden, bright, brilliant, and unending pain.

She went to her office to claim her coffee cup, filled it at the snack station, and then dragged herself to the conference room. As she entered, her stomach turned over at the scent of one of Jack Stone's Frito pies.

Most of her creative team looked at her. Some didn't: a few hadn't arrived, and Jack was devoting himself to eating his breakfast with a plastic spoon. Dagmar took a place at the head of the table, put her handheld down, and opened her notes on the display.

She was too nervous to sit still. While she waited for the late arrivals, she got up and looked out the window to make certain that Joe Clever wasn't across the highway with his laser eavesdropper.

No James Bond vans lurked.

She turned on the white-noise generator to baffle any eavesdroppers she hadn't spotted. As she returned to her seat, she passed behind Jack and wondered if the sound of Fritos being masticated, echoing over the Big Ears, was enough to make Joe Clever crazy.

It wasn't doing much for Dagmar's nerves, that was for certain sure. Said the big wall monitor,

> *Read the Schedule*
> *Know the Schedule*
> *Love the Schedule*

The last few members of the team wandered in with apologies. Dagmar looked down at her notes again, then looked up.

"Charlie's decided to move the game in an interesting direction," she said.

There were no actual groans. She supposed that was the best she could hope for.

"What he's found," she said, "is that there are un-authorized copies of AvN Soft agents floating around. Specifically Rialto. He wants us to get the players to take them out."

Suddenly they were all interested.

Out of the corner of her eye, she saw BJ listening intently, his eyes staring sightlessly into the shiny finish of the table, one big hand fiddling with the pearl buttons of his new shirt.

Dagmar explained the plan she had worked out over the weekend. When IP addresses came in, the players would have to perform certain acts, and in a certain order.

First, they'd try sending Charlie's patch to the gold-farming bots at each IP address. If the computer was inadequately firewalled, the bots would rewrite them-selves, reboot, send a message to the player indicating that the patch had been installed, and then erase them-selves.

Before wiping themselves out, the bots would liquidate their accounts and send the results to the Forlorn Hope account, though the players wouldn't know that.

If the patch bounced off a firewall, then the player would have to try to find out who the IP address belonged to, contact that person, and tell him that there might be unauthorized software on his machine and how to get rid of it, referencing the AvN Soft patch, which would be found on that person's Web page.

"Do we have solutions for any of those problems?" Helmuth asked.

"No. The players will have to dig around in reality."

"You mean," said Jack, "that we're going to send millions of people Dumpster-diving in every major brokerage in the world? And following that, we're going to organize the largest coordinated hacking attempt in the history of the Internet?"

Tension stiffened Dagmar's spine.

"Yes," she said.

Helmuth absorbed this, looked at Jack, and nodded.

"Cool," he said.

Jack nodded back.

"Wicked cool," he confirmed, and took a spoonful of Frito pie.

Dagmar felt her tension ebb.

"It *is* pretty cool," she said. "Isn't it?"

"I have another whole idea, a better one," Charlie said. "I'm working on Patch 2.0."

It was Tuesday morning, and Dagmar was talking to Charlie on the phone. He was in his Moorish extravaganza of a hotel room, and she was in the break room at Great Big Idea, watching her plastic cup of beef barley soup rotating in the microwave.

"Tell me," Dagmar said.

The cup of soup rotated. The microwave hummed. The odor of beef stock crept into the room.

"The agents are linked in a peer-to-peer network, right?" Charlie said. "So Patch 2.0 rewrites the program to spread *the patch itself* along the network. It'll be like a killer virus aimed right at the whole population of agents."

Dagmar considered this.

"You mean," she said, "we only have to succeed once? And then the whole network gets infected and goes down?"

"No," Charlie said. "The peer-to-peer network is organized into smaller groups, and there are bound to be gaps even in those. Gaps where the program's been wiped by an alert systems administrator, or where a disk drive blew up, or where the computer was shut down and stuck in a closet somewhere, or where the machine was just tossed away.

"Redundancy," he said, "is still our friend."

"But it'll make the job easier."

"A *lot* easier."

World saved, Dagmar thought. *Charlie still rich, game still cool.*

What could possibly go wrong?

The microwave gave a chime. Dagmar opened the door, gingerly took out her cup of soup by the handle, and put it on the counter.

"Okay," she said. "When can you have the new patch ready?"

"Tomorrow," he said, "I hope."

After the call ended, Dagmar stirred her soup with the plastic spoon, then returned to her office. She found BJ there, peering at her computer screen, his fingers poised over her keyboard.

"What do you need?" she asked.

"I'm looking for the script for Week Six, Part One," BJ

said. "I wanted to make sure I included the bit about Carlo leaving the matchbook behind in the Russian restaurant for David to find."

"I *think* you did," she said, stirring.

BJ was still staring at the screen, his hand busy on her trackball.

"Can we make sure? Because I don't want to leave that detail out."

"Let me," said Dagmar. She put down her lunch, and BJ rolled her office chair out of the way. Dagmar bent over the computer and said, "Open file *Briana Assets 6.1*." When the file popped open, she instituted a search for *matchbook*.

"Yeah," she said. "There it is."

She pointed. BJ followed her finger, then nodded.

"Okay. Good."

She picked up her soup and tasted it.

"What are you doing here, anyway?" she asked.

"I just got back from a lunch with Helmuth," BJ said. His blue eyes glittered mischievously from behind his spectacles. "I'm thinking of stealing him to work for me at Katanyan Associates."

She looked at him.

"Not funny, Boris," she said.

"I was kidding," he said.

"Uh-huh."

He smiled up at her. "I just got interested in how he does what he does. Making Web sites disappear, hiding stuff in the code."

"Be careful around Helmuth," Dagmar said. "Especially if you're planning on collecting a big salary from this new job of yours. Helmuth will corrupt you faster than hanging with any twenty rock stars."

BJ was impressed.

"I had no idea," he said.

"He'll tell you so himself," Dagmar said.

There was another update later in the afternoon. It was intended that after the last puzzle was solved, there was going to be a clue hunt in *Planet Nine*, with the players' avatars zooming around the rust-colored surface of Titan on flying scooters.

Except that the clue hunt didn't happen. The players got hung up on one of the online puzzles and never progressed to Titan.

At the end of the day, there was a meeting concerning how to nudge the players loose.

"Okay," Dagmar said. "The misunderstanding is all to do with the recording of Omar in the safe house. He's saying, 'I need what's on the banana split.' And so the players are trying to figure out what's on a banana split, and how to get it to Omar, instead of noticing that 'Banana Split' is a *feature* on *Titan* in *Planet Nine*."

"They've all got the Titan map," Jack said.

"The problem," said BJ, "is that they haven't memorized it."

"And so they're trying to get Omar a maraschino cherry," said Dagmar.

"Or whipped cream," Jack said.

"Or jimmies," Helmuth said. "They mentioned jimmies." He looked at Dagmar. "What *are* jimmies?"

"Little bits of candy," Dagmar said, "in the shape of mouse turds."

Lines formed between Helmuth's brows.

"If I go into an ice cream store and ask for a banana split with jimmies," he said, "they'll give to me these candy mouse turds?"

"Yes," said Dagmar.

Helmuth gave a slow nod. "Interesting," he said.

He had learned something new about America. Dagmar concealed a smile.

"What about Banana Split in the game?" BJ asked.

Dagmar decided she was too tired to make any major decisions right now.

"Next update's on Saturday," she said. "And that's a big one, because we've got players with Tapping the Source machines sampling every water puddle in the world. So we've got to get the Titan adventure over before then—let's say by Thursday night."

"Okay," said Jack. "Good."

"The players could crack the Banana Split thing anytime between now and then. So let's give them the chance, and if they don't, we'll think of a clever way to tell them—or failing that, we'll just go into one of the forums under a pseudonym and give them the answer."

The others were happy to put off the decision, and Dagmar called an end to the mission. BJ rose and looked at the others.

"Anyone interested in dinner?" he asked.

Dagmar pushed her chair back from the long table. "Not me," she said. "I'm for a long night's sleep."

She said her good-byes and left as BJ and Helmuth and some others planned a trip to a restaurant.

The reek of the ginkgo trees filled the parking lot.

Dagmar looked carefully behind bushes and trees for Siyed or any other lurker, then went through the gate unmolested and went to her apartment. She warmed a frozen meal of chicken and pasta in alfredo sauce—despite the appetizing name, it was alleged to be low in calories—and idly wondered when she had last actually cooked something on the stove.

Weeks ago, at least.

She turned on CNN and ate in front of the television. Charlie's bots had been busy wrecking South American currencies—Bolivia and Chile had just been a warm-up. Brazil and Argentina were taking a hammering.

The IMF and the World Bank weren't offering any help. They'd already lost billions trying to prop up other currencies, and now they had removed themselves from the bot wars altogether.

The talking heads speculated that they were keeping what remained of their reserves to prop up the U.S. dollar if it came under attack.

If the dollar fell, it was bad news even for people who weren't U.S. citizens. The dollar was the world's reserve currency—it was the currency that foreign governments used when trading with one another, or when buying commodities like gold and oil. Other currencies were coupled to the dollar and would collapse when the dollar fell. And Bolivia and Chile had saved a little of their citizens' savings by coupling their own money to the dollar. If the dollar fell, they'd be ruined twice over.

It was all too depressing. Dagmar switched the channel and watched a program about a gallant teenager who fought crime with her extrasensory powers. The program's lack of any connection to reality was a comfort.

She went to bed early and slept late. When she rose, she started the coffee machine and cooked some oatmeal in the microwave, then took a shower. She ate breakfast while CNN reported that South American currencies were still under attack. Dagmar muted the volume on the television while she booted her laptop and checked her email.

FROM: BJSKI
SUBJECT: Corrupiton

Oh hai!

U waz rite about Hellmouth. We haz been out all nite and I iz now throughly corrupited.

Ai think her nbame was Beverly. She and Hellmouth goze way back. She drinkz mojitos.

Have you ever haz mojitos? 3 and you can not walk rite. Ai do not know how Ai gotz home.

Ai just write to let you knowz that I iz going to be lait with the deliverabblies.

Bj

PS Ai haz spent all mai dollarz. Kin I haz a raze?

Dagmar laughed, saw that the email had been sent at 4:42 A.M., and figured she wouldn't be hearing from BJ till midafternoon at the earliest.

At least some people in Great Big Idea were having fun.

FROM: Charlie
SUBJECT: Patch 2.0

Hi. I'm attaching the second version of the patch. I've tested it on my own machines and it works.

I'm also attaching files from an assortment of online brokers giving the IP addresses of computers making suspicious trades.

Talk to ya soon!

Charlie

That email had been sent at 5:08, so BJ wasn't the only person having an all-nighter.

It's like they're undergraduates again, Dagmar thought.

She shifted in her seat, and out of the corner of her eye she saw a familiar piece of downtown Los Angeles on the television screen.

The brick facade of the Figueroa Hotel.

Her mouth went dry. She lunged for the television remote to bring up the sound.

"—believed to be one fatality in the early morning blast," said the reporter. "It has not been officially stated whether the explosion was an accident or the result of a bomb, but sources report that Homeland Security has been called in."

Dagmar's heart sank. The reporter hadn't said where in the hotel the explosion had been, or given the name of the casualty, but Dagmar already knew.

She knew.

The Russians had found Charlie.

She looked at the screen of her laptop and saw Charlie's emails, with the attachments listed.

This might be the only copy left of Patch 2.0.

She turned back to the television and listened. The explosion had occurred just before six o'clock, a short time after Charlie had sent her the email. The hotel had been evacuated and the fire department called, but the fire had been minor and easily put out. One body had been found, and there were believed to be no further casualties.

She should find out, Dagmar thought. She should try to confirm what she felt she already knew.

Dagmar turned to the laptop, took it from the kitchen table, and connected it to the cable modem on her desk. She found the Figueroa's home page, got the number for the front desk, and called it.

"Figueroa Hotel." The desk clerk's voice was hoarse. He'd probably been answering a lot of phone calls in the past few hours.

"Can you connect me to the Medina Suite, please?"

There was a moment's hesitation.

"I'm afraid there's been an accident," the clerk said.

"The accident was *in* the Medina Suite?" Dagmar asked.

"Yes." Another hesitation. "May I know the name of the person you wished to contact?"

"By 'accident,'" Dagmar said, relentless, "you mean the bomb, right?"

"Yes."

"Thank you." Dagmar pressed End.

She stared at the phone for a long moment while CNN ran a commercial for Viagra.

Her mind seemed to have nothing in it. Just a big empty warehouse space, with fading footsteps echoing.

Both her fingertips and her mind seemed to be numb as she downloaded Patch 2.0 to her computer, then copied both it and the broker files to a memory stick.

Now there were three copies. She put the memory stick in the pocket of her jeans.

She gave a galvanic leap as the phone began to ring in her hand. The number on the display was area code 818, but she didn't recognize it.

She muted the sound on the television, then pressed Send and put the handheld to her ear.

"Yes?"

"Dagmar." Joe Clever's voice was breathless. "I've found the Russian!"

Dagmar let breath whisper from her lips in a sigh. If only Clever had found Litvinov twenty-four hours ago.

"He's in the pool, swimming laps!" Joe Clever said. "I'm watching him now!"

"Where are you?" Dagmar asked.

"Oceanside Motel, in Santa Monica. Near Pacific Palisades."

That wasn't anywhere near downtown Los Angeles, but then of course the bomb could have been carried to the Figueroa from wherever Litvinov had assembled it.

"Charlie Ruff lives in Santa Monica, right?" Joe Clever said. "I think the Russian was probably still trying to stake out Charlie's house."

"Yes," Dagmar said. Her mind turned in sluggish circles. She didn't seem to be processing this at all.

"Man!" Joe Clever said. "I thought I'd never be able to get back to my cell phone! I've been watching his door since six thirty last night, and I had no way of contacting you!"

Dagmar suddenly found herself in a timeless space, the long, soft period between two of her heartbeats extending to infinity in all directions while Joe Clever's words echoed in her brain.

"You'd better tell me," Dagmar said.

"I've been going to every hotel and motel in Greater Los Angeles," said Joe Clever. "I've got pictures I made of Litvinov, and I show them to the desk clerks. I photoshop beards and so on in case he's trying to disguise himself." He laughed. "It's old-fashioned detective work! I tried emailing the pictures, you know, but the hotels don't always respond, so I have to go in person. And the desk clerks work in shifts, you know, so I don't always get them all, and I have to come back."

Dagmar tried to picture Joe Clever driving his old van from one motel to the next, talking to one bemused desk clerk after another. How many thousands of hours would it take to hit every motel in the Los Angeles area? Even LAPD didn't have that much manpower, that many hours.

"Good work," Dagmar said. It seemed inadequate praise.

"I keep coming back to the motels around Santa Monica," Joe Clever said. "I checked the hotels in the Valley, too, but I figured Litvinov wouldn't go back to AvN Soft, not after you increased security the way you did. Anyway, I got lucky . . . Yesterday around dinnertime I got to the Oceanside just an hour after Litvinov checked in."

"You're sure it's him?"

"Oh yes, once I got a look at him! When the clerk told me he'd checked in, I got a room across the motel court from his. Then I ran to the van and got my Big Ears and video camera and went to my room to set up.

"I was going to call you, but I realized I'd left my cell phone in the van, and I didn't dare leave until I was sure that it really was Litvinov. I didn't want him to disappear the way he did last time.

"I didn't have your number with me, so I couldn't use the phone in the room. So I employed the Big Ears and I got some conversations of Litvinov talking on the phone."

"When did you confirm it was really him?"

Joe Clever was so excited that his words began to stumble over one another. "Just this morning! S-someone came to the door to give him a package, and I got a good look!"

"Who was the messenger?"

"Just some guy. They talked in Russian! I got some good pictures of him."

"And you're sure that Litvinov didn't go out all night?"

"That's right! I was awake the whole time! And even if I fell asl—if I drowsed off, I was wearing my Big Ear headphones and I had my camera running, so if his door had opened, I would have known it. He stayed in all night and watched the *CSI* marathon on the Crime Channel."

Doing his homework, no doubt, learning about all the forensic science that might trip him up when he committed his next murder.

"Anyway," Joe Clever said, "I didn't want to lose him, so I stayed in the room until he came out and started doing laps. I figured he wasn't going to run off wearing just a pair of swim trunks, so I snuck out to the van and got the cell phone and came back to the room and called you. And the Russian's still doing laps."

"Oceanside Motel," Dagmar said. "Which room?"

"One one four. Or do you mean Litvinov's?"

"His."

"One one seven. Are you coming over?"

"I'm going to call the police."

"Well," Joe Clever said, "tell them to hurry and not screw up like last time. Litvinov isn't going to stay in the damn pool forever."

He sounded disappointed that Dagmar wasn't driving to Santa Monica to take down the Russian herself, with his help.

"I'll call you right back," Dagmar said.

Dagmar called the North Hollywood Station and asked for Lieutenant Murdoch. The receptionist said that he was away from the station, and asked if she wanted his voice mail.

Dagmar's body shivered with anxiety. This was taking too long.

"Tell Murdoch," Dagmar said, "that I've located Litvinov, the murderer of Austin Katanyan. Litvinov is in the Oceanside Motel in Santa Monica, room one one seven. But he might not be there long, so the police need to respond quickly."

"And your name, ma'am?"

"Dagmar Shaw. He knows who I am."

"Stay on the line," the receptionist said quickly. "I'll contact the officer."

"Good idea," said Dagmar.

Dagmar couldn't sit still any longer and got up to march back into the kitchen. She looked down at her cold bowl of oatmeal and then turned and marched back to her desk again.

Her heart throbbed like a racing turbine in her chest. She felt charged with energy and wondered why her knees felt weak.

Charlie hadn't been killed by Litvinov. Joe Clever had just provided him an alibi.

And he hadn't been killed by anyone else in the Maffya, either. Probably there were plenty of Russian gangsters in Los Angeles who were willing to kill people, but bombing the hotel room was too awkward a plan, not when they could have gunned him down on his way to dinner or simply kicked down the door and shot him in his bed.

There was some reason it was a bomb, and some other person who had planted it.

Dagmar was absolutely certain that, when it came time to fill out Charlie's death certificate, the cause of death should be listed as Patch 2.0.

CHAPTER TWENTY-THREE

This Is Not a Dream

Litvinov submitted quietly to arrest when the Santa Monica police used their battering ram to knock his motel room door off its hinges. Dagmar was sorry to hear it: she had hoped he'd resist and be shot full of holes.

Unless the Russian pleaded guilty, there would be a trial, and Dagmar would testify. And so she was asked to come to the police station and give a statement.

Murdoch was interviewing someone else, so Dagmar was given a ten-ounce foam cup of coffee and a white and red plastic stir stick and then asked to wait on a chair of shiny tube steel and gray plastic. She did so.

The North Hollywood Station was quiet on a Wednesday morning. Doubtless the drunks and other flotsam of the previous night were sleeping it off or being processed somewhere else.

Find out who knew Charlie was staying at the Fig, Dagmar thought, *and you find the bomber.*

Phones rang. Detectives answered. Fingers tapped keyboards.

She called AvN Soft and asked for Karin, Charlie's secretary.

"Hi," she said. "This is Dagmar."

"Hi, Dagmar," Karin said. "Charlie still isn't in."

"Do you know where he's staying?"

"Yes," she said. Then she added, "I'm not sure if I can tell you without his permission."

Apparently she hadn't heard the news that morning. Dagmar lacked the energy to tell her.

"That's all right," Dagmar said. "I was wondering if anyone besides you knows where he's at."

She could hear the uncertainty in Karin's voice.

"I haven't *heard* that he's told anyone else," she said.

"*You* haven't told anyone?"

"No. The only reason I know myself is that I have to drive down every few days to bring him paperwork he needs to sign."

"Okay, I just wondered. Thanks."

After she ended the conversation, she considered Karin. She'd been Charlie's secretary since the early days of the company and, like Dagmar, was in her early thirties. She seemed to be deeply competent, and Charlie had always praised her.

Karin had just returned from maternity leave. She had bleached-blond hair, a rectangular butt that jutted out like a Lego block beneath her jackets, and wore a nursing bra. She just didn't seem bomb-thrower material.

Well, she thought. *That leaves me as the only remaining suspect.*

She didn't seem to be prospering as a detective.

A door opened and Murdoch came out with Joe Clever and a woman in a gray pantsuit. Joe Clever seemed a little more wild-eyed than usual.

"If you can wait for a few minutes," Murdoch said, "we'll have your statement printed for you, and you can check it." He looked up at Dagmar. "Miss Shaw? Can you speak to us now?"

Joe Clever grinned. "Hi, Dagmar." He gave a thumbs-up. "We make a good team, don't we?"

"We sure do, Andy," Dagmar said. Joe Clever's expression clouded.

Finding out Joe Clever's real name had been an unanticipated bonus of this adventure. *She could find out where he lived.*

Let him misbehave again, and she'd send Richard the Assassin to throw bricks through his windows.

Dagmar went with the detectives into the interview room. It had functional furniture and an official poster telling suspects of their rights. The metal desk was bolted to the floor and had shiny steel loops for handcuffs. There was an antiseptic smell.

Murdoch introduced the woman, who was a detective from the Santa Monica PD. Dagmar, Murdoch, and the woman were given lapel mics, and as they spoke, a computer turned the words into letters and projected them on a monitor.

Dagmar simply answered questions. She still wasn't processing very well and felt that her answers, while factual, lacked the concrete specificity that she preferred in her prose.

She reported that she'd seen Austin killed, and that

she'd turned to the players—"programmed" them, in Murdoch's words—to hunt for Litvinov.

The woman detective, who didn't talk much, seemed surprised at all this.

Dagmar went on to state that Andy Claremont— which was Joe Clever's real name—had located Litvinov the previous night and called her that morning, and that she'd called Murdoch right away.

She said that she had no reason to believe that Austin Katanyan had anything to do with the Russian Maffya.

The interview didn't take very long. At the end, a printer in the squad room printed out the interview, after which Dagmar corrected the occasional spelling error and signed it.

"We got to him just in time," Murdoch volunteered. "The accomplice who visited this morning seems to have dropped off Litvinov's new ID. With that, Litvinov could have walked across the border into Tijuana and then flown from there to . . ." He shrugged. "To somewhere else. There are biometric scanners at the border that might have ID'd him, or they might not—and even if they did, he might have been in Mexico before the border patrol could react."

"Do you know who the courier was?" Dagmar asked.

"We're forwarding Mr. Claremont's video to the Organized Crime Task Force, along with the sound recordings. We'll get Litvinov's cell phone records, so that might help us as well." He paused, and then added, "We found a motorcycle in the parking lot that we think was stolen, probably by Litvinov. It wasn't the same motor- cycle that was used in the murder—but that one was probably stolen, too, then abandoned."

Dagmar jumped again as her phone rang. She chided herself for being too nervous and glanced at Murdoch to see if he'd noticed.

His face retained the same bland professionalism it always wore. To give her privacy, he turned and ambled toward the coffee machine.

Dagmar looked at the display and saw that it was Karin.

"This is Dagmar," she answered.

"Dagmar," Karin said, "they say Charlie's been in a bombing."

She looked up at Murdoch's bland back. "Who says?"

"The FBI. They're here. They're taking everything from Charlie's office."

Dagmar was astonished. "Why are they doing that?"

Distress flooded Karin's voice. "They won't say!"

"Have you called our lawyers?"

"Lawyers?" Karin sounded as if she'd never heard the word before.

"Call the firm's attorneys," Dagmar said. "If they're taking company property, there needs to be an inventory. And probably a warrant—I don't know."

"Okay. Should I do that now?"

"Yes," Dagmar said.

Karin clicked off. Dagmar looked at her phone and saw the AvN Soft number glow for a moment, then vanish as the screen went to black.

She tried to work out what to do next. Rush to the office to prevent the FBI from taking Charlie's things? Tell Murdoch what had just happened? Do nothing?

Try to play detective and solve the crime?

It had to be admitted that this last approach hadn't worked well so far.

Murdoch was stirring white powder into a cup of coffee with one of the red and white stir sticks. Dagmar holstered her handheld and approached him. He looked up.

"My boss has been killed," she told him. "Charles Ruff, you might remember him. In a bombing."

She realized as the words left her lips that Karin hadn't actually given her all this information, and there followed a thrill of fear as she realized that Murdoch might trip her up.

But then, she thought, Karin wouldn't remember what she'd said and what she hadn't. And there wasn't anything wrong with Dagmar's knowing what she knew.

She was safe.

The crinkles around Murdoch's eyes softened and then re-formed themselves, something Dagmar took to be an expression of interest.

"Is this the bombing downtown?" he asked. "In the Fig?"

"I . . ." Dagmar hesitated. "She didn't say. She only said that the FBI turned up at the office."

His eyes held hers for a moment, and then he looked down and gave a long sigh.

"Well," he said, "if it's the Russians, the FBI might be the best agency for it." His tone suggested that he made this statement against his better judgment. He made a vague gesture with the hand that held the stir stick.

"I'll make some calls," he said, "and we'll see what we can find out."

*

In the end, Murdoch took Dagmar to the FBI's blue glass tower on Wilshire, where Dagmar talked to a special agent named Landreth, a woman with perfect makeup, an immaculate gray suit, and a Tidewater accent. She seemed completely comfortable with the idea that Charlie was a terrorist who had blown himself up with his own bomb. When Dagmar pointed out that Charlie was a multimillionaire entrepreneur with no ideological ax to grind, Landreth gave her a green-eyed look that made her realize that it was her credibility, not Landreth's, that was in question.

A fact that pointed to Charlie's guilt, Landreth was convinced, was that he had checked into the hotel under a false name, Neville Longbottom. Dagmar pointed out that this was a character in the Harry Potter books. Landreth didn't seem to think that mattered.

Dagmar didn't tell her about the patch. Landreth would probably have confiscated it as a possible tool in Charlie's terrorist plot, and Dagmar wasn't going to allow that to happen.

After the futile interview, Dagmar was tasked to identify Charlie's body. Charlie's other associates suddenly seemed unavailable, and Karin had refused.

It would probably sour her breast milk, Dagmar thought. Sourly.

Murdoch, who seemed to be doubling today as her chauffeur, took her to the morgue. The attendants weren't yet ready with Charlie's body, and Dagmar waited with Murdoch in the corridor. A fluorescent light buzzed overhead. Air-conditioning efficiently suppressed any odor: the place smelled like nothing at all.

"Harlem Nocturne" began to chime from Dagmar's belt. She looked at the display and saw that it was Helmuth.

"Dagmar," she said.

"We need to know what to do about the Banana Split mix-up," Helmuth said.

"Jesus," Dagmar said. "Do you know where I *am?*"

"We know that Charlie's been killed," Helmuth said. "But even if he has, we still can't update till the players solve the Banana Split puzzle."

She mashed her free hand against her forehead, then scrubbed her palm over her face, as if she were hoping that might help her mind to jump from one track to another.

"I can't think," she said. "You'll just have to handle it yourselves."

"Should I call Boris?"

"Sure. Why not? He's devious."

"He can't hold his liquor very well."

Dagmar didn't remember that about him. It seemed to her that BJ had been pretty good with alcohol—better anyway than Dagmar.

"He and I went out clubbing last night," Helmuth said. "My God! He turned into some kind of rampaging disco monster."

Dagmar remembered the email BJ had sent her at four in the morning. *Oh hai . . .*

"You were with someone named Beverly?" she asked.

"Yes. Boris seemed . . . fond of her."

"He didn't pass out or anything?" she asked.

"No. He just . . . had more fun than the situation called for."

"Well, he's had good news lately. I'll talk to you later, okay?"

"Sure. And we're very sorry about Charlie, by the way."

"Yes," she said. "So am I."

Dagmar put her phone away. To give her privacy, Murdoch had turned away and taken a few steps down the corridor, just as he had during the phone call at the North Hollywood Station that morning.

"Someone from work," she said.

Murdoch turned around and gave her a diffident look.

"Do people at your office pass out very often?" he asked.

A reluctant laugh bubbled like champagne up her nose.

"They do when they're drinking with Helmuth," she said.

Murdoch nodded.

A door opened and an attendant came out. He had glossy black skin, was dressed in pale green surgical scrubs, and had shaved his head.

"We're ready, ma'am," he said. "I should tell you a few things first."

Dagmar nodded dumbly. Her insides were trying to climb up her throat.

"The victim's face," said the attendant, "has been badly damaged." Then, speaking quickly as he gauged Dagmar's horrified expression: "We're not going to show you the face. We're going to show you as much of the body as we can, so that maybe you'll recognize the hands or feet or a birthmark or something."

"Okay," Dagmar said.

"The victim has also been autopsied. There is a large Y-shaped incision on the trunk. It has been sewn up and has nothing to do with the accident."

Accident. Indeed.

"Let's go," she said.

Dagmar had expected a scene from the movies, with a wall full of sliding trays with bodies in them, but the viewing room wasn't like that. It was small, with subdued light, and the body was actually in an adjacent chamber, with glass in between. A woman attendant, also in scrubs, was in the room with the body.

The body was very white, and naked except for a cloth covering the face, and a towel folded over the genitals. The front of the torso had been blackened, and there were deep circular wounds dished over the arms and torso. The Y-shaped incision of the autopsy had been closed with large stitches.

Only the legs seemed normal.

Dagmar felt a lightness wash over her, a floating sensation as if she were on the very edge of sleep. She continued walking toward the body, but her feet felt as if she were walking on pillows, reaching a long way before they met the ground.

The shaven-headed attendant stayed behind her, quite close. To catch her if she fainted dead away.

She came up to the glass and stopped. She looked at the wounds on the arms and torso. It looked as if someone had gone into the flesh with a melon baller.

"What are those?" she said, pointing.

Murdoch understood her vague question.

"Shrapnel wounds," he said. "The bomb was packed with nails, probably dipped in rat poison."

Dagmar looked at Murdoch in utter surprise. *The bomb wasn't* enough? she thought.

"Rat poison prevents clotting," Murdoch said.

"Ma'am?" The woman attendant's voice came through a speaker. "Can you identify the victim?"

Dagmar felt herself sway. She turned to the body again, flesh the color of raw dough except where it had been burned or wounded, and realized that this was the only time she had seen Charlie without his clothes.

It was clearly Charlie. The tall, thin body reeked of Charlieness. But she didn't know how she knew this.

"I can't really tell," she said. "But I'm sure it's him."

"We need a definite identification, ma'am," the male attendant said.

"In that case," Dagmar said, "I can't."

The woman attendant took a step closer to the body. Dagmar noticed that she was wearing surgical gloves.

"The face is badly—there really isn't a face left," she said. "But if I remove the cover, maybe you can identify the shape of the face or the—"

"No," said Dagmar. "No, I won't look at that."

She turned and walked out. Her vision seemed to have narrowed; she felt as if she were walking down the length of a telescope.

The intensity of the light in the corridor startled her. She stood blinking on the green and white tile floor. Murdoch stood at her elbow. The fact of his presence was shocking—it was as if he hadn't walked there but had somehow materialized at that instant.

"Do you think you might want to sit down?" he asked.

"Just get me out of here," Dagmar said.

Murdoch's Crown Victoria smelled of leather and gun oil. Hissing voices spoke inscrutable ten-codes from the police radio. Dagmar closed her eyes and leaned against the headrest as he accelerated onto I-5.

"Damn," he said in his mild voice. She opened her eyes and saw the flashes of taillights, long rows of them.

Rush hour had commenced. They were probably going to spend the next hour trapped on the freeway.

"Don't worry about the identification," Murdoch said. "They can do a DNA with hair from his bathroom at home or something. Though that will take a while."

"Mm," said Dagmar. She wasn't paying attention; she was just relieved that she had avoided the Phantom of the Opera moment, the unmasking of Charlie's mutilated face.

The car crawled at about ten miles an hour toward the San Fernando Valley. Dagmar thought of Charlie's plaster-white flesh and the horrible gouges of the shrapnel.

"Why did they do it?" she found herself saying.

"The Maffya?" Murdoch's pinched mouth gave a twist. "Money. It's why they do anything."

"I mean," Dagmar began, and realized that she had no idea what she had meant.

"I mean"—starting again—"why a bomb?"

Murdoch considered this. "Because the killer can be somewhere else when the bomb goes off," he said. "A bomb is a lot more anonymous than a gun. With a gun you have to be on the scene when the killing takes place."

"But you need a lot of technical knowledge to make a bomb."

"Not for a gunpowder bomb, and this was a gunpowder bomb." She looked at him. "The smell," he said. "That was powder."

Dagmar didn't remember a gunpowder smell, or any kind of smell at all, but then she supposed she could trust a police officer to know what gunpowder smelled like.

"You can legally buy up to a pound of smokeless powder at a time," Murdoch said. "You can buy it at any gun store. You can buy it at Wal-Mart. For use in reloading ammunition."

Dagmar thought idly about getting the players to track gunpowder sales in Greater Los Angeles.

"You can get a fuse from a model rocket kit," Murdoch said. "You can find the instructions for the whole thing on the Internet."

"It's that easy?" Dagmar asked.

Murdoch's unsurprised eyes gazed out over the hood of the Crown Victoria.

"Just google *Anarchist Cookbook*," he said.

The trip to the North Hollywood Station took more than an hour. Dagmar thanked Murdoch for driving and got into her Prius. She didn't feel like continuing the crawl along the 101, so she took back streets toward her apartment.

She realized she didn't want to be alone in her rooms and wondered if she should stop somewhere and have dinner. But she didn't have an appetite, so she stopped at a coffee shop and ordered a chai tea latte and bought a copy of that morning's *New York Times* and read every

page, even the sports news, which she usually skipped.
The fact that none of the news was local was a comfort.
She didn't want to think about L.A. or the bombing or
the wounds in Charlie's bloodless body.

By the time she finished the paper, it was after dark
and she felt the stirrings of hunger. She drove to a
Chinese place and had twice-cooked pork, half of which
she carried away in a white cardboard take-out box.

She went to her apartment and to her room. She took
a shower, and when she finished toweling, her phone
began its song. She looked at the display and saw that it
was Siyed.

After the misery of these past few days, Dagmar found
Siyed too pathetic a distraction to think about. She
pressed the End button to divert Siyed to voice mail.

A few minutes later the phone chimed to let her know
that someone had left a message. She turned the phone
off.

Dagmar fell onto the bed and slept. She dreamed.
Somewhere in her awareness was a sense of gratitude
that she didn't dream about Charlie, or his body, or what
was behind the cloth tented over his face.

She dreamed about a lake, blue under blue skies. The
shore was green with birch and poplar. It was a scene
from her girlhood in Ohio, and in the dream she was a
girl, gliding over a green lawn as she ran from a lakeside
cabin to a sagging wooden picnic table. Little gold and
brown butterflies flew ahead of her on tangled Brownian
bearings.

Dagmar's experience of the scene was strangely
bifurcated. She was Girl Dagmar, running through the

butterflies, and a smaller part of her was Grown-up Dagmar, the vigilant puppetmaster, supervising the scene to make certain that untoward, disturbing elements of her more recent past did not intrude.

Her father sat at the picnic table, smoking a cigarette, a glass of amber liquid by his hand. He wore cutoff jeans and a faded Metallica T-shirt. He wasn't the sad, sly, frustrated man he became later, the man who pawned her computer to buy vodka, but a warm, smiling, benign parent whose breath was scented with tobacco and Irish whiskey.

Girl Dagmar hugged her father, climbed onto his lap. Grown-up Dagmar, watching the scene, felt a shock as she recognized Girl Dagmar's Sport Girl denim skirt, with its narrow pockets and cartoony appliquéd bird. Girl Dagmar had actually worn that skirt.

Dagmar's father kissed Girl Dagmar's cheek, and she felt the bristles on his chin. A motorboat raced over the blue water.

Out of the cabin, with its asphalt-shingled walls, came Dagmar's mother, carrying a plate in either hand. Grown-up Dagmar felt that her mother's appearance was anachronistic—with her hair pinned back and her lipstick and an apron over the straight skirt that fell to below her knees, she looked like a late 1940s movie mom, not the Reagan-era parent that she actually was.

Dream Mom put the plates on the table, and Dagmar saw that they held sloppy joes. Grown-up Dagmar hadn't eaten a sloppy joe since she had left Cleveland.

Girl Dagmar could smell the onions and tomato sauce. She slipped off her father's knees and picked up her fork and ate.

The tastes of her childhood flooded her palate. Grown-up Dagmar approved.

The dream, or memory, floated serenely on. Grown-up Dagmar, watching from her corner of the sky, approved of everything: the lake, the motorboat, the spicy sauce on the ground beef, the soft texture of the bun. The sun on Girl Dagmar's arms, the smile on her father's face.

When she woke, she was smiling.

The sunny Ohio afternoon stayed with her as she rose, took her shower, and poured her first cup of coffee.

It wasn't until she looked out her kitchen window and saw the parking lot with its flashing lights and yellow crime-scene tape that the last of the dream faded into the Valley's hard, snarling morning light.

CHAPTER TWENTY-FOUR

This Is Not a Suspect

FROM: Chatsworth Osborne Jr.

According to <u>this online article</u> from the *L.A. Times,* Arkady Petrovich Litvinov has been arrested in SoCal. So that thread of the game has now been wound up— assuming of course that it *was* really a part of the game somehow, and not a way of turning us into a posse.

FROM: Corporal Carrot

Did any of us have anything to do with catching him?

FROM: Chatsworth Osborne Jr.

The article doesn't say.

FROM: Consuelo

Not to brag or anything, but it was me.

I tracked him down at the Oceanside Motel in Santa Barbara. Dagmar alerted the police. I've posted a <u>video of the arrest</u>.

FROM: Chatsworth Osborne Jr.

Mild applause. Kudos to the Clever, etc.

FROM: Hippolyte

Whoa! Next to Chatty's article is <u>this item</u>, *just posted,* that says that the victim in the L.A. bombing this morning in the Figueroa Hotel has been tentatively identified as Charles Ruff, founder of Great Big Idea!

FROM: LadyDayFan

??!!??

FROM: Consuelo

Did this happen before Tuesday evening? Because that's when I had Litvinov under surveillance.

FROM: Corporal Carrot

This is weird. I was in that hotel just the other day.

FROM: Chatsworth Osborne Jr.

Passing strange. Is this another piece of metafiction? I wonder if we will be asked to find the bomber.

FROM: LadyDayFan

If we're going to solve anything, it better be after Saturday, when we have to sample every source of water in the world!

FROM: LadyDayFan

Looking at the article, it seems clear that Charlie Ruff is really dead.

FROM: Vikram

What difference does that make?

Dagmar's car was in the part of the parking lot cordoned off by the crime-scene tape. Police cars with flashing lights sat parked in the street. Uniformed officers and detectives clumped in the parking lot, and a photographer's flash briefly lit the palm trees near the street. An ambulance waited nose-in to the parking lot. Several of Dagmar's neighbors, none known to her by name, stood outside the tape barrier, impatient to get to work.

"What's happening?" she asked.

"Sandy found a body," someone said.

Dagmar felt her spirits deflate like the air sighing out

of a tire. It was too much of a coincidence to believe that this brand-new dead person was not somehow known to her.

A whiff of the ginkgo fruit floated through the air and turned Dagmar's stomach.

She looked at the detectives for Murdoch but didn't see him. She called to one of the uniformed officers.

"Can I see the body?" she asked. "I might know him."

There was a consultation, and a young detective came over. He was Asian, with bad acne.

"You think you might know the victim?" he said.

"I know lots of people," Dagmar said.

"You can't go too close," the detective said. "We haven't finished processing the crime scene."

He held up the tape so that she could pass under it, and he took her elbow and gingerly took her past the trunk of her white Prius to where the body was visible between an old Buick and a Volvo station wagon.

Dagmar felt her vision narrow, darkness approaching from all directions, just as it had in the morgue.

"I know him," she said. "Siyed Prasad."

The detective produced a PDA. With his stylus he tapped a part of the screen that said Record, and then took notes on the screen.

"Could you spell that?"

Dagmar spelled it.

"Did he live in this building?" the detective asked.

"No. He was an actor flown in for a commercial. I think he was at the Chateau Marmont."

"Was he from India?"

"No. He was British."

She kept looking at the body. It was tiny, crumpled between the two cars as if it had fallen there from out of the sky. Siyed wore a white shirt and white Dockers, both soiled with dirt and with blood. One foot was bare, and the sandal lay upside down on the asphalt a few feet away.

"How did you know him?"

For the first time she looked away from Siyed, into the detective's hardened, acne-scarred face.

"He was stalking me," she said.

The detective's expression changed in some unfathomable but definitive way.

For the first time, Dagmar realized that she might be in trouble. There were three bodies, and she was the only connection between them.

If the police thought like police, which they most likely did, she had just jumped the quantum gap from witness to suspect.

"Could you call Detective Murdoch?" she said. "He knows me."

"Do I need a lawyer?" Dagmar asked.

"Why would you think that?" asked Murdoch.

Dagmar looked at the interrogation room, the plain walls in depressing institutional colors, the metal table with its loops for handcuffs, the poster informing suspects of their rights, and the mirror behind which, if television was to be trusted, there was a camera.

"Why would I need a lawyer?" she repeated. "Let's just say I'm getting that vibe."

Murdoch and the Asian cop, whose name was Kim, had asked Dagmar to come to the station and make another statement. She had declined Kim's offer of a ride and followed him to the station in her Prius. They'd provided the same equipment as last time, the lapel mics, computer, and screen that broadcast her words as text.

Vibe, she saw, was flagged as a suspect word. *Vice, vile*, and *tribe* were suggested as alternatives.

This interrogation was different from the other. The detectives were much more interested in her answers, for one thing.

"But," said Kim, "why would you *think*—"

"I'm not going to speculate about my intuitions," Dagmar said. "Why don't you ask your questions?"

They complied. She told them that she had hired Siyed Prasad for a game called *Curse of the Golden Nagi*, which had ended five months before in India. She had to spell out *nagi* and explain what a nagi was. She told them she'd been sexually involved with Siyed but had broken it off when she'd discovered he was married.

"Did that make you angry?" Kim asked.

What the fuck do you *think?* Dagmar wanted to respond, but she settled for, "Yes."

There were more questions about the state of her emotions, all of which seemed somehow askew, as if the detectives had never actually experienced emotions themselves and were trying to figure out what they were and how they worked. She began to suspect that her actual feelings meant less than the theory into which they could jack her answers. After a while, she worked out the equation into which they were trying to fit her.

$E+R=3H$. In which E was emotion, R rage, and the rest multiple homicide.

She pointed at the transcription machine.

"Just have your transcript read, 'Shaw shrugs.'" She looked at Murdoch. "Why don't you ask me when I next heard from Siyed?"

Kim seemed a little taken aback by this, but Murdoch, without surprise, replied in his bland professional way.

"All right," he said. "When did you hear from him next?"

"Just after Austin was killed," Dagmar said. "Siyed sent me emails saying he was coming to Los Angeles to do a commercial and he wanted to meet me. I told him I wouldn't be available."

There was a flicker of interest behind Murdoch's blue eyes.

"Do these emails still exist?" he asked.

"I think so. I'll provide copies if so."

She didn't think there was anything in the emails that would send her to the gas chamber.

She said that more emails had followed, and phone calls. And a lot of flowers. She said she hadn't responded to it, or had told Siyed to leave.

"I called his wife," she said. "I told her that Siyed had gone crazy and that she should call him and get him to come home." She shrugged. "I guess it didn't work."

Kim looked interested.

"Did you tell her that her husband was involved with you?"

"*Had been* involved," Dagmar corrected. "And no, I didn't." She felt immediately that she'd given the wrong answer. The wronged woman might always make a good suspect.

"It's possible that she knew anyway," she said. "Siyed was acting pretty strange."

Murdoch considered this.

"You didn't at any time see Siyed in person?" he asked.

Dagmar took a breath. She'd been hoping this question wouldn't come up.

"Yes," she said. "A few days ago. He turned up at my apartment and tried to talk to me when I came home from work. I told him to go home, and the next day I called his wife."

"What did he say?"

"He told me he loved me. He told me he had told his wife about us, but I later learned he'd lied about that."

"How did that make you feel?" Kim asked.

Again with the feelings, as if they alone would justify a charge of murder.

Act on our feelings, she thought, *and who would 'scape hanging?*

Dagmar looked at Kim.

"It made me feel terrified," she said.

"And angry?"

"And *terrified*," said Dagmar. "I'd never told him where I lived. He'd tracked me down and ambushed me in my own parking lot."

There were a few more questions, but they were just variations on the questions the detectives had already asked. She figured they weren't after clarification; they were just hoping her answers would start contradicting one another, and then they could start picking her story to bits. She stood up.

"I really have to go to work," she said. "Call for an appointment, and I'll try to get you those emails."

The two detectives looked at each other.

"Siyed's wife is named Manjari," Dagmar said. "I don't know exactly how to spell it, but I know they're in the London phone directory."

"We'll terminate the interview, then," Murdoch said. He looked at his watch and gave the time and then turned off the dictation machine. Dagmar took off her lapel mic.

"How was Siyed killed?" she asked.

"We won't know till the autopsy," Murdoch said, "but it looks as if he was beaten to death."

Dagmar's reaction, for which she hoped she would later feel ashamed, was relief. She looked down at her hands, her knuckles—no bruises, no cuts. She held the hands up for the others to see.

"Well," she said, "doesn't look like I've been in a fist-fight, does it?"

"The killer," said Kim, "might have used a club or a pipe or something."

"Or something," Dagmar repeated pointlessly. Relief blew through her like a warm desert wind. She walked around the table to the door, then stopped.

"My God," she said. "Siyed left voice mail last night. I'd forgot."

She got out her phone, thumbed buttons, brought up voice mail.

"Not yet," said Murdoch. He reached for the transcription machine. "Can you put the phone on speaker?"

Dagmar could. She waited for Murdoch to engage the

transcription device, punched up the volume, and called up voice mail.

"Dagmar, my darling." Siyed's voice was distorted and tinny, a reminder that he was speaking from the afterlife.

"I'm sorry, but I couldn't stay away," he said. "I just wanted to see you. I watched you go through the gate. I know that's naughty. I promise I won't approach you again."

Words advanced on the screen, then paused. Dagmar's eyes, tracking the screen, focused on the word *naughty*.

"There's another man here," he said. "A man watching. I wanted to call you about it, but your phone won't answer. He is very interested in you. After you went inside, he got out and walked around your car and then looked under it. Now he's watching again . . ."

The voice trailed away. The transcription machine waited patiently. Dagmar's heart filled the silence with sudden thunder.

Siyed's voice turned impatient. "I'm going to talk to him," Siyed said. "I didn't like the way he was looking at your machine."

Just before the phone call ended came the sound of a car door opening, Siyed marching to his death.

He was such a little man, Dagmar remembered. Five foot three or something. Even the average American couch potato could have given him a thrashing without breaking a sweat.

Damn actors and their egos, Dagmar thought. Siyed thought he was a superhero and had walked right up to the man who killed him.

With adrenaline-clumsy fingers, Dagmar punch. buttons on her phone and saved the voice mail. Ki. turned off the transcription machine.

All the tension seemed to have drained out of the room.

"You'll forward that to us?" Murdoch asked.

"If I can find out how to do that," Dagmar said.

"Who's your carrier?" Kim asked.

Dagmar told him. He wrote it down.

Murdoch's blue eyes seemed to look at her from a hundred miles away.

"Do you have any idea," he asked, "who this other watcher might be?"

She shook her head.

The man who was waiting to kill me, she thought. Fire licked along her nerves.

"I've got to leave," she said suddenly.

But where, she thought, would she go?

She didn't want to think about the killer who was tracking her. She decided to deal with another problem, one that Special Agent Landreth had declined to help her with.

Richard the Assassin sat quietly in his fifth-floor office, his white-noise generator hissing quietly from the window. A series of screens curved around him like a heads-up display the size of the room. The ninja action figures posed in a long glass case on top of his bookshelf.

"Yes," he said. "I can get you Charlie's emails, at least providing he was using his AvN Soft email address. Our email clients use IMAP protocol, not POP3. All emails stored on the server unless they're specifically deleted." He glanced up. "It makes it easier for people who use different computers in different locations to get their email."

"Charlie was in touch with people at brokerage houses," Dagmar said. "He'd discovered that someone was using illegal copies of Rialto, and he wanted to send a patch to those copies to shut them down."

Richard looked at her.

"That's kind of interesting," he said. "I heard that from one of the Great Big Idea people, and when I told some folks on the AvN Soft side, they said they hadn't heard anything about it."

"You're hearing about it now," said Dagmar.

Richard drew a finger down the side of his jaw.

"Okayyy," he said slowly.

Dagmar reached into her jeans pocket and took out the memory stick.

"Here's the final version of Charlie's patch," she said, "along with all the IP addresses that have been harvested so far. There will be more on Monday, when Tapping the Source goes into play."

Richard took the portable memory and looked at it.

"What do you want me to do with this?" he asked.

"Copy it to a secure location," Dagmar said, "because I think that's what got Charlie killed."

The white-noise generator hissed as Richard looked at the memory stick in his hand.

"Maybe," he said, "we should find out if this thing works."

"How?"

"We've got the patch. We've got IP addresses. Let's send it out and see what happens."

Dagmar considered this.

"Firewall the hell out of it," she said, "and let's go for a drive."

Dagmar moved one of the office chairs so that she could watch over Richard's shoulder. He plugged the memory stick into one of his sliver-thin state-of-the-art laptops and downloaded the patch onto a virtual drive that he created especially for the program. He made certain his firewalls were in place and then ran the program.

A window appeared on his display.

>**Insert target address.**
>

"Well," Dagmar said, "the display's a classic."

Richard opened one of the files of addresses and typed.

>**161.148.066.255**

Richard hit Enter, and another prompt appeared. Richard clicked on another window, one of his firewalls, and gave permission for a message to go out.

"It sent some kind of ping," he said.

Richard typed in another address, hit Enter, and then repeated the procedure several times.

One of the firewall windows opened.

"That first address is responding," he said.

He gave permission for the firewall to let the message enter.

>161.148.066.255 infected. Patch sent.

"Damn," Richard said. "We got lucky first time out."

He had to give permission for the patch to clear the firewall. Less than a minute later, another message appeared.

>161.148.066.255 clean.

And not only was 161.148.066.255 clean, Dagmar knew, but it was now busy scrubbing other computers, spreading the patch to every machine in its network.

They had done all this, she reminded herself, without knowing where the target computer was or who it belonged to. Who *any* of them belonged to.

She and Richard spent the next half hour sending the patch to IP addresses on Charlie's list. Twenty-eight percent were infected and were cleansed with Charlie's patch.

Charlie's plan, his demented plan, was working.

Richard pushed his chair back from the machine and rolled his shoulders.

"How many IP addresses left?"

"Thousands. Maybe hundreds of thousands—I haven't looked."

Richard blinked. It was one thing to test your ninja mettle against a cunning opponent; it was another to slave over a keyboard in order to type in zillions of addresses.

"Let's call it a day's work, shall we?" he said.

"Now you understand," said Dagmar, "why we wa[nt] millions of players to work with these IP addresses."

He nodded.

She raised her arms and stretched, opening her chest, filling her lungs with air.

One of Richard's other machines gave a chime. He wheeled his office chair to another part of his desk and frowned at the display.

"Someone's trying to go through the firewall," he said.

"Not one of the targets?"

"No. They'd be identified by IP address only. This is someone at the company." He paused as he read the monitor, then turned to look over his shoulder at Dagmar.

"It's you," he said.

She looked at him in surprise.

"What do you mean?" she asked.

"It's someone using your account."

She bolted out of her chair to look at the display. "Who?"

Richard shrugged. "He's calling from off-site," he said. He frowned at the screen for a moment. "We could let him do what he wants," he said, "and find out what he's after."

"Have you got a secure copy of the patch?"

Richard wheeled to the computer with the patch on it, pulled the memory stick, and held it so that Dagmar could see it. She took the stick from his hand. That left only the copy on the hard drive.

Richard let the intruder through the firewall, and

y watched as Patch 2.0 was overwritten by something
se.

"Slightly smaller file size," Richard said after a few
minutes' analysis. "Still an executable file. Best guess is
that it's an earlier version of the patch."

"Or a patch that's been rewritten."

Richard frowned. "Let's do a comparison."

More firewalls, software run, code rolling at near light
speed on the monitors.

"There's a difference," Richard said, pointing. Code
highlighted in blinking red. Dagmar narrowed her eyes,
looked from one screen to the next.

"It's a bank routing code," Dagmar said. "The . . .
intruder"—*the other me*—"he's changing the program to
send money to a different account." She looked at the
prefix. "An account in a different country, I think."

Richard's scanning program found other changes.
Dagmar scanned the symbols and compared one to the
next and tried to summon the programming skills she'd
once possessed.

You could tell the difference between the programmers. The original code was elegant and concise; the new
stuff consisted of code laid down in huge swaths, clumsy
and overhasty.

But it would work, this new code. It would work perfectly well.

"Charlie's patch," she said, "sends the patch to every
other bot the program knows about, then turns the bot
off. But that feature has been deleted in this new one. It
just lets the program run."

"But it changes the bot's owner."

"Yes. All the profits get sent to the new account."

Richard nodded. "Elegant," he said. "Meet the new boss, same as the old boss."

The new boss kills people, she thought. *Dips nails in rat poison and packs them around explosive cores.*

He looked at her. "Which one of the bosses is the bomber? Which is the Maffya?"

She thought about it. "Does it matter?"

Richard's face took on a grim cast. He rolled his chair to a third machine and began typing.

"I'm going to find out what our intruder's been up to."

He scanned data for a moment, then turned to Dagmar again.

"You've been in all sorts of places where you're not allowed," he said. "Someone's given you superuser status."

"Who can do that?" Dagmar asked.

"Me. And Charlie Ruff, but he's dead."

"Can you find out who made me a superuser?"

More tapping. He frowned. "Someone who shouldn't be a superuser, either, but he is. He has the handle CRAPJOB."

A thousand pieces fell into place in Dagmar's head, an action like a reverse explosion, a million bits of shrapnel flying together to form a perfect, seamless platonic solid.

She was astonished there was no sound. She should have heard the universe cracking.

Her heart and the jolt of adrenaline caught up long after the moment of comprehension, too late, useless for anything except making her hands tremble . . .

Richard tapped his keyboard. "Man!" he said. "That CRAPJOB account is only three days old! And then all

APJOB did was grant you superuser status, and since
en all the activity's been on *your* account."

He turned, looked over his shoulder. "Any idea who
this is?"

Dagmar shook her head. Unconvincingly, she thought.

Richard turned back to his machine. "I'll cancel that
account," he said. "And yours. And then we'll give you a
new account."

"*No!*" Dagmar lunged from her chair and put her
hand over his. Richard looked at her in surprise.

"What's the matter?"

"When you're played," Dagmar said, "you play back."

Richard's eyes narrowed in thought.

"We tell him what he wants to know," Dagmar said.
"And then we pull the rug out from under him."

Richard the Assassin looked at her with a growing
admiration.

"Excellent," he said.

ACT 3

CHAPTER TWENTY-FIVE

This Is Not a Place to Hide

Dagmar cleaned her office. Dropping Siyed's faded flowers, one pot after another, into the trash can, the series of clangs ringing off the walls, echoing down the hall.

A warning Klaxon.

Dagmar on the warpath. Stay away.

She picked up the trash can with its ceramic, earth, and plant matter and carried it away in a swirl of dry petals. She didn't have a place to put it, really, so she took it to the break room and swapped it for the trash can there. It held only used tea bags, foil packets that had once contained instant hot chocolate, and an empty donut box.

It was a lot lighter.

He had trapdoors everywhere, Charlie had said. *He'd been thinking about doing a scorched-earth on the company long before I took control . . . Wiping out everything before the creditors could have it, or lurking in the computers in order to sabotage our successors or to steal things. Bad as the damn Soong. He could have ended up in jail!*

Except that Charlie had locked him out before he could do any damage. It had been Dagmar herself who gave him a computer, an account, and a paycheck. Once he had access, he used one of his trapdoors to create CRAPJOB and alter Dagmar's own account so that he could use it to go anywhere in AvN Soft's system.

The balance of the account, as of 1600 hours Cayman time yesterday, was $12,344,946,873.23, all in U.S. dollars.

That had been posted on Our Reality Network, where anyone could read it. The players assumed the numbers had been made up, but Dagmar had known they were real.

And one other person had seen that number and realized right away what Charlie had done, and had known how to turn the whole thing to his own advantage.

Figueroa? That's on Figueroa, right?

My God, she'd spoken Charlie's location aloud right in front of him.

She remembered him standing ten feet away, sipping his coffee, pretending he wasn't listening.

She remembered him in the steak house, the dull fury in his eyes as he talked about Charlie stealing his company.

Dagmar went into her office and dropped the trash can next to her desk. Another clang.

She grabbed a dusty stack of papers from her shelf and, without looking at them, dumped them in the trash. They'd been there for months: if they were important, she'd have needed them by now.

You are *helping*, she'd said. *You're the only person I can talk to.*

And then she'd handed him all he needed in order to kill Charlie and collect millions. Billions.

He had played her. He had played her totally.

His games back at Caltech had always been about deviousness and betrayal. All the nonplayer characters in the games had their own agenda. They all functioned within ruthless, logical parameters. They were all treacherous, all faithless, all false. Charlie, Dagmar, and Austin had grown to trust the fact that they would be stabbed in the back sooner or later.

Dagmar hadn't realized that the games were *autobiography*. All those false-hearted mercenaries, recreant knights, and traitorous grandmothers were the same person.

They were all BJ.

All along he had been telling the world how his mind worked, and everyone had thought it was fiction.

She could reconstruct his chain of logic.

Charlie and BJ had worked on Rialto *together*. They *both* created the algorithm that the agents used to acquire knowledge and evolve new strategies.

Why, he must have wondered, should Charlie be the only one to profit?

Charlie had *cheated* him. Let the company go into bankruptcy just so that he could buy it with money he'd earned on the sly.

Charlie *owed* him. Owed him on the business, the money, the clothes, the cars, the homes. Owed him half of everything.

Charlie wasn't paying that debt—and the debt was

greater than BJ had ever imagined, half of twelve *billion*, as he had just discovered. So when chance made the opportunity not only desirable but profitable, Charlie was punished by having his face shredded from his skull with sixpenny nails.

Which didn't quite solve the problem, because it only reduced the number of people who knew about the gold-farming bots from three to two.

Dagmar had to be dealt with, too.

Because, in this line of utilitarian reasoning, Dagmar was just another obstacle.

Dagmar found another pile of old papers and heaved them into the trash. The can rocked; a small cloud of dust rose.

She looked at the rocking trash can and dared it to tip over.

It chose obedience and returned to an upright setting.

Richard entered the room on his silent white Converse sneaks, a laptop in his hands. His nose wrinkled at the scent of dust.

"I've got your new machine. And your new account."

"Very good."

She dumped another stack of papers to clear a space on the desk, and Richard put the machine down.

By then, Richard had found out how Dagmar's account had been compromised. A keystroke monitor had been installed on her office computer, one that recorded every single letter or numeral that she typed and made it available for download by someone else. It had given away her passwords, which were the keys to everything else. BJ had found Patch 2.0 on the IMAP server and acted to replace it with his own, searching through the entire system for the patch and its copies, then overwriting them with the patch that had the number of his own offshore account.

I'm looking for the script for Week Six, Part One, BJ had said. She'd found him using her computer. He had just installed the keystroke monitor.

Dagmar should have recognized BJ's careless, sloppy coding. He was always in too much of a hurry for elegant code.

Richard set up the computer and connected it with a cable to the AvN Soft network.

"You don't use the wireless network now," Richard said. "You don't know who's going to be listening."

"Check," Dagmar said.

Her old computer would be used entirely for routine correspondence, and for anything she wanted BJ to know.

Richard handed her a portable memory card. "Here's all the details of Charlie's correspondence with the brokerage firms."

"Thanks."

The new computer, with her new online identity, would be used for anything important.

She booted the new computer, paged through Charlie's email on the memory card, and wrote the first of several emails to the officers of various brokerage firms. She let them know that, after Mr. Ruff's unfortunate death, she was now handling the matter of the bootleg Rialto programs, and she hoped to continue the same degree of cooperation, particularly in the matter of the trades for Tapping the Source Ltd. on the following Monday.

She sent that letter eighteen times. A brief business letter, eighteen times, to help save the world.

She got out a notepad and wrote a list of things to do.

- *Contact players*
- *Follow up emails to brokers*
- *Manage Saturday upload*
- *Hide*

With someone—with *BJ*, since she had to think of him as the enemy now—with BJ staking out her apartment, there was no way she'd return there. She'd have to find a hotel or something and hope it worked out better for her than for Charlie.

BJ, she thought, could have killed Siyed easily. With his big hands and powerful arms and shoulders, he could have hammered the little man to the ground with only his fists.

Dagmar wondered if he had bruises and cuts. If so, he would be avoiding her until he healed.

She stared out the window into the parking lot. Sudden hot rage flooded her. BJ had reached through *her* to kill Charlie. He had used her—*used her very own tools*—to deceive, to manipulate, and to kill.

She tilted her head back and *screamed,* a hoarse cry of fury and frustration and grief. Her ears rang with the sound.

After her shriek, the silence of the building seemed profound.

In a storm of anger she reached for her pen and added a new item to the list.

• *Fuck up BJ*

Her actual job title was executive producer, but the players called her puppetmaster.

She hadn't lived up to the name. She'd been dancing at the ends of someone else's strings, a perfect, cooperative pawn in someone else's fantasy of power and murder.

It was time to show BJ just who the real puppetmaster was.

Then she put the pen down on the desk and thought about nothing else for a long while.

"Are you all right?"

Dagmar considered her answer while she turned the notebook over so that Helmuth couldn't read her notes.

It was safe to say, she thought, that she was not all right.

She swung her chair around to face him. He stood in the doorway, a concerned look on his handsome blond head.

"I had to identify Charlie's body," she said. Explaining about Siyed, she'd decided, would have taken too much energy.

"I'm sorry," Helmuth said.

"I couldn't identify him," Dagmar said. "He was too torn up."

Helmuth seemed not to know where to go from there. He took a step into the room and raised his arms. Dagmar rose from her chair and hugged him.

Perhaps she felt a little better.

They surrendered their embrace. "Some of us are going out for pizza," Helmuth said. "Want to come?"

She shook her head. "I have too much work."

"Should we bring some pizza back for you?"

"That would be nice, yes."

"Your friend Boris did well last night."

The words sent a shock through her. Her mind whirled. Her shock must have been clear, because Helmuth clarified.

"The mix-up about Banana Split," he said.

"Oh." A hollow laugh rose from her chest. "I'd forgotten about all that."

"Boris went into one of the chat rooms on *Planet Nine* and waited for some of the players to come in— they've started hanging around Joe's Joint and the Galaxy, like they were real clubs. Desi was there, and Corporal Carrot, and some others. And Boris started up a conversation about hauling asteroid ore to the smelters at the New Dome on Mars, and along the way he mentioned he'd like to ski the Banana Split someday." He laughed. "You should have seen how fast they all left the room! Boris was all alone, talking to himself!"

"He's slick," Dagmar said.

Helmuth nodded approvingly.

"He calls you Hellmouth, by the way," Dagmar said. "After the other night."

Helmuth smiled. "I bait the hook of temptation," he said, "but do they bite?"

"How late were you out?"

"Three or four, I think."

"Well," Dagmar said, "be careful he doesn't corrupt *you*."

After Helmuth left, Dagmar sat before her computer again. BJ had been out with Helmuth all of Wednesday night and well into Thursday morning, when Charlie had died.

BJ had gone out with Helmuth to establish his alibi, and then compounded the alibi by sending Dagmar a letter filled with Internet cant, one that arrived in her mailbox at a certain time. Charlie died a short time afterward, which gave BJ a small window to actually plant the bomb himself, but BJ had probably intended the bomb to explode sometime Wednesday night.

The killer can be somewhere else when the bomb goes off, Murdoch had said. *A bomb is a lot more anonymous than a gun. With a gun you have to be on the scene when the killing takes place.*

Do they really do what you tell them to? BJ had asked.

Yes, Dagmar had said. *They do.*

She called up the complete list of players who had registered for *The Long Night of Briana Hall.* They had all provided their phone numbers, email addresses, and street addresses.

It was possible to sort the list for all those who were in one category or other, an area code or zip code. She sorted for area codes in the Los Angeles area, 213, 818, 747, 323, and the others, including those used by cell phones. She made a point of excluding BJ's number, and then she sent the rest the same email.

FROM: Dagmar Shaw
SUBJECT: L.A. Games

Greetings:

This is Dagmar Shaw, executive producer of Great Big
Idea games.

It's come to our attention that someone may be piggybacking their own game off our own game about Briana
Hall. This person may have sent some of you on a live
event on Wednesday afternoon or evening.

These missions were not a part of our own game.

We hope that those of you who took these missions had
a good time, but we want to make certain that none of
you were defrauded or humiliated in some way. If you
were contacted by anyone about this event or any other
that has not appeared on our *Briana Hall* site, I would like
to know about it.

If you have been contacted, please email me at this address.

And please don't tell anyone else or put this online,
because we don't want people to start distrusting our
genuine messages, puzzles, and clues.

Sincerely,

Dagmar Shaw

It didn't take long for the email to generate an answer.

FROM: Desi
SUBJECT: re: L.A. Games

I was part of the live event on Wednesday night. I was supposed to be working for David. He called me and asked me to carry a disk with information from Cullen's firm that Briana would need to expose the rogue traders.

I took it from Topanga Canyon over to Venice. I hope that's okay.

Disk? Dagmar thought. *Venice?*

For a moment her whole fantasy seemed to tremble on the edge of dissolution. She looked up Desi's number and called. A woman answered.

"Is Desi there?" Dagmar asked.

"Desi?" The woman seemed genuinely puzzled.

"I'm sorry," Dagmar said. "Desi is his handle. Is there someone in the house who plays online games?"

"Oh." The woman's voice was amused. "That would be Jeremiah."

Jeremiah? Dagmar thought. She heard the sound of a phone being picked up by another hand.

"Yes?" The deep baritone had a resonant James Earl Jones quality to it that suggested an actor or disk jockey, a singer or a preacher, someone used to projecting a trained voice to an audience.

"This is Dagmar Shaw," she said. "Thanks for responding to my email."

"No problem," said Desi. "I hope what I did was all right."

"Oh, we're not worried about that. We just hope you weren't the victim of some kind of practical joke."

"No," Desi said. "It was kind of fun, actually."

"Tell me what happened."

"Well," said Desi, "it started when I got a call from David."

David was a fictional character, Maria Perry's gay friend. His part in Briana's story was minor, which made David a good choice, because he never appeared on any of the game's audio files. When BJ called, he wouldn't have had to worry about matching an actor's voice.

"David asked me if I was willing to perform a special favor for Briana on Wednesday night. I was asked to pick up a disk that had been hidden by Maria in Topanga Canyon. I got the disk and put it in a bag from Burger King as I was instructed to do, and then I carried it to Venice Beach and put it in a certain trash can there. Then I went home.

"I was asked not to talk about it or write about it online, and I haven't."

For players not to post online about their game experiences was very unusual. ARGs were social games; sharing the experience was a part of the game's raison d'être.

"What reason did David give?" she asked.

"He said it was a special mission, just for me. Sort of a reward for being a special friend of Briana's, and that if I told anyone about it, they might get jealous."

Dagmar considered this. "Did you copy what was on the disk?" she asked.

"I thought about it, but I was told it was encrypte and that I couldn't read it, so I didn't."

"All right," she said. "Well, thanks."

There was a moment of silence, and then the deep voice spoke.

"What should I do if David calls again?"

"Say yes, if you like. But call me to let me know what you're being asked to do."

She gave Desi her mobile number and then said good-bye.

She turned back to her computer and saw that two more people had answered her email. She didn't think she knew either of them personally, though it was possible they'd been in the crowd at certain live events.

Dagmar called them and got more of the story. By the time she'd finished with them, others had responded to her email.

Within an hour she had laid out the entire plot.

David had asked the players to help get Briana some of the IP addresses that would be used to perpetrate the bad guys' stock manipulation. Since IP addresses would turn up in the game the following Wednesday as part of the players' bot hunt, this was actually a plausible thing for the players to do.

Different players were asked to do different things. Some were asked to move the data on its disk from one place to another. Others were asked to shuttle a PC tower from Griffith Observatory to the deserted Cathay Bank parking lot in Chinatown. Others were asked to help move a flat-screen monitor. Still others hand-carried a greeting card from place to place.

"Did you read the greeting card?" Dagmar asked.

"Yes. The envelope was open."

"What kind of card was it?"

"One of those 'Thinking of You' cards. It had some poetry on it. I copied it down—"

"No, that doesn't matter. Was there a message?"

"Yeah, I copied that, too. It said, *You want to play this on this.* With *this* being underlined. And it was signed, *Love, D.*"

Dagmar stared in cold horror at the wall opposite her chair. The players would have read *D.* for David, but Charlie would have thought it stood for Dagmar.

Charlie knew the Maffya was after him and might have hesitated to plug in an anonymous computer that appeared magically on his doorstep. But if he'd thought it was from Dagmar, he'd have tried to play the disk without question.

Dagmar felt her skin tighten in a wave of cold fear.

"Dagmar?" asked the player. "Are you still there?"

"Yes. I'm still here." She rubbed her forehead. "Was the note handwritten?"

"Yes. Blue ballpoint."

She hadn't known one way or another if BJ had any talents as a forger, but there were enough samples of her handwriting around the Great Big Idea offices to give him a good start.

Her calls continued. She found that it was Corporal Carrot who had carried the united PC, monitor, greeting card, and data disk, all packed in a single box, to the Figueroa Hotel.

"I got instructions to put the box at a particular place,"

he said. He sounded like a teenager. "Right at the doc
outside the Medina Suite." There was a pause. "Thi
didn't have anything to do with the bombing, did it? I've
been worried about that ever since I saw that Charles
Ruff had been killed."

Dagmar unclenched her jaw muscles.

"Don't worry about that," she said.

"Oh, good!" The relief in Carrot's voice was clear.
"That's great!"

The last thing Dagmar needed was speculation about
whether players in one of her games had been used in a
terrorist event.

Even if it was true. *Especially* if it was true. It would
cast every future ARG under suspicion, it wouldn't do the
players any good, and it wouldn't help to catch the killer.

She told Carrot that if David called again, he was free
to say yes, but that he should call her right away.

She could see now how Charlie had died. He'd finished
his work on Patch 2.0, emailed the result to Dagmar, and
then gone out for breakfast, or to put one of his empty
Cokes in the flat, or left the room for some other reason.
The box had been placed right in front of his door.
Computer, monitor, disk, and greeting card. He'd read the
note allegedly from Dagmar, then attached the monitor to
the computer, plugged it in, and turned the computer on.

That's when the bomb went off. Or maybe BJ had
worked it so that the bomb was detonated when Charlie
opened the door to insert the data disk. Charlie would
have been right there, peering at the machine at close
range through his glasses, when the gunpowder detonated.

Pain brought Dagmar out of her reverie. She looked

own at her hands and saw that her fists had been clenched so hard that her fingernails had dug hard into her palms.

Killing was too good for BJ.

From outside the office, Dagmar heard the chime of the elevator. She looked out the windows and saw that it had gotten dark, that long lines of red and white auto lights were pouring past on the 101.

She heard footsteps coming toward her across the tile floor, and then she remembered that she was alone in the Great Big Idea offices, and that she'd given BJ access to the building.

Her heart gave a sickening lurch. She jumped out of her chair so quickly that her chair shot backward along its rollers and crashed into a shelf. Her nerves leaped.

Great, she thought. She'd just told him where she was.

She darted around the office looking for a weapon. She clutched at a pair of scissors and then thought of how useless they'd be against BJ's powerful arms and big hands. Hands that had already broken Siyed's body.

Belatedly she realized she could call for help. She reached for her phone with the hand that wasn't holding scissors, punched 911, and was in the process of pressing Send when Helmuth appeared in the doorway carrying a pizza box.

They stared at each other for a moment in mutual surprise.

"God in heaven, Dagmar," Helmuth said. "You look like hell."

Carefully, Dagmar pressed End before the operator could pick up.

"Sorry," she said. "I forgot you were coming back."

Helmuth smiled. "Who did you think I was, Jack the Ripper?"

"Close enough."

He offered the pizza box. "There's pepperoni, there's a slice with mushrooms, and a couple slices of a rather tasty Hawaiian barbecue chicken with pineapple."

"Great," Dagmar said. She summoned the will not to faint dead away.

"Sorry I scared you," Helmuth said.

She put down the scissors and pressed her trembling hands together.

"I think I'm getting used to it," she said.

CHAPTER TWENTY-SIX

This Is Not Desperation

FROM: Dagmar Shaw
SUBJECT: L.A. Games

This is Dagmar Shaw, of Great Big Idea Productions, the company that is bringing you the ARG about Briana Hall.

We've managed to confirm that someone else is running live events that are piggybacking off our game about Briana Hall. These games do not seem to be pranks, but genuine live events running in parallel with our own.

Players should feel free to participate in these events if they feel so inclined, but please be aware that Great Big Idea does not sponsor them, and that discoveries made during the course of these adventures may or may not constitute actual answers to Great Big Idea puzzles.

We would like to continue monitoring this situation, however, so if you hear from anyone asking you to participate in a live event in the next few weeks, please contact me by responding to this email, and please include your phone number.

Please do not post about this on any of the regular forums, because it might confuse our other players about what's going on.

Thank you,

Dagmar Shaw

This Is Not Finance

Dagmar spent Thursday night in the Best Western in Chinatown, a short distance from the Cathay Bank parking lot that had briefly held components of the bomb that had killed Charlie. She had left her Prius in the AvN Soft parking lot, parked directly under the glassy eye of a security camera, and had rented one of the new Mercedes two-seater sports cars from Enterprise, which delivered the vehicle right to the doors of the office tower. She had redlined the Mercedes as she drove out of the Valley, probably tripping half a dozen automatic cameras and generating a couple of thousand dollars in the outrageous fines that California's broken government extorted from its citizens, but at least she knew she hadn't been followed.

The morning news was full of alarmed chatter about the assault on the Chinese yuan, something that Dagmar had missed in the traumas of the previous day. The

arkets in China, where it was already Saturday, were
osed, but the fury continued on other exchanges.

The yuan seemed to be in serious danger. Political
pressure had forced the yuan to decouple from the dollar
a few years earlier, and now a currency much abused by
China's slowing growth, political demands, and inflation
was showing its vulnerability. No one knew whether
China's economic statistics were genuine or mere vapor.
Maybe the Chinese themselves didn't know. In any case
they were now paying the cost of their lack of trans-
parency.

Chinese sovereign wealth funds were dumping bonds,
American and others, in order to free the cash to defend
the yuan, and bond markets were tottering worldwide. As
a consequence the American dollar was plunging, and
the dollar wasn't even the target of the attack. The
Chinese government had been reduced to uttering
threats against whatever foreign governments were
behind the attacks. Dagmar wondered if an actual war
could start over this.

The talking heads on CNN were surprised over the
attack, since it had been widely assumed that it had been
Chinese traders who had led the assault on other currencies. Were the Chinese attacking their own currency?
Were other traders attacking China by way of retalia-
tion? Or was the whole Chinese trader story a myth?

Dagmar, with better information, wondered how the
actual Chinese traders—the ones who had followed
Charlie's gold-mining bots in the currency markets—were
responding to the crisis. Patriotic traders would surely
pour their profits into defending the yuan, risking their

money. Pragmatic traders would follow the bots aga
risking lives and livelihoods if the Chinese governmer
chose to take their resentment out of the electronic worlc
and convert it to real-world shackles and bullets.

Whatever was going on behind the scenes in China,
Dagmar imagined that there was cheering in Jakarta.

After checking out of the hotel, she bought new
clothes and a traveling case, changed in the restroom of a
coffee shop that served her a peculiarly Filipino version of
an American breakfast, bacon and eggs Luzonized, and
showed up late for work to find that no one had missed
her.

She spent half the day writing scripts for *Briana Hall*
and the other half dealing with emails from brokerage
houses. She had a midafternoon meal of vaguely Thai
noodles—chicken, chiles, and cilantro—from the coffee
shop on the ground floor and was walking across Finnish
porphyry to the elevator when "Harlem Nocturne"
began to sound from her handheld. She looked at the
display and saw it was BJ.

She felt a prickle of heat across her skin, and her knees
seemed briefly to buckle. She took a breath of air and it
felt like her first breath in hours.

She sat down on the polished granite ledge that separated the elevator area from the atrium. Her heart beat in
her ribs like a prisoner throwing herself headfirst against
the bars.

BJ had been unable to restrain his curiosity, she told
herself. He'd been staking out her apartment last night
and he hadn't seen her come home. He didn't know
about her reaction to Siyed's death or to Charlie's.

Dagmar told herself that he was going to try to get information from her so that he could kill her. She admonished herself to keep this surmise in the forefront of her mind.

She put the phone to her ear. "This is Dagmar."

"Hey," said BJ. "How's it going?"

"Life sucks," Dagmar said with perfect truth.

"Yeah," BJ said. "I'm sorry if what happened to Charlie is causing you grief."

"That's two of my best friends murdered," Dagmar said. Fury rose in her as she spoke. One of her fists punched the granite ledge on which she sat. Gratifying pain crackled from her knuckles.

"Well, you know," BJ said, "I won't pretend that I'm in mourning over Charlie, but I care about *you*. Do you want to get together and talk?"

"I can't," Dagmar said. "I've got too fucking much to do."

"I could get Chinese takeout and bring it to your apartment," he said.

"I'm not at my apartment anymore. I'm hiding out at a hotel."

There was a moment's silence.

"Why?" he asked.

"Two reasons," Dagmar said. "First, I think I might be next on the killer's agenda."

"I thought the killer was caught," BJ said.

"*One* of them was," Dagmar said.

"But . . ." He hesitated while he tried to decide which of several possible scripts to follow. "Why would the Russian Maffya be after you?" he said finally.

"I can't tell you. But I have another reason—which that the police have pretty much told me that I'm a suspect in three murders. So if I meet with you and I'm being followed, it might lead the cops to you."

Chew on that, she thought.

Maybe it would keep him from following her.

"I can bring Chinese to your hotel," he said.

What he should have said, Dagmar told herself, was *Three murders?* Because he wasn't supposed to know about Siyed.

That, Dagmar thought, was a misstep.

"Maybe some other time," she said. "I've really got to run right now."

"See you tomorrow," BJ said.

An alarm jolted through her nerves. "Tomorrow?" she said.

"The update."

"Oh. Right. Bye."

After the call ended, she stared at the phone's display until it went dark.

Tomorrow, she thought.

She would have to meet BJ face-to-face and hope that he couldn't guess what she knew.

This Is Not a Dinner

"You have a cut on your face," Dagmar said.

The cut was just below BJ's left eye, a thin little half circle of red. Probably made by Siyed's fingernail as he tried to push BJ away while BJ pounded the life out of him.

"Kitchen accident," BJ said.

"With what?" She was feeling reckless and wanted to torment him or at least make him improvise.

"Oh," he said. He scratched a sideburn with one blunt finger. "I have this sort of magnet thingy over the sink where I stick my knives, and I bumped into the counter and knocked one of the knives off, and it hit me."

"You could have lost your eye," Dagmar said.

BJ shrugged. "Maybe," he said.

He had progressed another step toward acquiring tycoon wear, with a soft cream-colored shirt, a sumptuous tie, and an Italian summer-weight jacket of pastel-colored linen. The fine clothing, rather than embellish his appearance, seemed rather to accent his thick neck and steelworker's shoulders and long arms.

"I've got to show you my new car," he said. "I've finally got rid of the Chevy."

"We've got an update to do," Dagmar said.

"I meant later."

Around them, Helmuth and the technical staff were monitoring the progress of the players as they sampled one body of water after another—thousands altogether, on five continents. A running count was kept of the number of times the Tapping the Source units detected phenolphthalein, which Dagmar's agents had added to streams, fountains, creeks, and ponds earlier in the day. The chemical itself was harmless, its chief property being to turn purple in an acid environment.

Every time six of the contaminated water sources were detected, another page was loaded to the *Briana Hall* site.

Each led to other pages filled with clues to puzzles that would keep the players busy, it was hoped, for at least a few hours.

This played out over the latter half of the morning and most of the afternoon. Early in the day, eating a tasteless cruller from the box she'd brought in, Dagmar had announced that everyone was invited to dine at a nearby Italian restaurant that night, courtesy of the company. She had already called and made the arrangements; she only needed a head count.

No one was immune to the attractions of free food. She called the restaurant and finalized the number.

"Twelve people," she said.

"Thirteen," said BJ, "counting you."

"Thirteen," Dagmar said.

Food and soft drinks were free, she explained to her guests, but she knew Helmuth and a few of the others too well to offer free alcohol.

The restaurant was a decoy. She had no intention of being the thirteenth person at that meal, but intended to call in sick. She wouldn't stiff the restaurant, which already had her business card number.

It was all a way of getting away from BJ so he wouldn't follow her home.

At some point, civility required that she view BJ's new car. Dagmar followed BJ to the elevator and rode with him in silence. He seemed aware that something was wrong, and she sensed wariness beneath the casual, pleasant pose. She looked at his hands and saw that a knuckle had been cut, but a cut could appear on a knuckle for all sorts of innocent reasons. There was a cut on one of

Dagmar's knuckles at that very moment, and she had no idea how it got there.

The killer might have used a club or a pipe or something.

Right. The thought of an angry BJ coming after her with a baseball bat sent a quaver along her nerves.

She turned her mind from nightmare imagination to analysis, a welcome shift. If, she considered, Siyed had cut BJ under the eye with a fingernail, would scrapings of that nail provide the DNA that could send him to prison?

Maybe. Maybe not.

The last thing she wanted was BJ investigated and then let go on grounds of insufficient evidence. That would be a triumph for him: that would be BJ killing Charlie and then rubbing her face in it.

The car was a Ford Phalanx, slightly used, with a locust-green low-slung monocoque body and a hard top that disappeared, on command, into what proved a surprisingly large trunk.

"Good lord," Dagmar said.

"V-eight, turbocharged." BJ was smiling as the wind tossed his fair hair. "The original owner put thirty-five hundred miles on it, and then his boss gave him a company car—a Bentley coupé, believe it or not, and this became redundant. Those thirty-five hundred miles cut the original price nearly in half."

He had said "coupé," not "coupe" as Americans do. She walked around the machine.

"It just screams, *Fuck the environment*, doesn't it?" she said.

He laughed. "I thought that was the California state motto. Oh no, my mistake—the motto is *I've got mine.*"

She looked at him. "Aram must be paying you well."

"So are you." BJ opened the passenger door. "Want to go for a ride?"

"Maybe later." She shaded her eyes with her hand and blinked. "I think I'm getting a headache."

"Sorry to hear it." His face softened into an expression of concern. He closed the door and approached her. "You've had a hard time."

He offered a comforting embrace and she took it, thinking as she gazed blankly over his big shoulder that her rented Mercedes two-seater would probably not be able to outrun the Ford, not with its body designed by French aeronautical engineers and housing eight cylinders of Detroit iron.

The Italian restaurant deception would be necessary, then.

"Speaking of Aram," he said as they returned to the office tower, "he's flying into town tomorrow night. I've got a meeting with him on Monday, and then he and I will have our first meeting with the staff at the company on Tuesday. Then he's throwing a welcome dinner and reception for me."

"Where?" she asked.

"At Katanyan Associates. The dinner will be catered."

She wondered about the meeting, if one of Austin's partners would ask, *Say, aren't you the BJ that Austin always said was, like, the worst businessman in the history of the world?*

How jolly the dinner would be afterward.

They could hear Helmuth's fury as soon as they arrived at the third floor.

"*Goddam it! What shit-head decided that HTML was going to be case sensitive!*"

Upload not going well, Dagmar concluded.

The afternoon ended with all pages, puzzles, sound files, and videos loaded and available to the gamers, and with the computers at Tapping the Source bulging with useful data.

They were going to be *very* surprised, Dagmar thought, by what happened to their stock on Monday.

"I'll meet you all at the restaurant," Dagmar said. "I've got to do some shopping in the meantime."

She waited in her office until she saw the green monocoque body cross the 101 and head toward Ventura, where the restaurant waited. She looked up, saw a familiar white Dodge van in the parking lot across the freeway. She got out her handheld and hit the speed dial.

"Andy," she said when Joe Clever answered, "I'm looking at you right now. And if you damage my retinas with that laser, I'm going to cross the highway and rip out your fucking lungs."

"I couldn't get *anything* with the Big Ears," Andy complained. "You've got too many computers pumping heat into the room."

Quiet triumph sizzled in Dagmar's heart.

"I got one of the puzzles on my own, though," he said. "The one about what happened to Cullen's hat."

"I have some questions," she said, "about the snoop-and-poop business."

She'd claimed to have shopping to do as a way of getting rid of BJ, and now she *did* have shopping to do, buying the gear on Joe Clever's list. Night-surveillance scopes, cameras, video recorders, little cameras on wires narrow enough to go down someone's gullet.

She called Helmuth and told him to give everyone her apologies. She had a headache, and she was going home. She'd see them all on Monday.

"Get a receipt from the restaurant at the end of the evening," she told him.

"Are you sure you're all right?" Helmuth asked.

"I'll be fine," she said.

Then came the search for the perfect motel. She found it finally off the Hollywood Freeway, a place that looked as if it had been built as a Ramada Inn or a Travelodge but, in the decades since its construction, had probably been sold to Arabs, who sold it to Indians, who sold it to Chinese, who sold it to Koreans, who sold it finally to refugees from Bangladesh. The white building, with its rust-colored stains, sprawled around a series of court-yards, and there was nothing to stop anyone from walking right off the street to any of the rooms. The large swimming pool, where she might have done laps, had been filled with earth and turned into a rather shabby garden.

When she checked in, the scent of Indian cuisine filled the office, cardamom and cloves, cumin and cinnamon. The manager, a small, dark man with well-oiled hair, sat behind bulletproof Perspex.

"What are you cooking?" she asked.

"Tacos," he said.

She ate her own dinner in a Teriyaki chicken joint as she thought wistfully of Bengali tacos, then returned to her motel room to set up and test her gear. Everything worked smoothly, as advertised.

She slept fitfully, if at all.

This Is Not a Trap

FROM: Dagmar Shaw
SUBJECT: Where I'm At

Hi, Mom,

I'm not at home right now, so if you called the landline you wouldn't have got me. I'm staying in a motel here in L.A., just to get away from distraction and get some work done. The game will be done in another couple weeks, and then I can take some time off.

I tried to call you on my cell phone but for some reason I couldn't get a signal. I'm at the New Hollywood Inn, rm 118, and the phone here is 818-733-3991.

I'll try to call you later today.

Love,

D.

Dagmar had logged on to the AvN Soft servers using her old ID and password. She imagined the message lying there on the IMAP server, waiting for CRAPJOB to log on and discover her secret location.

Except that the email was a lie. She wasn't actually sleeping in room 118—inspired by the way that Joe Clever had stalked Litvinov, she had taken a room across the courtyard, 115, separated from it by the shrubs of the filled-in swimming pool. She had rented 118 as well, paying in cash shoved beneath the bulletproof screen, because she didn't want to be responsible for the lives of any innocent tourists who might camp there.

Now, though, she considered shifting to the decoy room, at least for the rest of the afternoon. She had a feeling that CRAPJOB might want to confirm her location.

She got her laptop and her room key, with its diamond-shaped plastic tag, and crossed the old swimming pool. She spent the afternoon working there, in the clean Lysol scent of the room, at the little round table by the window, where she became sufficiently engrossed in her work to give a start when the phone rang.

Her pulse raging, Dagmar stepped across the room and picked up the old-fashioned heavy black handset.

"This is Dagmar," she said, and was answered only by a soft click.

"Hello to you, too," she responded, fear turning in an instant to fury.

She mussed the bed in order to convince any enemy reconnaissance, and the maids, that the bed had been slept in. She drew the drapes, left a light on above the stained vanity mirror in the back of the room, and then withdrew to the safety of room 115.

The scout crept in a little after ten. The court was well-enough lit at night that the night-vision camera was hardly necessary; the video monitor clearly showed the wide-shouldered man enter from the street and slowly stroll the length of the walk in front of room 118. On the return journey, a few minutes later, the man stopped near

118 and studied the steel door in its orange steel frame. Fair hair glinted from beneath a dark cap.

Dagmar was amazed by her sudden rage. It was all she could do to keep herself from hurling open her door, striding across the swimming pool, ripping the cap from BJ's head, and slapping him across the face.

Only the remains of her sanity, dangling above the abyss with quivering fingers, kept her still.

BJ, having seen what he came to see, ambled back to the street. A few minutes later she heard the big V-8 thunder into life, then roar away.

Dagmar began to take full breaths again. Her hands shivered as the anger receded, like the tide, in waves—the fury building, then falling, then returning, but each time diminished, with the pulses of lucidity lasting longer.

Coldly she considered what evidence she had just collected. BJ had come to her motel room, had stalked around outside, had left. Dagmar understood the homicidal intent, but would Murdoch? Would a jury?

She was inclined to think not.

She doubted that BJ would have bomb-building supplies in his apartment—if he wasn't hiding them from the police, he was certainly hiding them from his roommate, Jacen. They might find evidence on his computer that he was CRAPJOB, but if he'd been smart, he would have used computers rented at Kinko's or borrowed at the library.

If he had been foolish enough to use his own phone when contacting the players he'd used to deliver the bomb to the Fig, he'd have hanged himself—but Dagmar knew that BJ was smarter than that. Dagmar knew he would have used what on TV crime shows was called a burner—a cell phone with prepaid hours, purchased anonymously and after the crime destroyed.

There was nothing in any of this that would indict BJ, let alone convict him.

A bigger demonstration would be required.

In the morning she took Hollywood Boulevard west, toward the ocean, and found a place to park near where it became Sunset Boulevard. Between two shabby old office buildings, and beneath a billboard for Ray Corrigan's new blockbuster, she found an old, steep stairway that connected Sunset and Santa Monica boulevards, and from this vantage viewed the building that contained Katanyan Associates.

She had been there many times, but she thought it might be useful to refresh her memory. The building was a four-story structure of dark glass. Austin's company occupied the second floor. Cars were parked on a kind of concrete shelf cantilevered out over the slope, with a view of Century City beyond. There was a booth for a gate guard, but it was manned only during working hours.

The building across the street had CCTV cameras on its roof, but these were drooping downward—broken or unused.

It's going to happen Tuesday night, she thought. *When you've got Aram for your alibi.*

It was lucky that Katanyan Associates was only a short distance from the New Hollywood Inn.

That would make things easier.

This Is Not an Assassin

Richard the Assassin sat behind his long, curving row of consoles, screen images winking in his eyes. Ninjas glared down from the upper shelves, fierce eyes gazing from masked faces.

"CRAPJOB's starting to scare me," he said. "He's using your account to build a program that's going to cause major damage. When he gives the word, it's going to trash every record on our servers, starting with all Great Big Idea's games, then going on to email and accounting files, then demolishing everything in AvN Soft that it can reach. We've got backups off-site, of course, but we can't swear that every single thing is backed up."

"He won't move till after the Wednesday update," Dagmar said. "He can't afford to destroy anything until the players send his patch out."

"I'm still worried," said Richard.

She looked at him. "All right," she said. "If we don't track this guy down by Tuesday six P.M., lock him out. Eliminate his account, wipe out his little data bomb, and make sure—" She leaned forward, intent. "Make sure it's *Charlie's* patch that goes out to the players, not anything else."

Richard shrugged. "Of course."

Dagmar began to speak, then hesitated, then spoke anyway. Any residual loyalty to BJ had vanished at the point at which she'd seen him stalking up and down outside her conjectural motel room.

"While you're doing that," she said, "eliminate Boris Bustretski's account."

Richard raised his eyebrows. "You think he's CRAPJOB?"

"CRAPJOB appeared after BJ came on as a freelancer."

The eyebrows lifted another millimeter.

"BJ?"

"He's an old friend," Dagmar said, "but I don't trust him."

Richard made a sweeping motion with his hand, clean as the slice of a ninja sword.

"It's done," he said.

FROM: Consuelo
SUBJECT: Porn Invasion

Hey, Dagmar—

Why has my hard drive filled up with this awful Asian porn?

Is this any way for a detective to treat his partner?

Joe

FROM: Dagmar Shaw
SUBJECT: Re: Porn Invasion

Andy,

Your hard drive should keep its fly zipped.

Good detectives don't go anywhere without a warrant.

Dagmar

FROM: Consuelo
SUBJECT: Re: re: Porn Invasion

Darn it, Dagmar, I thought we were friends!

FROM: Hippolyte
SUBJECT: Re: L.A. Games

Hi, Dagmar,

I've got the phone call from David! I'm supposed to help deliver data to Maria so that she can get it to Briana.

I told David yes. He said it's going down Tuesday night.

My phone is (714) 756-0578.

H.

"Okay," said Dagmar. "So the data stick is going to be hidden in a vase of flowers?"

She was speaking not to Hippolyte, to whom she had talked earlier in the day, but to a player named GIAWOL, whom she did not know. GIAWOL had a clenched-sounding voice, as if he were afraid to let his lower teeth get too far from his upper. Possibly, Dagma[r] thought, he had a pipe in his mouth.

"Yes," GIAWOL said. Dagmar knew that his name was an acronym for *Gaming is a way of life.*

"I don't know that it's a data stick, exactly," he said, "only that I'm supposed to put it in the vase. And that once I deliver it to Maria, I'm supposed to text-message David at a certain number."

"Can you give me the number?"

GIAWOL did. Dagmar wrote it down. It was a number she didn't recognize.

BJ's latest cell phone burner.

"Where are you supposed to deliver the flowers?" Dagmar asked.

"Someplace called the New Hollywood Inn," GIAWOL said. "Room one one eight."

Dagmar felt the flush of anger on her skin.

"Anything else?" she asked.

"Just that I'm to say it's from the management."

"Of the motel?"

"Yes. It's supposed to be thanks for staying there for so long." There was a hesitation. "Can I make a request?"

"Of course."

"More mathematical puzzles," GIAWOL said. "I love those."

She smiled. "I'll make a note of it."

"Also, the destegging program you people use only works with a PC. I'm a Mac user."

"I'll pass that on to them."

Over Monday afternoon she had tracked the evolution of BJ's plot. It featured sending players along the ame wandering courses that he'd used in his last scheme, followed by a player's uniting the data with the "package"—in this case a vase of flowers—and delivering them to a motel room door.

His bomb-making skills had evolved, clearly. The last bomb had been triggered when Charlie turned on the computer or opened the door to the CD player. This one would be command-detonated, presumably by cell phone. It would have to be assumed that Dagmar would be averse to plugging in any strange computers delivered to her door, so when GIAWOL sent the text message that the flowers had been delivered, BJ in turn would call the cell phone hidden in the flower vase. Which would trigger the bomb, thus ending BJ's problems. And Dagmar's, of course.

An abstract kind of pity, devoid of genuine sadness or compassion, floated through Dagmar's mind.

Poor BJ, she thought. *He's only got the one trick. He's not puppetmaster enough to save himself.*

FROM: Maria Perry
SUBJECT: Ford Phalanx

I've located Cullen's briefcase. It's in a late-model Ford Phalanx parked in the Coolomb Corporation garage!

Is there any way I can break into the car without setting off the alarm? I don't need to steal the car, I just need to get into it!

Maria

FROM: Desi
SUBJECT: Re: Ford Phalanx

Maria,

This company sells custom lockpick sets for specific models of cars.

If the Phalanx has keyless entry, then of course this won't work.

FROM: ReVerb
SUBJECT: Re: Ford Phalanx

Pity it's not the late nineties, when GM cars had keys so interchangeable that you could randomly insert your key into a strange lock with a 50% chance it would open. Of course the Phalanx isn't GM, but I can't resist an interesting bit of trivia!

You might try ordering some of these tools from this online catalog. These are the tools used by professionals, legit and otherwise, to break into cars.

The tools don't seem to have names, just catalog numbers.

FROM: Atenveldt
SUBJECT: Re: Ford Phalanx

Maria, the Phalanx has keyless entry. There isn't a conventional lock anywhere on the vehicle. The driver carries a sort of seedpod-shaped cartridge with an active (battery-operated) RFID tag that scanners in the car will recognize. The car won't start without the RFID tag inside.

RFIDs, of course, have a well-known problem, which is that they broadcast to all the wrong scanners as well as the right ones.

What I would do is this: I'd get an RFID scanner somewhere near that car to record the signal the pod emits when it tells the Phalanx to open its doors. Then you create an electronic duplicate of the signal, and the car is yours!

And the car is mine, Dagmar thought.

Two players she'd never heard from had jumped out of the electronic world to answer Maria's question. She could always count on the Group Mind.

It was time for another visit to the electronics store.

This Is Not Breakfast

It was typical of L.A. that the surveillance store was open till midnight—after all, one never knew at what hour one's husband, or one's banker, would choose to cheat. The clerk sold her a battery-powered RFID scanner and a device for cloning the captured signals. Both boxes were compact and idiotproof—stupid criminals, after all, used them every day, usually to steal someone's identity when the victim swiped a credit card while making a purchase, or when they were carrying one of the new American passports, which the government had insisted could only be detected at a range of four inches, even in the face of objective tests that demonstrated their vulnerability at a range of ten meters or more.

The clerk gazed at her from sad, idiotproof eyes. "You must promise to use this only for good," he told her.

She looked at him.

"I'm innocent as chocolate syrup," she told him.

She drove to BJ's apartment. She'd never been there before, but the address was available in the contract he'd signed with Great Big Idea.

It wasn't in a good part of L.A. The small building, with clapboard walls and a shake roof, was ramshackle and contained no more than four apartments. Two vehicles sat in the parking lot on concrete blocks. In this district her Mercedes coupe glowed like a beacon.

Dagmar circled the apartment and saw neither the Phalanx nor BJ's old Chevy. She parked half a block away, in a place where her car was shaded from the streetlight by an overgrown willow, and shifted to the passenger seat. She remembered reading somewhere that a person sitting in the passenger seat was less conspicuous than someone behind the wheel.

She reclined the seat as far as possible, pulled her panama hat partly down her face, and waited for the rumble of the Ford's V-8. When BJ arrived and went to bed, she intended to slip out and put the RFID scanner beneath his car to catch the signals from his remote, then retrieve the scanner after he left.

The Phalanx didn't come. She waited for hours, enduring the occasional scrutiny of young men walking past along the broken sidewalk. When they began to crowd the Mercedes, either to admire the car or to steal it, she raised her seat to make herself more visible and pretended to be talking on the phone. The young men, surprised and suddenly self-conscious, retreated. No one really bothered her.

Eventually even the drifting knots of young men went to bed. Dagmar drowsed and periodically scanned the apartment building with night binoculars. BJ hadn't come home.

He was wherever he was building the bomb, she thought. Where he was carefully crafting the instrument that would kill her.

When dawn began to feather the leaves of the willow tree overhead, Dagmar got out of the car and stretched aching limbs. She retreated to her motel room for a shower and an hour's jangled sleep, and the alarm function in her phone woke her promptly at seven.

Dagmar looked at the phone and dreaded what was going to happen next. She tasted stomach acid in the back of her throat.

She took a deep breath and pressed buttons for the speed dial.

When BJ answered, she said, "Let's have breakfast. I need to talk to someone."

He cleared his throat, and when his voice emerged it was thick with sleep.

"Dagmar? Are you all right?"

"No," she said. "I'm not."

The morning news was about the continued attack on the yuan. The Chinese currency had lost at least half its value, neatly canceling half the value of the obsessive savings of hundreds of millions of people, most of them poor. Rioters had trashed a train station in Guangzhou and broken bank windows on the Shanghai Bund. The dollar was losing value as well, and the Chinese government was still uttering threats.

She wondered if anyone other than she and BJ had yet realized that the attacks were coming from a botnet.

Dagmar and BJ met near Koreatown, in the egg-themed restaurant where they'd dined before Charlie had been killed. BJ had been planning to kill Charlie then, Dagmar thought, because the twelve-billion-dollar figure had shown up on Our Reality Network earlier in the day, and BJ would have known at once what it meant.

Dagmar arrived at the restaurant first and sat with her back to the wall and ordered coffee. BJ arrived fifteen minutes later, heralded by the bass vibrato of the Ford. He was unshaven and dressed in worn jeans and a faded T. Apparently, she thought, tycoon wear and bomb factories did not mix.

Dagmar managed not to hurl the coffee in his face. Instead she steeled herself and rose to embrace him. She smelled the familiar lavender soap and her stomach turned over.

"What's going on?" he asked. "You look awful."

She seated herself. "Three friends dead. Cops on my tail. No sleep. And the game updates tomorrow."

This time BJ remembered he wasn't supposed to know about Siyed.

"*Three* friends?" he asked.

She told him about Siyed, and while she did, she watched him. The calculation behind his reactions emed plain, the falsity enormous. There was a little delay behind every response, as he tried to decide how to react. He did everything but wave a placard saying "Murderous Sociopath."

How, she wondered, had she not noticed any of this till now?

They had known each other for thirteen or fourteen years. They had been lovers for nine months of that. She had adored him at the start of the relationship, had been secretly relieved when he broke it off, and had been twisted enough by the rejection to marry a man she didn't love.

She and BJ had been working together for weeks, and she'd sat opposite him at desks and tables and heard his stories of the fall of AvN Soft and seen his blue eyes glitter with anger at Charlie, and she hadn't seen any of the mendacity, any of the self-interest, any of the plotting.

Charlie had told her over and over about BJ. So had Austin. She hadn't thought they were lying; she had just thought they were prejudiced.

She hadn't seen any of what BJ had created. She, so good at plots, at hiding and detecting, had gone on thinking of BJ as her friend—and not only that, but her friend of last resort.

Dagmar could only conclude that she was as broken as he was.

"Staying out of sight is probably a good idea," BJ said. "It'll give them time to find out who really did it. And you should get some rest, you look like you haven't slept in a week."

Go stay in your hotel room, Dagmar translated, *where I can get to you with my bomb.*

"Yeah," she said. "But there's the big update tomorro

"It's all set up, right?" he said. "You don't even nee
be there. Any last-minute writing or anything, I'll hand
it."

"You're spending the day with Aram, I thought."

He gave one of his big-shouldered shrugs. "I'll work
all night, if I have to."

BJ went on to talk about Aram Katanyan, about how
he'd made the connection at Austin's memorial service,
then kept in touch. He'd known that Aram would have a
lot to say about what happened to Katanyan Associates,
and so BJ had kept stressing his qualifications for the job.
He'd talked about how long he'd known Austin, how
they'd met over gaming. Eventually it was Aram, not BJ,
who had first brought up the matter of his coming in as
acting head of the firm.

BJ was bouncy and confident and pleased with himself. A
few weeks ago, she'd seen him baffled and defeated. Now he
was much more like the BJ she'd met at Caltech, the one
who'd walk up to you and tell you how smart he was and
how successful he was going to be.

All it took to create this change, she thought, was
killing a couple of people and getting away with it.

Suddenly she realized why she'd been so blind. *I haven't
been in his way till now.* She'd been trying to help BJ, not
prevent him from doing anything he'd wanted to do.
What little she'd had, she'd offered freely. She'd never
thwarted him, and he'd never turned into any of those
people in his games, the two-faced gutter crawlers that
stood ready to betray everyone in sight.

She looked down at the table. BJ's plate was empty.

own blueberry and pecan pancakes had been more
n to shreds than eaten. The smell of candied pepper
acon hung in the air.

She'd never be able to eat candied pepper bacon
again.

"Can we go for a ride in your car?" she asked.

Surprise blinked in his blue eyes.

"Sure," he said.

"Can I drive?"

She left money on the table for breakfast, and they
stepped out into yet another brilliant Los Angeles morning. She held out a hand.

"The key?" she asked.

BJ fished in his pocket and found the remote.

"You press the—"

"I know."

She had the scanner in her handbag. She held the bag
out and the remote next to it and pressed the button to
open the car.

Inches away, the scanner should have picked up the
signal.

The car folded around her like a body stocking. The
whole vehicle shivered to the big engine. She took the car
through the parking lot, then hurled it onto the street like
a lioness accelerating after an antelope.

"Jeez," BJ said, surprised.

The back end swung around, clawing for traction, as
she turned onto Interstate 10. There was a hesitation,
and then the turbocharger kicked in and punched her
back in the seat. Lips skinned back from her teeth in a
reckless grin. Methodically she clocked through the gears,

and she headed for Pomona as fast as the V-8 would take her. If the automated traffic cameras clocked her at 120, BJ could just suck the fines.

From his damn jail cell.

It had occurred to Dagmar that BJ might try to kill her when they were alone. She doubted it, however. He would view it as too risky: someone could see him, something could go wrong. Better to have his puppets deliver Dagmar's death later, in the sanctuary that she didn't realize had been compromised.

But just in case he was tempted to do something, Dagmar wanted him too terrified to act.

She got off the freeway, fishtailed around a couple of intersections, and returned to the interstate, heading west into L.A. She returned to the restaurant parking lot, put the Phalanx in neutral, and pulled the parking brake.

"As expensive mechanical substitute penises go," she said, "this one's the cat's pajamas."

"Uh, yeah," BJ said. His eyes were wide.

She looked at him. "See you tomorrow," she said. "At the update."

His blue eyes looked into hers with perfect certainty.

"See you there," he said.

See you in hell, she thought.

This Is Not a Florist

From room 115 in the New Hollywood Inn, Dagmar waited while BJ's plot unfolded. Her room smelled of the Thai takeout she hadn't been able to bring herself to eat. The cameras reported only the usual tourists—a worried

...iinese mother with a pack of small children, a solemn ...outh American with a camera, a disorganized family, ...unning between their room and their car, chattering in Finnish or Estonian or some other unlikely language.

She'd received a message from Richard the Assassin that CRAPJOB's online privileges had been canceled. So had BJ's. So had Dagmar's old account. All copies of Charlie's patch had been reverted to the archived copy of Patch 2.0.

Dagmar supposed that BJ wouldn't have discovered any of these changes as yet. Not if he was being feted by Aram.

CNN informed her that the attacks on the Chinese yuan had ceased. The bots had done as much damage as they could and left riots and anger behind.

Dagmar watched the monitor. More children, more tourists.

At last came a stout man staggering under a huge burden of flowers. Dagmar opened her door and met him on the doorstep of room 118. She put her key in the door.

"Maria?" he asked. "Maria Perry?"

She looked up. "Yes?"

He was a portly man around sixty, with white hair tied in a ponytail, gold-rimmed spectacles, and a cheerful red face. Dots of sweat marked his forehead.

"The management"—pant—"wanted me to give you this." Panting. "It's for being"—pant—"such a good customer."

Dagmar tried to feign surprise. The vase was large and ugly, black ceramic, with reliefs of strange Polynesian tiki monsters. A huge spray of long-stemmed roses fanned from the opening at the top, the flowers white but rimmed delicately with pink. Below was a crazed mix of colorful blossoms: mums and carnations and black and yellow lilies, plus baby's breath and other flowers that Dagmar couldn't identify.

Dagmar opened the door of 118 and took the vase from GIAWOL, who immediately dissolved into a paroxysm of coughing. The vase was heavy with its presumed cargo of nails and gunpowder, and Dagmar wrestled it into the room and put it on the scarred old table. The scent of the roses mixed strangely with the Lysol smell of the room.

She turned back to GIAWOL, who had recovered from his coughing fit.

"Thank you," she said, and raised a finger to her lips. "Remember not to send that text. And don't tell anyone—they might be jealous."

His grin was infectious. "Sure. Enjoy the flowers—Maria."

Still grinning, he walked away. Dagmar watched him go, then closed the door and contemplated the enormous floral display.

Flowers, she thought, were really Siyed's weapon, not BJ's. BJ was running out of ideas.

She returned to 115, got her panama hat and a cardigan against the growing October chill. She went back to 118, collected the enormous vase with its extravagant spray of blossoms, and walked toward the street, flowers bobbing over her head like the feathers of a Lakota headdress.

Her rented car was a two-seater, so she secured the vase between the passenger seat and the shelf behind, then drove to Hollywood. Progress along the famous ɔoulevard was slow, the pavement packed with traffic and mobs of tourists who looked even more bewildered than they did in daylight. Out-of-work actors walked up and down the sidewalks dressed as superheroes and offered to let visitors take their picture for a small fee.

Fly this bomb to where it belongs, Tony Stark, she thought. But Tony was busy posing with a couple of kids from the Midwest and failed to hear her mental command.

Eventually she got to the top of the street, where Hollywood became Sunset, and found a place to park. She took out the vase, hesitated, then opened the trunk and dumped all the flowers inside. With the vase itself swinging at the end of her arm, she located the two office buildings and walked down the dark, narrow old stair to Santa Monica Boulevard.

The blue-windowed office building stood across the street. There were lots of lights on the second floor, where Katanyan Associates was hosting a party for its new manager. Dagmar shifted the vase from the arm that was cramping to the arm that was not.

Its green color fluorescing in the light of a streetlamp, BJ's Phalanx sat in the parking lot.

Dagmar took a breath, tilted her hat so that anyone on the second floor couldn't see her face, and stepped into the night street.

This Is Not a Game

She felt the flush of danger on her skin. Her pulse was rapid but not frantic. She remembered being far more frightened in Jakarta.

She'd learned a few things since then. And besides, L.A. was *her* town.

Dagmar wanted the bomb *inside* BJ's car because that would indicate that the bomb belonged to him. If she put the bomb underneath the Phalanx, he would be a victim.

She didn't want him victimized. She wanted him indicted.

She would plant the bomb in his car and then send a text to the number that David had given to GIAWOL. BJ, assuming that Dagmar had been given the bomb, would use his burner to call the phone in the bomb and would then turn in surprise and shock as the Katanyan Associates windows reflected the orange flower of flame that burst from his own vehicle, and all his hopes and expectations were blown to smithereens.

Even Special Agent Landreth of the FBI would realize that there had to be a connection between this bomb and the identical weapon that had killed Charlie Ruff. The easiest explanation was that BJ had accidentally blown up his own vehicle with his own weapon.

There would be an investigation. In time, bomb materials would be found, as well as the place where BJ had assembled the bomb. And Dagmar would be questioned again.

BJ always had a grudge against Charlie, she would say. *He thought Charlie had cheated him out of his company.*

BJ would go to prison, possibly the gas chamber. He'd lose his job with Aram, and his attempt to subvert the gold-farming bots would fail.

He'd have nothing. He'd have less than he had when this whole adventure started.

Dagmar would tangle him in his own puppet strings and hang him out to twist slowly in the wind.

She glanced at the CCTV on the neighboring building and saw the cameras still dangling at a useless angle. Dagmar passed the empty guard box standing sentry in the parking lot and walked to BJ's car. He had parked on the south side of the parking ramp, with a view of his new domain. L.A. shimmered below her, a skein of lights stretching all the way to the Pacific. Dagmar reached into her pocket and pulled out her cloned Phalanx remote, and she pressed the button.

Dagmar heard the solid chunk of a door lock opening. She pulled the sleeve of her cardigan over her fingers, crouched down by the low car, and opened the door without leaving fingerprints. She tilted the seat forward, scrubbed fingerprints off the vase with her cardigan, and tucked the vase behind the driver's seat. She pushed the seat back into place.

She looked up at the building. Silhouettes wandered behind the lit windows. She didn't recognize BJ or anyone else.

She rose, tilted her hat again to obscure her face from the new direction, and left the parking lot. Success tingled in her fingers and toes.

Her feet bounded up the old concrete stair. She neared the top, and breathing with exertion, she turned and gazed down over the parking lot.

The neon-green Phalanx was visible, its color brilliant under the light. She reached into a pocket for the cell phone she'd bought just that afternoon, her very own burner.

"What are we going to do tonight, Brain?" she asked.

The answer seemed to hang pregnant in the air, so she spoke it aloud.

"What we do every night, Pinky," she said. "Try to take over the world!"

Flowers delivered. Maria delighted.

She texted to the number GIAWOL had sent her, and pressed Send.

Cars hissed by on Sunset. Her heart beat double-time in her throat. Nothing happened.

Several minutes went by while Dagmar's unease increased. She wondered frantically if she had miscalculated completely, if this was all some insane fantasy she'd cobbled together out of stray facts and paranoia.

Maybe it wasn't a command-detonated bomb at all, she thought. Maybe it was a time bomb, scheduled to go off at 2 A.M. or something.

But in that case, why the text message? That was a breach in security, though a small one. There was no reason for it unless it was timed somehow to the bomb's detonation.

A figure appeared in the parking lot below, and she recognized BJ at once. His big body moved with a jaunty stride, as if he were on top of the world. He was wearing tycoon clothes, a dark suit. A bright tie glowed at his throat in the light of the streetlamps.

BJ stepped toward the Phalanx and reached into a pocket for a remote. He opened the car door, put the remote away, reached into a pocket for something else. Something small.

Dagmar felt her insides twist. She stopped herself from calling out.

BJ dropped into the car. It lurched under his considerable weight. Seconds ticked by. Perhaps he was gazing through the windshield at his new domain, at the Los Angeles that lay before him, spread out like a harlot on a mattress.

In the merest fragment of a second, the explosion happened. The explosion was faster than in movies. In films, Dagmar realized, explosions are slowed down so you can see them. In reality, they're too fast for the eye to catch.

Clangs echoed up the stair as pieces of the Phalanx began raining down. The part of the car that remained on the ground caught fire instantly and burned with a brilliant flame. Little fiery pellets fell over the parking lot, burning with bright chemical fire, and Dagmar realized they were incendiaries.

If the bomb hadn't killed her directly, she realized, she was meant to burn to death in her motel room or choke to death on smoke.

She couldn't see BJ amid the flames. She knew only that he hadn't gotten out of the car.

She wondered if he had died happy. Knowing that he was a fraction of a second from erasing the last obstacle between him and his prospects. Pleased with his new job, with the billions that the software agents would soon be dropping into his account, with his future as a tycoon.

Or in that last fragment of a second, had he heard the cell phone detonator chirp from behind his driver's seat and realized that it had all gone horribly wrong?

Dagmar returned to her own car, which was filled by now with a horrid rose scent. She stopped at a filling station and hurled all the flowers into a rubbish can, along with the cloned remote and the cell phone burner, both rubbed clean of fingerprints.

When she got to her motel room, she began taking apart all her surveillance gear. She thought that maybe she should erase all the evidence she'd gathered, in case it ended up pointing toward her.

Then she thought she might want to keep it, to prove that BJ was whatever it was that BJ was.

"This is not a game," she reminded herself.

CHAPTER TWENTY-SEVEN

This Is Not Remorse

So, she thought. What else could she have done?

There wasn't, and would probably never be, enough evidence to convict BJ of anything. At least not until the bomb went off in his car, which would precipitate a very thorough investigation by some rather thorough government agencies. And by then, BJ being in the car, it was too late.

If she had saved him, then what? He would have beaten her to death and thrown her off the parking jetty into the darkness below.

She could have been smarter or less distracted by events. But she hadn't been, and instead she had been who she was, so caught up in events that she had never caught up to the truth.

And the truth was four dead by violence, here in L.A. And countless others, in Bolivian mining towns, Indonesian kampungs, burning Cantonese passenger trains . . .

Her own well-meaning fictions, layered page by page on the so-called World Wide Web, differed from the web of the real world in that they lacked genuine malice. No matter how depraved her imagination when it came to *Briana Hall* or blood-crazed revenge-maddened nagis, her own work was practically wholesome compared with anything served up by Southeast Asian generals, Chinese mobs, or Arkady Petrovich Litvinov, the scope of whose iniquity had been reduced to the county jail.

These thoughts drifted through Dagmar's mind as she drowsed amid the disassembled spyware in her Lysol-scented motel room. Throughout her reflections drifted slumber itself, half-submerged on a slow-moving tide of perception.

She woke craving waffles and hearing the sound of rain on the walk outside.

Dagmar ate waffles in a coffee shop on Ventura while the rain turned the street outside into a canal. On the way to the Great Big Idea office, the radio informed her that the assault on the dollar had begun. As soon as the tech team had assembled, she told them to begin the update to *The Long Night of Briana Hall*. Normally they waited until noon, but the gold-farming bots had not delayed, and neither would she.

"If I were you," Helmuth said, "I'd slip out and buy as many euros as I could." He gave her a significant look. "I already did that on Monday."

"I don't have that much in cash," Dagmar said.

"Still." *Still.*

Sipping from an insulated mug of Darjeeling tea, Dagmar watched the update from over Helmuth's shoulder. The well-practiced tech team loaded the day's series puzzles. Because the real job came after the puzzles were solved, the puzzles themselves weren't all that difficult, and the players devoured them with the Internet equivalent of roars of gusto.

Then they encountered the long lists of IP addresses and paused.

LadyDayFan says:
What the hell???

Vikram says:
We're supposed to cope with all these addresses? Seriously?

Corporal Carrot says:
I'm game! Let's divide up the numbers!

LadyDayFan says:
Ohmygoddess! This is madness!

Vikram says:
All right, let's have a show of hands! Who wants a job?

Dagmar watched as the players divided the thousands of numbers among themselves and began posting their successes and failures. They argued about which successes belonged to whom and offered methods of locating the owners of firewalled computers.

The dollar was down 35 percent since the start of the day.

Dagmar bought a sesame chicken salad in the coffee

shop downstairs, and the largest, most elaborate latte for dessert afterward. She thought she might as well spend her money now, before it was no longer worth the paper it was printed on.

Chatsworth Osborne Jr. says:
This has to be the biggest feat of social engineering in the history of the Internet! Or possibly anywhere!

Corporal Carrot says:
It's pure hackage, man! This is soooooo freaking cool!

No doubt, Dagmar thought, some of the players were decompiling and reverse-engineering Charlie's patch to figure out what it did and how it worked. But they wouldn't discover much: it was a patch, not a whole program. It altered some modest bits of code to other bits of code. It gave the address of the Cayman account, but the players already had that address. It didn't offer any insights into what the original gold-farming bot was for.

Reverse engineering would show that it was a patch designed to tell one piece of a network to shut the entire network down. That was all. And that information happened to fit right in with the premise of *Briana Hall,* in which the players were called upon to shut down networks of villains.

It was all, amazingly, fitting together.

"Miss Shaw?"
"Yes?"

Dagmar recognized the voice of Detective Murdoch. She left the conference room and returned to her office.

"Do you know a Boris Bustretski?" he asked.

"Yes."

There was a little pause—the length, perhaps, of an explosion.

"I'm sorry to tell you he's been killed in another bombing."

She let another explosion-pause go by.

"Why would anyone kill BJ?" she asked. "He wasn't . . . *anybody.*"

"Can you tell us more about him?"

"He was my boyfriend ten years ago, before my marriage. We were good friends with Charlie Ruff and Austin Katanyan. But BJ and Charlie started their business together, and they ended up hating each other. BJ acted crazy, and Charlie fired him. Austin didn't get along with him, either, after that. BJ is—was—still angry about it, after all these years.

"I recently gave BJ a job because I felt sorry for him. But"—she hoped she was convincing—"I don't know why anyone would kill him. That's just crazy."

There was another little pause, another little explosion.

"Had Boris—BJ—ever made threats against Mr. Ruff?"

"None that I took seriously," Dagmar said.

"What were the nature of the threats?"

In her mind, Dagmar replayed the Phalanx flying apart in flames, one image following the other like frames on a film reel.

"He said that if he could figure out a way to kill Charlie, he would," Dagmar said. "But he wouldn't do it if it meant being caught."

The car burned in Dagmar's mind, a smear of brilliant orange against the night web of Los Angeles.

"But BJ wasn't a violent man," she said. "He wasn't serious."

"Can you come down to the station and talk to us?"

"No," Dagmar said. "Maybe later. Right now I'm in the middle of something at work."

Whole networks of bots vanished from the world. The threat to the dollar faded by late afternoon, along with the morning's rainstorm. The Federal Reserve had an emergency meeting; the IMF stepped in; so did European banks; so did sovereign wealth funds from a number of American allies. The value of the dollar began to rise.

Billions, Dagmar thought, were pouring into the United Bank of Cayman as the botnets shut down. At some point, Dagmar was going to have to call Charlie's parents and tell them how rich they were and urge them to continue Charlie's generous donations to charities worldwide.

They could keep a billion or two. What the hell.

By evening the dollar was regaining value on Pacific exchanges, where it was already Thursday morning. Eventually it stabilized at about 85 percent of its former value.

On Thursday morning, Dagmar went to a meeting with Murdoch and Special Agent Landreth of the FBI, who managed at length to convince her, against her will, that BJ was a killer. That he'd hired Litvinov to kill Austin, that he was responsible for the bomb that killed Charlie, that he'd beaten Siyed to death in a jealous rage, and that finally he'd blown himself up accidentally.

"It doesn't make any sense!" Dagmar protested, and she was right; but she knew it made all the sense that it had to.

> *Read the Schedule*
> *Know the Schedule*
> *Love the Schedule*

Dagmar looked at the words tracking endlessly on the flat-screen wall monitor and permitted herself a small smile. The mass hacking was the last big event of *The Long Night of Briana Hall,* and after that the game would grow manageable, both for her and her staff.

On Saturday, the Tapping the Source modules had told the players which water sources would be targeted by the terrorists, and allowed them to foil the terror plot. On Wednesday, they had destroyed the financial networks of the money men who had planned to profit from the disruption.

With both sets of major villains defeated, the game turned more intimate. It would all be about Briana Hall's trying to convince the police that she was innocent in the deaths of her two former boyfriends.

Briana Hall's life, Dagmar thought, was not unlike her own. Born a refugee in a hotel room, ending as words in a police file.

*

The web of Los Angeles spread out below her, lines yellow and red, incandescents and neon and billboards.

The crime-scene tape was gone. The rubble had been swept into boxes to be stared at by experts. A few lights were on at Katanyan Associates, and a few cars remained in the parking lot.

Dagmar stood where the Phalanx had been and looked out at the city. The wind coming up the slope stirred her hair and brought with it the faint scent of eucalyptus.

Her phone sang. She answered.

"Miss Shaw?"

A wry smile touched Dagmar's lips at the sound of the familiar voice. "You know, Lieutenant Murdoch," she said, "I believe you know me well enough by now that you might as well call me by my first name."

"If you like," Murdoch said.

"How can I help you?"

"I called because I have news," Murdoch said. "Rather sad news, I'm afraid."

Police sirens wailed somewhere down in Los Angeles. Billboards flashed, transmitting the code that was commerce.

"Yes?" she said.

"Preliminary DNA evidence has confirmed that it was Mr. Ruff that was killed in the hotel explosion," Murdoch said. "The preliminary evidence will be confirmed later, when a more thorough analysis is performed, but I've never known the preliminary to be wrong."

"I understand," Dagmar said.

Murdoch was only telling her what she already knew. Charlie, who despite his best efforts was not Victor von Doom, had not substituted another body for his own and had not gone underground in order to mastermind the collapse of world economies. That was the sort of thing that happened only in fiction—including the sort of fiction Dagmar wrote.

"We've also found the place where the bombs were assembled," Murdoch said. "A hotel room. The tenant had asked not to be disturbed, but after three days the management decided to open the door. When they looked into the tenant's luggage, they found bomb-making materials and instructions downloaded from the Internet, and called us. Prints taken at the scene match prints taken from Boris Bustretski's apartment."

"If there was a late-model laptop, it belongs to my company," Dagmar said.

"You'll have to contact the FBI about that," Murdoch said. "Homeland Security has it all now."

"Ah," Dagmar said.

Great Big Idea would probably get the computer back only after time had made it thoroughly obsolete.

"Thank you for calling," she said.

She holstered her phone and looked out over Los Angeles, feeling the wind lift her hair.

This was what BJ had played for, the view from the corner office, the tycoon car, the tycoon clothes, the tycoon bank account, and all Los Angeles at his feet.

Played and lost. All the brilliant game mastering, the devious plots, the ninja tactics played in *World of Cinnabar*, hadn't helped BJ in the end.

The world was just too big. BJ hadn't been defeated by Dagmar so much as by the Group Mind, lots of little autonomous agents out in the world, each with a skill set and a knowledge set, each with her own motivations, her own joys, her own alternate reality, all networked together in the great gestalt, the great becoming, that was the world.

Dagmar turned, Los Angeles at her back, and walked to her car.

FROM: LadyDayFan

Motel Room Blues, or *The Long Night of Briana Hall,* will end on Saturday with a live event in Griffith Park. Presumably we'll meet Briana, and maybe some of her friends, and help them tidy up the last few bits of plot before the happy ending that we see on the near horizon.

What are we to make of this game?

We're used to ARGs wandering in and out of the real world, but this one took more twists and sharp turns than any I can remember. We've had real-life death wound into the narrative, and we've done some real-life detection. We've also skied down glaciers on Titan, got drunk in the bars of Mars Port, and engaged in the most outrageous public hacking event in world history.

Is this a model for ARGs of the future? Will we be asked to aid real-world problem solvers with their agendas? And if so, can such a thing possibly be classified as entertainment?

We're used to following the whims of puppetmasters, but puppetmasters with real-world policies are another matter. Is this a good idea? Should we follow *anyone* who provides what they say is entertainment, even if it comes with an ideology?

Does it become dangerous when This Is *Really* Not A Game?

The chatter of players filled the rooms of the Fajita Hut with a constant roar. Dagmar recognized LadyDayFan, Hippolyte, GIAWOL—and of course Joe Clever, who sat alone at his table. No one, in this highly networked group, wanted to be seen talking to him. Even helping to catch Litvinov had not persuaded the others not to shun him, at least in public.

The Griffith Park event had gone well. Despite a day of drizzle, five or six hundred players had turned out to publicly solve a few last-minute puzzles. Briana, played by the actress Terri Griff, had appeared to thank the players for their efforts and then rumbled away in a vintage red Mustang convertible, the personal wheels of Richard the Assassin, who had lent the car for the occasion.

Dagmar watched the event on the live feed. To attend in person would have broken the fourth wall.

The players, buoyed and sad, their collective dream fading, reassembled in the nearby Fajita Hut, a large fast-food place with obsessively clean counters and containers of freshly made tortillas on the buffet. Dagmar, Jack Stone, the puzzle designer, and a few of the minor actors joined them. The fourth wall had, by this time, crumbled to dust.

"What's coming up next?" asked a young man with bright red hair.

Dagmar finished chewing her pollo asado, swallowed, and spoke.

"Wait and see," she said. A puppetmaster never revealed anything, not in public.

"I've never done one of these before," he said. "I'm totally stoked."

Dagmar dabbed a bit of sour cream from her upper lip.

"Are you Corporal Carrot, by any chance?" she asked.

He grinned. "That's me!"

"I thought I recognized your voice. Big Terry Pratchett fan?"

"Oh! He's *huge!*"

In truth, Dagmar had no idea what game project was coming next. There seemed to be a lull in demand for Great Big Idea's product. She'd have to get out and start stirring the pot.

And furthermore, she had no idea what might become of her job. She didn't expect that Mr. and Mrs. Ruff would want to run Charlie's business. They'd sell their interest to someone else, and that someone would send some stern vice president or other with instructions to "rationalize" the business, which was usually done by firing as many people as possible.

Charlie's main business was his software, of course. The game business would stick out by contrast—the *two*

,ame businesses, actually, since Great Big Idea and *Planet Nine* were effectively separate companies.

Of the two, *Planet Nine* had already generated eight or nine million players. Most of those had joined for free under the eight-week special offer, courtesy of *Briana Hall,* but a lot of them had sampled *Planet Nine*'s pleasures while waiting for updates from Dagmar and would probably stay. *Planet Nine* would most likely have at least a million revenue-generating subscribers.

By contrast, Great Big Idea had just lost a huge amount of money. Millions. Dagmar could always explain that those millions were lost on Charlie Ruff's direct orders, and that he had *provided* the millions in question out of his own funds, but this distinction might well be lost on any Harvard MBA intent on proving his worth by slashing costs and jobs.

She supposed that Great Big Idea might be sold to some other, larger game company, where it would remain a square peg in a round hole or be spun off into a company of its own.

In any case, Dagmar had reason to be worried about her professional future.

She could survive, of course, by theft. Nobody knew about Atreides LLC but her, and there were nearly fourteen million dollars left in that account, even after all her lavish spending. But she had every intention of returning the money to AvN Soft.

When all was said and done, she wasn't a thief. She was a puppetmaster, and she had blown up a former boyfriend, but it had to be said in her favor that stealing was quite beneath her.

Besides, a forensic accountant could turn up that money without a lot of trouble, and Dagmar had no intention of going to jail, not after all this.

"May I join you?"

She recognized the gamer she knew as Hippolyte—a scrawny young woman with straw-blond hair. "Of course."

Hippolyte arranged her thin body on a chair. Her hair was frizzed by the day's humidity, and she had a smudge of pale green eye shadow between her eyes, which suggested that she'd put on her makeup in great haste that morning, before she'd quite come awake.

"That was a phenomenal game!" Hippolyte said.

"Thank you."

"Everyone's talking about how it staked out new ground, solving a crime in the real world and running down an actual criminal." Hippolyte smiled. "But then you know that, since you read all the posts on Our Reality Network."

Dagmar, Woman of Mystery, gave an ambiguous shrug.

"But it didn't solve *all* the mysteries, did it?" Hippolyte said. "Those other deaths."

"You couldn't help," Dagmar said. "We didn't have the clues to give you. Nobody had a picture of the perpetrator."

"They were all your friends, right?" Hippolyte asked. "Even the bomber."

Dagmar allowed herself a moment of sadness.

"Even the bomber," she said. "We all knew each other."

Hippolyte shook her head. "That's kind of amazing."

"We all met in college," Dagmar said. "We were in the same gaming group."

And then, in front of that audience, she found herself telling that story, about BJ and Austin and Charlie, and the treacherous, devious worlds they had created, when they were all young and games were all they knew of life.

Acknowledgments

With thanks to Daniel Abraham, Sage Walker, Melinda Snodgrass, Emily Mah, Ty Franck, Ian Tregillis, Terry England, Victor Milán, Corie Conwell, David Levine, Allen Moore, Deborah Roggie, Ben Francisco, Brian Lowe, and Steve Stirling, who read drafts of this work with their usual active intelligence.

Special thanks to poker buddies Sean Stewart, Maureen McHugh, Elan Lee, and Jordan Weisman, for introducing me to the subject matter of this book.

extras

about the author

Walter Jon Williams has been nominated repeatedly for every major SF award, including Hugo and Nebula Award nominations for his novel *City on Fire*. His most recent books are *The Sundering*, *The Praxis*, *Destiny's Way* and *The Rift*. He lives near Albuquerque, New Mexico, with his wife.

Find out more about Walter Jon Williams and other Orbit authors by registering for the free monthly newsletter at www.orbitbooks.net

if you enjoyed
THIS IS NOT A GAME

look out for

THE EXECUTION
CHANNEL

by

Ken MacLeod

1.

The day it happened Travis drove north. The back of the Land Rover held a spare fuel tank and five jerrycans, filled years ago and now a standing violation of several laws; an air rifle, an air pistol, a first-aid kit, stacks of bottled water, MREs, camping gear, and a stash of trade goods: a wad of euros, twenty gold coins, and ten kilos of rolling tobacco. Travis kept the radio switched off. He didn't need the information and he didn't want the distraction. He watched the road and the sky, and the crawling blip on his phone's Galileo monitor. From his seat he could see over the hedgerows. Early May morning mist obscured the distance. The mist lay low, around trees and in hollows, under a clear sky. The only contrails visible were high up. No civil aviation was landing or taking off. Now and then a fighter jet flashed above the damp fields, vapour trailing from its wing-tips like cartoon streaks. He saw helicopters often, their throb a seldom absent background. Some were big twin-engined, tandem-rotor troop carriers; most were ground-attack choppers. He avoided looking at them. If you looked too long at an attack helicopter, someone might look back.

It took him a while to realise why so many military aircraft were airborne. They were being kept off the airfields.

Two calls had come in the middle of the night. The red numbers on his alarm clock read 4.13. On the bedside table his mobile buzzed and jittered, then stopped as he reached for it. Text message, he guessed. Down the hall the landline phone was ringing. Landlines triggered an older reflex of urgency. Travis jumped out of bed, stubbed his toe on the door and stumbled down the hallway in streetlight.

'Yes?'

'Dad, I'm all right.' Roisin didn't sound all right at all.

'What? What's wrong?'

'I'm just ringing to say I'm all right.'

'That's good, that's good.' Travis licked his dry lips with a sticky tongue. 'Why should—?'

'There's been a bomb—'

'Oh, Christ! Are you all right?'

'I just said—'

'Just hang tight and call the cops, OK? Stay where you are, lie low. Whoever attacked you might still be out there.'

'Dad,' said Roisin, in a pitying, patient tone that took him back about five years, 'it wasn't a bomb on the *camp*. It was a bomb on the *base*.'

'Shit! What kind of bomb?'

Roisin took a deep, sniffling breath and let it out shakily. 'I think it was a nuke.'

Travis almost dropped the handset. He heard beeps and the sound of coins being shoved in.

'Still there?' Roisin asked.

'Yes, yes – if you run out of money just stay and I'll call you back. Where are you?'

'Some wee village gas station. I can't stay. We're just going.'

'Why do you think it was a nuke?'

'Dad, I'm looking at a fucking mushroom cloud. I saw the flash.'

'Are you all right?'

'Yes, I told you. I have to go.'

'Was the camp—?'

'We weren't in the camp. Nobody was, thanks to— Thank God. We're on the road.'

'Where are you going?'

'Wherever.'

Travis paused. Wherever. That word had been agreed between them.

'I'll come for you.'

'Don't, Dad, please don't. I have to go. I'm all right. Take care. Bye.'

She'd put the phone down. Travis dialled 1471 and heard a chip voice. 'You were called . . . today . . . at oh four fourteen hours. The caller withheld—'

He slammed the phone down and ran back to the bedroom. He speed-dialled the number for Roisin's mobile and got another chip voice, telling him the number was unobtainable. Travis guessed that if there really had been a nuke the mobile might have got fried by the electromagnetic pulse. As he ended the call he saw the flashing envelope symbol and keyed up the text message:

sell apls buy orngs

Travis stared at it for a moment in blank puzzlement, then recognised it. His hand shook a little. He knew better than to call or text back. It wasn't even worth memorising the number before he deleted it. After he'd deleted it he ran a soft wipe: it was the best he could do short of trashing the chip. For a while he sat on the side of the bed and stared at the phone's blank screen. The text message had left him more disturbed than the phone call. The bomb, assuming it wasn't an opening shot in the big one, would in time become another date that marked a *before*. Before 9/11. Before the bombing. Before the Iraq war. Before 7/7. Before the Iran war. Before the nukes. Before the flu. Before the Straits. Before Rosyth. Before . . . and so you could go on, right up to now: 5/5, the first nuke on Britain. Yet another date that changed everything.

The text message was different. Every new shock, no matter how long dreaded, was unexpected when it came. Travis had been expecting this text message for a long time. It was no surprise.

He thumbed the phone to television and tuned it to Sky News. The two presenters looked grave.

'. . . confirmation of an incident at RAF Leuchars . . .'

The caption read BREAKING NEWS: BASE EXPLOSION. The scrolling update read *so far no reports of casualties*.

The male presenter glanced down and said, 'Ah, we're just getting the first pictures . . .'

A digital low-res image. Travis couldn't make it ⟨
on the phone screen. He grabbed the remote an⟨
flicked on the television on the far wall.

'. . . viewer on a North Sea oil rig . . .'

A crescent Moon high above the sea. Faint background voice, male, Newcastle accent: 'Look at the Moon, love, and—'

The screen went white, then faded to a glare reflected on the sea, the rig's shadow long and skeletal stretched before.

'What the *fuck!*'

A glimpse of the roustabout as he whirled around, turning his phone camera to—

'Holy fucking shit!'

Travis had seen enough on-screen nuclear explosions to recognise a kiloton yield. So, it seemed, had the roustabout.

'Tac nuke on Leuchars, love,' he said. 'Best I get inside. Stay safe . . . love you too . . . bye.'

'As yet there has been no official confirmation,' said the presenter.

Travis turned the television off. He could hear a faint ringing sound from outside. Wallingford at night was normally so quiet you could hear a snail climbing the window. After a while he worked out that the ringing sound came from his neighbours' phones. After another while the ringing was drowned out by a deeper tone that came from the sky. The heavy bombers were lifting from Brize Norton.

Time to move.

*

This was what had happened.

Roisin Travis crept among dark conifers, towards a light. She carried a heavy camera with a long-range lens. She had to make an effort not to laugh: she felt like some daft UFO-chaser, following a light seen through trees. She knew she looked like an alien herself in a thin, hooded coverall, with gloves and face-masking scarf of the same insulating black material. Even worn over nothing but jeans and T-shirt, the coverall was far too warm to be comfortable. The notion was that, by containing her body's heat, it made her less visible in the infrared. She suspected a flaw in this reasoning.

She stopped just before the edge of the forest. The trees and undergrowth remained dense right up to that line, beyond which they had been clear-cut some years earlier. The base at RAF Leuchars had expanded along with the war; though it had kept its name, it had long since been turned over to the USAF. The rent was unknown but was rumoured to go a long way to mollify any objections from the Scottish Executive. The only gesture of independence from that quarter was to tolerate a token peace-protest camp a kilometre away from the base's eastern perimeter, on the other side of what was left of the forest. From that huddle of shelters and vans a fluctuating dozen or so people made sorties to monitor activity at the base and to wave indignant placards at indifferent motorists. Roisin had spent six months with this ineffectual crew and had accomplished little beyond learning how to live rough through winter. With the Gulf Stream halfway to shut-down this was useful for the foreseeable future, but nothing to her

purpose. Others had drifted off; the camp was dov
six.

The other thing she had learned was how to ta
photographs on film and develop them. She ha
learned this from Mad Jack Armitage. It was a thing he
did. He was quite old and he mistrusted digital cameras.
He was not actually mad. In fact he was not even
Armitage. His real name, he claimed, was Norman
Cunningham. 'Mad Jack Armitage' was what he said
was his pirate name, and he insisted on answering to no
other, including during his appearances in court. He
was given to attributing his politics and his persistent
petty offences to attention-deficit disorder. It was not
that he refused to hold down a job, pay taxes, vote, pay
utility bills, or always put his clothes on before going
out. He merely forgot. In a similar manner he claimed
to be not actually a peace campaigner but a plane-
spotter. This was not one of the claims he made in court.
Plane-spotting was not in itself illegal but almost all the
activities involved in it were.

Roisin flattened herself on the ground and crawled
forward on elbows and knees until she was lying under
the overhang of a gorse bush on the very edge of the
clear-cut area. A hundred metres ahead of her was the
fence, then some grass, and beyond that the tarmac of a
runway. Hangars and towers a kilometre away. She
checked the viewfinder and the settings and waited. A
perimeter patrol paced by, behind the wire. Twenty
minutes later, another. A surveillance drone buzzed
overhead, then landed like a toy. Each time Roisin lowered her head and held her breath.

omething *was* in the air. Roisin heard it above the
f and the sound of the wind. She rolled on her
ack, opened her mouth wide, eased the sides of the
hood from her face and turned her head this way and
that until she identified the sound. A big heavy jet aircraft, coming in low over the North Sea. A bomber –
no, a transport plane. A C17 Globemaster. It was surprising how much she had learned from Armitage.
She rolled prone again and lost her night vision as the
runway lights flared. Roisin heard the change in the
engines' sound as the aircraft banked, way out over St
Andrews Bay, and then another change as it dug in the
flaps for its approach. She could hear it behind her
and felt a tension in the back of her neck; she was
lying right under its flight path. It passed over her in a
rush and flash and she heard the rubber hit the
tarmac.

Before the aircraft had come to a halt she was looking through the viewfinder and zooming the lens. It was
almost as if she was hauling the plane back as it moved
away. So she saw what happened after the aircraft came
to a halt, outside the hangars. The tailgate opened, the
ramp lowered, and an object whose main component
was a black cylinder that looked about a metre in diameter and four metres long was rolled out on a gurney. A
utility vehicle drew up, and the gurney was towed away
into the nearest hangar.

Roisin kept clicking the shutter until the film ran
out. She replaced the spool and waited. A couple of jet
fighters took off and screamed away over the North
Sea. A Chinook landed and a dozen soldiers deplaned.

They took up positions in front of the hangar. So‐ what later a few cars drove up and a handful of me some in uniform, some not, passed through the cordo into the hangar. She photographed all that. Two military policemen with dogs passed in front of her, a hundred metres away behind the perimeter fence. The next such patrol followed a few minutes later. She heard voices.

Guessing that security had been stepped up, Roisin backed away into the bushes, then rose to a low crouch which she maintained until she was deep in among the trees. With relief she threw back her hood, took off her scarf and unzipped the front of the coverall. Her T-shirt was damp and sticky with sweat. She let the faint breeze from the west cool her for a moment. The stars were very clear overhead in the darkness, the Milky Way like a cold breath hanging. A satellite crawled across the firmament from south to north. A meteor rushed down the sky.

Roisin had no difficulty making her way through the wood. The floor was springy with pine needles. She walked slowly and carefully.

When her phone vibrated she nearly dropped the camera. She ducked to put the camera on the ground. The phone was in her back pocket and if she didn't catch it in five seconds it would start ringing. She tried to reach through the open front of the coverall, then swore under her breath and tugged her right arm up out of the sleeve. Her hand darted to her pocket and she slid the phone out just as the vibration stopped. It was only a message after all. But it was tagged as urgent:

little bead that glowed on the side of the casing was
n. She flipped the screen open. It showed her brother
Alec's standard e-card shot of himself grinning in his
beret in front of a mountain range. Scrawled across it
was the text:

> *Get away from that base asap Rosh expect big security*
> *sweep any minute I mean NOW!!! xxx*

Roisin stared at it. If it was true, how would Alec
know? Of course he would – he worked in comms.

Away to her left, to the north, she heard the baying
of dogs.

The camp was located in a clearing that had once been
a picnic-area car park, at the end of a single-track road
off from the back of the military housing and the civilian part of town. A concrete litter-bin that they used for
the fire. Half-rotted tables with built-in benches that
should have been put on the fire long ago but were
never quite dry enough. Two vans, one a plain white
Transit, the other an ancient VW camper painted with
rainbows and peace signs. Two timber-and-plastic shelters and Mad Jack's bivouac. The old man was sitting
cross-legged outside it, smoking, when Roisin ran out of
the trees.

He stubbed the roll-up and stood up, quite limber.
'What's up?'
She told him. He showed no surprise about her
brother.

'You take this seriously?'

'Very,' she said. 'Listen.'

He cocked his head and cupped his ear. 'What?'

'Drones, dogs, a chopper lifting . . .'

'Fuck. All right.'

He strode to the nearest shelter, the one that held three students from St Andrews, and rattled the plywood door. Roisin heard raised voices as she stepped inside the shelter she shared with Claire Moyle. She shook her friend in the sleeping bag.

'Where you been?' Claire asked, drowsy.

Roisin swung the camera. 'Night photography. Doesn't matter. We got to go before we get chased out.'

'Why?' asked Claire. 'We haven't done anything wrong.'

It took too long to explain. By the time Roisin and Claire had come out of the shelter Mad Jack's bivouac and belongings had vanished into the back of the Transit and the students were slinging things into the camper. The sounds of search hadn't come closer – they seemed to be in the woods and farther along the perimeter.

'Move!' Jack said, not too loud.

'I still think we should just wait,' Claire grumbled, then dashed back into the hut and emerged with an armful. 'OK,' she said. 'OK.' She grinned at Roisin like she was suddenly in full agreement, threw her stuff in the Transit and walked over to talk to the three students, who sounded like they needed more explanation than they'd got.

Roisin grabbed up some gear, food, two-litre bottles of water. She used one to douse the fire, then took the

…ver's seat of the Transit. Claire climbed in on the …assenger side, Mad Jack jumped in the back and …lammed the doors. The sound seemed to echo.

'Sorry,' he said. 'Forgot.' They were worn words from him. Roisin glared over her shoulder.

The two-van convoy lurched up the potholed track, the Transit in the lead. They reached the junction with a back road.

'Take the right,' said Claire, looking up from a map. 'I've worked out a route.'

'Good work,' said Roisin.

Claire laughed. 'Johnny, Mike and Irena' – the students – 'were going to drive straight through Leuchars!'

Roisin checked the wing mirror. The camper had followed them.

'Uh-huh. So what's the route?'

'Head up for the Point, then cut across past Newport. We can head west on the back roads, then south to the coast. Park in a back street in Pittenweem or another of the wee villages. The camper's going to go on to Dundee. They have friends there.'

'They'll get picked up,' said Mad Jack.

'Yes, if there's anything to this at all.' Claire glanced across at Roisin, who looked straight ahead. 'But we won't,' Claire added.

'There's a lot to be said for a white van,' said Mad Jack.

'Can you see anything back there?' asked Roisin.

Mad Jack shuffled on his knees through camping gear and photographic equipment and peered out the back window.

'Lights in the sky,' he reported. 'Flashing light bac
where we were, I can just make it out. No signs of pursuit.'

He crawled forward. 'It's ahead you have to watch
out.'

'Yeah, yeah,' said Roisin.

But there was no pursuit and no roadblock. Within
half an hour they had reached their turning point,
parted from the northbound camper, and were making
their way along a maze of back roads through farm-
land. Claire, in the passenger seat, was exchanging text
messages with the students. Jack, behind her, was also
intent on his phone, no doubt online and browsing conspiracy sites. Roisin was negotiating a corner blind with
hedgerows and dipping the headlamp beams when
Claire said: 'Shit, the phone—'

The road, the hedge, and the whole landscape
around became for a moment bright as day.

The day it happened was not the day it began. For
Travis it had begun two and a half years earlier, in the
Red Lion in Westminster. He'd spent the day investigat-
ing the feasibility of a large-scale software project with
Alain Gauthier, who was over from Paris looking to out-
source various tasks that had overloaded the IT
department of the French state electricity company, EdF.
The company for which Travis worked, Result, had
made a strong pitch; Travis and his colleagues had
answered every question. There had been many questions. At seven in the evening Travis and Gauthier had at
the same moment stepped back from a much-scrawled

whiteboard, nodded, then looked at each other and laughed. Each man's drawn face mirrored how the other felt.

'Call it a day?' Travis said.

'Yes,' said Gauthier. He thumbed a line or two into his PDA, nodded to himself again, then closed the device with a click of finality. 'As far as I am concerned, the deal is as good as done. But of course . . .'

'I know. Over to the bean-counters.'

'Pardon?'

'The guys who count the costs.'

'Yes. Still . . .' Gauthier shrugged. 'Until then, let us presume.'

'Sure.' Travis brushed flecks of dried ink from his hands. 'Do you have a plane or train to catch?'

'No, no, a hotel for the night. Red-eye from Heathrow in the morning.'

'Fancy a drink?'

'That's very kind. You do not wish to go home?'

Travis shuffled papers into his briefcase. 'No rush,' he said. He blinked, spun the locks, looked up and smiled. 'Let's go.'

The Red Lion smelled of sweat from suits and steam from food. Travis bought a bitter for himself and a lager for Gauthier and made his way to the pillar with a shelf on which the Frenchman had positioned an elbow. On the big screen in the corner boys capered around a burning Humvee in Aleppo. At the nearest table a thin fortyish English guy in heavy-framed glasses, with a gold pound sign on his lapel, talked in rapid monotone to a stout young American in T-shirt and combat pants.

As Travis sidled past the American's seat back he caught five seconds of a long story involving Muslims, heroin, and Soviets.

Gauthier stopped giving that pair the evil eye and took his pint.

'Thanks,' he said. He glanced sideways again. 'Cunts.'

Travis flinched and backed away a little around the pillar, toeing his briefcase.

'What?'

Gauthier re-closed the gap. 'Sorry.' He smiled across the top of his glass. 'Five minutes of overhearing these liberals mouthing off about the French.'

'I thought it was all about the Muslims and the Soviets. I gathered the guy thinks the latter still exist.'

'Indeed, and supposedly controlling France and . . .' Gauthier jerked a thumb at the television.

'The man's a nut. Ignore it.'

Gauthier sighed and sipped. 'I would,' he said, 'but I hear that canard too often.'

'You do? I've never heard it before.'

'Ah.' Gauthier looked embarrassed for a moment. He spread his fingers and waggled his left hand. 'Well.'

'You're married,' said Travis, catching a gold glint. Gauthier took the opportunity to change the subject and displayed photos of his wife and small son.

'And yourself?' he asked, slipping his wallet back.

'I was,' Travis said. 'Until the flu pandemic.'

'I'm sorry.'

Travis nodded. 'It's all right. Well, no, it's not, but . . .'

'I understand,' said Gauthier. 'I lost my mother to it, and . . . but I know, it's not the same.'

They agreed it was not the same.

'Any children?' asked Gauthier.

'Two,' said Travis. 'Son in the Army, daughter at university. Both doing well.'

'Where is your son?'

'Iranian Kurdistan.'

Gauthier's glance flicked to the television, and back. 'It must be a great concern.'

'I worry more about my daughter, to tell you the truth,' said Travis, not telling the truth. 'She's at SOAS. It's a bit of a hotbed.'

Gauthier smiled. 'Explain, please.'

'School of Oriental and African Studies. Full of noisy Islamists, Zionists, anti-war agitators. Roisin – that's my daughter – she likes getting into all these arguments. She's a pacifist, at the moment.'

'And therefore hated by everyone?'

'That's about it, yes.'

'What do you think about . . . all that? If that is not too direct a question!'

'I disagree with both my children,' said Travis. 'If that is not too indirect an answer.'

'It's very precise,' said Gauthier. 'You are against this war, but not against every war?'

'Nah, I just hate the Yanks,' said Travis, in an idle tone.

The young American, standing up and pulling on a big padded jacket, overheard him and gave him a look. Travis held his gaze until the American turned away.

About a dozen other people joined the American and his English companion in a sudden hubbub as they made their way to the door. Off to a meeting or function, Travis guessed.

'Ah,' said Gauthier. He placed his empty glass on the shelf. 'Permit me to buy you another drink.'

And that was how it began.